THE CLASSROOM DOORS SWING OPEN TO REVEAL . . .

A high school teacher trying to shape his student's thoughts and control his own feelings in John Updike's TOMORROW AND TOMORROW AND SO FORTH . . .

A child suffering the tortures of the damned in the very proper hell of an English boarding school in George Orwell's SUCH, SUCH WERE THE JOYS . . .

A teacher making a supreme effort to turn English into a dead language for a future prose master in James Thurber's HERE LIES MISS GROBY . . .

A street kid finding his way out of the Brooklyn slums in Alfred Kazin's A WALKER IN THE CITY . . .

Youth in rebellion and a teacher fighting for his life in Evan Hunter's THE BLACKBOARD JUNGLE . . .

From England . . . from France . . . from Greece . . . from Ireland . . . from all parts of America . . . a whole world opens up before our eyes in—

GOING TO SCHOOL

ABRAHAM H. LASS, formerly principal of Abraham Lincoln High School in Brooklyn, New York, numbers among his notable anthologies *The Secret Sharer and Other Great Stories* and *Twenty-One Great Stories* (with Norma Tasman), *Masters of the Short Story* and *Stories of the American Experience* (with Leonard Kriegel), and *The Mentor Book of Short Plays* (with Richard H. Goldstone), all available in Mentor editions.

NORMA L. TASMAN is former chairperson of the English Department at Sheepshead Bay High School in Brooklyn, New York.

MENTOR Books of Special Interest

GOING TO SCHOOL

An Anthology of Prose About Teachers and Students

edited by

ABRAHAM H. LASS
AND NORMA L. TASMAN

A MENTOR BOOK
NEW AMERICAN LIBRARY

TIMES MIRROR
NEW YORK AND SCARBOROUGH, ONTARIO
THE NEW ENGLISH LIBRARY LIMITED, LONDON

*To Janet, Paul, Miranda, and Bethany
and Terry and Angelo*

Copyright © 1980 by Abraham H. Lass and Norma L. Tasman

Library of Congress Catalog Card Number: 80-83490

MENTOR TRADEMARK REG. U.S. PAT. OFF. AND FOREIGN COUNTRIES
REGISTERED TRADEMARK—MARCA REGISTRADA
HECHO EN CHICAGO, U.S.A.

SIGNET, SIGNET CLASSICS, MENTOR, PLUME, MERIDIAN and
NAL BOOKS are published *in the United States* by The New American
Library, Inc., 1633 Broadway, New York, New York 10019, *in Canada*
by The New American Library of Canada Limited, 81 Mack Avenue,
Scarborough, Ontario M1L 1M8, *in the United Kingdom* by The New
English Library Limited, Barnard's Inn, Holborn, London EC1N 2JR,
England.

First Printing, January, 1981

1 2 3 4 5 6 7 8 9

PRINTED IN THE UNITED STATES OF AMERICA

CONTENTS

GOING TO SCHOOL

An Anthology of Prose
About Teachers and Students

INTRODUCTION

Going to School spans almost four thousand years of recorded history—from ancient Sumer (circa 2000 B.C.) to the present. The selections in this book mirror something of the variety and complexity of the universally bittersweet school experience. They reflect the thoughts and feelings of men and women at various times and in various places. The writers range from the obscure to Nobel Laureates and world literary figures. But they have one quality in common: From their deeply felt engagements and encounters, they write compellingly about school.

From earliest times, students have regarded school as an inescapable, generally melancholy, dull, repressive, and frequently traumatic experience—to be endured in quiet desperation, resigned indifference, or met with open rebellion—but rarely to be enjoyed or remembered with affection. Given a choice, most would have opted for anything other than school.

For those who have not been privileged to teach and care for the young, it may come as something of a shock to learn that by and large most children don't like school and teachers at all. Their feelings run from simple ennui to lethal hostility. They are not consumed by an unslakable thirst for learning. They come to school because their parents and society force them to, because they are afraid not to, and because they are too weak to revolt against those whom they see as their oppressors.

Writing in *L'Ecolier* in 1841, an anonymous contributor sums up the enduring, quintessential postures of teachers and students:

". . . The Schoolboy systematically maintains a struggle against authority, a struggle full of hate and as relentless as that of the Guelphs and Ghibellines, which carries on uninterrupted from generation to generation. The pupil brings to bear all his lack of submission, his cantankerousness, his vexatious mockery, his intransigence, while the teacher responds with all the authority he has been granted. . . ."

Almost one hundred years later, B.C. Beresford in his *Schooldays with Kipling* (1936) sounds a startlingly similar note:

"There was, of course, never any question of mutual aid and cooperation in the business of education. Such an idea never came into our heads. We were at school to fight the masters."

Most of the time, teachers aren't exactly enamored of their students either. They know (for they remember their own schooldays) that their students don't really like or respect them, that often they hate them.

To make matters worse, teaching has always attracted its share of inadequate, incompetent, hapless, cruel men and women—some doing successful battle with the children, others bruised and broken, and eventually driven out of teaching into less taxing, less hazardous careers.

Locked in hostile, involuntary embrace, teachers and students have done and continue to do unkind and sometimes terrifying things to each other. Some of the writers in *Going to School* offer vivid testimony to the nature of this virtually changeless struggle and confrontation. In "A Schoolboy's Life in Ancient Sumer," we see that teachers were caning their charges almost four thousand years ago. The same primitive practice finds horrifying expression in "The Caning" from James Joyce's *A Portrait of the Artist as a Young Man*. In George Orwell's "Such, Such Were the Joys," the masters are at the flogging game again—with some especially sadistic refinements added.

But there are hurts that teachers inflict upon their helpless students that are, in some respects, more lasting than the application of the cane or whip. Thomas Gradgrind in Dickens' *Hard Times* achieved immortality practicing his cruel arts unchecked by any authority other than his flinty conscience. Philip Carey in Somerset Maugham's *Of Human Bondage* is scarred by the "impatient and choleric" and cruelly insensitive Reverend B.B. Gordon.

Predictably, the students strike back at their teachers and tormentors in this unequal contest of wills, in which most of the time the students come out at the losing end. And when the oppressed rise up against their oppressors, they give no quarter and no mercy, as we see in "The Ordeal of Ursula

Brangwen" from D.H. Lawrence's *The Rainbow* and "Mr. Dadier's First Days at North Manual Trades High School" from Evan Hunter's *The Blackboard Jungle*.

But not all teachers find teaching and children an unbearable vexation of spirit. Many are skillful, loving, caring people. They love their students. They love teaching them. And they are remembered with a deep and enduring fondness. In the words of Henry Adams, they "affect eternity." Some of this special light and love radiates from Christopher Morley's "In Memoriam: Francis Barton Gummere," James Thurber's "Here Lies Miss Groby," Francis Gray Patton's *Good Morning, Miss Dove*, Hortense Calisher's "A Wreath for Miss Totten," Elie Wiesel's "My Teachers," Leo Rosten's "Dear Miss O'Neill," Theodore White's "Fond Memories of Schooldays," Francine du Plessix Gray's "For Lycidas Is Dead."

Going to school isn't all tears and frustration. It has a special kind of joy, even hilarity. Some of this is captured in "Happy Hours" from Mark Twain's *Tom Sawyer*, Booth Tarkington's "Joys of School," Stephen Leacock's "My Memories and Miseries as a Schoolmaster," Wolcott Gibbs' "Ring Out, Wild Bells," S.J. Wilson's "Miss Diamond's Difficult Day."

We have found much pleasure putting *Going to School* together. We hope that it will bring to our readers a deeper appreciation of what it means and has always meant to be a teacher and a student.

Abraham H. Lass
Norma L. Tasman

MORRIS ROSENBLUM

Morris Rosenblum (1900–1978) was an American teacher, writer, linguist, classicist, and world traveler. Rosenblum was a graduate of the College of the City of New York and Columbia University. It was at Columbia that he studied with the great classical scholar, Moses Hadas. Hadas had a profound effect on the young Rosenblum's literary and intellectual life.

Rosenblum taught Latin, Spanish, French, and English in the New York City public high schools. His published works include *Heroes of Israel, Heroes of Mexico, How to Build a Better Vocabulary* (with Maxwell Nurnberg).

A Schoolboy's Life in Ancient Sumer—Circa 2000 B.C.

◆◆◆

On May 7, 1949, Professor Samuel Noah Kramer (Clark research professor of Assyriology and curator of the Tablet Collection of the University Museum, University of Pennsylvania) read a paper before the annual convention of the American Oriental Society at Yale University. This paper contained a translation of the text of twenty-one tablets and fragments, twenty of which were excavated in Nippur, a city of ancient Sumer (part of Babylonia), situated near the Euphrates River. Some of these tablets are now in the University Museum, others in the Istanbul Museum of the Ancient Orient and in the Louvre. Dr. Kramer realized that the fragments in the different museums were part of one document and pieced them together.

Dr. Kramer's foreword follows in part:

"To date very little had been uncovered about education in ancient Sumer. Oriental scholars generally realized that the learning of the three 'R's' was not universal in the land,

Reprinted from Morris Rosenblum, "The Antiquarian's Corner," *High Points*, October 1949.

but was probably confined to those boys and young men who aimed to become professional scribes, or as the Sumerians themselves called them, 'tablet writers.' But we had practically no details of the activities carried on in these ancient Sumerian schools, which may not inaptly be described as the oldest educational centers known to man. It is therefore a real privilege to be in a position to sketch at least tentatively the contents of a Sumerian document describing in considerable detail the experiences and reactions of an ancient Sumerian schoolboy, as purported to be told in large part by the boy himself.

"This ninety-line semi-biographical composition, which was probably first written in 2000 B.C., is one of the most 'human' documents excavated in the Near East; its relatively simple, straightforward words reveal how little human nature has really changed through the millennia. Thus we find our ancient schoolboy, not unlike his modern counterpart, terribly afraid of coming late to school 'lest his teacher cane him.' When he awakes he hurries his mother to prepare his lunch. In school he misbehaves and is caned more than once by the teacher and his assistants; the text does not reveal the spot on which the cane was laid, but in all likelihood it is the same that has been reserved throughout the ages for that purpose. As for the teacher or professor, his pay seems to have been as meager then as it is now; at least he seems to be only too happy to make a 'little extra' from the parents to eke out his earnings."

Dr. Kramer's text follows. All italicized words are, according to him, doubtful translations; the number of dots indicates a break of so many words.

* * *

"Schoolboy, where did you go *from earliest days?*"
"I went to school."
"What did you do in school?"
"I *recited* my tablet, ate my lunch,
prepared my (new) tablet, wrote it, finished it; then
they *assigned me my oral work,*
(and in) the afternoon, they *assigned me my written work.*
Upon the dismissal of the school, I went home,
entered the house, (there) was my father sitting.
I *spoke* to my father *of my written work,* then
read the tablet to him, (and) my father was pleased;
truly I *found favor with my father.*

'I am thirsty, give me drink,
I am hungry, give me bread,
wash my feet, set up the bed, I want to go to sleep;
wake me early in the morning,
I must not be late, (or) my teacher will cane me.'
When I awoke early in the morning,
I faced my mother, and
said to her: 'Give me my lunch, I want to go to the school.'
my mother gave me two rolls, I *left* her;
My mother gave me two rolls, I went to school.
In school, the *monitor* said to me: 'Why are you late?' I was
      afraid, my heart pounded.
I entered before my teacher, greeted him respectfully.
My tablet-father *read* my tablet to me,
(said) 'the . . *is cut off*,' caned me.
I . . d him to lunch . . . . lunch.
The teacher (while) supervising the activities of the school,
looked into *house and street in order to pounce upon* some
      one, (said) 'Your . . is not . . ,' caned me.
My tablet-father brought me my tablet.
The man (in charge) of the courtyard *said* 'Write,' . . . . *a
      peaceful place.*
I took my tablet, ...
I write my tablet, ... my . . .
Its uninspected part my . . . . *does* not know.
Who was in charge of . . . (said) 'Why when I was not here
      did you talk?' caned me.
Who was in charge of the . . . (said) 'Why when I was not
      here did you not *raise a firm head?*' caned me.
Who was in charge of *drawing* (said) 'Why when I was not
      here did you stand up?' caned me.
Who was in charge of the gate (said) 'Why when I was not
      here did you *go* out?' caned me.
Who was in charge of the . . (said) 'Why when I was not
      here did you take the . . ?' caned me.
Who was in charge of Sumerian (said) 'You spoke . . ,' caned
      me.
My teacher (said) 'Your hand [that is "copy"] is not good,'
      caned me.
'You have neglected the scribal art, ... the scribal art.'

CHARLES LAMB

Charles Lamb (1775–1834), British essayist and man of letters, earned his living as a clerk in the East India House for thirty-three years, until he was pensioned in 1825. Readers still find delight in the quaintness and leisurely autobiographical qualities of his style. A student of sixteenth- and seventeenth-century literature, he wrote *Tales from Shakespeare* (1807) with his sister, and *Specimens of English Dramatic Poets* (1808). It was the *Essays of Elia* (1823) and *Last Essays of Elia* (1833), however, that established Lamb's position in the literary world. Among the best-known of the essays are "The Two Races of Men" (borrowers and lenders), "A Chapter on Ears" (his own lack of a musical ear), "The Superannuated Man" (the problems of a pensioner), the "Dissertation on Roast Pig" (the origin of the dish), and the touching "Dream Children."

FROM The Old and New Schoolmaster

Why are we never quite at our ease in the presence of a schoolmaster?—because we are conscious that he is not quite at ease in ours. He is awkward and out of place in the society of his equals. He comes like Gulliver from among his little people, and he cannot fit the stature of his understanding to yours. . . . He is so used to teaching, that he wants to be teaching *you*. . . .

———◆◆◆———

The modern schoolmaster is expected to know a little of every thing, because his pupil is required not to be entirely ignorant of anything. He must be superficially, if I may so say, omniscient. He is to know something of pneumatics; of

From *Essays of Elia* by Charles Lamb, 1823.

chemistry; of whatever is curious, or proper to excite the attention of the youthful mind; an insight into mechanics is desirable, with a touch of statistics; the quality of soils, etc., botany, the constitution of his country, *cum multis aliis*. You may get a notion of some part of his expected duties by consulting the famous Tractate on Education, addressed to Mr. Hartlib.

All these things—these, or the desire of them—he is expected to instil, not by set lessons from professors, which he may charge in the bill, but at school-intervals, as he walks the streets, or saunters through green fields (those natural instructors), with his pupils. The least part of what is expected from him, is to be done in school-hours. He must insinuate knowledge at the *mollia tempora fandi*. He must seize every occasion—the season of the year—the time of the day—a passing cloud—a rainbow—a waggon of hay—a regiment of soldiers going by—to inculcate something useful. He can receive no pleasure from a casual glimpse of Nature, but must catch at it as an object of instruction. He must interpret beauty into the picturesque. He cannot relish a beggar-man, or a gipsy, for thinking of the suitable improvement. Nothing comes to him, not spoiled by the sophisticating medium of moral uses. The Universe—that Great Book, as it has been called—is to him indeed, to all intents and purposes, a book, out of which he is doomed to read tedious homilies to distasting schoolboys.—Vacations themselves are none to him, he is only rather worse off than before; for commonly he has some intrusive upper-boy fastened upon him at such high times; some cadet of a great family; some neglected lump of nobility, or gentry; that he must drag after him to the play, to the Panorama, to Mr. Bartley's Orrery, to the Panopticon, or into the country, to a friend's house, or his favourite watering-place. Wherever he goes, this uneasy shadow attends him. A boy is at his board, and in his path, and in all his movements. He is boy-rid, sick of perpetual boy. . . .

Why are we never quite at our ease in the presence of a schoolmaster?—because we are conscious that he is not quite at his ease in ours. He is awkward, and out of place, in the society of his equals. He comes like Gulliver from among his little people, and he cannot fit the stature of his understanding to yours. He cannot meet you on the square. He wants a point given him, like an indifferent whist-player. He is so used to teaching, that he wants to be teaching *you*. One of these professors, upon my complaining that these little sketches of mine were any thing but methodical, and that I was unable to make them otherwise, kindly offered to instruct me in the method by which young gentlemen in *his* seminary were taught to compose English themes.—The jests of a schoolmaster are coarse, or thin. They do not *tell* out of school. He is under the restraint of a formal and didactive hypocrisy in company, as a clergyman is under a moral one. He can no more let his intellect loose in society, than the other can his inclinations.—He is forlorn among his co-evals; his juniors cannot be his friends.

"I take blame to myself," said a sensible man of this profession, writing to a friend respecting a youth who had quitted his school abruptly, "that your nephew was not more attached to me. But persons in my situation are more to be pitied, than can well be imagined. We are surrounded by young, and, consequently, ardently affectionate hearts, but *we* can never hope to share an atom of their affections. The relation of master and scholar forbids this. *How pleasing this must be to you, how I envy your feelings*, my friends will sometimes say to me, when they see young men, whom I have educated, return after some years' absence from school, their eyes shining with pleasure, while they shake hands with their old master, bringing a present of game to me, or a toy to my wife, and thanking me in the warmest terms for my care of their education. A holiday is begged for the boys; the house is a scene of happiness; I, only, am sad, at heart.—This fine-spirited and warmhearted youth, who fancies he repays his master with gratitude for the care of his boyish years—this young man—in the eight long years I watched over him with a parent's anxiety, never could repay me with one look of genuine feeling. He was proud, when I praised; he was submissive, when I reproved him; but he did never *love* me—and what he now mistakes for gratitude and kindness for me, is but the pleasant sensation, which all persons feel at revisiting the scene of their boyish hopes and fears; and the seeing on equal terms the man they were accustomed to look up to with reverence.

CHARLES DICKENS

Charles Dickens (1812–1870), the best-loved and most widely read of English novelists, was born into a lower-middle-class family. His father was an ineffectual naval clerk whose fortunes continually fluctuated. When Charles was nine years old, the family fortunes took a catastrophic turn for the worse. Dickens' father was imprisoned for debt, and the boy suffered the humiliation of working in a London blacking factory pasting labels on bottles. These early experiences left an indelible mark on him and shaped much of the fiction he was later to write.

In 1835 Dickens became a parliamentary reporter for a newspaper and began to contribute sketches of London life, which were published in 1836 as *Sketches by Boz*. Later that year, when *The Pickwick Papers* began appearing in monthly installments, the name Dickens became a household word. The success of *Pickwick* enabled Dickens to marry Catherine Hogarth, the sister of the girl he really loved. (The unhappy marriage ended in separation in 1856.) *Oliver Twist* appeared in 1838, followed by *Nicholas Nickleby* in 1839 and *The Old Curiosity Shop* and *Barnaby Rudge* in 1841.

In 1856 Dickens' public readings from his works enhanced his reputation even further. A born actor, he put so much of himself into these dramatic readings that they totally exhausted him.

The novels of Dickens' middle period, *David Copperfield* (1850), *Bleak House* (1852), *Hard Times* (1854), and *A Tale of Two Cities* (1859), show the author concerned with social injustice and the evils of industrialism.

Dickens' novels reflect the zeal of the reformer, and a strong didactic purpose directs most of them. The theatrical element is strong in his work; he is often melodramatic and his character presentations often verge on caricature. But there remain a freshness of sympathy, a vigor of imagination, a depth of humor and goodwill, a keenness of satire, and a faith in humankind which ensure him a devoted following accorded no other English writer.

The Unexpected Half-Holiday
FROM *The Old Curiosity Shop*

What rebellious thoughts . . . kept tempting and urging
that sturdy boy who sat fanning his flushed face with a
spelling book, wishing himself a whale, or a minnow, or
a fly, or anything but a boy at school, on that hot, broiling day.

———◆◆◆———

Shortly after the schoolmaster had arranged the forms and
taken his seat behind his desk, a small white-headed boy with
a sunburnt face appeared at the door, and, stopping there to
make a rustic bow, came in and took his seat upon one of
the forms. He then put an open book, astonishingly dog's-
eared, upon his knees, and thrusting his hands into his pockets,
began counting the marbles with which they were filled; dis-
playing, in the expression of his face, a remarkable capacity
of totally abstracting his mind from the spelling on which his
eyes were fixed.

Soon afterward, another white-headed little boy came
straggling in, and after him, a red-headed lad, and then one
with a flaxen poll, until the forms were occupied by a dozen
boys, or thereabouts, with heads of every color but gray, and
ranging in their ages from four years old to fourteen years or
more; for the legs of the youngest were a long way from the
floor, when he sat upon the form; and the eldest was a heavy,
good-tempered fellow, about half a head taller than the schoolmaster. . . .

Then began the hum of conning over lessons and getting
them by heart, the whispered jest and stealthy game, and all
the noise and drawl of school; and in the midst of the din,
sat the poor schoolmaster, vainly attempting to fix his mind
upon the duties of the day. . . . His thoughts were rambling
from his pupils—it was plain.

None knew this better than the idlest boys, who, growing
bolder with impunity, waxed louder and more daring; playing
"odd or even" under the master's eye; eating apples openly
and without rebuke; pinching each other in sport or malice,

From *The Old Curiosity Shop* by Charles Dickens, 1841.

without the least reserve; and cutting their initials in the very legs of his desk. The puzzled dunce, who stood beside it to say his lesson "off the book," looked no longer at the ceiling for forgotten words, but drew closer to the master's elbow, and boldly cast his eye upon the page; the wag of the little troop squinted and made grimaces (at the smallest boy, of course), holding no book before his face, and his approving companions knew no constraint in their delight. If the master did chance to rouse himself, and seem alive to what was going on, the noise subsided for a moment, and no eye met his but wore a studious and deeply humble look; but the instant he relapsed again, it broke out afresh, and ten times louder than before.

Oh! how some of those idle fellows longed to be outside, and how they looked at the open door and window, as if they half meditated rushing violently out, plunging into the woods, and being wild boys and savages from that time forth. What rebellious thoughts of the cool river, and some shady bathing place, beneath willow trees with branches dipping in the water, kept tempting and urging that sturdy boy, who, with his shirt collar unbuttoned, and flung back as far as it could go, sat fanning his flushed face with a spelling book, wishing himself a whale, or a minnow, or a fly, or anything but a boy at school, on that hot, broiling day.

Heat! ask that other boy, whose seat being nearest to the door, gave him opportunities of gliding out into the garden, and driving his companions to madness, by dipping his face into the bucket of the well, and then rolling on the grass,— ask him if there was ever such a day as that, when even the bees were diving down into the cups of the flowers, and stopping there, as if they had made up their minds to retire from business, and be manufacturers of honey no more. The day was made for laziness, and lying on one's back in green places, and staring at the sky, till its brightness forced the gazer to shut his eyes and go to sleep. And was this a time to be poring over musty books in a dark room, slighted by the very sun itself? Monstrous!

The lessons over, writing time began. This was a more quiet time; for the master would come and look over the writer's shoulder, and mildly tell him to observe how such a letter was turned up, in such a copy on the wall . . . and bid him take it as a model. . . .

"I think, boys," said the schoolmaster, when the clock struck twelve, "that I shall give you an extra half holiday this afternoon." At this intelligence, the boys, led on and headed by the tall boy, raised a great shout, in the midst of which the master was seen to speak, but could not be heard. As he held up his hand, however, in token of his wish that they should be silent, they were considerate enough to leave off, as soon as the longest-winded among them were quite out of breath. "You must promise me, first," said the schoolmaster, "that you'll not be noisy, or at least, if you are, that you'll go away first, out of the village, I mean. . . ."

There was a general murmur (and perhaps a very sincere one, for they were but boys) in the negative; and the tall boy, perhaps as sincerely as any of them, called those about him to witness, that he had only shouted in a whisper. "Then pray don't forget, there's my dear scholars," said the schoolmaster, "what I have asked you, and do it as a favor to me. Be as happy as you can, and don't be unmindful that you are blessed with health. Good-by, all."

"Thank'ee, sir," and "Good-by, sir," were said a great many times in a great variety of voices, and the boys went out very slowly and softly. But there was the sun shining and there were birds singing, as the sun only shines and the birds only sing on holidays and half holidays; there were the trees waving to all free boys to climb, and nestle among their leafy branches; the hay, entreating them to come and scatter it to the pure air; the green corn, gently beckoning toward wood and stream; the smooth ground, rendered smoother still by blending lights and shadows, inviting to runs and leaps, and long walks, nobody knows whither. It was more than boy could bear, and with a joyous whoop, the whole cluster took to their heels, and spread themselves about, shouting and laughing as they went. " 'Tis natural, thank Heaven!" said the poor schoolmaster, looking after them. "I am very glad they didn't mind me."

The Rout of Mr. Mell
FROM *David Copperfield*

If I could associate the idea of a bull or a bear with any one so mild as Mr. Mell, I should think of him, in connection with that afternoon when the uproar was at its

From *David Copperfield* by Charles Dickens, 1850.

height, as of one of those animals baited by a thousand dogs. . . . there were laughing boys, singing boys, talking boys, dancing boys, howling boys; boys shuffled with their feet, boys whirled about him, grinning, making faces, mimicking him behind his back and before his eyes— mimicking his poverty, his boots, his coat, his mother, everything belonging to him that they should have had consideration for.

———◆◆———

It was probably a half-holiday, being Saturday; but as the noise in the playground would have disturbed Mr. Creakle, and the weather was not favourable for going out walking, we were ordered into school in the afternoon, and set some lighter tasks than usual, which were made for the occasion. It was the day of the week on which Mr. Sharp went out to get his wig curled; so Mr. Mell, who always did the drudgery, whatever it was, kept school by himself.

If I could associate the idea of a bull or a bear with any one so mild as Mr. Mell, I should think of him, in connection with that afternoon when the uproar was at its height, as of one of those animals baited by a thousand dogs. I recall him bending his aching head, supported on his bony hand, over the book on his desk, and wretchedly endeavouring to get on with his tiresome work, amidst an uproar that might have made the Speaker of the House of Commons giddy. Boys started in and out of their places, playing at puss-in-the-corner with other boys; there were laughing boys, singing boys, talking boys, dancing boys, howling boys; boys shuffled with their feet, boys whirled about him, grinning, making faces, mimicking him behind his back and before his eyes— mimicking his poverty, his boots, his coat, his mother, everything belonging to him that they should have consideration for.

"Silence!" cried Mr. Mell, suddenly rising up and striking his desk with the book. "What does this mean? It's impossible to bear it. It's maddening. How can you do it to me, boys?"

It was my book that he struck his desk with; and as I stood beside him, following his eye as it glanced round the room, I saw the boys all stop, some suddenly surprised, some half afraid, and some sorry perhaps.

Steerforth's place was at the bottom of the school, at the opposite end of the long room. He was lounging with his back against the wall, and his hands in his pockets, and looked at Mr. Mell with his mouth shut up as if he were whistling, when Mr. Mell looked at him.

"Silence, Mr. Steerforth!" said Mr. Mell.

"Silence yourself," said Steerforth, turning red. "Whom are you talking to?"

"Sit down," said Mr. Mell.

"Sit down yourself," said Steerforth, "and mind your business."

There was a titter, and some applause. But Mr. Mell was so white that silence immediately succeeded; and one boy, who had darted out behind him to imitate his mother again, changed his mind, and pretended to want a pen mended.

"If you think, Steerforth," said Mr. Mell, "that I am not acquainted with the power you can establish over any mind here"—he laid his hand, without considering what he did (as I supposed), upon my head—"or that I have not observed you, within a few minutes, urging your juniors on to every sort of outrage against me, you are mistaken."

"I don't give myself the trouble of thinking at all about you," said Steerforth coolly; "so I'm not mistaken, as it happens."

"And when you make use of your position of favouritism here, sir," pursued Mr. Mell, with his lip trembling very much, "to insult a gentleman——"

"A what?—where is he?" said Steerforth.

Here somebody cried out, "Shame, J. Steerforth! Too bad!" It was Traddles, whom Mr. Mell instantly discomfited by bidding him hold his tongue.

"To insult one who is not fortunate in life, sir, and who never gave you the least offence, and the many reasons for not insulting whom you are old enough and wise enough to understand," said Mr. Mell, with his lip trembling more and more, "you commit a mean and base action. You can sit down or stand up as you please, sir—Copperfield, go on."

"Young Copperfield," said Steerforth, coming forward up the room, "stop a bit. I tell you what, Mr. Mell, once for all: when you take the liberty of calling me mean or base, or anything of that sort, you are an impudent beggar. You are always a beggar, you know; but when you do that, you are an impudent beggar."

I am not clear whether he was going to strike Mr. Mell, or Mr. Mell was going to strike him, or there was any such intention on either side. I saw a rigidity come upon the whole school as if they had been turned into stone, and found

Mr. Creakle in the midst of us, with Tungay at his side, and Mrs. and Miss Creakle looking in at the door as if they were frightened. Mr. Mell, with his elbows on his desk and his face in his hands, sat for some moments quite still.

"Mr. Mell," said Mr. Creakle, shaking him by the arm—and his whisper was so audible now that Tungay felt it unnecessary to repeat his words—"you have not forgotten yourself, I hope?"

"No, sir, no," returned the Master, showing his face, and shaking his head, and rubbing his hands in great agitation. "No, sir, no. I have remembered myself; I—no, Mr. Creakle, I have not forgotten myself; I—I have remembered myself, sir. I—I—could wish you had remembered me a little sooner, Mr. Creakle. It—it—would have been more kind, sir, more just, sir. It would have saved me something, sir."

Mr. Creakle, looking hard at Mr. Mell, put his hand on Tungay's shoulder, and got his feet upon the form close by, and sat upon the desk. After still looking hard at Mr. Mell from his throne, as he shook his head and rubbed his hands, and remained in the same state of agitation, Mr. Creakle turned to Steerforth, and said,—

"Now, sir, as he don't condescend to tell me, what *is* this?"

Steerforth evaded the question for a little while, looking in scorn and anger on his opponent, and remaining silent. I could not help thinking even in that interval, I remember, what a noble fellow he was in appearance, and how homely and plain Mr. Mell looked opposed to him.

"What did he mean by talking about favourites, then?" said Steerforth at length.

"Favourites?" repeated Mr. Creakle, with the veins in his forehead swelling quickly. "Who talked about favourites?"

"He did," said Steerforth.

"And pray, what did you mean by that, sir?" demanded Mr. Creakle, turning angrily on his assistant.

"I meant, Mr. Creakle," he returned in a low voice, "as I said—that no pupil had a right to avail himself of his position of favouritism to degrade me."

"To degrade *you?*" said Mr. Creakle. "My stars! But give me leave to ask you, Mr. What's-your-name" (and here Mr. Creakle folded his arms, cane and all, upon his chest, and made such a knot of his brows that his little eyes were hardly visible below them), "whether, when you talk about favourites, you showed proper respect to me? To me, sir," said Mr. Creakle, darting his head at him suddenly, and drawing it back again, "the principal of this establishment, and your employer."

"It was not judicious, sir, I am willing to admit," said Mr. Mell. "I should not have done so if I had been cool."

Here Steerforth struck in.

"Then he said I was mean, and then he said I was base; and then I called him a beggar. If I had been cool, perhaps I shouldn't have called him a beggar; but I did, and I am ready to take the consequences of it."

Without considering, perhaps, whether there were any consequences to be taken, I felt quite in a glow at this gallant speech. It made an impression on the boys too, for there was a low stir among them, though no one spoke a word.

"I am surprised, Steerforth—although your candour does you honour," said Mr. Creakle, "does you honour, certainly —I am surprised, Steerforth, I must say, that you should attach such an epithet to any person employed and paid in Salem House, sir."

Steerforth gave a short laugh.

"That's not an answer, sir," said Mr. Creakle, "to my remark. I expect more than that from you, Steerforth."

If Mr. Mell looked homely in my eyes before the handsome boy, it would be quite impossible to say how homely Mr. Creakle looked.

"Let him deny it," said Steerforth.

"Deny that he is a beggar, Steerforth?" cried Mr. Creakle, "Why, where does he go a-begging?"

"If he is not a beggar himself, his near relation's one," said Steerforth. "It's all the same."

He glanced at me, and Mr. Mell's hand gently patted me upon the shoulder. I looked up with a flush upon my face and remorse in my heart; but Mr. Mell's eyes were fixed on Steerforth. He continued to pat me kindly on the shoulder, but he looked at him.

"Since you expect me, Mr. Creakle, to justify myself," said Steerforth, "and to say what I mean: what I have to say is, that his mother lives on charity in an alms-house."

The Unforgettable Thomas Gradgrind
FROM *Hard Times*

"In this life, we want nothing but Facts, Sir; nothing but Facts!" The speaker, and the schoolmaster, and the third grown person, all backed a little, and swept with their eyes the inclined plane of little vessels then and there arranged in order, ready to have imperial gallons of facts poured into them until they were full to the brim.

---◆◆◆---

CHAPTER I

THE ONE THING NEEDFUL

"Now, what I want is Facts. Teach these boys and girls nothing but Facts. Facts alone are wanted in life. Plant nothing else, and root out everything else. You can only form the minds of reasoning animals upon Facts: nothing else will ever be of any service to them. This is the principle on which I bring up my own children, and this is the principle on which I bring up these children. Stick to Facts, Sir!"

The scene was a plain, bare, monotonous vault of a schoolroom, and the speaker's square forefinger emphasized his observations by underscoring every sentence with a line on the schoolmaster's sleeve. The emphasis was helped by the speaker's square wall of a forehead, which had his eyebrows for its base, while his eyes found commodious cellarage in two dark caves, overshadowed by the wall. The emphasis was helped by the speaker's mouth, which was wide, thin, and hard set. The emphasis was helped by the speaker's voice, which was inflexible, dry, and dictatorial. The emphasis was helped by the speaker's hair, which bristled on the skirts of his bald head, a plantation of firs to keep the wind from its shining surface, all covered with knobs, like the crust of a plum pie, as if the head had scarcely warehouse-room for the hard facts stored inside. The speaker's obstinate carriage,

From *Hard Times* by Charles Dickens, 1854.

square coat, square legs, square shoulders—nay, his very neckcloth, trained to take him by the throat with an unaccommodating grasp, like a stubborn fact, as it was—all helped the emphasis.

"In this life, we want nothing but Facts, Sir; nothing but Facts!"

The speaker, and the schoolmaster, and the third grown person present, all backed a little, and swept with their eyes the inclined plane of little vessels then and there arranged in order, ready to have imperial gallons of facts poured into them until they were full to the brim.

CHAPTER II

MURDERING THE INNOCENTS

Thomas Gradgrind, Sir. A man of realities. A man of facts and calculations. A man who proceeds upon the principle that two and two are four, and nothing over, and who is not to be talked into allowing for anything over. Thomas Gradgrind, Sir—peremptorily Thomas—Thomas Gradgrind. With a rule and a pair of scales, and the multiplication table always in his pocket, Sir, ready to weigh and measure any parcel of human nature, and tell you exactly what it comes to. It is a mere question of figures, a case of simple arithmetic. You might hope to get some other nonsensical belief into the head of George Gradgrind, or Augustus Gradgrind, or John Gradgrind, or Joseph Gradgrind (all supposititious, non-existent persons), but into the head of Thomas Gradgrind—no, Sir!

In such terms Mr. Gradgrind always mentally introduced himself, whether to his private circle of acquaintance, or to the public in general. In such terms, no doubt, substituting the words "boys and girls," for "Sir," Thomas Gradgrind now presented Thomas Gradgrind to the little pitchers before him, who were to be filled so full of facts.

Indeed, as he eagerly sparkled at them from the cellarage before mentioned, he seemed a kind of cannon loaded to the muzzle with facts, and prepared to blow them clean out of the regions of childhood at one discharge. He seemed a galvanizing apparatus, too, charged with a grim mechanical substitute for the tender young imaginations that were to be stormed away.

"Girl number twenty," said Mr. Gradgrind, squarely point-ing with his square forefinger, "I don't know that girl. Who is that girl?"

"Sissy Jupe, Sir," explained number twenty, blushing, stand-ing up, and curtseying.

"Sissy is not a name," said Mr. Gradgrind. "Don't call yourself Sissy. Call yourself Cecilia."

"It's father as calls me Sissy, Sir," returned the young girl in a trembling voice, and with another curtsey.

"Then he has no business to do it," said Mr. Gradgrind. "Tell him he mustn't. Cecilia Jupe. Let me see. What is your father?"

"He belongs to the horse-riding, if you please, Sir."

Mr. Grandgrind frowned, and waved off the objectionable calling with his hand.

"We don't want to know anything about that, here. You mustn't tell us about that, here. Your father breaks horses, don't he?"

"If you please, Sir, when they can get any to break, they do break horses in the ring, Sir."

"You mustn't tell us about the ring, here. Very well, then. Describe your father as a horsebreaker. He doctors sick horses, I dare say?"

"Oh yes, Sir."

"Very well, then. He is a veterinary surgeon, a farrier, and horsebreaker. Give me your definition of a horse."

(Sissy Jupe thrown into the greatest alarm by this demand.)

"Girl number twenty unable to define a horse!" said Mr. Gradgrind, for the general behoof of all the little pitchers. "Girl number twenty possessed of no facts, in reference to one of the commonest of animals! Some boy's definition of a horse. Bitzer, yours."

The square finger, moving here and there, lighted sud-denly on Bitzer, perhaps because he chanced to sit in the same ray of sunlight which, darting in at one of the bare win-dows of the intensely whitewashed room, irradiated Sissy. For the boys and girls sat on the face of the inclined plane in two compact bodies, divided up the centre by a narrow in-terval; and Sissy, being at the corner of a row on the sunny side, came in for the beginning of a sunbeam, of which Bitzer, being at the corner of a row on the other side, a few rows in advance, caught the end. But whereas the girl was so dark-eyed and dark-haired that she seemed to receive a deeper and more lustrous colour from the sun when it shone upon her, the boy was so light-eyed and light-haired that the self same rays appeared to draw out of him what little colour he ever possessed. His cold eyes would hardly have been eyes but for the short ends of lashes which, by bringing them into immediate contrast with something paler than themselves, expressed their form. His shortcropped hair might have been a mere continuation of the sandy freckles on his forehead and face. His skin was so unwholesomely deficient in the natural tinge, that he looked as though, if he were cut, he would bleed white.

"Bitzer," said Thomas Gradgrind. "Your definition of a horse."

"Quadruped. Graminivorous. Forty teeth, namely twenty-four grinders, four eye-teeth, and twelve incisive. Sheds coat in the spring; in marshy countries, sheds hoofs, too. Hoofs hard, but requiring to be shod with iron. Age known by marks in mouth." Thus (and much more) Bitzer.

"Now girl number twenty," said Mr. Gradgrind. "You know what a horse is."

She curtseyed again, and would have blushed deeper, if she could have blushed deeper than she had blushed all this time. Bitzer, after rapidly blinking at Thomas Gradgrind with both eyes at once, and so catching the light upon his quivering ends of lashes that they looked like the antennæ of busy insects, put his knuckles to his freckled forehead, and sat down again.

The third gentleman now stepped forth. A mighty man at cutting and drying, he was; a government officer; in his way (and in most other people's too), a professed pugilist; always in training, always with a system to force down the general throat like a bolus, always to be heard of at the bar of his little public-office, ready to fight all England. To continue in fistic phraseology, he had a genius for coming up to the scratch, wherever and whatever it was, and proving himself an ugly customer. He would go in and damage any subject whatever with his right, follow up with his left, stop, exchange, counter, bore his opponent (he always fought All England) to the ropes, and fall upon him neatly. He was certain to knock the wind out of common sense, and render that unlucky adversary deaf to the call of time. And he had it in charge from high authority to bring about the great public-office Millennium, when Commissioners should reign upon earth.

"Very well," said this gentleman, briskly smiling, and folding his arms. "That's a horse. Now let me ask you girls and boys: Would you paper a room with representations of horses?"

After a pause, one half of the children cried in chorus, "Yes, Sir!" Upon which the other half, seeing in the gentlemen's face that Yes was wrong, cried out in chorus, "No, Sir!"—as the custom is in these examinations.

"Of course, No. Why wouldn't you?"

A pause. One corpulent slow boy, with a wheezy manner of breathing, ventured the answer, Because he wouldn't paper a room at all, but would paint it.

"You *must* paper it," said the gentleman, rather warmly.

"You must paper it," said Thomas Gradgrind, "whether you like it or not. Don't tell *us* you wouldn't paper it. What do you mean, boy?"

"I'll explain to you, then," said the gentleman, after another and a dismal pause, "why you wouldn't paper a room with representations of horses. Do you ever see horses walking up and down the sides of rooms in reality—in fact? Do you?"

"Yes, Sir!" from one half. "No, Sir!" from the other.

"Of course, No," said the gentleman, with an indignant look at the wrong half. "Why, then, you are not to see anywhere what you don't see in fact; you are not to have anywhere what you don't have in fact. What is called Taste is only another name for Fact."

Thomas Gradgrind nodded his approbation.

"This is a new principle, a discovery, a great discovery," said the gentleman. "Now, I'll try you again. Suppose you were going to carpet a room. Would you use a carpet having a representation of flowers upon it?"

There being a general conviction by this time that "No, Sir!" was always the right answer to this gentleman, the chorus of No was very strong. Only a few feeble stragglers said Yes, among them Sissy Jupe.

"Girl number twenty," said the gentleman, smiling in the calm strength of knowledge.

Sissy blushed, and stood up.

"So you would carpet your room—or your husband's room, if you were a grown woman, and had a husband—with representations of flowers, would you?" said the gentleman. "Why would you?"

"If you please, Sir, I am very fond of flowers," returned the girl.

"And is that why you would put tables and chairs upon them, and have people walking over them with heavy boots?"

"It wouldn't hurt them, Sir. They wouldn't crush and wither, if you please, Sir. They would be the pictures of what was very pretty and pleasant, and I would fancy——"

"Ay, ay, ay! But you mustn't fancy," cried the gentleman, quite elated by coming so happily to his point. "That's it! You are never to fancy."

"You are not, Cecilia Jupe," Thomas Gradgrind solemnly repeated, "to do anything of that kind."

"Fact, fact, fact!" said the gentleman. And "Fact, fact, fact!" repeated Thomas Gradgrind.

"You are to be in all things regulated and governed," said the gentleman, "by fact. We hope to have, before long, a board of fact, composed of commissioners of fact, who will force the people to be a people of fact, and of nothing but fact. You must discard the word Fancy altogether. You have nothing to do with it. You are not to have, in any object of use or ornament, what would be a contradiction in fact. You don't walk upon flowers in fact; you cannot be allowed to walk upon flowers in carpets. You don't find that foreign birds and butterflies come and perch upon your crockery; you cannot be permitted to paint foreign birds and butterflies upon your crockery. You never meet with quadrupeds going up and down walls; you must not have quadrupeds represented upon walls. You must see," said the gentleman, "for all these purposes, combinations and modifications (in primary colours) of mathematical figures which are susceptible of proof and demonstration. This is the new discovery. This is fact. This is taste."

The girl curtseyed, and sat down. She was very young, and she looked as if she were frightened by the matter-of-fact prospect the world afforded.

"Now, if Mr. M'Choakumchild," said the gentleman, "will proceed to give his first lesson here, Mr. Gradgrind, I shall be happy, at your request, to observe his mode of procedure."

Mr. Gradgrind was much obliged. "Mr. M'Choakumchild, we only wait for you."

So, Mr. Choakumchild began in his best manner. He and some one hundred and forty other schoolmasters had been lately turned at the same time, in the same factory, on the same principles, like so many pianoforte legs. He had been put through an immense variety of paces, and had answered volumes of head-breaking questions. Orthography, etymology, syntax, and prosody, biography, astronomy, geography, and general cosmography, the sciences of compound proportion, algebra, land-surveying and levelling, vocal music, and drawing from models, were all at the ends of his ten chilled fingers. He had worked his stony way into Her Majesty's most Honourable Privy Council's Schedule B, and had taken the bloom off the higher branches of mathematics and physical science, French, German, Latin and Greek. He knew all about all the water-sheds of all the world (whatever they are), and all the histories of all the peoples, and all the names of all the rivers and mountains, and all the productions, manners, and customs of all the countries, and all their boundaries and bearings on the two-and-thirty points of the compass. Ah, rather overdone, M'Choakumchild. If he had only learnt a little less, how infinitely better he might have taught much more!

He went to work in this preparatory lesson, not unlike Morgiana in the Forty Thieves: looking into all the vessels ranged before him, one after another, to see what they contained. Say good M'Choakumchild— When from thy boiling store, thou shalt fill each jar brim full by-and-by, dost thou think that thou wilt always kill outright the robber Fancy lurking within—or sometimes only maim him and distort him!

THOMAS HUGHES

Thomas Hughes (1822–1896), an English jurist, reformer, and writer, was active in the Christian Socialist movement, working to improve the conditions of the poor. He founded the Working Man's College and became its principal (1872–1873). Hughes is best known as the author of *Tom Brown's School Days* (1857).

The "doctor" in the following selection is the famous Thomas Arnold.

The Awesome Doctor
FROM *Tom Brown's School Days*

And then came that great event in his, as in every Rugby boy's life of that day—the first sermon from the doctor. . . . What was it that moved and held us . . . three hundred reckless, childish boys, who feared the doctor with all our hearts, and very little besides in heaven and earth . . . ? It was . . . the warm, living voice of one who was fighting for us and by our sides, and calling on us to help him and ourselves and one another.

—◆—

The chapel-bell began to ring at a quarter to eleven, and Tom got in early and took his place in the lowest row, and watched all the other boys come in and take their places, filling row after row: and tried to construe the Greek text which was inscribed over the door with the slightest possible success, and wondered which of the masters, who walked down the chapel and took their seats in the exalted boxes at the end, would be his lord. And then came the closing of the doors, and the doctor in his robes, and the service, which, however, didn't impress him much, for his feeling of wonder and

From *Tom Brown's School Days* by Thomas Hughes, 1857.

curiosity was too strong. And the boy on one side of him was scratching his name on the oak paneling in front, and he couldn't help watching to see what the name was, and whether it was well scratched; and the boy on the other side went to sleep and kept falling against him; and on the whole, though many boys even in that part of the school were serious and attentive, the general atmosphere was by no means devotional; and when he got out into the close again, he didn't feel at all comfortable, or as if he had been to church.

But at afternoon chapel it was quite another thing. He had spent the time after dinner in writing home to his mother, and so was in a better frame of mind; and his first curiosity was over, and he could attend more to the service. As the hymn after the prayers was being sung, and the chapel was getting a little dark, he was beginning to feel that he had been really worshipping. And then came that great event in his, as in every Rugby boy's life of that day—the first sermon from the doctor.

More worthy pens than mine have described that scene. The oak pulpit standing out by itself above the school seats. The tall gallant form, the kindling eye, the voice, now soft as the low notes of a flute, now clear and stirring as the call of the light infantry bugle, of him who stood there Sunday after Sunday, witnessing and pleading for his Lord, the King of righteousness and love and glory, with whose spirit he was filled, and in whose power he spoke. The long lines of young faces, rising tier above tier down the whole length of the chapel, from the little boy's who had just left his mother to the young man's who was going out next week into the great world rejoicing in his strength. It was a great and solemn sight, and never more so than at this time of year, when the only lights in the chapel were in the pulpit and at the seats of the præposters of the week, and the soft twilight stole over the rest of the chapel, deepening into darkness in the high gallery behind the organ.

But what was it after all which seized and held these three hundred boys, dragging them out of themselves, willing or unwilling, for twenty minutes, on Sunday afternoon? True, there always were boys scattered up and down the school, who in heart and head were worthy to hear and able to carry away the deepest and wisest words there spoken. But these were a minority always, generally a very small one, often so small a one as to be countable on the fingers of your hand.

What was it that moved and held us, the rest of the three hundred reckless, childish boys, who feared the doctor with all our hearts, and very little besides in heaven or earth: who thought more of our sets in the school than of the Church of Christ, and put the traditions of Rugby and the public opinion of boys in our daily life above the laws of God? We couldn't enter into half that we heard; we hadn't the knowledge of our own hearts or the knowledge of one another; and little enough of the faith, hope, and love needed to that end. But we listened, as all boys in their better moods will listen (aye, and men too, for the matter of that), to a man who we felt to be, with all his heart and soul and strength, striving against whatever was mean and unmanly and unrighteous in our little world. It was not the cold clear voice of one giving advice and warning from serene heights to those who were struggling and sinning below, but the warm, living voice of one who was fighting for us and by our sides, and calling on us to help him and ourselves and one another. And so, wearily and little by little, but surely and steadily on the whole, was brought home to the young boy for the first time, the meaning of his life: that it was no fool's or sluggard's paradise into which he had wandered by chance, but a battle-field ordained from of old, where there are no spectators, but the youngest must take his side, and the stakes are life and death. And he who roused his consciousness in them showed them at the same time, by every word he spoke in the pulpit, and by his whole daily life, how that battle was to be fought; and stood there before them their fellow soldier and the captain of their band. The true sort of captain, too, for a boy's army, one who had no misgivings and gave no uncertain word of command, and, let who would yield or make a truce, would fight the fight out (so every boy felt) to the last gasp and the last drop of blood. Other sides of his character might take hold of and influence boys here and there, but it was this thoroughness and undaunted courage which more than anything else won his way to the hearts of the great mass of those on whom he left his mark, and made them believe first in him, and then in his Master.

It was this quality above all others which moved such boys as our hero, who had nothing whatever remarkable about him except excess of boyishness; by which I mean animal life in its fullest measure, good nature and honest impulses, hatred of injustice and meanness and thoughtlessness enough to sink a three-decker. And so, during the next two years, in which it was more than doubtful whether he would get good or evil from the school, and before any steady purpose or principle grew up in him, whatever his week's sins and shortcomings might have been, he hardly ever left the chapel on Sunday evenings without a serious resolve to stand by and follow the doctor, and a feeling that it was only cowardice (the incarnation of all other sins in such a boy's mind) which hindered him from doing so with all his heart.

MARK TWAIN

Mark Twain, pen name of Samuel Langhorne Clemens (1835–1910), the most thoroughly American of our writers, was a product of the frontier. He grew up in Hannibal, Missouri, the town he was later to use as the setting for *Tom Sawyer*. In 1867, with experience as a miner, printer, newspaperman, and Mississippi steamboat pilot behind him, he published *The Celebrated Jumping Frog of Calaveras County and Other Sketches*. The book launched him on what was to become one of the most distinguished American literary careers. Among Twain's most widely read books are *Tom Sawyer* (1876), *Life on the Mississippi* (1883), and *The Adventures of Huckleberry Finn* (1884).

Happy Hours
FROM *Tom Sawyer*

Tom lay thinking. Presently it occurred to him that he wished he was sick; then he could stay home from school. Here was a vague possibility. He canvassed his system. No ailment was found, and he investigated again.

———◆◆———

Monday morning found Tom Sawyer miserable. Monday morning always found him so—because it began another week's slow suffering in school. He generally began that day with wishing he had no intervening holiday, it made the going into captivity and fetters again so much more odious.

Tom lay thinking. Presently it occurred to him that he wished he was sick; then he could stay home from school. Here was a vague possibility. He canvassed his system. No ailment was found, and he investigated again. This time he thought he could detect colicky symptoms, and he began to

From *Tom Sawyer* by Mark Twain, 1876.

encourage them with considerable hope. But they soon grew feeble, and presently died wholly away. He reflected further. Suddenly he discovered something. One of his upper front teeth was loose. This was lucky; he was about to begin to groan, as a "starter," as he called it, when it occurred to him that if he came into court with that argument, his aunt would pull it out, and that would hurt. So he thought he would hold the tooth in reserve for the present, and seek further. Nothing offered for some little time, and then he remembered hearing the doctor tell about a certain thing that laid up a patient for two or three weeks and threatened to make him lose a finger. So the boy eagerly drew his sore toe from under the sheet and held it up for inspection. But now he did not know the necessary symptoms. However, it seemed well worth while to chance it, so he fell to groaning with considerable spirit.

But Sid slept on unconscious.

Tom groaned louder, and fancied that he began to feel pain in the toe.

No result from Sid.

Tom was panting with his exertions by this time. He took a rest and then swelled himself up and fetched a succession of admirable groans.

Sid snored on.

Tom was aggravated. He said, "Sid, Sid!" and shook him. This course worked well, and Tom began to groan again. Sid yawned, stretched, then brought himself up on his elbow with a snort, and began to stare at Tom. Tom went on groaning. Sid said:

"Tom! Say, Tom!" (No response.) "Here, Tom! *Tom!* What is the matter, Tom?" And he shook him and looked in his face anxiously.

Tom moaned out:

"Oh, don't, Sid. Don't joggle me."

"Why, what's the matter, Tom? I must call auntie."

"No—never mind. It'll be over by and by, maybe. Don't call anybody."

"But I must! *Don't* groan so, Tom, it's awful. How long you been this way?"

"Hours. Ouch! Oh, don't stir so, Sid, you'll kill me."

"Tom, why didn't you wake me sooner? Oh, Tom, *don't!* It makes my flesh crawl to hear you. Tom, what *is* the matter?"

"I forgive you everything, Sid. (Groan.) Everything you've ever done to me. When I'm gone——"

"Oh, Tom, you ain't dying, are you? Don't, Tom—oh, don't. Maybe——"

"I forgive everybody, Sid. (Groan.) Tell 'em so, Sid. And Sid, you give my window sash and my cat with one eye to that new girl that's come to town, and tell her——"

But Sid had snatched his clothes and gone. Tom was suffering in reality, now, so handsomely was his imagination working, and so his groans had gathered quite a genuine tone.

Sid flew downstairs and said:

"Oh, Aunt Polly, come! Tom's dying!"

"Dying!"

"Yes'm. Don't wait—come quick!"

"Rubbage! I don't believe it!"

But she fled upstairs, nevertheless, with Sid and Mary at her heels. And her face grew white, too, and her lip trembled. When she reached the bedside she gasped out:

"You, Tom! Tom, what's the matter with you?"

"Oh, auntie, I'm——"

"What's the matter with you—what *is* the matter with you, child?"

"Oh, auntie, my sore toe's mortified!"

The old lady sank down into a chair and laughed a little, then she cried a little, then did both together. This restored her and she said:

"Tom, what a turn you did give me. Now you shut up that nonsense and climb out of this."

The groans ceased and the pain vanished from the toe. The boy felt a little foolish, and he said:

"Aunt Polly, it *seemed* mortified, and it hurt so I never minded my tooth at all."

"Your tooth, indeed! What's the matter with your tooth?"

"One of them's loose, and it aches perfectly awful."

"There, there, now, don't begin that groaning again. Open your mouth. Well—your tooth *is* loose, but you're not going to die about that. Mary, get me a silk thread, and a chunk of fire out of the kitchen."

Tom said:

"Oh, please auntie, don't pull it out. It don't hurt any more. I wish I may never stir if it does. Please don't, auntie. *I* don't want to stay home from school."

"Oh, you don't, don't you? So all this row was because you thought you'd get to stay home from school and go a-fishing? Tom, Tom, I love you so, and you seem to try every way you can to break my old heart with your outrageousness." By this time the dental instruments were ready. The old lady made one end of the silk thread fast to Tom's tooth with a loop and tied the other to the bedpost. Then she seized the chunk of fire and suddenly thrust it almost into the boy's face. The tooth hung dangling by the bedpost, now.

But all trials bring their compensations. As Tom wended to school after breakfast, he was the envy of every boy he met because the gap in his upper row of teeth enabled him to expectorate in a new and admirable way. He gathered quite a following of lads interested in the exhibition; and one that had cut his finger and had been a center of fascination and homage up to this time, now found himself suddenly without an adherent, and shorn of his glory. His heart was heavy, and he said with a disdain which he did not feel, that it wasn't anything to spit like Tom Sawyer; but another boy said "Sour grapes!" and he wandered away a dismantled hero.

FINLEY PETER DUNNE

Finley Peter Dunne (1867–1936) was an American news-paperman, editor, and humorist. "Mr. Dooley," created while Dunne was writing for the Chicago *Post*, was pictured as a Chicago Irishman who presided over a small saloon on Archey Road. Mr. Dooley regarded the events of the world with his own brand of wit and wisdom, addressing his re-flections to his friend Malachi Hennessey, whom Dooley described as "a post to hitch y'er silences to." "Mr. Dooley" was widely read and respected by a large and diverse audience, including both Henry Adams and Henry James.

Lickin' and Larnin'
FROM Mr. Dooley's Opinions

". . . I believe 'tis as Father Kelly says: 'Childer shudden't be sent to school to larn, but to larn how to larn. I don't care what ye larn thim so long as 'tis onpleasant to thim.' "

◆◆◆

". . . I dhropped in on Cassidy's daughter, Mary Ellen, an' see her kindygartnin'. Th' childher was settin' ar-round on th' flure an' some was moldin' dachshunds out iv mud an' wipin' their hands on their hair, an' some was carvin' figures iv a goat out iv paste-board an' some was singin' an' some was sleepin' an' a few was dancin' an' wan la-ad was pullin' another la-ad's hair. 'Why don't ye take th' coal shovel to that little barbaryan, Mary Ellen?' says I. 'We don't believe in corporeal punishment,' says she. 'School shud be made pleasant f'r th' childher,' she says. 'Th' child who's hair is bein' pulled is larnin' patience,' she says, 'an' th' child that's pullin' th' hair is discovrin' th' footility iv human indeavor,' says she. 'Well, oh, well,' says I, 'times has changed since I was a boy,' I says.

From Mr. Dooley's Opinions (1901). Reprinted from *Mr. Dooley on Ivrything and Ivrybody* by Finley Peter Dunne. Copyright © 1963 by Dover Publications.

'Put thim through their exercises,' says I. 'Tommy,' says I, 'spell cat,' I says. 'Go to th' divvle,' says th' cheerub. 'Very smartly answered,' says Mary Ellen. 'Ye shud not ask thim to spell,' she says. 'They don't larn that till they go to colledge,' she says, 'an',' she says, 'sometimes not even thin,' she says. 'An' what do they larn?' says I. 'Rompin',' she says, 'an' dancin',' she says, 'an' indepindance iv speech, an' beauty songs, an' sweet thoughts, an' how to make home home-like,' she says. 'Well,' says I, 'I didn't take anny iv thim things at colledge, so ye needn't unblanket thim,' I says. 'I won't put thim through anny exercise to-day,' I says. 'But whisper, Mary Ellen,' says I, 'don't ye niver feel like bastin' th' seeraphims?' 'Th' teachin's iv Freebull and Pitzotly is conthrary to that,' she says. 'But I'm goin' to be marrid an' lave th' school on Choosdah, th' twinty-sicond iv Janooary,' she says, 'an' on Mondah, th' twinty-first, I'm goin' to ask a few iv th' little darlin's to th' house an',' she says, 'stew thim over a slow fire,' she says. Mary Ellen is not a German, Hinnissy.

"Well, afther they have larned in school what they ar-re licked f'r larnin' in th' back yard that is squashin' mud with their hands—they're conducted up through a channel iv free an' beautiful thought till they're r-ready f'r colledge. Mamma packs a few doylies an' tidies into son's bag, an' some silver to be used in case iv throuble with th' landlord, an' th' la-ad throts off to th' siminary. If he's not sthrong eniough to look f'r high honors as a middle weight pugilist he goes into th' thought departmint. Th' prisidint takes him into a Turkish room, gives him a cigareet an' says: 'Me dear boy, what special branch iv larnin' wud ye like to have studied f'r ye be our compitint profissors? We have a chair iv Beauty an' wan iv Puns an' wan iv Pothry on th' Changin' Hues iv the Settin' Sun, an' wan on Platonic Love, an' wan on Nonsense Rhymes, an' wan on Sweet Thoughts, an' wan on How Green Grows th' Grass, an' wan on th' Relation iv Ice to th' Greek Idee iv God,' he says. 'This is all ye'll need to equip ye f'r th' perfect life, onless,' he says, 'ye intind bein' a dintist, in which case,' he says, 'we won't think much iv ye, but we have a good school where ye can larn that disgraceful thrade,' he says. An' th' la-ad makes his choice, an' ivry mornin' whin he's up in time he takes a whiff iv hasheesh an' goes off to hear Profissor Maryanna tell him that 'if th' dates iv human knowledge must be rejicted as subjictive, how much more must they be subjicted as rejictive if, as I think, we keep our thoughts fixed upon th' inanity iv th' finite in comparison with th' onthinkable truth with th' ondivided an' onimaginable reality. Boys ar-re ye with me?'

"That's at wan colledge—Th' Colledge iv Speechless Thought, Thin there's th' Colledge iv Thoughtless Speech, where th' la-ad is larned that th' best thing that can happen to annywan is to be prisident iv a railroad consolidation. Th' head iv this colledge believes in thrainin' young men f'r th' civic ideel, Father Kelly tells me. Th' on'y thrainin' I know f'r th' civic ideel is to have an alarm clock in ye'er room on iliction day. He believes 'young men shud be equipped with Courage, Discipline, an' Loftiness iv Purpose'; so I suppose Packy, if he wint there, wud listen to lectures fr'm th' Profissor iv Courage an' Erasmus H. Noddle, Doctor iv Loftiness iv Purpose. I loft, ye loft, he lofts. I've always felt we needed some wan to teach our young th' Courage they can't get walkin' home in th' dark, an' th' loftiness iv purpose that doesn't start with bein' hungry an' lookin' f'r wurruk. An' in th' colledge where these studies are taught, it's undhershtud that even betther thin gettin' th' civic ideel is bein' head iv a thrust. Th' on'y trouble with th' coorse is that whin Packy comes out loaded with loftiness iv purpose, all th' lofts is full iv men that had to figure it out on th' farm."

"I don't undherstand a wurrud iv what ye're sayin'," said Mr. Hennessy.

"No more do I," said Mr. Dooley. "But I believe 'tis as Father Kelly says: 'Childher shudden't be sint to school to larn, but to larn how to larn. I don't care what ye larn thim so long as 'tis onpleasant to thim.' 'Tis thrainin' they need, Hinnissy. That's all. I niver cud make use iv what I larned in colledge about thrigojoomethry an'—an'—grammar an' th' welts I got on th' skull fr'm the schoolmaster's cane I have nivver been able to turn to anny account in th' business, but 'twas th' bein' there and havin' to get things to heart without askin' th' meanin' iv thim an' goin' to school cold an' comin' home hungry, that made th' man iv me ye see befure ye."

"That's why th' good woman's throubled about Packy," said Hennessy.

"Go home," said Mr. Dooley.

ROMAIN ROLLAND

Romain Rolland (1866–1944), French novelist, music and
art critic, was educated in Paris and continued his studies
in Rome. In 1895, he returned to France to teach the history
of fine arts at the Ecole Normale Supérieure, and the history
of music at the Sorbonne.

Rolland's great work, *Jean-Christophe*, runs to ten volumes.
The first volume appeared in 1904 and the last in 1913. It
established him as one of the major writers of his time. *Jean-
Christophe* is a hymn to the creative spirit of man, a social
and intellectual picture of Europe during the years that pre-
ceded World War I. Critics see in Jean-Christophe, the pro-
tagonist, an embodiment of Beethoven, Mozart, Gluck, and
other great musical figures. Jean-Christophe is one of the
most vigorously, most variously alive characters in twentieth-
century literature.

The Foiled Suicide
FROM *Jean-Christophe*

He went home, pale and storming. . . . He declared frigidly that he would not go to school again. They paid no
attention to what he said. Next morning, when his mother
reminded him that it was time to go, he replied quietly
that he had said that he was not going any more.

———◆–◆———

. . . one day at school, when Jean-Christophe was spending
his time watching the flies on the ceiling, and thumping his
neighbors, to make them fall off the form, the schoolmaster,
who had taken a dislike to him, because he was always fidget-

ing and laughing, and would never learn anything, made an unhappy allusion. Jean-Christophe had fallen down himself, and the schoolmaster said he seemed to be like to follow brilliantly in the footsteps of a certain well-known person [a reference to Jean-Christophe's father, frequently drunk—ed.]. All the boys burst out laughing, and some of them took upon themselves to point the allusion with comment both lucid and vigorous. Jean-Christophe got up, livid with shame, seized his ink-pot, and hurled it with all his strength at the nearest boy whom he saw laughing. The schoolmaster fell on him and beat him. He was thrashed, made to kneel, and set to do an enormous imposition.

He went home, pale and storming, though he said never a word. He declared frigidly that he would not go to school again. They paid no attention to what he said. Next morning, when his mother reminded him that it was time to go, he replied quietly that he had said that he was not going any more. In vain Louisa begged and screamed and threatened; it was no use. He stayed sitting in his corner, obstinate. Melchior thrashed him. He howled, but every time they bade him go after the thrashing was over he replied angrily, "No!" They asked him at least to say why. He clenched his teeth, and would not. Melchior took hold of him, carried him to school, and gave him into the master's charge. They set him on his form, and he began methodically to break everything within reach—his inkstand, his pen. He tore up his copy-book and lesson-book, all quite openly, with his eye on the schoolmaster, provocative. They shut him up in a dark room. A few moments later the schoolmaster found him with his handkerchief tied round his neck, tugging with all his strength at the two ends of it. He was trying to strangle himself.

They had to send him back.

BOOTH TARKINGTON

Booth Tarkington (1869–1946), American novelist and play-wright, founded the Triangle Club at Princeton, but left the university without being graduated. In 1920 and 1923, he was a member of the Indiana house of representatives. His interest in legislation and the political process is reflected in *The Gentleman from Indiana* (1899) and *In the Arena* (1905). *Monsieur Beaucaire* (1900) caught the public fancy, but Tarkington's greatest success was *Penrod* (1914), a story about a twelve-year-old boy whose antics rivaled those of Tom Sawyer. *Seventeen* (1916) concerns Willie Baxter in the throes of his first love affair.

Tarkington wrote more than forty novels, and won Pulitzer prizes for *The Magnificent Ambersons* (1918; filmed by Orson Welles, 1941) and *Alice Adams* (1921). He also wrote twenty-five plays. In spite of the speed with which he worked, writing never came easily to him. Tarkington described writing as "a very painful job, worse than having the measles." In 1930 his eyesight failed completely, and only after a series of operations did he regain partial sight. *The World Does Move* (1928) is his autobiography.

The Joys of School
FROM *Penrod*

The nervous monotony of the schoolroom inspires a sometimes unbearable longing for something astonishing to happen, and as every boy's fundamental desire is to do something astonishing himself, so as to be the center of all human interest and awe, it was natural that Penrod should discover in fancy the delightful secret of self-levitation.

---◆◆◆---

CHAPTER VIII

SCHOOL

Next morning, when he had once more resumed the dreadful burden of education, it seemed infinitely duller. And yet what pleasanter sight is there than a schoolroom well filled with children of those sprouting years just before the 'teens? The casual visitor, gazing from the teacher's platform upon these busy little heads, needs only a blunted memory to experience the most agreeable and exhilarating sensations. Still, for the greater part, the children are unconscious of the happiness of their condition; for nothing is more pathetically true than that we "never know when we are well off." The boys in a public school are less aware of their happy state than are the girls; and of all the boys in his room, probably Penrod himself had the least appreciation of his felicity.

He sat staring at an open page of a textbook, but not studying; not even reading; not even thinking. Nor was he lost in a reverie: his mind's eye was shut, as his physical eye might well have been, for the optic nerve, flaccid with *ennui*, conveyed nothing whatever of the printed page upon which the orb of vision was partially focused. Penrod was doing something very unusual and rare, something almost never accomplished except . . . by a boy in school on a spring day: he was doing really nothing at all. He was merely a state of being.

From the street a sound stole in through the open window, and abhorring Nature began to fill the vacuum called Penrod Schofield; for the sound was the spring song of a mouth-organ, coming down the sidewalk. The windows were intentionally above the level of the eyes of the seated pupils; but the picture of the musician was plain to Penrod, painted for him by a quality in the runs and trills, partaking of the oboe, of the calliope, and of cats in anguish; an excruciating sweetness obtained only by the wallowing, walloping yellow-pink palm of a hand whose back was Congo black and shiny. The music came down the street and passed beneath the window, accompanied by the carefree shuffling of a pair of old shoes scuffing syncopations on the cement sidewalk. It passed into the distance; became faint and blurred; was gone. Emotion stirred in Penrod a great and poignant desire, but (perhaps fortunately) no fairy godmother made her appearance. Otherwise Penrod would have gone down the street in a black skin, playing the mouth-organ, and an unprepared colored youth would have found himself enjoying educational advantages for which he had no ambition whatever.

Roused from perfect apathy, the boy cast about the school-room an eye wearied to nausea by the perpetual vision of the neat teacher upon the platform, the backs of the heads of the pupils in front of him, and the monotonous stretches of blackboard threateningly defaced by arithmetical formulæ and other insignia of torture. Above the blackboard, the walls of the high room were of white plaster—white with the qualified whiteness of old snow in a soft coal town. This dismal expanse was broken by four lithographic portraits, votive offerings of a thoughtful publisher. The portraits were of good and great men, kind men; men who loved children. Their faces were noble and benevolent. But the lithographs offered the only rest for the eyes of children fatigued by the everlasting sameness of the schoolroom. Long day after long day, interminable week in and interminable week out, vast month on vast month, the pupils sat with those four portraits beaming kindness down upon them. The faces became permanent in the consciousness of the children; they became an obsession—in and out of school the children were never free of them. The four faces haunted the minds of children falling asleep; they hung upon the minds of children waking at night; they rose forebodingly in the minds of children waking in the morning; they became monstrously alive in the minds of children lying sick of fever. Never, while the children of that schoolroom lived, would they be able to forget one detail of the four lithographs: the hand of Longfellow was fixed, for them, forever, in his beard. And by a simple and unconscious association of ideas, Penrod Schofield was accumulating an antipathy for the gentle Longfellow and for James Russell Lowell and for Oliver Wendell Holmes and for John Greenleaf Whittier, which would never permit him to peruse a work of one of those great New Englanders without a feeling of personal resentment.

His eyes fell slowly and inimically from the brow of Whittier to the braid of reddish hair belonging to Victorine Riordan, the little octoroon girl who sat directly in front of him. Victorine's back was as familiar to Penrod as the necktie of Oliver Wendell Holmes. So was her gayly colored plaid waist. He hated the waist as he hated Victorine herself, without knowing why. Enforced companionship in large quantities and on an equal basis between the sexes appears to sterilize the affections, and schoolroom romances are few.

Victorine's hair was thick, and the brickish glints in it were beautiful, but Penrod was very tired of it. A tiny knot of green ribbon finished off the braid and kept it from unravelling; and beneath the ribbon there was a final wisp of hair which was just long enough to repose upon Penrod's desk when Victorine leaned back in her seat. It was there now. Thoughtfully, he took the braid between thumb and forefinger, and without disturbing Victorine, dipped the end of it and the green ribbon into the ink-well of his desk. He brought hair and ribbon forth dripping purple ink, and partially dried them on a blotter, though, a moment later when Victorine leaned forward, they were still able to add a few picturesque touches to the plaid waist.

Rudolph Krauss, across the aisle from Penrod, watched the operation with protuberant eyes, fascinated. Inspired to imitation, he took a piece of chalk from his pocket and wrote "RATS" across the shoulder-blades of the boy in front of him, then looked across appealingly to Penrod for tokens of congratulations. Penrod yawned. It may not be denied that at times he appeared to be a very self-centered boy.

CHAPTER IX

SOARING

Half the members of the class passed out to a recitation-room, the empurpled Victorine among them, and Miss Spence started the remaining half through the ordeal of trial by mathematics. Several boys and girls were sent to the blackboard, and Penrod, spared for the moment, followed their operations a little while with his eyes, but not with his mind; then, sinking deeper in his seat, limply abandoned the effort. His eyes remained open, but saw nothing; the routine of the arithmetic lesson reached his ears in familiar, meaningless sounds, but he heard nothing; and yet, this time, he was profoundly occupied. He had drifted away from the painful land of facts, and floated now in a new sea of fancy which he had just discovered.

Maturity forgets the marvelous realness of a boy's daydreams, how colorful they glow, rosy and living, and how opaque the curtain closing down between the dreamer and the actual world. That curtain is almost sound-proof, too, and causes more throat-trouble among parents than is suspected.

The nervous monotony of the schoolroom inspires a some-times unbearable longing for something astonishing to happen, and as every boy's fundamental desire is to do something astonishing himself, so as to be the center of all human interest and awe, it was natural that Penrod should discover in fancy the delightful secret of self-levitation. He found, in this curious series of imaginings, during the lesson in arithmetic, that the atmosphere may be navigated as by a swimmer under water, but with infinitely greater ease and with perfect comfort in breathing. In his mind he extended his arms gracefully, at a level with his shoulders, and delicately paddled the air with his hands, which at once caused him to be drawn up out of his seat and elevated gently to a position about midway between the floor and the ceiling, where he came to an equilibrium and floated; a sensation not the less exquisite because of the screams of his fellow pupils, appalled by the miracle. Miss Spence herself was amazed and frightened, but he only smiled down carelessly upon her when she commanded him to return to earth; and then, when she climbed upon a desk to pull him down, he quietly paddled himself a little higher, leaving his toes just out of her reach. Next, he swam through a few slow somersaults to show his mastery of the new art, and, with the shouting of the dumb-founded scholars ringing in his ears, turned on his side and floated swiftly out of the window, immediately rising above the housetops, while people in the street below him shrieked, and a trolley car stopped dead in wonder.

With almost no exertion he paddled himself, many yards at a stroke, to the girls' private school where Marjorie Jones was a pupil—Marjorie Jones of the amber curls and the golden voice! Long before the "Pageant of the Table Round," she had offered Penrod a hundred proofs that she considered him wholly undesirable and ineligible. At the Friday Afternoon Dancing Class she consistently incited and led the laughter at him whenever Professor Bartet singled him out for ad-monition in matters of feet and decorum. And but yesterday she had chid him for his slavish lack of memory in daring to offer her a greeting on the way to Sunday-school. "Well! I expect you must forgot I told you never to speak to me again! If I was a boy, I'd be too proud to come hanging around peo-ple that don't speak to me, even if I *was* the Worst Boy in

Town!" So she flouted him. But now, as he floated in through the window of her classroom and swam gently along the ceiling like an escaped toy balloon, she fell upon her knees beside her little desk, and, lifting up her arms toward him, cried with love and admiration:

"Oh, *Pen*rod!"

He negligently kicked a globe from the high chandelier, and, smiling coldly, floated out through the hall to the front steps of the school, while Marjorie followed, imploring him to grant her one kind look.

In the street an enormous crowd had gathered, headed by Miss Spence and a brass band; and a cheer from a hundred thousand throats shook the very ground as Penrod swam overhead. Marjorie knelt upon the steps and watched adoringly while Penrod took the drum-major's baton and, performing sinuous evolutions above the crowd, led the band. Then he threw the baton so high that it disappeared from sight; but he went swiftly after it, a double delight, for he had not only the delicious sensation of rocketing safely up and up into the blue sky, but also that of standing in the crowd below, watching and admiring himself as he dwindled to a speck, disappeared and then, emerging from a cloud, came speeding down, with the baton in his hand, to the level of the treetops, where he beat time for the band and the vast throng and Marjorie Jones, who all united in the "Star-spangled Banner" in honor of his aerial achievements. It was a great moment.

It was a great moment, but something seemed to threaten it. The face of Miss Spence looking up from the crowd grew too vivid—unpleasantly vivid. She was beckoning him and shouting, "Come down, Penrod Schofield! Penrod Schofield, come down here!" He could hear her above the band and the singing of the multitude; she seemed intent on spoiling everything. Marjorie Jones was weeping to show how sorry she was that she had formerly slighted him, and throwing kisses to prove that she loved him; but Miss Spence kept jumping between him and Marjorie, incessantly calling his name.

He grew more and more irritated with her; he was the most important person in the world and was engaged in proving it to Marjorie Jones and the whole city, and yet Miss Spence seemed to feel she still had the right to order him about as she did in the old days when he was an ordinary schoolboy. He was furious; he was sure she wanted him to do something disagreeable. It seemed to him that she had screamed "Penrod Schofield!" thousands of times.

From the beginning of his aerial experiments in his own schoolroom, he had not opened his lips, knowing somehow that one of the requirements for air floating is perfect silence on the part of the floater; but, finally, irritated beyond measure by Miss Spence's clamorous insistence, he was unable to restrain an indignant rebuke—and immediately came to earth with a frightful bump.

Miss Spence—in the flesh—had directed toward the physical body of the absent Penrod an inquiry as to the fractional consequences of dividing seventeen apples, fairly, among three boys, and she was surprised and displeased to receive no answer although to the best of her knowledge and belief, he was looking fixedly at her. She repeated her question crisply, without visible effect; then summoned him by name with increasing asperity. Twice she called him, while all his fellow pupils turned to stare at the gazing boy. She advanced a step from the platform.

"Penrod Schofield!"

"Oh, my goodness!" he shouted suddenly. "Can't you keep still a *minute?*"

CHAPTER X

UNCLE JOHN

Miss Spence gasped. So did the pupils. The whole room filled with a swelling conglomerate *"O-o-o-o-h!"*

As for Penrod himself, the walls reeled with the shock. He sat with his mouth open, a mere lump of stupefaction. For the appalling words that he had hurled at the teacher were as inexplicable to him as to any other who heard them.

Nothing is more treacherous than the human mind; nothing else so loves to play the Iscariot. Even when patiently bullied into a semblance of order and training, it may prove but a base and shifty servant. And Penrod's mind was not his servant; it was a master, with the April wind's whims; and it had just played him a diabolical trick. The very jolt with which he came back to the schoolroom in the midst of his fancied flight jarred his day-dream utterly out of him; and he sat, open-mouthed in horror at what he had said.

The unanimous gasp of awe was protracted. Miss Spence,

however, finally recovered her breath, and, returning deliberately to the platform, faced the school. "And then, for a little while," as pathetic stories sometimes recount, "everything was very still." It was so still, in fact, that Penrod's newborn notoriety could almost be heard growing. This grisly silence was at last broken by the teacher.

"Penrod Schofield, stand up!"

The miserable child obeyed.

"What did you mean by speaking to me in that way?"

He hung his head, raked the floor with the side of his shoe, swayed, swallowed, looked suddenly at his hands with the air of never having seen them before, then clasped them behind him. The school shivered in ecstatic horror, every fascinated eye upon him; yet there was not a soul in the room but was profoundly grateful to him for the sensation—including the offended teacher herself. Unhappily, all this gratitude was unconscious and altogether different from the kind which results in testimonials and loving-cups On the contrary!

"Penrod Schofield!"

He gulped.

"Answer me at once! Why did you speak to me like that?"

"I was——" He choked, unable to continue.

"Speak out!"

"I was just—thinking," he managed to stammer.

"That will not do," she returned sharply. "I wish to know immediately why you spoke as you did."

The stricken Penrod answered helplessly:

"Because I was just thinking."

Upon the very rack he could have offered no ampler truthful explanation. It was all he knew about it.

"Thinking what?"

"Just thinking."

Miss Spence's expression gave evidence that her power of self-restraint was undergoing a remarkable test. However, after taking counsel with herself, she commanded:

"Come here!"

He shuffled forward, and she placed a chair upon the platform near her own.

"Sit there!"

Then (but not at all as if nothing had happened) she continued the lesson in arithmetic. Spiritually the children may have learned a lesson in very small fractions indeed as they gazed at the fragment of sin before them on the stool of penitence. They all stared at him attentively with hard and passionately interested eyes, in which there was never one trace of pity. It cannot be said with precision that he writhed; his movement was more a slow, continuous squirm, effected with a ghastly assumption of languid indifference; while his gaze, in the effort to escape the marble-hearted glare of his schoolmates, affixed itself with apparent permanence to the waistcoat button of James Russell Lowell just above the "U" in "Russell."

Classes came and classes went, grilling him with eyes. Newcomers received the story of the crime in darkling whispers; and the outcast sat and sat and sat, and squirmed and squirmed and squirmed. (He did one or two things with his spine which a professional contortionist would have observed with real interest.) And all this while of freezing suspense was but the criminal's detention awaiting trial. A known punishment may be anticipated with some measure of equanimity; at least, the prisoner may prepare himself to undergo it; but the unknown looms more monstrous for every attempt to guess it. Penrod's crime was unique; there were no rules to aid him in estimating the vengeance to fall upon him for it. What seemed most probable was that he would be expelled from the school in the presence of his family, the mayor, and council, and afterward whipped by his father upon the State House steps, with the entire city as audience by invitation of the authorities.

Noon came. The rows of children filed out, every head turning for a last unpleasingly speculative look at the outlaw. Then Miss Spence closed the door into the cloakroom and that into the big hall, and came and sat at her desk, near Penrod. The tramping of feet outside, the shrill calls and shouting and the changing voices of the older boys ceased to be heard—and there was silence. Penrod, still affecting to be occupied with Lowell, was conscious that Miss Spence looked at him intently.

"Penrod," she said gravely, "what excuse have you to offer before I report your case to the principal?"

The word "principal" struck him to the vitals. Grand Inquisitor, Grand Khan, Sultan, Emperor, Tsar, Cæsar Augustus—these are comparable. He stopped squirming instantly, and sat rigid.

"I want an answer. Why did you shout those words at me?"

"Well," he murmured, "I was just—thinking."

"Thinking what?" she asked sharply.

"I don't know."

"That won't do!"

He took his left ankle in his right hand and regarded it helplessly.

"That won't do, Penrod Schofield," she repeated severely. "If that is all the excuse you have to offer I shall report your case this instant!"

And she rose with fatal intent.

But Penrod was one of those whom the precipice inspires. "Well, I *have* got an excuse."

"Well" — she paused impatiently — "what is it?"

He had not an idea, but he felt one coming, and replied automatically, in a plaintive tone:

"I guess anybody that had been through what *I* had to go through, last night, would think they had an excuse."

Miss Spence resumed her seat, though with the air of being ready to leap from it instantly.

"What has last night to do with your insolence to me this morning?"

"Well, I guess you'd see," he returned, emphasizing the plaintive note, "if you knew what *I* know."

"Now, Penrod," she said, in a kinder voice, "I have a high regard for your mother and father, and it would hurt me to distress them, but you must either tell me what was the matter with you or I'll have to take you to Mrs. Houston."

"Well, ain't I going to?" he cried, spurred by the dread name. "It's because I didn't sleep last night."

"Were you ill?" The question was put with some dryness.

He felt the dryness. "No'm; *I* wasn't."

"Then if someone in your family was so ill that even you were kept up all night, how does it happen they let you come to school this morning?"

"It wasn't illness," he returned, shaking his head mournfully. "It was lots worse'n anybody's being sick. It was—it was—well, it was jest awful."

"*What* was?" He remarked with anxiety the incredulity in her tone.

"It was about Aunt Clara," he said.

"Your Aunt Clara!" she repeated. "Do you mean your mother's sister who married Mr. Farry of Dayton, Illinois?"

"Yes—Uncle John," returned Penrod sorrowfully. "The trouble was about him."

Miss Spence frowned a frown which he rightly interpreted as one of continued suspicion. "She and I were in school together," she said. "I used to know her very well, and I've always heard her married life was entirely happy. I don't——"

"Yes, it was," he interrupted, "until last year when Uncle John took to running with traveling men——"

"What?"

"Yes'm." He nodded solemnly. "That was what started it. At first he was a good, kind husband, but these traveling men would coax him into a saloon on his way from work, and they got him to drinking beer and then ales, wines, liquors, and cigars——"

"Penrod!"

"Ma'am?"

"I'm not inquiring into your Aunt Clara's private affairs; I'm asking you if you have anything to say which would palliate——"

"That's what I'm tryin' to *tell* you about, Miss Spence," he pleaded,—"if you'd jest only let me. When Aunt Clara and her little baby daughter got to our house last night——"

"You say Mrs. Farry is visiting your mother?"

"Yes'm—not just visiting—you see, she *had* to come. Well of course, little baby Clara, she was so bruised up and mauled, where he'd been hittin' her with his cane——"

"You mean that your uncle had done such a thing as *that!*" exclaimed Miss Spence, suddenly disarmed by this scandal.

"Yes'm, and mamma and Margaret had to sit up all night nursin' little Clara—and *Aunt* Clara was in such a state *somebody* had to keep talkin' to *her*, and there wasn't anybody but me to do it, so I——"

"But where was your father?" she cried.

"Ma'am?"

"Where was your father while——"

"Oh—papa?" Penrod paused, reflected; then brightened. "Why, he was down at the train, waitin' to see if Uncle John would try to follow 'em and make 'em come home so's he could persecute 'em some more. I wanted to do that, but they said if he did come I mightn't be strong enough to hold him, and——" The brave lad paused again, modestly. Miss Spence's expression was encouraging. Her eyes were wide with astonishment, and there may have been in them, also, the mingled beginnings of admiration and self-reproach. Penrod, warming to his work, felt safer every moment.

"And so," he continued, "I had to sit up with Aunt Clara. She had some pretty big bruises, too, and I had to——"

"But why didn't they send for a doctor?" However, this question was only a flicker of dying incredulity.

"Oh, they didn't want any *doctor*," exclaimed the inspired realist promptly. "They don't want anybody to *hear* about it because Uncle John might reform—and then where'd he be if everybody knew he'd been a drunkard and whipped his wife and baby daughter?"

"Oh!" said Miss Spence.

"You see, he used to be upright as anybody," he went on explanatively. "It all begun——"

"Began, Penrod."

"Yes'm. It all commenced from the first day he let those traveling men coax him into the saloon." Penrod narrated the downfall of his Uncle John at length. In detail he was nothing short of plethoric; and incident followed incident, sketched with such vividness, such abundance of color, and such verisimilitude to a drunkard's life as a drunkard's life should be, that had Miss Spence possessed the rather chilling attributes of William J. Burns himself, the last trace of skepticism must have vanished from her mind. Besides, there are two things that will be believed of any man whatsoever, and one of them is that he has taken to drink. And in every sense it was a moving picture which, with simple but eloquent words, the virtuous Penrod set before his teacher.

His eloquence increased with what it fed on; and as with the eloquence so with self-reproach in the gentle bosom of the teacher. She cleared her throat with difficulty once or twice, during his description of his ministering night with Aunt Clara. "And I said to her, 'Why, Aunt Clara, what's the use of takin' on so about it?' And I said, 'Now, Aunt Clara, all the crying in the world can't make things any better.' And then she'd just keep catchin' hold of me, and sob and kind of holler, and I'd say, '*Don't* cry, Aunt Clara—*please* don't cry.'"

Then, under the influence of some fragmentary survivals of the respectable portion of his Sunday adventures, his theme became more exalted; and, only partially misquoting a phrase from a psalm, he related how he had made it of comfort to Aunt Clara, and how he had besought her to seek Higher guidance in her trouble.

The surprising thing about a structure such as Penrod was erecting is that the taller it becomes the more ornamentation it will stand. Gifted boys have this faculty of building magnificence upon cobwebs—and Penrod was gifted. Under the spell of his really great performance, Miss Spence gazed more and more sweetly upon the prodigy of spiritual beauty and goodness before her, until at last, when Penrod came to the explanation of his "just thinking," she was forced to turn her head away.

"You mean, dear," she said gently, "that you were all worn out and hardly knew what you were saying?"

"Yes'm."

"And you were thinking about all those dreadful things so hard that you forgot where you were?"

"I was thinking," he said simply, "how to save Uncle John."

And the end of it for this mighty boy was that the teacher kissed him!

W. SOMERSET MAUGHAM

William Somerset Maugham (1874–1965) was an English novelist, short-story writer, and playwright. His unhappy youth was plagued by a stammer, incipient tuberculosis, shyness, and loneliness. Although he began as a practicing physician, he always wanted to write rather than care for patients. In 1907 he realized his ambition. His first play, *Lady Frederick*, was an immediate success and made him immensely popular. He grew rich on the royalties of his plays and embarked on what was to be a lifelong series of travels that took him all over the world and provided him with materials for his writings.

Maugham's finest novel, *Of Human Bondage* (1915), brought him recognition and appreciation. Partly autobiographical, *Of Human Bondage* is still widely read. Maugham's work is marked by skillful craftsmanship, a lightly satirical and cynical tone, and a characteristically ironic detachment.

The Names That Maim
FROM *Of Human Bondage*

From the first day Mr. Gordon struck terror in his heart; and the master, quick to discern the boys who were frightened of him, seemed on that account to take a peculiar dislike to him. Philip had enjoyed his work, but now he began to look upon the hours passed in school with horror.

———◆◆◆———

The Rev. B. B. Gordon was a man by nature ill-suited to be a schoolmaster: he was impatient and choleric. No master could have been more unfitted to teach things to so shy a boy as Philip. He had come to the school with fewer terrors than he had when first he went to Mr. Watson's. He knew a good many boys who had been with him at the preparatory school. He felt more grown-up, and instinctively realised that among the larger numbers his deformity would be less noticeable. But from the first day Mr. Gordon struck terror in his heart; and the master, quick to discern the boys who were frightened of him, seemed on that account to take a peculiar dislike to him. Philip had enjoyed his work, but now he began to look upon the hours passed in school with horror. Rather than risk an answer which might be wrong and excite a storm of abuse from the master, he would sit stupidly silent, and when it came towards his turn to stand up and construe he grew sick and white with apprehension. His happy moments were those when Mr. Perkins took the form. He was able to gratify the passion for general knowledge which beset the headmaster; he had read all sorts of strange books beyond his years, and often Mr. Perkins, when a question was going round the room, would stop at Philip with a smile that filled the boy with rapture, and say:

"Now, Carey, you tell them."

The good marks he got on these occasions increased Mr. Gordon's indignation. One day it came to Philip's turn to translate, and the master sat there glaring at him and furiously biting his thumb. He was in a ferocious mood. Philip began to speak in a low voice.

"Don't mumble," shouted the master.

Something seemed to stick in Philip's throat.

"Go on. Go on. Go on."

Each time the words were screamed more loudly. The effect was to drive all he knew out of Philip's head, and he looked at the printed page vacantly. Mr. Gordon began to breathe heavily.

"If you don't know why don't you say so? Do you know it or not? Did you hear all this construed last time or not? Why don't you speak? Speak, you blockhead, speak!"

The master seized the arms of his chair and grasped them as though to prevent himself from falling upon Philip. They knew that in past days he often used to seize boys by the throat till they almost choked. The veins in his forehand stood out and his face grew dark and threatening. He was a man insane.

Philip had known the passage perfectly the day before, but now he could remember nothing.

"I don't know it," he gasped.

"Why don't you know it? Let's take the words one by one. We'll soon see if you don't know it."

Philip stood silent, very white, trembling a little, with his head bent down on the book. The master's breathing grew almost stertorous.

"The headmaster says you're clever. I don't know how he sees it. General information." He laughed savagely. "I don't know what they put you in his form for. Blockhead."

He was pleased with the word, and he repeated it at the top of his voice.

"Blockhead! Blockhead! Club-footed blockhead!"

That relieved him a little. He saw Philip redden suddenly. He told him to fetch the Black Book. Philip put down his Caesar and went silently out. The Black Book was a sombre volume in which the names of boys were written with their misdeeds, and when a name was down three times it meant a caning. Philip went to the headmaster's house and knocked at his study-door. Mr. Perkins was seated at his table.

"May I have the Black Book, please, sir?"

"There it is," answered Mr. Perkins, indicating its place by a nod of his head. "What have you been doing that you shouldn't?"

"I don't know, sir."

Mr. Perkins gave him a quick look, but without answering went on with his work. Philip took the book and went out. When the hour was up, a few minutes later, he brought it back.

"Let me have a look at it," said the headmaster. "I see Mr. Gordon has black-booked you for 'gross impertinence.' What was it?"

"I don't know, sir. Mr. Gordon said I was a club-footed blockhead."

Mr. Perkins looked at him again. He wondered whether there was sarcasm behind the boy's reply, but he was still much too shaken. His face was white and his eyes had a look of terrified distress. Mr. Perkins got up and put the book down. As he did so he took up some photographs.

"A friend of mine sent me some pictures of Athens this morning," he said casually. "Look here, there's the Akropolis."

He began explaining to Philip what he saw. The ruin grew vivid with his words. He showed him the theatre of Dionysus and explained in what order the people sat, and how beyond they could see the blue Aegean. And then suddenly he said:

"I remember Mr. Gordon used to call me a gipsy counterjumper when I was in his form."

And before Philip, his mind fixed on the photographs, had time to gather the meaning of the remark, Mr. Perkins was showing him a picture of Salamis, and with his finger, a finger of which the nail had a little black edge to it, was pointing out how the Greek ships were placed and how the Persian.

D. H. LAWRENCE

David Herbert Lawrence, (1885–1930) was born in the mining village of Eastwood, Nottinghamshire. His father was a coal miner, his mother a teacher. For a short time, he taught school. He gave up teaching after the publication of his first novel, *The White Peacock* (1911). From that point on, he devoted his time to writing. He traveled widely through India, Australia, New Mexico, Mexico, and Europe. He died in France of tuberculosis.

Lawrence is recognized as one of the most gifted of English prose writers—a fine stylist with a highly sensitive mind capable of extraordinary empathy for the world around him. His almost uncanny insight into men and women is revealed in his autobiographical novel *Sons and Lovers* (1913), and in *Women in Love* (1920) and *Lady Chatterley's Lover* (1928).

The Ordeal of Ursula Brangwen
FROM *The Rainbow*

She stood before her class not knowing what to do. She waited painfully. Her block of children, fifty unknown faces, watched her, hostile, ready to jeer. . . . They were so many, that they were not children. They were a squadron. She could not speak as she would to a child, because they were not individual children, they were a collective, inhuman thing.

———◆◆◆———

She was walking down a small, mean, wet street, empty of people. The school squatted low within its railed, asphalt yard, that shone black with rain. The building was grimy, and horrible, dry plants were shadowily looking through the windows.

She entered the arched doorway of the porch. The whole place seemed to have a threatening expression, imitating the church's architecture, for the purpose of domineering, like a gesture of vulgar authority. She saw that one pair of feet had paddled across the flagstone floor of the porch. The place was silent, deserted, like an empty prison waiting the return of tramping feet.

Ursula went forward to the teachers' room that burrowed in a gloomy hole. She knocked timidly.

"Come in!" called a surprised man's voice, as from a prison cell. She entered the dark little room that never got any sun. The gas was lighted naked and raw. At the table a thin man in shirt-sleeves was rubbing a paper on a jelly-tray. He looked up at Ursula with his narrow, sharp face, said "Good morning," then turned away again, and stripped the paper off the tray, glancing at the violet-coloured writing transferred, before he dropped the curled sheet aside among a heap. . . .

"Am I early?" she asked.

The man looked first at a little clock, then at her. His eyes seemed to be sharpened to needle-points of vision.

"Twenty-five past," he said. "You're the second to come. I'm first this morning."

Ursula sat down gingerly on the edge of a chair, and watched his thin red hands rubbing away on the white surface of the paper, then pausing, pulling up a corner of the sheet, peering, and rubbing away again. There was a great heap of curled white-and-scribbled sheets on the table.

"Must you do so many?" asked Ursula. . . .

"Sixty-three," he answered.

"It is too many," she said sympathetically.

"You'll get about the same," he said.

That was all she received. She sat rather blank, not knowing how to feel. . . .

The door opened, and a short, neutral-tinted young woman of about twenty-eight appeared.

"Oh, Ursula!" the newcomer exclaimed. "You are here early! My word, I'll warrant you don't keep it up. That's Mr. Williamson's peg. *This* is yours. Standard Five teacher always has this. Aren't you going to take your hat off?"

Miss Violet Harby removed Ursula's waterproof from the peg on which it was hung, to one a little farther down the row. She had already snatched the pins from her own stuff

hat, and jammed them through her coat. She turned to
Ursula, as she pushed up her frizzed, flat, dun-coloured hair.

"Isn't it a beastly morning," she exclaimed, "beastly!
And if there's one thing I hate above another it's a wet
Monday morning;—pack of kids trailing in anyhow-nohow,
and no holding 'em———"

She had taken a black pinafore from a newspaper package,
and was tying it round her waist.

"You've brought an apron, haven't you?" she said jerkily,
glancing at Ursula. "Oh—you'll want one. You've no idea
what a sight you'll look before half-past four, what with chalk
and ink and kids' dirty feet.—Well, I can send a boy down
to mamma's for one."

"Oh, it doesn't matter," said Ursula.

"Oh, yes—I can send easily," cried Miss Harby.

Ursula's heart sank. Everybody seemed so cocksure and
so bossy. How was she going to get on with such jolty, jerky,
bossy people? And Miss Harby had not spoken a word to
the man at the table. She simply ignored him. Ursula felt
the callous crude rudeness between the two teachers.

The two girls went out into the passage. A few children
were already clattering in the porch.

"Jim Richards," called Miss Harby, hard and authoritative.
A boy came sheepishly forward.

"Shall you go down to our house for me, eh?" said Miss
Harby, in a commanding, condescending, coaxing voice. She
did not wait for an answer. "Go down and ask mamma to
send me one of my school pinas, for Miss Brangwen—shall
you?"

The boy muttered a sheepish "Yes, miss," and was moving
away.

"Hey," called Miss Harby. "Come here—now what are
you going for? What shall you say to mamma?"

"A school pina———" muttered the boy.

" 'Please, Mrs. Harby, Miss Harby says will you send her
another school pinafore for Miss Brangwen, because she's
come without one.' "

"Yes, miss," muttered the boy, head ducked, and was
moving off. Miss Harby caught him back, holding him by
the shoulder.

"What are you going to say?"

"Please, Mrs. Harby, Miss Harby wants a pinny for Miss
Brangwin," muttered the boy very sheepishly.

"Miss *Brangwen!*" laughed Miss Harby, pushing him away. "Here, you'd better have my umbrella—wait a minute."

The unwilling boy was rigged up with Miss Harby's umbrella, and set off.

"Don't take long over it," called Miss Harby, after him. Then she turned to Ursula, and said brightly:

"Oh, he's a caution, that lad—but not bad, you know."

"No," Ursula agreed, weakly.

The latch of the door clicked, and they entered the big room. Ursula glanced down the place. Its rigid, long silence was official and chilling. Half-way down was a glass partition, the doors of which were open. A clock ticked re-echoing, and Miss Harby's voice sounded double as she said:

"This is the big room—Standard Five-Six-and-Seven.— Here's your place—Five——"

She stood in the near end of the great room. There was a small high teacher's desk facing a squadron of long benches, two high windows in the wall opposite.

It was fascinating and horrible to Ursula. The curious, unliving light in the room changed her character. She thought it was the rainy morning. Then she looked up again, because of the horrid feeling of being shut in a rigid, inflexible air, away from all feeling of the ordinary day; and she noticed that the windows were of ribbed, suffused glass.

The prison was round her now! She looked at the walls, colour washed, pale green and chocolate, at the large windows with frowsy geraniums against the pale glass, at the long rows of desks, arranged in a squadron, and dread filled her. This was a new world, a new life, with which she was threatened. But still excited, she climbed into her chair at her teacher's desk. It was high, and her feet could not reach the ground, but must rest on the step. Lifted up there, off the ground, she was in office. How queer, how queer it all was! How different it was from the mist of rain blowing over Cossethay. As she thought of her own village, a spasm of yearning crossed her, it seemed so far off, so lost to her.

She was here in this hard, stark reality—*reality*. It was queer that she should call this the reality, which she had never known till to-day, and which now so filled her with dread and dislike, that she wished she might go away. This was the reality, and Cossethay, her beloved, beautiful, well-known Cossethay, which was as herself unto her, that was minor reality. This prison of a school was reality. Here, then, she would sit in state, the queen of scholars! Here she would realise her dream of being the beloved teacher bringing light and joy to her children! But the desks before her had an abstract angularity that bruised her sentiment and made her shrink. She winced, feeling she had been a fool in her anticipations. She had brought her feelings and her generosity to where neither generosity nor emotion were wanted. And already she felt rebuffed, troubled by the new atmosphere, out of place.

She slid down, and they returned to the teachers' room. It was queer to feel that one ought to alter one's personality. She was nobody, there was no reality in herself, the reality was all outside of her, and she must apply herself to it.

Mr. Harby was in the teachers' room, standing before a big, open cupboard, in which Ursula could see piles of pink blotting-paper, heaps of shiny new books, boxes of chalk, and bottles of coloured inks. It looked a treasure store.

The schoolmaster was a short, sturdy man, with a fine head, and a heavy jowl. Nevertheless he was good-looking, with his shapely brows and nose, and his great, hanging moustache. He seemed absorbed in his work, and took no notice of Ursula's entry. There was something insulting in the way he could be so actively unaware of another person, so occupied.

When he had a moment of absence, he looked up from the table and said good-morning to Ursula. There was a pleasant light in his brown eyes. He seemed very manly and incontrovertible, like something she wanted to push over.

"You had a wet walk," he said to Ursula.

"Oh, I don't mind, I'm used to it," she replied, with a nervous little laugh.

But already he was not listening. Her words sounded ridiculous and babbling. He was taking no notice of her.

"You will sign your name here," he said to her, as if she were some child—"and the time when you come and go."

Ursula signed her name in the time book and stood back. No one took any further notice of her. She beat her brains for something to say, but in vain.

"I'd let them in now," said Mr. Harby to the thin man, who was very hastily arranging his papers.

The assistant teacher made no sign of acquiescence, and went on with what he was doing. The atmosphere in the room grew tense. At the last moment Mr. Brunt slipped into his coat.

"You will go to the girls' lobby," said the schoolmaster to Ursula, with a fascinating, insulting geniality, purely official and domineering.

She went out and found Miss Harby, and another girl teacher, in the porch. On the asphalt yard the rain was falling. A toneless bell tang-tang-tanged drearily overhead, monotonously, insistently. It came to an end. Then Mr. Brunt was seen, bare-headed, standing at the other gate of the school yard, blowing shrill blasts on a whistle and looking down the rainy, dreary street.

Boys in gangs and streams came trotting up, running past the master and with a loud clatter of feet and voices, over the yard to the boys' porch. Girls were running and walking through the other entrance.

In the porch where Ursula stood there was a great noise of girls, who were tearing off their coats and hats, and hanging them on the racks bristling with pegs. There was a smell of wet clothing, a tossing out of wet, draggled hair, a noise of voices and feet.

The mass of girls grew greater, the rage around the pegs grew steadier, the scholars tended to fall into little noisy gangs in the porch. Then Violet Harby clapped her hands, clapped them louder, with a shrill "Quiet, girls, quiet!"

There was a pause. The hubbub died down but did not cease.

"What did I say?" cried Miss Harby, shrilly.

There was almost complete silence. Sometimes a girl, rather late, whirled into the porch and flung off her things.

"Leaders—in place," commanded Miss Harby shrilly.

Pairs of girls in pinafores and long hair stood separate in the porch.

"Standard Four, Five, and Six—fall in," cried Miss Harby.

There was a hubbub, which gradually resolved itself into three columns of girls, two and two, standing smirking in the passage. In among the peg-racks, other teachers were putting the lower classes into ranks.

Ursula stood by her own Standard Five. They were jerking their shoulders, tossing their hair, nudging, writhing, staring, grinning, whispering and twisting.

A sharp whistle was heard, and Standard Six, the biggest girls, set off, led by Miss Harby. Ursula, with her Standard Five, followed after. She stood beside a smirking, grinning row of girls, waiting in a narrow passage. What she was herself she did not know.

Suddenly the sound of a piano was heard, and Standard Six set off hollowly down the big room. The boys had entered by another door. The piano played on, a march tune. Standard Five followed to the door of the big room. Mr. Harby was seen away beyond at his desk. Mr. Brunt guarded the other door of the room. Ursula's class pushed up. She stood near them. They glanced and smirked and shoved.

"Go on," said Ursula.

They tittered.

"Go on," said Ursula, for the piano continued.

The girls broke loosely into the room. Mr. Harby, who had seemed immersed in some occupation, away at his desk, lifted his head and thundered:

"Halt!"

There was a halt, the piano stopped. The boys who were just starting through the other door, pushed back. The harsh, subdued voice of Mr. Brunt was heard, then the booming shout of Mr. Harby, from far down the room:

"Who told Standard Five girls to come in like that?"

Ursula crimsoned. Her girls were glancing up at her, smirking their accusation.

"I sent them in, Mr. Harby," she said, in a clear, struggling voice. There was a moment of silence. Then Mr. Harby roared from the distance.

"Go back to your places, Standard Five girls."

The girls glanced up at Ursula, accusing, rather jeering, fugitive. They pushed back. Ursula's heart hardened with ignominious pain.

"Forward—march," came Mr. Brunt's voice, and the girls set off, keeping time with the ranks of boys.

Ursula faced her class, some fifty-five boys and girls, who stood filling the ranks of the desks. She felt utterly nonexistent. She had no place nor being there. She faced the block of children.

Down the room she heard the rapid firing of questions. She stood before her class not knowing what to do. She waited painfully. Her block of children, fifty unknown faces, watched her, hostile, ready to jeer. She felt as if she were in torture over a fire of faces. And on every side she was naked to them. Of unutterable length and torture the seconds went by.

Then she gathered courage. She heard Mr. Brunt asking questions in mental arithmetic. She stood near to her class, o that her voice need not be raised too much, and faltering, uncertain, she said:

"Seven hats at twopence ha'penny each?"

A grin went over the faces of the class, seeing her commence. She was red and suffering. Then some hands shot up like blades, and she asked for the answer.

The day passed incredibly slowly. She never knew what to do, there came horrible gaps, when she was merely exposed to the children; and when, relying on some pert little girl for information, she had started a lesson, she did not know how to go on with it properly. The children were her masters. She deferred to them. She could always hear Mr. Brunt. Like a machine, always in the same hard, high, inhuman voice he went on with his teaching, oblivious of everything. And before this inhuman number of children she was always at bay. She could not get away from it. There it was, this class of fifty collective children, depending on her for command, for command it hated and resented. It made her feel she could not breathe: she must suffocate, it was so inhuman. They were so many, that they were not children. They were a squadron. She could not speak as she would to a child, because they were not individual children, they were a collective, inhuman thing.

Dinner-time came, and stunned, bewildered, solitary, she went into the teachers' room for dinner. Never had she felt such a stranger to life before. It seemed to her she had just disembarked from some strange horrible state where everything was as in hell, a condition of hard, malevolent system. And she was not really free. The afternoon drew at her like some bondage.

The first week passed in a blind confusion. She did not know how to teach, and she felt she never would know. Mr. Harby came down every now and then to her class, to see what she was doing. She felt so incompetent as he stood by, bullying and threatening, so unreal, that she wavered, became neutral and non-existent. But he stood there watching with the listening-genial smile of the eyes, that was really threatening; he said nothing, he made her go on teaching, she felt she had no soul in her body. Then he went away, and his going was like a derision. The class was his class. She was a wavering substitute. He thrashed and bullied, he was hated. But he was master. Though she was gentle and always considerate of her class, yet they belonged to Mr. Harby, and they did not belong to her. Like some invincible source of the mechanism he kept all power to himself. And the class owned his power. And in school it was power, and power alone that mattered. . . .

So she taught on. She made friends with the Standard Three teacher, Maggie Schofield. Miss Schofield was about twenty years old, a subdued girl who held aloof from the other teachers. She was rather beautiful, meditative, and seemed to live in another, lovelier world.

Ursula took her dinner to school, and during the second week ate it in Miss Schofield's room. Standard Three classroom stood by itself and had windows on two sides, looking on to the playground. It was a passionate relief to find such a retreat in the jarring school. For there were pots of chrysanthemums and coloured leaves, and a big jar of berries: there were pretty little pictures on the wall, photogravure reproductions from Greuze, and Reynolds's "Age of Innocence," giving an air of intimacy; so that the room, with its window space, its smaller, tidier desks, its touch of pictures and flowers, made Ursula at once glad. Here at last was a little personal touch, to which she could respond.

It was Monday. She had been at school a week and was getting used to the surroundings, though she was still an entire foreigner in herself. She looked forward to having dinner with Maggie. That was the bright spot in the day. Maggie was so strong and remote, walking with slow, sure steps down a hard road, carrying the dream within her. Ursula went through the class teaching as through a meaningless daze.

Her class tumbled out at midday in haphazard fashion. She did not realise what host she was gathering against herself by her superior tolerance, her kindness and her *laisser-aller*. They were gone, and she was rid of them, and that was all. She hurried away to the teachers' room.

Mr. Brunt was crouching at the small stove, putting a little rice-pudding into the oven. . . .

"Don't you think it's rather jolly bringing dinner?" she said to Mr. Brunt.

"I don't know as I do," he said, spreading a serviette on a corner of the table, and not looking at her.

"I suppose it is too far for you to go home?"

"Yes," he said. Then he rose and looked at her. He had the bluest, fiercest, most pointed eyes that she had ever met. He stared at her with growing fierceness.

"If I were you, Miss Brangwen," he said, menacingly, "I should get a bit tighter hand over my class."

Ursula shrank.

"Would you?" she asked, sweetly, yet in terror. "Aren't I strict enough?"

"Because," he repeated, taking no notice of her, "they'll get you down if you don't tackle 'em pretty quick. They'll pull you down, and worry you, till Harby gets you shifted—that's how it'll be. You won't be here another six weeks"—and he filled his mouth with food—"if you don't tackle 'em and tackle 'em quick."

"Oh, but——" Ursula said, resentfully, ruefully. The terror was deep in her.

"Harby'll not help you. This is what he'll do—he'll let you go on, getting worse and worse, till either you clear out or he clears you out. It doesn't matter to me, except that you'll leave a class behind you as *I* hope I shan't have to cope with."

She heard the accusation in the man's voice, and felt condemned. . . .

"I do feel frightened," said Ursula. "The children seem so——"

"What?" said Miss Harby, entering at that moment.

"Why," said Ursula, "Mr. Brunt says I ought to tackle my class," and she laughed uneasily.

"Oh, you have to keep order if you want to teach," said Miss Harby, hard, superior, trite.

Ursula did not answer. She felt non valid before them.

"If you want to be let to *live*, you have," said Mr. Brunt.

"Well, if you can't keep order, what good *are* you?" said Miss Harby.

"An' you've got to do it by yourself,"—his voice rose like the bitter cry of the prophets. "You'll get no *help* from anybody."

"Oh, indeed!" said Miss Harby. "Some people can't be helped." And she departed.

The air of hostility and disintegration, of wills working in antagonistic subordination, was hideous. Mr. Brunt, subordinate, afraid, acid with shame, frightened her. Ursula wanted to run. She only wanted to clear out, not to understand.

Then Miss Schofield came in, and with her another, more restful note. Ursula at once turned for confirmation to the newcomer. . . .

"Is Mr. Harby really horrid?" asked Ursula, venturing into her own dread.

"He!—why, he's just a bully," said Miss Schofield, raising her shamed dark eyes, that flamed with tortured contempt. "He's not bad as long as you keep in with him, and defer to him, and do everything in his way—but—it's all so *mean!* It's just a question of fighting on both sides—and those great louts——"

She spoke with difficulty and with increased bitterness. She had evidently suffered. Her soul was raw with ignominy. Ursula suffered in response.

"But why is it so horrid?" she asked, helplessly.

"You can't do *anything,*" said Miss Schofield. "He's against you on one side and he sets the children against you on the other. The children are simply awful. You've got to *make* them do everything. Everything, everything has got to come out of you. Whatever they learn, you've got to force it into them—and that's how it is."

Ursula felt her heart fail inside her. Why must she grasp all this, why must she force learning on fifty-five reluctant children, having all the time an ugly, rude jealousy behind her, ready to throw her to the mercy of the herd of children, who would like to rend her as a weaker representative of authority. A great dread of her task possessed her. She saw Mr. Brunt, Miss Harby, Miss Schofield, all the school-teachers, drudging unwillingly at the graceless task of compelling many children into one disciplined, mechanical set, reducing the whole set to an automatic state of obedience and attention, and then of commanding their acceptance of various pieces of knowledge. The first great task was to reduce sixty children to one state of mind, or being. This state must be produced automatically, through the will of the teacher, and the will of the whole school authority, imposed upon the will of the children. The point was that the headmaster and the teachers should have one will in authority, which should bring the will of the children into accord. But the headmaster was narrow and exclusive. The will of the teachers could not agree with his, their separate wills refused to be so subordinated. So there was a state of anarchy, leaving the final judgment to the children themselves, which authority should exist.

So there existed a set of separate wills, each straining itself to the utmost to exert its own authority. Children will never naturally acquiesce to sitting in a class and submitting to knowledge. They must be compelled by a stronger, wiser will. Against which will they must always strive to revolt. So that the first great effort of every teacher of a large class must be to bring the will of the children into accordance with his own will. And this he can only do by an abnegation of his personal self, and an application of a system of laws, for the purpose of achieving a certain calculable result, the imparting of certain knowledge. Whereas Ursula thought she was going to become the first wise teacher by making the whole business personal, and using no compulsion. She believed entirely in her own personality.

So that she was in a very deep mess. In the first place she was offering to a class a relationship which only one or two of the children were sensitive enough to appreciate, so that the mass were left outsiders, therefore against her. Secondly, she was placing herself in passive antagonism to the one fixed authority of Mr. Harby, so that the scholars could more safely harry her. She did not know, but her instinct gradually warned her. She was tortured by the voice of Mr. Brunt. On it went, jarring, harsh, full of hate, but so monotonous, it nearly drove her mad: always the same set, harsh monotony. The man was become a mechanism working on and on and on. But the personal man was in subdued friction all the time. It was horrible—all hate! Must she be like this? She could feel the ghastly necessity. She must become the same —put away the personal self, become an instrument, an abstraction, working upon a certain material, the class, to achieve a set purpose of making them know so much each day. And she could not submit. Yet gradually she felt the invincible iron closing upon her. The sun was being blocked out. Often when she went out at playtime and saw a luminous blue sky with changing clouds, it seemed just a fantasy, like a piece of painted scenery. Her heart was so black and tangled in the teaching, her personal self was shut in prison, abolished, she was subjugate to a bad, destructive will. How then could the sky be shining? There was no sky, there was no luminous atmosphere of out-of-doors. Only the inside of the school was real—hard, concrete, real and vicious.

She would not yet, however, let school quite overcome her. She always said, "It is not a permanency, it will come to an end." She could always see herself beyond the place, see the time when she had left it. On Sundays and on holidays, when she was away at Cossethay or in the woods where the beech-leaves were fallen, she could think of St. Philip's Church

School, and by an effort of will put it in the picture as a dirty
little low-squatting building that made a very tiny mound
under the sky, while the great beech-woods spread immense
about her, and the afternoon was spacious and wonderful.
Moreover the children, the scholars, they were insignificant
little objects far away, oh, far away. And what power had
they over her free soul? A fleeting thought of them, as she
kicked her way through the beech-leaves, and they were gone.
But her will was tense against them all the time.

All the while, they pursued her. She had never had such
a passionate love of the beautiful things about her. Sitting
on top of the tram-car, at evening, sometimes school was
swept away as she saw a magnificent sky settling down. And
her breast, her very hands, clamoured for the lovely flare of
sunset. It was poignant almost to agony, her reaching for it.
She almost cried aloud seeing the sundown so lovely.

For she was held sway. It was no matter how she said to
herself that school existed no more once she had left it. It
existed. It was within her like a dark weight, controlling her
movement. It was in vain the high-spirited, proud young girl
flung off the school and its association with her. She was Miss
Brangwen, she was Standard Five teacher, she had her most
important being in her work now. . . .

She went on doggedly, blindly, waiting for a crisis. Mr.
Harby had now begun to persecute her. Her dread and hatred
of him grew and loomed larger and larger. She was afraid he
was going to bully her and destroy her. He began to persecute her because she could not keep her class in proper condition, because her class was the weak link in the chain which
made up the school.

One of the offences was that her class was noisy and disturbed Mr. Harby, as he took Standard Seven at the other
end of the room. She was taking composition on a certain
morning, walking in among the scholars. Some of the boys
had dirty ears and necks, their clothing smelled unpleasantly,
but she could ignore it. She corrected the writing as she went.

"When you say 'their fur is brown,' how do you write
'their'?" she asked.

There was a little pause; the boys were always jeeringly
backward in answering. They had begun to jeer at her
authority altogether.

"Please, miss, t-h-e-i-r," spelled a lad, loudly, with a note of
mockery.

At that moment Mr. Harby was passing.

"Stand up, Hill!" he called, in a big voice.

Everybody started. Ursula watched the boy. He was evidently poor, and rather cunning. A stiff bit of hair stood straight off his forehead, the rest fitted close to his meagre head. He was pale and colourless.

"Who told you to call out?" thundered Mr. Harby.

The boy looked up and down, with a guilty air, and a cunning, cynical reserve.

"Please, sir, I was answering," he replied, with the same humble insolence.

"Go to my desk."

The boy set off down the room, the big black jacket hanging in dejected folds about him, his thin legs, rather knocked at the knees, going already with the pauper's crawl, his feet in their big boots scarcely lifted. Ursula watched him in his crawling, slinking progress down the room. He was one of *her* boys! When he got to the desk, he looked round, half furtively, with a sort of cunning grin and a pathetic leer at the big boys in Standard VII. Then, pitiable, pale, in his dejected garments, he lounged under the menace of the headmaster's desk, with one thin leg crooked at the knee and the foot stuck out sideways, his hands in the low-hanging pockets of his man's jacket.

Ursula tried to get her attention back to the class. The boy gave her a little horror, and she was at the same time hot with pity for him. She felt she wanted to scream. She was responsible for the boy's punishment. Mr. Harby was looking at her handwriting on the board. He turned to the class.

"Pens down."

The children put down their pens and looked up.

"Fold arms."

They pushed back their books and folded arms.

Ursula, stuck among the back forms, could not extricate herself.

"What is your composition about?" asked the headmaster. Every hand shot up. "The ——" stuttered some voice in its eagerness to answer.

"I wouldn't advise you to call out," said Mr. Harby. He would have a pleasant voice, full and musical, but for the detestable menace that always tailed in it. He stood unmoved, his eyes twinkling under his bushy black eyebrows, watching the class. There was something fascinating in him, as he stood, and again she wanted to scream. She was all jarred, she did not know what she felt.

"Well, Alice?" he said.

"The rabbit," piped a girl's voice.

"A very easy subject for Standard Five."

Ursula felt a slight shame of incompetence. She was exposed before the class. . . . She looked over the silent, attentive class that seemed to have crystallised into order and rigid, neutral form. This he had it in his power to do, to crystallise the children into hard, mute fragments, fixed under his will: his brute will, which fixed them by sheer force. She too must learn to subdue them to her will: she must. For it was her duty, since the school was such. He had crystallised the class into order. But to see him, a strong, powerful man, using all his power for such a purpose, seemed almost horrible. There was something hideous about it. . . .

The lesson was finished, Mr. Harby went away. At the far end of the room she heard the whistle and the thud of the cane. Her heart stood still within her. She could not bear it, no, she could not bear it when the boy was beaten. It made her sick. She felt that she must go out of this school, this torture-place. And she hated the schoolmaster, thoroughly and finally. The brute, had he no shame? He should never be allowed to continue the atrocity of this bullying cruelty. Then Hill came crawling back, blubbering piteously. There was something desolate about this blubbering that nearly broke her heart. For after all, if she had kept her class in proper discipline, this would never have happened, Hill would never have called out and been caned.

She began the arithmetic lesson. But she was distracted. The boy Hill sat away on the back desk, huddled up, blubbering and sucking his hand. It was a long time. She dared not go near, nor speak to him. She felt ashamed before him. And she felt she could not forgive the boy for being the huddled, blubbering object, all wet and snivelled, which he was.

She went on correcting the sums. But there were too many children. She could not get round the class. And Hill was on her conscience. At last he had stopped crying, and sat bunched over his hands, playing quietly. Then he looked up at her. His face was dirty with tears, his eyes had a curious washed look, like the sky after rain, a sort of wanness. He bore no malice. He had already forgotten, and was waiting to be restored to the normal position.

"Go on with your work, Hill," she said.

The children were playing over their arithmetic, and, she knew, cheating thoroughly. She wrote another sum on the blackboard. She could not get round the class. She went again to the front to watch. Some were ready. Some were not. What was she to do?

At last it was time for recreation. She gave the order to cease working, and in some way or other got her class out of the room. Then she faced the disorderly litter of blotted, uncorrected books, of broken rulers and chewed pens. And her heart sank in sickness. The misery was getting deeper.

The trouble went on and on, day after day. She had always piles of books to mark, myriads of errors to correct, a heart-wearying task that she loathed. And the work got worse and worse. When she tried to flatter herself that the composition grew more alive, more interesting, she had to see that the handwriting grew more and more slovenly, the books more filthy and disgraceful. She tried what she could, but it was of no use. But she was not going to take it seriously. Why should she? Why should she say to herself, that it mattered, if she failed to teach a class to write perfectly neatly? Why should she take the blame unto herself?

Pay day came, and she received four pounds two shillings and one penny. She was very proud that day. She had never had so much money before. And she had earned it all herself. She sat on the top of the tram-car fingering the gold and fearing she might lose it. She felt so established and strong, because of it. . . .

She had a standing ground now apart from her parents. She was something else besides the mere daughter of William and Anna Brangwen. She was independent. She earned her own living. She was an important member of the working community. . . .

She had another self, another responsibility. She was no longer Ursula Brangwen, daughter of William Brangwen. She was also Standard Five teacher in St. Philip's School. And it was a case now of being Standard Five teacher, and nothing else. For she could not escape.

Neither could she succeed. That was her horror. As the weeks passed on, there was no Ursula Brangwen, free and jolly. There was only a girl of that name obsessed by the fact that she could not manage her class of children. At week-ends there came days of passionate reaction, when she went mad with the taste of liberty, when merely to be free in the morning, to sit down at her embroidery and stitch the coloured silks was a passion of delight. For the prison house was always awaiting her! This was only a respite, as her chained heart knew well. So that she seized hold of the swift hours of the week-end, and wrung the last drop of sweetness out of them, in a little, cruel frenzy.

She did not tell anybody how this state was a torture to her. She did not confide . . . how horrible she found it to be a school-teacher. But when Sunday night came, and she felt the Monday morning at hand, she was strung up tight with dreadful anticipation, because the strain and the torture was near again. . . .

[Mr. Harby] was now beginning a regular attack on her, to drive her away out of his school. She could not keep order. Her class was a turbulent crowd, and the weak spot in the school's work. Therefore, she must go, and someone more useful must come in her place, someone who could keep discipline.

The headmaster had worked himself into an obsession of fury against her. He only wanted her gone. She had come, she had got worse as the weeks went on, she was absolutely no good. His system, which was his very life in school, the outcome of his bodily movement, was attacked and threatened at the point where Ursula was included. She was the danger that threatened his body with a blow, a fall. And blindly, thoroughly, moving from strong instinct of opposition, he set to work to expel her.

When he punished one of her children as he had punished the boy Hill, for an offence against *himself*, he made the punishment extra heavy with the significance that the extra stroke came in because of the weak teacher who allowed all these things to be. When he punished for an offence against *her*, he punished lightly, as if offences against her were not significant. Which all the children knew, and they behaved accordingly.

Every now and again Mr. Harby would swoop down to examine exercise books. For a whole hour, he would be going round the class, taking book after book, comparing page after page, whilst Ursula stood aside for all the remarks and fault-finding to be pointed at her through the scholars. It was true, since she had come, the composition books had grown more and more untidy, disorderly, filthy. Mr. Harby pointed to the pages done before her régime, and to those done after, and fell into a passion of rage. Many children he sent out to the front with their books. And after he had thoroughly gone through the silent and quivering class he caned the worst offenders well, in front of the others, thundering in real passion of anger and chagrin.

"Such a condition in a class, I can't believe it! It is simply disgraceful! I can't think how you have been let to get like it! Every Monday morning I shall come down and examine these books. So don't think that because there is nobody paying any attention to you, that you are free to unlearn everything you ever learned, and go back till you are not fit for Standard Three. I shall examine all books every Monday——"

Then in a rage, he went away with his cane, leaving Ursula to confront a pale, quivering class, whose childish faces were shut in blank resentment, fear, and bitterness, whose souls were full of anger and contempt for *her* rather than of the master, whose eyes looked at her with the cold, inhuman accusation of children. And she could hardly make mechanical words to speak to them. When she gave an order they obeyed with an insolent off-handedness, as if to say: "As for you, do you think we would obey *you*, but for the master?" She sent the blubbering, caned boys to their seats, knowing that they too jeered at her and her authority, holding her weakness responsible for what punishment had overtaken them. And she knew the whole position, so that even her horror of physical beating and suffering sank to a deeper pain, and became a moral judgment upon her, worse than any hurt.

She must, during the next week, watch over her books, and punish any fault. Her soul decided it coldly. Her personal desire was dead for that day at least. She must have nothing more of herself in school. She was to be Standard Five teacher only. That was her duty. In school, she was nothing but Standard Five teacher. Ursula Brangwen must be excluded.

So that, pale, shut, at last distant and impersonal, she saw no longer the child, how his eyes danced, or how he had a queer little soul that could not be bothered with shaping handwriting so long as he dashed down what he thought. She saw no children, only the task that was to be done. And keeping her eyes there, on the task, and not on the child, she was impersonal enough to punish where she could otherwise only have sympathized, understood, and condoned, to approve where she would have been merely uninterested before. But her interest had no place any more.

It was agony to the impulsive, bright girl of seventeen to

become distant and official, having no personal relationship
with the children. For a few days, after the agony of the
Monday, she succeeded, and had some success with her class.
But it was a state not natural to her, and she began to relax.

Then came another infliction. There were not enough pens
to go round the class. She sent to Mr. Harby for more. He
came in person.

"Not enough pens, Miss Brangwen?" he said, with the
smile and calm of exceeding rage against her.

"No, we are six short," she said, quaking.

"Oh, how is that?" he said menacingly. Then, looking
over the class, he asked:

"How many are there here to-day?"

"Fifty-two," said Ursula, but he did not take any notice,
counting for himself.

"Fifty-two," he said. "And how many pens are there,
Staples?"

Ursula was now silent. He would not heed her if she
answered, since he had addressed the monitor.

"That's a very curious thing," said Mr. Harby, looking over
the silent class with a slight grin of fury. All the childish
faces looked up at him blank and exposed.

"A few days ago there were sixty pens for this class—now
there are forty-eight. What is forty-eight from sixty, Williams?" There was a sinister suspense in the question. A thin,
ferret-faced boy in a sailor suit started up exaggeratedly.

"Please, sir!" he said. Then a slow, sly grin came over
his face. He did not know. There was a tense silence. The
boy dropped his head. Then he looked up again, a little
cunning triumph in his eyes. "Twelve," he said.

"I would advise you to attend," said the headmaster
dangerously. The boy sat down.

"Forty-eight from sixty is twelve: so there are twelve pens
to account for. Have you looked for them, Staples?"

"Yes, sir."

"Then look again."

The scene dragged on. Two pens were found: ten were
missing. Then the storm burst.

"Am I to have you thieving, besides your dirt and bad
work and bad behaviour?" the headmaster began. "Not content with being the worst-behaved and dirtiest class in the
school, you are thieves into the bargain, are you? It is a very
funny thing! Pens don't melt into the air: pens are not in

the habit of mizzling away into nothing. What has become of them then? They must be somewhere. What has become of them? For they must be found, and found by Standard Five. They were lost by Standard Five, and they must be found."

Ursula stood and listened, her heart hard and cold. She was so much upset, that she felt almost mad. Something in her tempted her to turn on the headmaster and tell him to stop, about the miserable pens. But she did not. She could not.

After every session, morning and evening, she had the pens counted. Still they were missing. And pencils and india-rubbers disappeared. She kept the class staying behind, till the things were found. But as soon as Mr. Harby had gone out of the room, the boys began to jump about and shout, and at last they bolted in a body from the school.

This was drawing near a crisis. She could not tell Mr. Harby because, while he would punish the class, he would make her the cause of the punishment, and her class would pay her back with disobedience and derision. Already there was a deadly hostility grown up between her and the children. After keeping in the class, at evening, to finish some work, she would find boys dodging behind her, calling after her: "Brangwen, Brangwen—Proud-acre."

When she went into Ilkeston of a Saturday morning with Gudrun, she heard again the voices yelling after her:

"Brangwen, Brangwen."

She pretended to take no notice, but she coloured with shame at being held up to derision in the public street. She, Ursula Brangwen of Cossethay, could not escape from the Standard Five teacher which she was. In vain she went out to buy ribbon for her hat. They called after her, the boys she tried to teach.

And one evening, as she went from the edge of the town into the country, stones came flying at her. Then the passion of shame and anger surpassed her. She walked on unheeding, beside herself. Because of the darkness she could not see who were those that threw. But she did not want to know.

Only in her soul a change took place. Never more, and never more would she give herself as individual to her class. Never would she, Ursula Brangwen, the girl she was, the person she was, come into contact with those boys. She would be Standard Five teacher, as far away personally from her class as if she had never set foot in St. Philip's school. She would just obliterate them all, and keep herself apart, take them as scholars only.

So her face grew more and more shut, and over her flayed, exposed soul of a younger girl who had gone open and warm to give herself to the children, there set a hard, insentient thing, that worked mechanically according to a system imposed.

It seemed she scarcely saw her class the next day. She could only feel her will, and what she would have of this class which she must grasp into subjection. It was no good, any more, to appeal, to play upon the better feelings of the class. Her swift-working soul realised this.

She, as teacher, must bring them all as scholars, into subjection. And this she was going to do. All else she would forsake. She had become hard and impersonal, almost avengeful on herself as well as on them, since the stone throwing. She did not want to be a person, to be herself any more, after such humiliation. She would assert herself for mastery, be only teacher. She was set now. She was going to fight and subdue.

She knew by now her enemies in the class. The one she hated most was Williams. He was a sort of defective, not bad enough to be so classed. He could read with fluency, and had plenty of cunning intelligence. But he could not keep still. And he had a kind of sickness very repulsive to a sensitive girl, something cunning and etiolated and degenerate. Once he had thrown an ink-well at her, in one of his mad little rages. Twice he had run home out of class. He was a well-known character.

And he grinned up his sleeve at this girl-teacher, sometimes hanging round her to fawn on her. But this made her dislike him more. He had a kind of leech-like power.

From one of the children she took a supple cane, and this she determined to use when real occasion came. One morning, at composition, she said to the boy Williams:

"Why have you made this blot?"

"Please, miss, it fell off my pen," he whined out, in the mocking voice that he was so clever in using. The boys near snorted with laughter. For Williams was an actor, he could tickle the feelings of his hearers subtly. Particularly he could tickle the children with him into ridiculing his teacher, or indeed, any authority of which he was not afraid. He had that peculiar gaol instinct.

"Then you must stay in and finish another page of composition," said the teacher.

This was against her usual sense of justice, and the boy resented it derisively. At twelve o'clock she caught him slinking out.

"Williams, sit down," she said.

And there she sat, and there he sat, alone, opposite to her, on the back desk, looking up at her with his furtive eyes every minute.

"Please, miss, I've got to go an errand," he called out insolently.

Bring me your book," said Ursula.

The boy came out, flapping his book along the desks. He had not written a line.

"Go back and do the writing you have to do," said Ursula. And she sat at her desk, trying to correct books. She was trembling and upset. And for an hour the miserable boy writhed and grinned in his seat. At the end of that time he had done five lines.

"As it is so late now," said Ursula, "you will finish the rest this evening."

The boy kicked his way insolently down the passage.

The afternoon came again. Williams was there, glancing at her, and her heart beat thick, for she knew it was a fight between them. She watched him.

During the geography lesson, as she was pointing to the map with her cane, the boy continually ducked his whitish head under the desk, and attracted the attention of other boys.

"Williams," she said, gathering her courage, for it was critical now to speak to him, "what are you doing?"

He lifted his face, the sore-rimmed eyes half smiling. There was something intrinsically indecent about him. Ursula shrank away.

"Nothing," he replied, feeling a triumph.

"What are you doing?" she repeated, her heart-beat suffocating her.

"Nothing," replied the boy, insolently, aggrieved, comic.

"If I speak to you again, you must go down to Mr. Harby," she said.

But this boy was a match even for Mr. Harby. He was so persistent, so cringing, and flexible, he howled so when he was hurt, that the master hated more the teacher who sent him than he hated the boy himself. For of the boy he was sick of the sight. Which Williams knew. He grinned visibly.

Ursula turned to the map again, to go on with the geog raphy lesson. But there was a little ferment in the class Williams' spirit infected them all. She heard a scuffle, and then she trembled inwardly. If they all turned on her this time, she was beaten.

"Please, miss——" called a voice in distress.

She turned round. One of the boys she liked was ruefully holding out a torn celluloid collar. She heard the complaint feeling futile.

"Go in front, Wright," she said.

She was trembling in every fibre. A big, sullen boy, not bad but very difficult, slouched out to the front. She went on with the lesson, aware that Williams was making faces at Wright, and that Wright was grinning behind her. She was afraid. She turned to the map again. And she was afraid.

"Please, miss, Williams——" came a sharp cry, and a boy on the back row was standing up, with drawn, pained brows, half a mocking grin on his pain, half real resentment against Williams—"Please, miss, he's nipped me,"—and he rubbed his leg ruefully.

"Come in front, Williams," she said.

The rat-like boy sat with his pale smile and did not move.

"Come in front," she repeated, definite now.

"I shan't," he cried, snarling, rat-like, grinning. Something went click in Ursula's soul. Her face and his eyes set, she went through the class straight. The boy cowered before her glowering, fixed eyes. But she advanced on him, seized him by the arm, and dragged him from his seat. He clung to the form. It was the battle between him and her. Her instinct had suddenly become calm and quick. She jerked him from his grip, and dragged him, struggling and kicking, to the front. He kicked her several times, and clung to the forms as he passed, but she went on. The class was on its feet in excitement. She saw it, and made no move.

She knew if she let go the boy he would dash to the door. Already he had run home once out of her class. So she snatched her cane from the desk, and brought it down on him. He was writhing and kicking. She saw his face beneath her, white, with eyes like the eyes of a fish, stony, yet full of hate and horrible fear. And she loathed him, the hideous writhing thing that was nearly too much for her. In horror lest he should overcome her, and yet at the heart quite calm, she brought down the cane again and again, whilst he struggled making inarticulate noises, and lunging vicious kicks at her.

With one hand she managed to hold him, and now and then the cane came down on him. He writhed, like a mad thing. But the pain of the strokes cut through his writhing, vicious, coward's courage, bit deeper, till at last, with a long whimper that became a yell, he went limp. She let him go, and he rushed at her, his teeth and eyes glinting. There was a second of agonised terror in her heart: he was a beast thing. Then she caught him, and the cane came down on him. A few times, madly, in a frenzy, he lunged and writhed, to kick her. But again the cane broke him, he sank with a howling yell on the floor, and like a beaten beast lay there yelling.

Mr. Harby had rushed up towards the end of this performance.

"What's the matter?" he roared.

Ursula felt as if something were going to break in her.

"I've thrashed him," she said, her breast heaving, forcing out the words on the last breath. The headmaster stood choked with rage, helpless. She looked at the writhing, howling figure on the floor.

"Get up," she said. The thing writhed away from her. She took a step forward. She had realised the presence of the headmaster for one second, and then she was oblivious of it again.

"Get up," she said. And with a little dart the boy was on his feet. His yelling dropped to a mad blubber. He had been in a frenzy.

"Go and stand by the radiator," she said.

As if mechanically, blubbering, he went.

The headmaster stood robbed of movement or speech. His face was yellow, his hands twitched convulsively. But Ursula stood stiff not far from him. Nothing could touch her now: she was beyond Mr. Harby. She was as if violated to death.

The headmaster muttered something, turned, and went down the room, whence, from the far end, he was heard roaring in a mad rage at his own class.

The boy blubbered wildly by the radiator. Ursula looked at the class. There were fifty pale, still faces watching her, a hundred round eyes fixed on her in an attentive, expressionless stare.

"Give out the history readers," she said to the monitors.

There was dead silence. As she stood there, she could hear again the ticking of the clock, and the chock of piles of books taken out of the low cupboard. Then came the faint flap of books on the desks. The children passed in silence, their

hands working in unison. They were no longer a pack, but
each one separated into a silent, closed thing.

"Take page 125, and read that chapter," said Ursula.

There was a click of many books opened. The children
found the page, and bent their heads obediently to read. And
they read, mechanically.

Ursula, who was trembling violently, went and sat in her
high chair. The blubbering of the boy continued. The strident
voice of Mr. Brunt, the roar of Mr. Harby, came muffled
through the glass partition. And now and then a pair o.
eyes rose from the reading-book, rested on her a moment
watchful, as if calculating impersonally, then sank again.

She sat still without moving, her eyes watching the class,
unseeing. She was quite still, and weak. She felt that she
could not raise her hand from the desk. If she sat there for
ever, she felt she could not move again, nor utter a command. It was a quarter-past four. She almost dreaded the
closing of the school, when she would be alone.

The class began to recover its ease, the tension relaxed.
Williams was still crying. Mr. Brunt was giving orders for
the closing of the lesson. Ursula got down.

"Take your place, Williams," she said.

He dragged his feet across the room, wiping his face on
his sleeve. As he sat down, he glanced at her furtively, his
eyes still redder. Now he looked like some beaten rat.

At last the children were gone. Mr. Harby trod by heavily,
without looking her way, or speaking. Mr. Brunt hesitated
as she was locking her cupboard.

"If you settle Clarke and Letts in the same way, Miss
Brangwen, you'll be all right," he said, his blue eyes glancing
down in a strange fellowship, his long nose pointing at her.

"Shall I?" she laughed nervously. She did not want anybody to talk to her.

As she went along the street, clattering on the granite
pavement, she was aware of boys dodging behind her. Something struck her hand that was carrying her bag, bruising her.
As it rolled away she saw that it was a potato. Her hand was
hurt, but she gave no sign. Soon she would take the tram.

She was afraid, and strange. It was to her quite strange
and ugly, like some dream where she was degraded. She would
have died rather than admit it to anybody. She could not
look at her swollen hand. Something had broken in her; she
had passed a crisis. Williams was beaten, but at a cost.

CLARENCE DAY

Clarence Day (1874–1935), American writer, published six books of humor which attracted little attention: *This Simian World* (1920), *The Crow's Nest* (1921), *Thoughts Without Words* (1928), *God and My Father* (1932), *In the Green Mountain Country* (1934) and *Scenes from the Mesozoic* (1935). With the publication of *Life with Father*, however, Day became famous. *Life with Mother* was published posthumously. The two books were made into stage plays and later into films. *Life with Father* opened on Broadway in 1939 and established a record run with 3,224 performances. Alexander Woollcott described Day's "Father" as "a part of American lore and seems likely to remain as familiar a legendary figure as Mr. Dooley or Uncle Remus or Huckleberry Finn."

The Noblest Instrument
FROM *Life with Father*

The violin is intended for persons with a passion for music. I wasn't that kind of person. . . . My teacher didn't know this. He greeted me as a possible genius.

◆◆◆

Father had been away, reorganizing some old upstate railroad. He returned in an executive mood and proceeded to shake up our home. In spite of my failure as a singer, he was still bound to have us taught music. We boys were summoned before him and informed that we must at once learn to play on something. We might not appreciate it now, he said, but we should later on. "You, Clarence, will learn the violin. George, you the piano. Julian—well, Julian is too young yet. But you older boys must have lessons."

I was appalled at this order. At the age of ten it seemed a disaster to lose any more of my freedom. The days were already too short for our games after school; and now here was a chunk to come out of playtime three days every week. A chunk every day, we found afterward, because we had to practice.

George sat at the piano in the parlor, and faithfully learned to pound out his exercises. He had all the luck. He was not an inspired player, but at least he had some ear for music. He also had the advantage of playing on a good robust instrument, which he didn't have to be careful not to drop, and was in no danger of breaking. Furthermore, he did not have to tune it. A piano had some good points.

But I had to go through a blacker and more gruesome experience. It was bad enough to have to come in from the street and the sunlight and go down into our dark little basement where I took my lessons. But that was only the opening chill of the struggle that followed.

The whole thing was uncanny. The violin itself was a queer, fragile, cigar-boxy thing, that had to be handled most gingerly. Nothing sturdy about it. Why, a fellow was liable to crack it putting it into its case. And then my teacher, he was queer too. He had a queer pickled smell.

I dare say he wasn't queer at all really, but he seemed so to me, because he was different from the people I generally met. He was probably worth a dozen of some of them, but I didn't know it. He was one of the violins in the Philharmonic, and an excellent player; a grave, middle-aged little man—who was obliged to give lessons.

He wore a black, wrinkled frock coat, and a discolored gold watch-chain. He had small, black-rimmed glasses; not tortoise-shell, but thin rims of metal. His violin was dark, rich, and polished, and would do anything for him.

Mine was balky and awkward, brand new, and of a light, common color.

The violin is intended for persons with a passion for music. I wasn't that kind of person. I liked to hear a band play a tune that we could march up and down to, but try as I would, I could seldom whistle such a tune afterward. My teacher didn't know this. He greeted me as a possible genius.

He taught me how to hold the contraption, tucked under my chin. I learned how to move my fingers here and there on its handle or stem. I learned how to draw the bow across the strings, and thus produce sounds. . . .

Does a mother recall the first cry of her baby, I wonder? I still remember the strange cry at birth of that new violin.

My teacher, Herr M., looked as though he had suddenly taken a large glass of vinegar. He sucked in his breath. His lips were drawn back from his teeth, and his eyes tightly shut. Of course, he hadn't expected my notes to be sweet at the start; but still, there was something unearthly about that first cry. He snatched the violin from me, examined it, readjusted its pegs, and comforted it gently, by drawing his own bow across it. It was only a new and not especially fine violin, but the sounds it made for him were more natural—they were classifiable sounds. They were not richly musical, but at least they had been heard before on this earth.

He handed the instrument back to me with careful directions. I tucked it up under my chin again and grasped the end tight. I held my bow exactly as ordered. I looked up at him, waiting.

"Now," he said, nervously.

I slowly raised the bow, drew it downward. . . .

This time there were *two* dreadful cries in our little front basement. One came from my new violin and one from the heart of Herr M.

Herr M. presently came to, and smiled bravely at me, and said if I wanted to rest a moment he would permit it. He seemed to think I might wish to lie down awhile and recover. I didn't feel any need of lying down. All I wanted was to get through the lesson. But Herr M. was shaken. He was by no means ready to let me proceed. He looked around desperately, saw the music book, and said he would now show me that. We sat down side by side on the window-seat, with the book in his lap, while he pointed out the notes to me with his finger, and told me their names.

After a bit, when he felt better, he took up his own violin, and instructed me to watch him and note how he handled the strings. And then at last, he nerved himself to let me take my violin up again. "Softly, my child, softly," he begged me, and stood facing the wall. . . .

We got through the afternoon somehow, but it was a ghastly experience. Part of the time he was maddened by the mistakes I kept making, and part of the time he was plain wretched. He covered his eyes. He seemed ill. He looked often at his watch, even shook it as though it had stopped; but he stayed the full hour.

That was Wednesday. What struggles he had with himself before Friday, when my second lesson was due, I can only dimly imagine, and of course I never even gave them a thought at the time. He came back to recommence teaching me, but he had changed—he had hardened. Instead of being cross, he was stern; and instead of sad, bitter. He wasn't unkind to me, but we were no longer companions. He talked to himself, under his breath; and sometimes he took bits of paper, and did little sums on them, gloomily, and then tore them up.

During my third lesson I saw the tears come to his eyes. He went up to Father and said he was sorry but he honestly felt sure I'd never be able to play.

Father didn't like this at all. He said he felt sure I would. He dismissed Herr M. briefly—the poor man came stumbling back down in two minutes. In that short space of time he had gallantly gone upstairs in a glow, resolved upon sacrificing his earnings for the sake of telling the truth. He returned with his earnings still running, but with the look of a lost soul about him, as though he felt that his nerves and his sanity were doomed to destruction. He was low in his mind, and he talked to himself more than ever. Sometimes he spoke harshly of America, sometimes of fate.

But he no longer struggled. He accepted this thing as his destiny. He regarded me as an unfortunate something, outside the human species, whom he must simply try to labor with as well as he could. It was a grotesque, indeed a hellish experience, but he felt he must bear it.

He wasn't the only one—he was at least not alone in his sufferings. Mother, though expecting the worst, had tried to be hopeful about it, but at the end of a week or two I heard her and Margaret talking it over. I was slaughtering a scale in the front basement, when Mother came down and stood outside the door in the kitchen hall and whispered, "Oh, Margaret!"

I watched them. Margaret was baking a cake. She screwed up her face, raised her arms, and brought them down with hands clenched.

"I don't know what we shall do, Margaret."

"The poor little feller," Margaret whispered. "He can't make the thing go."

This made me indignant. They were making me look like a lubber. I wished to feel always that I could make anything go. . . .

I now began to feel a determination to master this thing. History shows us many examples of the misplaced determinations of men—they are one of the darkest aspects of human life, they spread so much needless pain: but I knew little history. And I viewed what little I did know romantically —I should have seen in such episodes their heroism, not their futility. Any role that seemed heroic attracted me, no matter how senseless.

Not that I saw any chance for heroism in our front basement, of course. You had to have a battlefield or something. I saw only that I was appearing ridiculous. But that stung my pride. I hadn't wanted to learn anything whatever about fiddles or music, but since I was in for it, I'd do it, and show them I could. A boy will often put in enormous amounts of his time trying to prove he isn't as ridiculous as he thinks people think him.

Meanwhile Herr M. and I had discovered that I was nearsighted. On account of the violin's being an instrument that sticks out in front of one, I couldn't stand close enough to the music book to see the notes clearly. He didn't at first realize that I often made mistakes from that cause. When he and I finally comprehended that I had this defect, he had a sudden new hope that this might have been the whole trouble, and that when it was corrected I might play like a human being at last.

Neither of us ventured to take up this matter with Father. We knew that it would have been hard to convince him that my eyes were not perfect, I being a son of his and presumably made in his image; and we knew that he immediately would have felt we were trying to make trouble for him, and would have shown an amount of resentment which it was best to avoid. So Herr M. instead lent me his glasses. These did fairly well. They turned the dim grayness of the notes into a queer bright distortion, but the main thing was they did make them brighter, so that I now saw more of them. How well I remember those little glasses. Poor, dingy old things. Herr M. was nervous about lending them to me; he feared that I'd drop them. It would have been safer if they had been spectacles: but no, they were pince-nez; and I had to learn to balance them across my nose as well as I could. I couldn't wear them up near my eyes because my nose was too thin there; I had to put them about half-way down where there was enough flesh to hold them. I also had to tilt my head back, for the music-stand was a little too tall for me. Herr M. sometimes mounted me on a stool, warning me not to step off. Then when I was all set, and when he without his glasses was blind, I would smash my way into the scales again.

All during the long winter months I worked away at this job. I gave no thought, of course, to the family. But they did to me. Our house was heated by a furnace, which had big warm air pipes; these ran up through the walls with wide outlets into each room, and sound traveled easily and ringingly through their roomy, tin passages. My violin could be heard in every part of the house. No one could settle down to anything while I was practicing. If visitors came they soon left. Mother couldn't even sing to the baby. She would wait, watching the clock, until my long hour of scale-work was over, and then come downstairs and shriek at me that my time was up. She would find me sawing away with my forehead wet, and my hair wet and stringy, and even my clothes slowly getting damp from my exertions. She would feel my collar, which was done for, and say I must change it. "Oh, Mother! Please!"—for I was in a hurry now to run out and play. But she wasn't being fussy about my collar, I can see, looking back; she was using it merely as a barometer or gauge of my pores. She thought I had better dry myself before going out in the snow.

It was a hard winter for Mother. I believe she also had fears for the baby. She sometimes pleaded with Father; but no one could ever tell Father anything. He continued to stand like a rock against stopping my lessons.

Schopenhauer, in his rules for debating, shows how to win a weak case by insidiously transferring an argument from its right field, and discussing it instead from some irrelevant but impregnable angle. Father knew nothing of Schopenhauer, and was never insidious, but, nevertheless, he had certain natural gifts for debate. In the first place his voice was powerful and stormy, and he let it out at full strength, and kept on letting it out with a vigor that stunned his opponents. As a second gift, he was convinced at all times that his opponents were wrong. Hence, even if they did win a point or two, it did them no good, for he dragged the issue to some other ground then, where he and Truth could prevail. When Mother said it surely was plain enough that I had no ear, what was his reply? Why, he said that the violin was the noblest instrument invented by man. Having silenced her with this solid premise he declared that it followed that any boy was lucky to be given the privilege of learning to play it. No boy should expect to learn it immediately. It required persistence. Everything, he had found, required persistence. The motto was, Never give up.

All his life, he declared, he had persevered in spite of discouragement, and he meant to keep on persevering, and he meant me to, too. He said that none of us realized what he had had to go through. If he had been the kind that gave up at the very first obstacle, where would he have been now— where would any of the family have been? The answer was, apparently, that we'd either have been in a very bad way, poking round for crusts in the gutter, or else nonexistent. We might have never even been born if Father had not persevered.

Placed beside this record of Father's vast trials overcome, the little difficulty of my learning to play the violin seemed a trifle. I faithfully spurred myself on again, to work at the puzzle. Even my teacher seemed impressed with these views on persistence. Though older than Father, he had certainly not made as much money, and he bowed to the experience of a practical man who was a success. If he, Herr M., had been a success he would not have had to teach boys; and sitting in this black pit in which his need of money had placed him, he saw more than ever that he must learn the ways of this world. He listened with all his heart, as to a god, when Father shook his forefinger, and told him how to climb to the heights where financial rewards were achieved. The idea he got was that perseverance was sure to lead to great wealth.

Consequently our front basement continued to be the home of lost causes.

Of course, I kept begging Herr M. to let me learn just one tune. Even though I seldom could whistle them, still I liked tunes; and I knew that, in my hours of practicing, a tune would be a comfort. That is, for myself. Here again I never gave a thought to the effect upon others.

Herr M., after many misgivings, to which I respectfully listened—though they were not spoken to me, they were muttered to himself, pessimistically—hunted through a worn old book of selections, and after much doubtful fumbling chose as simple a thing as he could find for me—for me and the neighbors.

It was spring now, and windows were open. That tune became famous.

What would the musician who had tenderly composed

this air, years before, have felt if he had foreseen what an end
it would have, on Madison Avenue; and how, before death,
it would be execrated by that once peaceful neighborhood. I
engraved it on their hearts; not in its true form but in my
own eerie versions. It was the only tune I knew. Consequently
I played and replayed it.

Even horrors when repeated grow old and lose part of their
sting. But those I produced were, unluckily, never the same.
To be sure, this tune kept its general structure the same, even
in my sweating hands. There was always the place where I
climbed unsteadily up to its peak, and that difficult spot
where it wavered, or staggered, and stuck; and then a sudden jerk of resumption—I came out strong on that. Every
afternoon when I got to that difficult spot, the neighbors
dropped whatever they were doing to wait for that jerk,
shrinking from the moment, and yet feverishly impatient for
it to come.

But what made the tune and their anguish so different each
day? I'll explain. The strings of a violin are wound at the
end around pegs, and each peg must be screwed in and
tightened till the string sounds just right. Herr M. left my
violin properly tuned when he went. But suppose a string
broke, or that somehow I jarred a peg loose. Its string then
became slack and soundless. I had to re-tighten it. Not having
an ear, I was highly uncertain about this.

Our neighbors never knew at what degree of tautness I'd
put such a string. I didn't myself. I just screwed her up tight
enough to make a strong reliable sound. Neither they nor I
could tell which string would thus appear in a new role each
day, nor foresee the profound transformations this would
produce in that tune.

All that spring this unhappy and ill-destined melody floated
out through my window, and writhed in the air for one hour
daily, in sunshine or storm. All that spring our neighbors and
I daily toiled to its peak, and staggered over its hump, so
to speak, and fell wailing through space.

Things now began to be said to Mother which drove her
to act. She explained to Father that the end had come at
last. Absolutely. "This awful nightmare cannot go on," she
said.

Father pooh-poohed her.

She cried. She told him what it was doing to her. He said
that she was excited, and that her descriptions of the sounds
I made were exaggerated and hysterical—must be. She was

always too vehement, he shouted. She must learn to be calm.

"But you're downtown, *you* don't have to hear it!"

Father remained wholly skeptical.

She endeavored to shame him. She told him what awful things the neighbors were saying about him, because of the noise I was making, for which he was responsible.

He couldn't be made to look at it that way. If there really were any unpleasantness then I was responsible. He had provided me with a good teacher and a good violin—so he reasoned. In short, he had done his best, and no father could have done more. If I made hideous sounds after all that, the fault must be mine. He said that Mother should be stricter with me, if necessary, and make me try harder.

This was the last straw. I couldn't try harder. When Mother told me his verdict I said nothing, but my body rebelled. Self-discipline had its limits—and I wanted to be out: it was spring. I skimped my hours of practice when I heard the fellows playing outside. I came home late for lessons—even forgot them. Little by little they stopped.

Father was outraged. His final argument, I remember, was that my violin had cost twenty-five dollars; if I didn't learn it the money would be wasted, and he couldn't afford it. But it was put to him that my younger brother, Julian, could learn it instead, later on. Then summer came, anyhow, and we went for three months to the seashore; and in the confusion of this father was defeated and I was set free.

In the autumn little Julian was led away one afternoon, and imprisoned in the front basement in my place. I don't remember how long they kept him down there, but it was several years. He had an ear, however, and I believe he learned to play fairly well. This would have made a happy ending for Herr M. after all; but it was some other teacher, a younger man, who was engaged to teach Julian. Father said Herr M. was a failure.

WILLA CATHER

Willa Sibert Cather (1876–1947) was born in Virginia. When she was five years old, her parents moved to Red Cloud, Nebraska. Here she became part of the immigrant homesteaders' struggle against the pitiless forces of nature and economics. Her later writings drew on these childhood experiences. After graduating from the University of Nebraska, she worked as reporter, editor, and high school teacher.

Three of Cather's novels deal memorably with the lives of the settlers as she knew them: *O Pioneers!* (1913), *The Song of the Lark* (1915), and *My Ántonia* (1918). Her work is marked by a deep affection and respect for the courage, dignity, and honesty of the pioneers.

In 1922, Miss Cather was awarded the Pulitzer prize. In her later years, she developed a profound dislike for the modern world. The literary critic Maxwell Geismar has called her a "defender of spiritual grace in the midst of an increasingly materialistic culture."

A Day to Remember
FROM Paul's Case

His teachers felt this afternoon that his whole attitude was symbolized by his shrug and his flippantly red carnation flower, and they fell upon him without mercy, his English teacher leading the pack.

◆•◆

It was Paul's afternoon to appear before the faculty of the Pittsburgh High School to account for his various misdemeanors. He had been suspended a week ago, and his father

Reprinted from *Youth and the Bright Medusa* by Willa Cather. Courtesy of Alfred A. Knopf. Copyright 1920 by Willa Cather. Copyright renewed 1948 by the executors of the Estate of Willa Cather.

had called at the Principal's office and confessed his perplexity about his son. Paul entered the faculty-room suave and smiling. His clothes were a trifle outgrown, and the tan velvet on the collar of his open overcoat was frayed and worn; but for all that there was something of the dandy about him, and he wore an opal pin in his neatly knotted black four-in-hand, and a red carnation in his buttonhole. This latter adornment the faculty somehow felt was not properly significant of the contrite spirit befitting a boy under the ban of suspension.

Paul was tall for his age and very thin, with high, cramped shoulders and a narrow chest. His eyes were remarkable for a certain hysterical brilliancy, and he continually used them in a conscious, theatrical sort of way, peculiarly offensive in a boy. The pupils were abnormally large, as though he were addicted to belladonna, but there was a glassy glitter about them which that drug does not produce.

When questioned by the Principal as to why he was there, Paul stated, politely enough, that he wanted to come back to school. This was a lie, but Paul was quite accustomed to lying; found it, indeed, indispensable for overcoming friction. His teachers were asked to state their respective charges against him, which they did with such a rancor and aggrievedness as evinced that this was not a usual case. Disorder and impertinence were among the offenses named, yet each of his instructors felt that it was scarcely possible to put into words the real cause of the trouble, which lay in a sort of hysterically defiant manner of the boy's; in the contempt which they all knew he felt for them, and which he seemingly made not the least effort to conceal. Once, when he had been making a synopsis of a paragraph at the blackboard, his English teacher had stepped to his side and attempted to guide his hand. Paul had started back with a shudder and thrust his hands violently behind him. The astonished woman could scarcely have been more hurt and embarrassed had he struck at her. The insult was so involuntary and definitely personal as to be unforgettable. In one way and another, he had made all his teachers, men and women alike, conscious of the same feeling of physical aversion. In one class he habitually sat with his hand shading his eyes; in another he always looked out of the window during the recitation; in another he made a running commentary on the lecture, with humorous intent.

His teachers felt this afternoon that his whole attitude was symbolized by his shrug and his flippantly red carnation flower, and they fell upon him without mercy, his English teacher leading the pack. He stood through it smiling, his pale lips parted over his white teeth. (His lips were continually twitching, and he had a habit of raising his eyebrows that was contemptuous and irritating to the last degree.) Older boys than Paul had broken down and shed tears under that ordeal, but his set smile did not once desert him, and his only sign of discomfort was the nervous trembling of the fingers that toyed with the buttons of his overcoat, and an occasional jerking of the other hand which held his hat. Paul was always smiling, always glancing about him, seeming to feel that people might be watching him and trying to detect something. This conscious expression, since it was so far as possible from boyish mirthfulness, was usually attributed to insolence or "smartness."

As the inquisition proceeded, one of his instructors repeated an impertinent remark of the boy's, and the Principal asked him whether he thought that a courteous speech to make to a woman. Paul shrugged his shoulders slightly and his eyebrows twitched.

"I don't know," he replied. "I didn't mean to be polite or impolite, either. I guess it's a sort of way I have, of saying things regardless."

The Principal asked him whether he didn't think that a way it would be well to get rid of. Paul grinned and said he guessed so. When he was told that he could go, he bowed gracefully and went out. His bow was like a repetition of the scandalous red carnation.

His teachers were in despair, and his drawing master voiced the feeling of them all when he declared there was something about the boy which none of them understood. He added: "I don't really believe that smile of his comes altogether from insolence; there's something sort of haunted about it. The boy is not strong, for one thing. There is something wrong about the fellow."

The drawing master had come to realize that, in looking at Paul, one saw only his white teeth and the forced animation of his eyes. One warm afternoon the boy had gone to sleep at his drawing-board, and his master had noted with amazement what a white, blue-veined face it was; drawn and wrinkled like an old man's about the eyes, the lips twitching even in his sleep.

His teachers left the building dissatisfied and unhappy; humiliated to have felt so vindictive towards a mere boy, to have uttered this feeling in cutting terms, and to have set each other on, as it were, in the gruesome game of intemperate reproach. One of them remembered having seen a miserable street cat set at bay by a ring of tormentors.

CHRISTOPHER MORLEY

Christopher Morley (1890–1957) was an American news-paperman, editor, and writer. His first book of poems, *The Eighth Sin* (1912), was published while Morley was at Oxford as a Rhodes scholar. After serving on the editorial staff of Doubleday, Page and Company and the *Ladies' Home Journal*, he became a columnist for the Philadelphia *Public Ledger* and the New York *Evening Post*. From 1924 to 1941 he was contributing editor of the *Saturday Review of Literature*. His first novels, *Parnassus on Wheels* (1917) and its sequel, *The Haunted Bookshop* (1919), were immediate successes. These were followed by books of poetry, essays, and plays. During the 1920s Morley worked in the literary spotlight of New York. *Kitty Foyle* (1939) became a best-selling novel; collections of verse appeared regularly, and Morley edited two revisions of *Bartlett's Familiar Quotations*.

Morley brought wit, erudition, and stylistic elegance to his work. His good friend Henry Seidel Canby called him "a rusher in and out, bubbling with ideas like a soda fountain, a wit, a wagster, an Elizabethan philosopher, with one of the few minds I have known that seemed to be perpetually enjoying its own versatility." *Plum Pudding*, the collection of essays which includes the tribute to Dr. Gummere, was published in 1921.

In Memoriam:
Francis Barton Gummere

We were the most unpromising material for the scholar's eye; comfortable, untroubled middle-class lads, most of us, to whom study was neither a privilege nor a passion, but only a sober and decent way of growing old enough

to enter business. . . . We were a hopelessly mediocre,
well fed, satisfied, and characteristically Quakerish lot.
As far as the battle of learning goes, we were pacifists—
conscientious objectors.

* * *

often wonder what inward pangs of laughter or despair he
.ay have felt as he sat behind the old desk in Chase Hall
.d watched us file in, year after year! Callow, juvenile, ig-
orant, and cocksure—grotesquely confident of our own
.anly fulness of worldly *savoir*—an absurd rabble of youths,
.iserable flintheads indeed for such a steel! We were the most
.npromising of all material for the scholar's eye; comfortable,
.ntroubled middle-class lads most of us, to whom study was
.either a privilege nor a passion, but only a sober and decent
.ay of growing old enough to enter business.

We did not realize how accurately—and perhaps a trifle
.rimly—the strong, friendly face behind the desk was search-
.g us and sizing us up. He knew us for what we were—a
.roup of nice boys, too sleek, too cheerfully secure, to show
.e ambition of the true student. There was among us no
.pecimen of the lean and dogged crusader of learning that
.indles the eye of the master; no fanatical Scot, such as re-
.ices, the Oxford or Cambridge don; no liquid-orbed and
.awk-faced Hebrew with flushed cheek bones, such as sets
.he pace in the class-rooms of our large universities. No:
.Ve were a hopelessly mediocre, well fed, satisfied, and char-
.cteristically Quakerish lot. As far as the battle of learning
.oes, we were pacifists—conscientious objectors.

It is doubtful whether any really great scholar ever gave the
.est years of his life to so meagerly equipped a succession of
.oungsters! I say this candidly, and it is well it should be said,
.or it makes apparent the true genius of Doctor Gummere's
.reat gift. He turned this following of humble plodders into
.overs and zealots of the great regions of English letters. There
.vas something knightly about him—he, the great scholar, who
.vould never stoop to scoff at the humblest of us. It might have
.een thought that his shining gifts were wasted in a small
.country college, where not one in fifty of his pupils could
.ollow him into the enchanted lands of the imagination where
.e was fancy free. But it was not so. One may meet man after
.nan, old pupils of his, who have gone on into the homely
.irudging rounds of business, the law, journalism—men whose
.aces will light up with affection and remembrance when

Doctor Gummere's name is mentioned. We may have forgotten much of our Chaucer, our Milton, our Ballads—though I am sure we have none of us forgotten the deep and thrilling vivacity of his voice reciting:

> O where hae ye been, Lord Randal, my son?
> O where hae ye been, my handsome young man?
> I hae been to the wild wood; mither, make my bed soon,
> For I'm weary wi' hunting and fain wald lie doun.

But what we learned from him lay in the very charm of his personality. It was a spell that no one in his classroom could escape. It shone from his sparkling eye; it spoke in his irresistible humor; it moved in every line of that well-loved face, in his characteristic gesture of leaning forward and tilting his head a little to one side as he listened, patiently, to whatever juvenile surmises we stammered to express. It was the true learning of which his favorite Sir Philip Sidney said:

"This purifying of wit, this enriching of memory, enabling of judgment, and enlarging of conceit, which commonly we call learning, under what name soever it come forth or to what immediate end soever it be directed, the final end is to lead and draw us to as high a perfection as our degenerate souls, made worse by their clay lodgings, can be capable of."

Indeed, just to listen to him was a purifying of wit, an enrichment of memory, an enabling of judgment, an enlarging of imagination. He gave us "so sweet a prospect into the way as will entice any man to enter into it."

He moved among all human contacts with unerring grace. He was never the teacher, always the comrade. It was his way to pretend that we knew far more than we did; so with perfect courtesy and gravity, he would ask our opinion on some matter of which we knew next to nothing; and we knew it was only his exquisiteness of good manners that impelled the habit, and we knew he knew the laughableness of it; yet we adored him for it. He always suited his strength to our weakness, would tell us things almost with an air of apology for seeming to know more than we; pretending that we doubtless had known it all along, but it had just slipped our memory. Marvelously he set us on our secret honor to do justice to this rare courtesy. To fail him in some task he had set became, in our boyish minds, the one thing most abhorrent in dealing with such a man—a discourtesy. He was a man of the rarest and most delicate breeding, the finest and truest gentleman we

had known. Had he been nothing else, how much we would
have learnt from that alone.

What a range, what a grasp, there was in his glowing,
various mind! How open it was on all sides, how it teemed
with interests, how different from the scholar of silly traditional belief! We used to believe that he could have taught us
history, science, economics, philosophy—almost anything; and
so indeed he did. He taught us to go adventuring among
masterpieces on our own account, which is the most any
teacher can do. Luckiest of all were those who, on one pretext
or another, found their way to his fireside of an evening. To
sit entranced, smoking one of his cigars,[1] to hear him talk of
Stevenson, Meredith, or Hardy—(his favorites among the
moderns) to marvel anew at the infinite scope and vivacity
of his learning—this was to live on the very doorsill of en-
chantment. Homeward we would go, crunching across the
snow to where Barclay crowns the slope with her evening
blaze of lights, one glimpse nearer some realization of the
magical colors and tissues of the human mind, the rich perplexity and many-sided glamour of life.

It is strange (as one reviews all the memories of that good
friend and master) to think that there is now a new generation
beginning at Haverford that will never know his spell. There
is a heavy debt on his old pupils. He made life so much richer
and more interesting for us. Even if we never explored for
ourselves the fields of literature toward which he pointed, his
radiant individuality remains in our hearts as a true exemplar
of what scholarship can mean. Gropingly we turn to little
pictures in memory. We see him crossing Cope Field in the
green and gold of spring mornings, on his way to class. We
see him sitting on the verandah steps of his home on sunny
afternoons, full of gay and eager talk on a thousand diverse
topics. He little knew, I think, how we hung upon his words.
I can think of no more genuine tribute than this: that in my
own class—which was a notoriously cynical and scoffish band
of young sophisters—when any question of religious doubt or
dogma arose for discussion among some midnight group,
someone was sure to say, "I wish I knew what Doctor Gum-

---

[1] It was characteristic of him that he usually smoked *Robin Hood*,
that admirable five-cent cigar, because the name and the picture of an
outlaw on the band, reminded him of the Fourteenth Century ballads
he knew by heart.

mere thought about it!" We felt instinctively that what he
thought would have been convincing enough for us.

He was truly a great man. A greater man than we deserved,
and there is a heavy burden upon us to justify the life that he
gave to our little college. He has passed into the quiet and
lovely tradition that surrounds and nourishes that place we all
love so well. Little by little she grows, drawing strength and
beauty from human lives around her, confirming herself in
honor and remembrance. The teacher is justified by his scholars. Doctor Gummere might have gone elsewhere, surrounded
by a greater and more ambitiously documented band of pupils.
He whom we knew as the greatest man we had ever seen,
moved little outside the world of learning. He gave himself to
us, and we are the custodians of his memory.

Every man who loved our vanished friend must know with
what realization of shamed incapacity one lays down the trib-
utary pen. He was so strong, so full of laughter and grace, so
truly a man, his long vacation still seems a dream, and we feel
that somewhere on the well-beloved campus we shall meet him
and feel that friendly hand. In thinking of him I am always
reminded of that fine old poem of Sir Henry Wotton, a
teacher himself, the provost of Eton, whose life has been so
charmingly written by another Haverfordian—(Logan Pear-
sall Smith).

THE CHARACTER OF A HAPPY LIFE
How happy is he born and taught
That serveth not another's will;
Whose armour is his honest thought,
And simple thought his utmost skill!

Whose passions not his masters are;
Whose soul is still prepared for death
Not tied into the world by care
Of public fame or private breath;

Who envies none that chance doth raise,
Nor vice; who never understood
How deepest wounds are given by praise;
Nor rules of state, but rules of good;

Who hath his life from rumours freed;
Whose conscience is his strong retreat;
Whose state can neither flatterers feed,
Nor ruin make oppressors great;

Who God doth late and early pray
More of His Grace than gifts to lend;
And entertains the harmless day
With a well-chosen book or friend;

This man is freed from servile bands
Of hope to rise or fear to fall:
Lord of himself, though not of lands,
And having nothing, yet hath all.

Such was the Happy Man as Sir Henry Wotton described him. Such, I think, was the life of our friend. I think it must have been a happy life, for he gave so much happiness to others.

STEPHEN LEACOCK

Stephen Leacock (1869–1944) was born in England and educated at Canadian and American universities. After receiving his Ph.D. in 1903, he became professor of economics at McGill University. His writings reflect his interest in political science and in humor. *Elements of Political Science* appeared in 1906 and the first book of humorous selections, *Literary Lapses*, in 1910.

Robert Benchley once remarked that his own writings were merely rewritten Leacock. George Ade said of Leacock: "He inherits the genial traditions of Lamb, Thackeray, and Lewis Carroll and has absorbed, across the Canadian border, the delightful unconventionalities of Oliver Wendell Holmes and Mark Twain, with possibly a slight flavor of Will Rogers."

Among Leacock's humorous books are *Nonsense Novels* (1911), *Frenzied Fiction* (1917), *College Days* (1923), *Hellements of Hickonomics in Hiccoughs of Verse* (1936), and *My Remarkable Uncle and Other Stories* (1942). His autobiography, *The Boy I Left Behind Me*, appeared in 1946.

My Memories and Miseries as a Schoolmaster

A school boy, while he is at school, regards his masters as a mixed assortment of tyrants and freaks. He plans vaguely that at some future time in life he will "get even" with them. . . . In the whole round of the school year, there was, as I remember it, but one bright spot—the arrival of the summer holidays. . . . If every day in the life of a school could be the last day but one, there would be little fault to find with it.

◆◆◆

Reprinted by permission of Dodd, Mead and Company, Inc. From *College Days* by Stephen Leacock. Copyright 1923 by Dodd, Mead, Inc. Copyright renewed 1950 by George Leacock. Also reprinted by permission of The Bodley Head.

For ten years I was a schoolmaster. Just thirty years ago I was appointed to the staff of a great Canadian school. It took me ten years to get off it. Being appointed to the position of a teacher is just as if Fate passed a hook through one's braces and hung one up against the wall. It is hard to get down again.

From those ten years I carried away nothing in money and little in experience; indeed, no other asset whatever, unless it be, here and there, a pleasant memory or two and the gratitude of my former pupils. There was nothing really in my case for them to be grateful about. They got nothing from me in the way of intellectual food, but a lean and perfunctory banquet; and anything that I gave them in the way of sound moral benefit I gave gladly and never missed.

But school boys have a way of being grateful. It is the decent thing about them. A school boy, while he is at school, regards his masters as a mixed assortment of tyrants and freaks. He plans vaguely that at some future time in life he will "get even" with them. I remember well, for instance, at the school where I used to teach, a little Chilian boy who kept a stiletto in his trunk with which he intended to kill the second mathematical master.

But somehow a schoolboy is no sooner done with his school and out in the business of life, than a soft haze of retrospect suffuses a new color over all that he has left behind. There is a mellow sound in the tones of the school bell that he never heard in his six years of attendance. There is a warmth in the color of the old red bricks that he never saw before; and such a charm and such a sadness in the brook or in the elm trees beside the school playground that he will stand beside them with a bowed and reverent head as in the silence of a cathedral. I have seen an "Old Boy" gaze into the open door of an empty class room and ask, "And those are the same old benches?" with a depth of meaning in his voice. He has been out of school perhaps five years and the benches already seem to him infinitely old. This, by the way, is the moment and this the mood in which the "Old Boy" may be touched for a subscription to the funds of the school. This *is* the way in fact, in which the sagacious head master does it. The foolish head master, who has not yet learned his business, takes the "Old Boy" round and shows him all the *new* things, the fine new swimming pool built since his day and the new gymnasium with up-to-date patent apparatus. But this is all wrong. There is nothing in it for the "Old Boy" but boredom. The wise head master takes him by the sleeve and says "Come"; he leads him out of a deserted corner of the playground and shows him an old tree behind an ash house and the "Old Boy" no sooner sees it than he says:

"Why, Great Caesar! that's the same old tree that Jack McEwen and I used to climb up to hook out of bounds on Saturday night! Old Jimmy caught us at it one night and licked us both. And look here, here's my name cut on the boarding at the back of the ash house. See? They used to fine us five cents a letter if they found it. Well, Well!"

The "Old Boy" is deep in his reminiscences examining the board fence, the tree and the ash house.

The wise head master does not interrupt him. He does not say that he knew all along that the "Old Boy's" name was cut there and that that's why he brought him to the spot. Least of all does he tell him that the boys still "hook out of bounds" by this means and that he licked two of them for it last Saturday night. No, no, retrospect is too sacred for that. Let the "Old Boy" have his fill of it and when he is quite down and out with the burden of it, then as they walk back to the school building, the head master may pick a donation from him that falls like a ripe thimbleberry.

And most of all, by the queer contrariety of things, does this kindly retrospect envelop the person of the teachers. They are transported in the alchemy of time into a group of profound scholars, noble benefactors through whose teaching, had it been listened to, one might have been lifted into higher things. Boys who never listened to a Latin lesson in their lives look back to the memory of their Latin teacher as the one great man that they have known. In the days when he taught them they had no other idea than to put mud in his ink or to place a bent pin upon his chair. Yet they say now that he was the greatest scholar in the world and that if they'd only listened to him they would have got more out of his lessons than from any man that ever taught. He wasn't and they wouldn't—but it is some small consolation to those who have been schoolmasters to know that after it is too late this reward at least is coming to them.

Hence it comes about that even so indifferent a vessel as I should reap my share of schoolboy gratitude. Again and again it happens to me that some unknown man, well on in middle life, accosts me with a beaming face and says: "You don't remember me. You licked me at Upper Canada College," and we shake hands with a warmth and heartiness as if I had been his earliest benefactor. Very often if I am at an evening reception or anything of the sort, my hostess says, "Oh, there is a man here so anxious to meet you," and I know at once why. Forward he comes, eagerly pushing his way among the people to seize my hand. "Do you remember me?" he says. "You licked me at Upper Canada College." Sometimes I anticipate the greeting. As soon as the stranger grasps my hand and says, "Do you remember me?" I break in and and say, "Why, let me see, surely I licked you at Upper Canada College." In such a case the man's delight is beyond all bounds. Can I lunch with him at his Club? Can I dine at his home? He wants his wife to see me. He has so often told her about having been licked by me that she too will be delighted.

I do not like to think that I was in any way brutal or harsh, beyond the practice of my time, in beating the boys I taught. Looking back on it, the whole practice of licking and being licked, seems to me mediaeval and out of date. Yet I do know that there are, apparently, boys that I have licked in all quarters of the globe. I get messages from them. A man says to me, "By the way, when I was out in Sumatra there was a man there that said he knew you. He said you licked him at Upper Canada College. He said he often thought of you." I have licked, I believe, two Generals of the Canadian Army, three Cabinet Ministers, and more Colonels and Mayors than I care to count. Indeed all the boys that I have licked seem to be doing well.

I am stating here what is only simple fact, not exaggerated a bit. Any schoolmaster and every "Old Boy" will recognize it at once; and indeed I can vouch for the truth of this feeling on the part of the "Old Boys" all the better in that I have felt it myself. I always read Ralph Connor's books with great interest for their own sake, but still more because, thirty-two years ago, the author "licked me at Upper Canada College." I have never seen him since, but I often say to people from Winnipeg, "If you ever meet Ralph Connor—he's Major Charles Gordon, you know—tell him that I was asking about him and would like to meet him. He licked me at Upper Canada College."

But enough of "licking." It is, I repeat, to me nowadays a painful and a disagreeable subject. I can hardly understand how we could have done it. I am glad to believe that at the present time it has passed or is passing out of use. I understand that it is being largely replaced by "moral suasion."

This, I am sure, is a great deal better. But when I was a teacher moral suasion was just beginning at Upper Canada College. In fact I saw it tried only once. The man who tried it was a tall, gloomy-looking person, a university graduate in psychology. He is now a well-known Toronto lawyer, so I must not name him. He came to the school only as a temporary substitute for an absent teacher. He was offered a cane by the College janitor whose business it was to hand them round. But he refused it. He said that a moral appeal was better: he said that psychologically it set up an inhibition stronger than the physical. The first day that he taught—it was away up in a little room at the top of the old college building on King Street—the boys merely threw paper wads at him and put bent pins on his seat. The next day they put hot bees-wax on his clothes and the day after that they brought screw drivers and unscrewed the little round seats of the class room and rolled them down the stairs. After that day the philosopher did not come back, but he has since written, I believe, a book called "Psychic Factors in Education"; which is very highly thought of.

But the opinion of the "Old Boy" about his teachers is only a part of his illusionment. The same peculiar haze of retrospect hangs about the size and shape and kind of boys who went to school when he was young as compared with the boys of to-day.

"How small they are!" is always the exclamation of the "Old Boy" when he looks over the rows and rows of boys sitting in the assembly hall. "Why, when I went to school the boys were ever so much bigger."

After which he goes on to relate that when he first entered the school as a youngster (the period apparently of maximum size and growth), the boys in the sixth form had whiskers! These whiskers of the sixth form are a persistent and perennial school tradition that never dies. I have traced them, on personal record from eye-witnesses, all the way from 1829 when the college was founded until to-day. I remember well, during my time as a schoolmaster, receiving one day a parent, an "Old Boy" who came accompanied by a bright little son of twelve whom he was to enter at the school. The boy was sent to play about with some new acquaintances while I talked with his father.

"The old school," he said in the course of our talk, "is greatly changed, very much altered. For one thing the boys are very much younger than they were in my time. Why, when I entered the school—though you will hardly believe it—the boys in the sixth form had whiskers!"

I had hardly finished expressing my astonishment and appreciation when the little son came back and went up to his father's side and started whispering to him. "Say, dad," he said, "there are some awfully big boys in this school. I saw out there in the hall some boys in the sixth form with whiskers."

From which I deduced that what is whiskers to the eye of youth fades into fluff before the disillusioned eye of age. Nor is there need to widen the application or to draw the moral.

The parents of the boys at school naturally fill a broad page in the schoolmaster's life and are responsible for many of his sorrows. There are all kinds and classes of them. Most acceptable to the schoolmaster is the old-fashioned type of British father who enters his boy at the school and says:

"Now I want this boy well thrashed if he doesn't behave himself. If you have any trouble with him let me know and I'll come and thrash him myself. He's to have a shilling a week pocket money and if he spends more than that let me know and I'll stop his money altogether." Brutal though this speech sounds, the real effect of it is to create a strong prejudice in the little boy's favor and when his father curtly says, "Good-bye, Jack," and he answers, "Good-bye, father," in a trembling voice, the schoolmaster would be a hound indeed who could be unkind to him.

But very different is the case of the up-to-date parent. "Now I've just given Jimmy fifty dollars," he says to the schoolmaster with the same tone as he would to an inferior clerk in his office, "and I've explained to him that when he wants more he's to tell you to go to the bank and draw for him what he needs." After which he goes on to explain that Jimmy is a boy of very peculiar disposition, requiring the greatest nicety of treatment; that they find if he gets in tempers the best way is to humor him and presently he'll come round. Jimmy, it appears can be led, if led gently, but never driven. During all of which time the schoolmaster, insulted by being treated as an underling (for the iron bites deep into the soul of every one of them), has already fixed his eye on the undisciplined young pup called Jimmy with a view to trying out the problem of seeing whether he can't be driven after all.

But the greatest nuisance of all to the schoolmaster is the parent who does his boy's home exercises and works his boy's sums. I suppose they mean well by it. But it is a disastrous thing to do for any child. Whenever I found myself correcting exercises that had obviously been done for the boys in their homes I used to say to them quite grandly:

"Paul, tell your father that he *must* use the ablative after pro."

"Yes, sir," says the boy.

"And Edward, you tell your grandmother that her use of the dative case simply won't do. She's getting along nicely and I'm well satisfied with the way she's doing, but I cannot have her using the dative right and left on every occasion. Tell her it won't do."

"Yes, sir," says little Edward.

I remember one case in particular of a parent who did not do the boy's exercise but, after letting the boy do it himself, wrote across the face of it a withering comment addressed to me and reading: "From this exercise you can see that my boy, after six months of your teaching, is completely ignorant. How do you account for it?"

I sent the exercise back to him with the added note: "I think it must be hereditary."

In the whole round of the school year, there was, as I remember it, but one bright spot—the arrival of the summer holidays. Somehow as the day draws near for the school to break up for holidays, a certain touch of something human pervades the place. The masters lounge round in cricket flannels smoking cigarettes almost in the corridors of the school itself. The boys shout at the play in the long June evenings. At the hour when, on the murky winter nights, the bell rang for night study, the sun is still shining upon the playground and the cricket match between House and House is being played out between daylight and dark. The masters— good fellows that they are—have canceled evening study to watch the game. The headmaster is there himself. He is smoking a briar-wood pipe and wearing his mortar-board sideways. There is a wonderful greenness in the new grass of the playground and a wonderful fragrance in the evening air. It is the last day of school but one. Life is sweet indeed in the anticipation of this summer evening.

If every day in the life of a school could be the last day but one, there would be little fault to find with it.

THOMAS WOLFE

Thomas Wolfe (1900–1938), the American writer of novels, short stories, and plays, is best known for the four autobiographical novels which chronicle his short but tumultuous life: *Look Homeward, Angel* (1929), *Of Time and the River* (1935), *The Web and the Rock* (1939), and *You Can't Go Home Again* (1940). Wolfe's father, a stonecutter, was fond of reciting Shakespeare to his son; his mother ran a boarding-house in Asheville, North Carolina.

Wolfe studied at the University of North Carolina, where he pursued his interest in literature and drama. After graduation, he went to Harvard, attracted by Professor George Pierce Baker's famous course in playwriting, Workshop 47. Under Baker's tutelage he wrote *Welcome to Our City* (produced at Harvard in 1923), set in a Southern city named Altamont, based on his native Asheville—the same Altamont that provides the background for *Look Homeward, Angel.*

Wolfe taught at New York University intermittently from 1924 to 1930, but devoted most of his energies to writing. In July 1938 he developed pneumonia and was hospitalized in Seattle; in September he developed a brain infection and died after surgery at Johns Hopkins Hospital in Baltimore. Both Maxwell Perkins, of Charles Scribner's Sons, and Edward C. Aswell, of Harper's, helped to shape the final versions of much of Wolfe's material, during his lifetime and after his death.

Look Homeward, Angel is an intense record of Wolfe's struggle for self and individuality. Readers identify with that struggle and feel the force of the novel's soaring prose in spite of Wolfe's verbosity.

A Desperate and Hunted Animal
FROM *Look Homeward, Angel*

At school, he was a desperate and hunted little animal.
The herd, infallible in its banded instinct, knew at once
that a stranger had been thrust into it, and it was merciless at the hunt.

───◆◆◆───

. . . he was not quite six, when, of his own insistence, he went
to school. Eliza did not want him to go, but his only close
companion, Max Isaac, a year his senior, was going, and
there was in his heart a constricting terror that he would be
left alone. She told him he could not go: she felt, somehow,
that school began the slow, the final loosening of the cords
that held them together, but as she saw him slide craftily out
the gate one morning in September and run at top speed to
the corner where the other little boy was waiting, she did
nothing to bring him back. Something taut snapped in her:
she remembered his furtive backward glance, and she wept.
And she did not weep for herself, but for him: the hour
after his birth she had looked in his dark eyes and had seen
something that would brood there eternally, she knew, un-
fathomable wells of remote and intangible loneliness: she
knew that in her dark and sorrowful womb a stranger had
come to life, fed by the lost communications of eternity, his
own ghost, haunter of his own house, lonely to himself and to
the world. O lost. . . .

Now the innumerable archipelago had been threaded, and
he stood, firm-planted, upon the unknown but waiting
continent.

He learned to read almost at once, printing the shapes of
words immediately with his strong visual memory; but it was
weeks later before he learned to write, or even to copy, words.
The ragged spume and wrack of fantasy and the lost world
still floated from time to time through his clear schoolday

morning brain, and although he followed accurately all the other instruction of his teacher, he was walled in his ancient unknowing world when they made letters. The children made their sprawling alphabets below a line of models, but all he accomplished was a line of jagged wavering spear-points on his sheet, which he repeated endlessly and rapturously, unable to see or understand the difference.

"I have learned to write," he thought.

Then, one day, Max Isaacs looked suddenly, from his exercise, on Eugene's sheet, and saw the jagged line.

"That ain't writin'," said he.

And clubbing his pencil in his warted grimy hand, he crawled a copy of the exercise across the page.

The line of life, that beautiful developing structure of language that he saw flowing from his comrade's pencil, cut the knot in him that all instruction failed to do, and instantly he seized the pencil, and wrote the words in letters fairer and finer than his friend's. And he turned, with a cry in his throat, to the next page, and copied it without hesitation, and the next, the next. They looked at each other a moment with that clear wonder by which children accept miracles, and they never spoke of it again.

"That's writin' now," said Max. But they kept the mystery caged between them. . . .

He fell now easily into the School-Ritual; he choked his breakfast with his brothers every morning, gulped scalding coffee, and rushed off at the ominous warning of the final bell, clutching a hot paper-bag of food, already spattered hungrily with grease blots. He pounded along after his brothers, his heart hammering in his throat with excitement and, as he raced into the hollow at the foot of the Central Avenue hill, grew weak with nervousness, as he heard the bell ringing itself to sleep, jerking the slatting rope about in its dying echoes.

Ben, grinning evilly and scowling, would thrust his hand against the small of his back and rush him screaming, but unable to resist the plunging force behind, up the hill.

In a gasping voice he would sing the morning song, coming in pantingly on the last round of a song the quartered class took up at intervals:

> "—*Merrily, merrily, merrily, merrily,*
> *Life is but a dream.*"

Or, in the frosty Autumn mornings:

> "Waken, lords and ladies gay,
> On the mountain dawns the day."

Or the Contest of the West Wind and the South Wind. Or the Miller's Song:

> "I envy no man, no, not I,
> And no one envies me."

He read quickly and easily; he spelled accurately. He did well with figures. But he hated the drawing lesson, although the boxes of crayons and paints delighted him. Sometimes the class would go into the woods, returning with specimens of flowers and leaves—the bitten flaming red of the maple, the brown pine comb, the brown oak leaf. These they would paint; or in Spring a spray of cherry-blossom, a tulip. He sat reverently before the authority of the plump woman who first taught him: he was terrified lest he do anything common or mean in her eyes.

The class squirmed: the little boys invented tortures or scrawled obscenities to the little girls. And the wilder and more indolent seized every chance of leaving the room, thus: "Teacher, may I be excused?" And they would go out into the lavatory, sniggering and dawdling about restlessly.

He could never say it, because it would reveal to her the shame of nature.

Once, deathly sick, but locked in silence and dumb nausea, he had vomited finally upon his cupped hands.

He feared and hated the recess periods, trembled before the brawling confusion of the mob and the playground, but his pride forbade that he skulk within, or secrete himself away from them. Eliza had allowed his hair to grow long; she wound it around her finger every morning into fat Fauntleroy curls: the agony and humiliation it caused him was horrible, but she was unable or unwilling to understand it, and mouth-pursingly thoughtful and stubborn to all solicitation to cut it. She had the garnered curls of Ben, Grover, and Luke stored in tiny boxes: she wept sometimes when she saw Eugene's, they were the symbol of his babyhood to her, and her sad heart, so keen in marking departures, refused to surrender them. Even when his thick locks had become the luxuriant colony of Harry Tarkinton's lice, she would not cut them:

e held his squirming body between her knees twice a day
d ploughed his scalp with a fine-toothed comb.

As he made to her his trembling passionate entreaties, she
ould smile with an affectation of patronizing humor, make a
ntering humming noise in her throat, and say: "Why, say—
u can't grow up yet. You're my baby." Suddenly baffled
efore the yielding inflexibility of her nature, which could be
riven to action only after incessant and maddening prods,
ugene, screaming-mad with helpless fury, would understand
e cause of Gant's frenzy.

At school, he was a desperate and hunted little animal. The
rd, infallible in its banded instinct, knew at once that a
ranger had been thrust into it, and it was merciless at the
unt. As the lunch-time recess came, Eugene, clutching his big
ease-stained bag, would rush for the playground pursued by
e yelping pack. The leaders, two or three big louts of ad-
anced age and deficient mentality, pressed closely about
m, calling out suppliantly, "You know me, 'Gene. You
now me"; and still racing for the far end, he would open
s bag and hurl to them one of his big sandwiches, which
ayed them for a moment, as they fell upon its possessor and
awed it to fragments, but they were upon him in a moment
ore with the same yelping insistence, hunting him down into
corner of the fence, and pressing in with outstretched paws
d wild entreaty. He would give them what he had, some-
mes with a momentary gust of fury, tearing away from a
eedy hand half of a sandwich and devouring it. When they
w he had no more to give, they went away. . . .

There was a boy named Otto Krause, a cheese-nosed, hair-
ced, inch-browed German boy, lean and swift in the legs,
oarse-voiced and full of idiot laughter, who showed him the
ardens of delight. There was a girl named Bessie Barnes, a
lack-haired, tall, bold-figured girl of thirteen years who
cted as model. Otto Krause was fourteen, Eugene was eight:
ey were in the third grade. The German boy sat next to
im, drew obscenities on his books, and passed his furtive
crawled indecencies across the aisle to Bessie.

And the nymph would answer with a lewd face, and a
ontemptuous blow against her shapely lifted buttock, a
esture which Otto considered as good as a promise, and
hich tickled him into hoarse sniggers.

Bessie walked in his brain.

In their furtive moments at school, he and Otto amused

each other by drawing obscenities in their geographies, be
stowing on the representations of tropical natives saggin
breasts and huge organs. And they composed on tiny scrap
of paper dirty little rhymes about teachers and principa
Their teacher was a gaunt red-faced spinster, with fierce gla
ing eyes: Eugene thought always of the soldier and th
tinder and the dogs he had to pass, with eyes like saucer
windmills, the moon. Her name was Miss Groody, and Otte
with the idiot vulgarity of little boys, wrote of her:

> *"Old Miss Groody*
> *Has Good Toody."*

And Eugene, directing his fire against the principal,
plump, soft, foppish young man whose name was Armstrong
and who wore always a carnation in his coat, which, afte
whipping an offending boy, he was accustomed to hold del
cately between his fingers, sniffing it with sensitive nostrils an
lidded eyes, produced in the first rich joy of creation scores o
rhymes, all to the discredit of Armstrong, his parentage, an
his relations with Miss Groody.

He was obsessed; he spent the entire day now in the com
position of poetry—all bawdy variations of a theme. And h
could not bring himself to destroy them. His desk was stuffe
with tiny crumpled balls of writing: one day, during th
geography lesson, the woman caught him. His bones turne
to rubber as she bore down on him glaring, and took from th
concealing pages of his book the paper on which he had bee
writing. At recess she cleared his desk, read the sequence, and
with boding quietness, bade him to see the principal afte
school.

"What does it mean? What do you reckon it means?" he
whispered dryly to Otto Krause.

"Oh you'll ketch it now!" said Otto Krause, laughing
hoarsely.

And the class tormented him slily, rubbing their bottom
when they caught his eye, and making grimaces of agony.

He was sick through to his guts. He had a loathing of physical humiliation which was not based on fear, from which he
never recovered. The brazen insensitive spirit of the boys he
envied but could not imitate: they would howl loudly unde
punishment, in order to mitigate it, and they were vain-
gloriously unconcerned ten minutes later. He did not think
he could endure being whipped by the fat young man with

the flower: at three o'clock, white-faced, he went to the man's office.

Armstrong, slit-eyed and thin lipped, began to swish the cane he held in his hand through the air as Eugene entered. Behind him, smoothed and flatted on his desk, was stacked the damning pile of rhymed insult.

"Did you write these?" he demanded, narrowing his eyes to little points in order to frighten his victim.

"Yes," said Eugene.

The principal cut the air again with his cane. He had visited Daisy several times, had eaten at Gant's plenteous board. He remembered very well.

"What have I ever done to you, son, that you should feel this way?" he said, with a sudden change to whining magnanimity.

"N-n-nothing," said Eugene.

"Do you think you'll ever do it again?" said he, becoming ominous again.

"N-no, sir," Eugene answered, in the ghost of a voice.

"All right," said God, grandly, throwing away his cane. "You can go."

His legs found themselves only when he had reached the playground.

WINSTON CHURCHILL

Sir Winston Churchill (1874–1965) was an English states-man, military strategist, soldier, and historian. Though he held many government posts, Churchill is best remembered in his role as Prime Minister of England during World War II. Then he stood as the symbol and embodiment of the indomitable British will to survive the onslaught of the Nazis. His eloquence and leadership rallied his country and its allies around the world in defense of civilization. At the age of eighty, Churchill was proclaimed "the greatest living Briton." In 1953, he was awarded the Nobel Prize for literature.

Master of a "grand," polished felicitous style, Churchill wrote many books. Among the most memorable are his *History of World War II* and the *History of the English Speaking Peoples*.

Danger! School Ahead!
FROM *A Roving Commission: My Early Life*

. . . now a much worse peril began to threaten. I was to go to school. . . . Much that I had heard about school had made a distinctly disagreeable impression on my mind, an impression, I may add, thoroughly borne out by actual experience.

———◆◆◆———

It was at "The Little Lodge" I was first menaced with Educa-tion. The approach of a sinister figure described as "the Gover-ness" was announced. Her arrival was fixed for a certain day. In order to prepare for this day Mrs. Everest produced a book

Reprinted by permission of Charles Scribner's Sons. From *A Roving Commission: My Early Life* by Winston Churchill. Copyright 1930, Charles Scribner's Sons. British rights: The Hamlyn Group, Ltd.

called *Reading Without Tears*. It certainly did not justify its title in my case. I was made aware that before the Governess arrived I must be able to read without tears. We toiled each day. My nurse pointed with a pen at the different letters. I thought it all very tiresome. Our preparations were by no means completed when the fateful hour struck and the Governess was due to arrive. I did what so many oppressed peoples have done in similar circumstances: I took to the woods. I hid in the extensive shrubberies—forests they seemed —which surrounded "The Little Lodge." Hours passed before I was retrieved and handed over to "the Governess." We continued to toil every day, not only at letters but at words, and also at what was much worse, figures. Letters after all had only got to be known, and when they stood together in a certain way one recognised their formation and that it meant a certain sound or word which one uttered when pressed sufficiently. But the figures were tied into all sorts of tangles and did things to one another which it was extremely difficult to forecast with complete accuracy. You had to say what they did each time they were tied up together, and the Governess apparently attached enormous importance to the answer being exact. If it was not right, it was wrong. It was not any use being "nearly right." In some cases these figures got into debt with one another: you had to borrow one or carry one, and afterwards you had to pay back the one you had borrowed. These complications cast a steadily gathering shadow over my daily life. They took one away from all the interesting things one wanted to do in the nursery or in the garden. They made increasing inroads upon one's leisure. One could hardly get time to do any of the things one wanted to do. They became a general worry and preoccupation. More especially was this true when we descended into a dismal bog called "sums." There appeared to be no limit to these. When one sum was done, there was always another. Just as soon as I managed to tackle a particular class of these afflictions, some other much more variegated type was thrust upon me. . . .

I have already described the dreaded apparition in my world of "The Governess." But now a much worse peril began to threaten. I was to go to school. I was now seven years old, and I was what grown-up people in their offhand way called "a troublesome boy." It appeared that I was to go away from home for many weeks at a stretch in order to do lessons under masters. The term had already begun, but still I should have to stay seven weeks before I could come home for

Christmas. Although much that I had heard about school had made a distinctly disagreeable impression on my mind, an impression, I may add, thoroughly borne out by the actual experience, I was also excited and agitated by this great change in my life. I thought in spite of the lessons, it would be fun living with so many other boys, and that we should make friends together and have great adventures. Also I was told that "school days were the happiest time in one's life." Several grown-up people added that in their day, when they were young, schools were very rough: there was bullying, they didn't get enough to eat, they had "to break the ice in their pitchers" each morning (a thing I have never seen done in my life). But now it was all changed. School life nowadays was one long treat. All the boys enjoyed it. Some of my cousins who were a little older had been quite sorry—I was told—to come home for the holidays. Cross-examined the cousins did not confirm this; they only grinned. Anyhow I was perfectly helpless. Irresistible tides drew me swiftly forward. I was no more consulted about leaving home than I had been about coming into the world.

It was very interesting buying all the things one had to have for going to school. No less than fourteen pairs of socks were on the list. Mrs. Everest thought this was very extravagant. She said that with care ten pairs would do quite well. Still it was a good thing to have some to spare, as one could then make sure of avoiding the very great dangers inseparable from "sitting in wet feet."

The fateful day arrived. My mother took me to the station in a hansom cab. She gave me three half-crowns which I dropped on to the floor of the cab, and we had to scramble about in the straw to find them again. We only just caught the train. If we had missed it, it would have been the end of the world. However, we didn't, and the world went on.

The school my parents had selected for my education was one of the most fashionable and expensive in the country. It modelled itself upon Eton and aimed at being preparatory for that Public School above all others. It was supposed to be the very last thing in schools. Only ten boys in a class; electric light (then a wonder); a swimming pond; spacious football and cricket grounds; two or three school treats, or "expeditions" as they were called, every term; the masters all M.A.'s in gowns and mortar-boards; a chapel of its own; no hampers allowed; everything provided by the authorities.

It was a dark November afternoon when we arrived at this establishment. We had tea with the Headmaster, with whom my mother conversed in the most easy manner. I was preoccupied with the fear of spilling my cup and so making "a bad start." I was also miserable at the idea of being left alone among all these strangers in this great, fierce, formidable place. After all I was only seven, and I had been so happy in my nursery with all my toys. I had such wonderful toys: a real steam engine, a magic lantern, and a collection of soldiers already nearly a thousand strong. Now it was to be all lessons. Seven or eight hours of lessons every day except half-holidays, and football or cricket in addition.

When the last sound of my mother's departing wheels had died away, the Headmaster invited me to hand over any money I had in my possession. I produced my three half-crowns which were duly entered in a book, and I was told that from time to time there would be a "shop" at the school with all sorts of things which one would like to have, and that I could choose what I liked up to the limit of the seven and sixpence. Then we quitted the Headmaster's parlour and the comfortable private side of the house, and entered the more bleak apartments reserved for the instruction and accommodation of the pupils. I was taken into a Form Room and told to sit at a desk. All the other boys were out of doors, and I was alone with the Form Master. He produced a thin greeny-brown-covered book filled with words in different types of print.

"You have never done any Latin before, have you?" he said.

"No, sir."

"This is a Latin grammar." He opened it at a well-thumbed page. "You must learn this," he said, pointing to a number of words in a frame of lines. "I will come back in half an hour and see what you know."

Behold me then on a gloomy evening, with an aching heart, seated in front of the First Declension.

Mensa	a table
Mensa	O table
Mensam	a table
Mensae	of a table
Mensae	to or for a table
Mensa	by, with or from a table

What on earth did it mean? Where was the sense of it? It seemed absolute rigmarole to me. However, there was one thing I could always do: I could learn by heart. And I thereupon proceeded, as far as my private sorrows would allow, to memorise the acrostic-looking task which had been set me.

In due course the Master returned.

"Have you learnt it?" he asked.

"I think I can *say* it, sir," I replied; and I gabbled it off.

He seemed so satisfied with this that I was emboldened to ask a question.

"What does it mean, sir?"

"It means what it says. Mensa, a table. Mensa is a noun of the First Declension. There are five declensions. You have learnt the singular of the First Declension."

"But," I repeated, "what does it mean?"

"Mensa means a table," he answered.

"Then why does mensa also mean O table," I enquired, "and what does O table mean?"

"Mensa, O table, is the vocative case," he replied.

"But why O table?" I persisted in genuine curiosity.

"O table,—you would use that in addressing a table, in invoking a table." And then seeing he was not carrying me with him, "You would use it in speaking to a table."

"But I never do," I blurted out in honest amazement.

"If you are impertinent, you will be punished, and punished, let me tell you, very severely," was his conclusive rejoinder.

Such was my first introduction to the classics from which, I have been told, many of our cleverest men have derived so much solace and profit.

The Form Master's observations about punishment were by no means without their warrant at St. James's School. Flogging with the birch in accordance with the Eton fashion was a great feature in its curriculum. But I am sure no Eton boy, and certainly no Harrow boy of my day, ever received such a cruel flogging as this Headmaster was accustomed to inflict upon the little boys who were in his care and power. They exceeded in severity anything that would be tolerated in any of the Reformatories under the Home Office. My reading in later life has supplied me with some possible explanations of his temperament. Two or three times a month the whole school was marshalled in the Library, and one or more delinquents were haled off to an adjoining apartment by the two head boys, and there flogged until they bled freely, while the rest sat quaking, listening to their screams. . . .

How I hated this school, and what a life of anxiety I lived there for more than two years. I made very little progress at my lessons, and none at all at games. I counted the days and the hours to the end of every term, when I should return home from this hateful servitude and range my soldiers in line of battle on the nursery floor. The greatest pleasure I had in those days was reading. When I was nine and a half my father gave me *Treasure Island*, and I remember the delight with which I devoured it. My teachers saw me at once backward and precocious, reading books beyond my years and yet at the bottom of the Form. They were offended. They had large resources of compulsion at their disposal, but I was stubborn. Where my reason, imagination or interest were not engaged, I would not or I could not learn. In all the twelve years I was at school no one ever succeeded in making me write a Latin verse or learn any Greek except the alphabet. I do not at all excuse myself for this foolish neglect of opportunities procured at so much expense by my parents and brought so forcibly to my attention by my Preceptors. Perhaps if I had been introduced to the ancients through their history and customs, instead of through their grammar and syntax, I might have had a better record.

JAMES T. FARRELL

James T. Farrell (1904–1979), American novelist, began writing his Studs Lonigan stories in 1932. Farrell's style revealed the crudities of life among the poor city people whom he knew well. His writing aroused much controversy, yet Farrell did not set out to be sensational. He worked sincerely, honestly, and candidly. He made it a practice to write five pages a day without fail, and published many books. *Young Lonigan* (1932), *The Young Manhood of Studs Lonigan* (1934), and *Judgment Day* (1935) are the Studs Lonigan group. Farrell's other books include *A World I Never Made* (1936), *No Star Is Lost* (1938), *Father and Son* (1940), *My Days of Anger* (1934), and literary criticism and short story collections. F. O. Matthiessen praised Farrell for his honesty, his "thoroughgoing and valid" psychology, and his understanding of social change.

The School as Jailhouse
FROM *Young Lonigan*

> He puffed, drew the fag out of his mouth, inhaled and said to himself: Well, I'm kissing the old dump goodbye tonight.

———— ◆◆◆ ————

Studs Lonigan, on the verge of fifteen, and wearing his first suit of long trousers, stood in the bathroom with a Sweet Caporal pasted in his mug. His hands were jammed in his trouser pockets, and he sneered. He puffed, drew the fag out of his mouth, inhaled and said to himself:

Well, I'm kissin' the old dump goodbye tonight.

Reprinted from *Young Lonigan* by James T. Farrell, by permission of the publisher, Vanguard Press, Inc. Copyright © 1932 by James T. Farrell. Copyright renewed 1963 by James T. Farrell.

Studs was a small, broad-shouldered lad. His face was wide and planed; his hair was a light brown. His long nose was too large for his other features; almost a sheeny's nose. His lips were thick and wide, and they did not seem at home on his otherwise frank and boyish face. He was always twisting them into his familiar tough-guy sneers. He had blue eyes; his mother rightly called them baby-blue eyes.

He took another drag and repeated to himself:

Well, I'm kissin' the old dump goodbye.

The old dump was St. Patrick's grammar school; and St. Patrick's meant a number of things to Studs. It meant school, and school was a jailhouse that might just as well have had barred windows. It meant the long, wide, chalk-smelling room of the seventh- and eighth-grade boys, with its forty or fifty squirming kids. It meant the second floor of the tan brick, undistinguished parish building on Sixty-first Street that had swallowed so much of Studs' life for the past eight years. It meant the black-garbed Sisters of Providence, with their rattling beads, their swishing strides, and the funny-looking wooden clappers they used, which made a dry snapping sound and which hurt like anything when a guy got hit over the head with one. It meant Sister Carmel, who used to teach fourth grade, but was dead now; and who used to hit everybody with the edge of a ruler because she knew they all called her the bearded lady. It meant Studs, twisting in his seat, watching the sun come in the windows to show up the dust on the floor, twisting and squirming, and letting his mind fly to all kinds of places that were not like school. It meant Battleaxe Bertha talking and hearing lessons, her thin, sunken-jawed face white as a ghost, and sometimes looking like a corpse. It meant Bertha yelling in that creaky old woman's voice of hers. It meant Bertha trying to pound lessons down your throat, when you weren't interested in them; church history and all about the Jews and Moses, and Joseph, and Daniel in the lion's den, and Solomon who was wiser than any man that ever lived, except Christ, and maybe the Popes, who had the Holy Ghost to back up what they said; arithmetic, and square and cube roots, and percentage that Studs had never been able to get straight in his bean; catechism lessons . . . the ten commandments of God, the six commandments of the church, the seven capital sins, and the seven cardinal virtues and that lesson about the sixth commandment, which didn't tell a guy anything at all about it and only had words that he'd found in the dictionary like

adultery which made him all the more curious; grammar
with all its dry rules, and its sentences that had to be diagrammed and were never diagrammed right; spelling, and
words like apothecary that Studs still couldn't spell; Palmer
method writing, that was supposed to make you less tired and
made you more tired, and the exercises of shaking your arm
before each lesson, and the round and round 〇〇〇〇〇〇〇〇〇
and straight and straight ΛΛΛΛΛΛΛΛ, and the copy book,
all smeared with ink, that he had gone through, doing exercise after exercise on neat sheets of Palmer paper so that he
could get a Palmer method certificate that his old man kicked
about paying for because he thought it was graft; history lessons from the dull red history book, but they wouldn't have
been so bad if America had had more wars and if a guy could
talk and think about the battles without having to memorize
their dates, and the dates of when presidents were elected,
and when Fulton invented the steamboat, and Eli Whitney
invented the cotton gin or whatever in hell he did invent.
School meant Bertha, and Bertha should have been put away
long ago, where she could kneel down and pray herself to
death, because she was old and crabby and always hauling
off on somebody; it was a miracle that a person as old as
Bertha could sock as hard or holler as loud as she could; even
Sister Bernadette Marie, who was the superior and taught the
seventh and eighth grade girls in the next room, sometimes
had to come in and ask Bertha to make less noise, because
she couldn't teach with all the racket going on; but telling
Bertha not to shout was like telling a bull that it had no
right to see red. And smart guys, like Jim Clayburn, who
did his homework every night, couldn't learn much from
her. And school meant Dan and Bill Donoghue and Tubby
and all the guys in his bunch, and you couldn't find a better
gang of guys to pal with this side of Hell. And it meant going to mass in the barn-like church on the first floor, every
morning in Lent, and to stations of the cross on Friday afternoons; stations of the cross were always too long unless Father
Doneggan said them; and marching on Holy Thursday morning in church with a lily in your hand, and going to com-
munion the third Sunday of every month at the eight o'clock
mass with the boys' sodality. It meant goofy young Danny
O'Neill, the dippy punk who couldn't be hurt or made cry,
no matter how hard he was socked, because his head was
made of hard stuff like iron and ivory and marble. It meant
Vinc Curley, who had water on the brain, and the doctors

must have taken his brains out, drowned and dead like a dead fish, that time they were supposed to have taken a quart of water from his oversized bean. The kids in Vinc's class said that Sister Cyrilla used to pound him on the bean with her clapper, and he'd sit there yelling he was going to tell his mother; and it was funny, and all the kids in the room laughed their guts out. They didn't have 'em as crazy as Vinc in Studs' class; but there was TB McCarthy, who was always getting his ears beat off, and being made to kneel up in front of the room, or to go in Sister Bernadette's room and sit with all the girls and let them laugh at him. And there was Reardon with horses' hoofs for feet. One day in geography in the fifth grade, Cyrilla called on Reardon and asked him what the British Isles consisted of. Reardon didn't know so Studs whispered to him to say iron, and Reardon said iron. Sister Cyrilla thought it was so funny she marked him right for the day's lesson. And St. Patrick's meant Weary Reilley, and Studs hated Weary. He didn't know whether or not he could lick Weary, and Weary was one tough customer, and the guys had been waiting for Studs and Weary to scrap ever since Weary had come to St. Patrick's in the third grade. Studs was a little leery about mixing it with Reilley . . . no, he wasn't . . . it was just . . . well, there was no use starting fights unless you had to . . . and he'd never backed out of a scrap with Weary Reilley or any other guy. And that time he had pasted Weary in the mush with an icy snowball, well, he hadn't backed out of a fight when Weary started getting sore. He had just not meant to hit Weary with it, and in saying so he had only told the truth.

St. Patrick's meant a lot of things.

WOLCOTT GIBBS

Wolcott Gibbs (1902–1958) was an American editor, reporter, fiction writer, and drama critic, as well as a short-story writer and parodist. Through most of his professional career he was associated with *The New Yorker* magazine, in which periodical his weekly play reviews were followed by a devoted public. He wrote *Bed of Neuroses* (1937) and one play, *Season in the Sun* (1950), which had a successful run.

Ring Out, Wild Bells

> My own costume was mysterious, but spectacular. . . .
> The whole thing was made out of silk in alternate green
> and red stripes, and (unquestionably my poor mother's
> most demented stroke) it was covered from head to foot
> with a thousand tiny bells. Because all our costumes
> were obviously perishable, we never wore them in re-
> hearsal, and naturally nobody knew that I was invested
> with these peculiar sound effects until I made my en-
> trance at the beginning of the second act.

When I finally got around to see Max Reinhardt's cinema
version of *A Midsummer-Night's Dream*, and saw a child
called Mickey Rooney playing Puck, I remembered suddenly
that long ago I had taken the same part.

Our production was given on the open-air stage at the
Riverdale Country School, shortly before the war. The
scenery was only the natural scenery of that suburban dell,
and the cast was exclusively male, ranging in age from eleven
to perhaps seventeen. While we had thus preserved the pure,
Elizabethan note of the original, it must be admitted that our
version had its drawbacks. The costumes were probably the

worst things we had to bear, and even Penrod, tragically arrayed as Launcelot in his sister's stockings and his father's drawers, might have been embarrassed for us. Like Penrod, we were costumed by our parents, and like the Schofields, they seemed on the whole a little weak historically. Half of the ladies were inclined to favor the Elizabethan, and they had constructed rather bunchy ruffs and farthingales for their offspring; others, who had read as far as the stage directions and learned that the action took place in an Athenian wood, had produced something vaguely Athenian, usually beginning with a sheet. Only the fairies had a certain uniformity. For some reason their parents had all decided on cheesecloth, with here and there a little ill-advised trimming with tinsel.

My own costume was mysterious, but spectacular. As nearly as I have ever been able to figure things out, my mother found her inspiration for it in a Maxfield Parrish picture of a court jester. Beginning at the top, there was a cap with three stuffed horns; then, for the main part, a pair of tights that covered me to my wrists and ankles; and finally slippers with stuffed toes that curled up at the ends. The whole thing was made out of silk in alternate green and red stripes, and (unquestionably my poor mother's most demented stroke) it was covered from head to foot with a thousand tiny bells. Because all our costumes were obviously perishable, we never wore them in rehearsal, and naturally nobody knew that I was invested with these peculiar sound effects until I made my entrance at the beginning of the second act.

Our director was a man who had strong opinions about how Shakespeare should be played, and Puck was one of his favorite characters. It was his theory that Puck, being "the incarnation of mischief," never ought to be still a minute, so I had been coached to bound onto the stage, and once there to dance up and down, cocking my head and waving my arms.

"I want you to be a little whirlwind," this man said.

Even as I prepared to bound onto the stage, I had my own misgivings about those dangerously abundant gestures, and their probable effect on my bells. It was too late, however, to invent another technique for playing Puck, even if there had been room for anything but horror in my mind. I bounded onto the stage.

The effect, in its way, must have been superb. With every leap I rang like a thousand children's sleighs, my melodies foretelling God knows what worlds of merriment to the enchanted spectators. It was even worse when I came to the middle of the stage and went into my gestures. The other ringing had been loud but sporadic. This was persistent, varying only slightly in volume and pitch with the vehemence of my gestures. To a blind man, it must have sounded as though I had recklessly decided to accompany myself on a xylophone. A maturer actor would probably have made up his mind that an emergency existed, and abandonded his gestures as impracticable under the circumstances. I was thirteen, and incapable of innovations. I had been told by responsible authorities that gestures went with this part, and I continued to make them. I also continued to ring—a silvery music, festive and horrible.

If the bells were hard on my nerves, they were even worse for the rest of the cast, who were totally unprepared for my new interpretation. Puck's first remark is addressed to one of the fairies, and it is mercifully brief.

I said, "How now, spirit! Whither wander you?"

This unhappy child, already embarrassed by a public appearance in cheesecloth and tinsel, was also burdened with an opening speech of sixteen lines in verse. He began bravely:

> *"Over hill, over dale,*
> *Thorough bush, thorough brier,*
> *Over park, over pale,*
> *Thorough flood, thorough fire . . ."*

At the word "fire," my instructions were to bring my hands up from the ground in a long, wavery sweep, intended to represent fire. The bells pealed. To my startled ears, it sounded more as if they exploded. The fairy stopped in his lines and looked at me sharply. The jingling, however, had diminished; it was no more than as if a faint wind stirred my bells, and he went on:

> *"I do wander every where,*
> *Swifter than the moone's sphere . . ."*

Here again I had another cue, for a sort of swoop and dip indicating the swiftness of the moone's sphere. Again the bells rang out, and again the performance stopped in its tracks. The fairy was clearly troubled by these interruptions. He had, however, a child's strange acceptance of the inscrutable, and was even able to regard my bells as a last-minute adult addition to the program, nerve-racking but not to be questioned. I'm sure it was only this that got him through that first speech.

My turn, when it came, was even worse. By this time the audience had succumbed to a helpless gaiety. Every time my bells rang, laughter swept the spectators, and this mounted and mingled with the bells until everything else was practically inaudible. I began my speech, another long one, and full of incomprehensible references to Titania's changeling.

"Louder!" said somebody in the wings. "You'll have to talk louder."

It was the director, and he seemed to be in a dangerous state.

"And for heaven's sake, stop that jingling!" he said.

I talked louder, and I tried to stop the jingling, but it was no use. By the time I got to the end of my speech, I was shouting and so was the audience. It appeared that I had very little control over the bells, which continued to jingle in spite of my passionate efforts to keep them quiet.

All this had a very bad effect on the fairy, who by this time had many symptoms of a complete nervous collapse. However, he began his next speech:

> *"Either I mistake your shape and making quite,*
> *Or else you are that shrewd and knavish sprite*
> *Call'd Robin Goodfellow: are you not he*
> *That . . ."*

At this point I forgot that the rules had been changed and I was supposed to leave out the gestures. There was a furious jingling, and the fairy gulped.

"Are you not he that, that . . ."

He looked miserably at the wings, and the director supplied the next line, but the tumult was too much for him. The unhappy child simply shook his head.

"Say anything!" shouted the director desperately. "Anything at all!"

The fairy only shut his eyes and shuddered.

"All right!" shouted the director. "All right, Puck. *You* begin *your* next speech."

By some miracle, I actually did remember my next lines, and had opened my mouth to begin on them when suddenly the fairy spoke. His voice was a high, thin monotone, and there seemed to be madness in it, but it was perfectly clear.

"Fourscore and seven years ago," he began, "our fathers brought forth on this continent a new nation, conceived . . ."

He said it right through to the end, and it was certainly the most successful speech ever made on that stage, and probably one of the most successful speeches ever made on any stage. I don't remember, if I ever knew, how the rest of us ever picked up the dull, normal thread of the play after that extraordinary performance, but we must have, because I know it went on. I only remember that in the next intermission the director cut off my bells with his penknife, and after that things quieted down and got dull.

GEORGE BERNARD SHAW

George Bernard Shaw (1856–1950) was born in Dublin, but moved to London in 1876. He began his career as a novelist, then joined the Fabian socialist movement and devoted himself to social propaganda. His novels did not sell, nor did his early plays, so he earned his living as a critic of music, art, and the theater. *Widowers' Houses* was his first play to be produced in an independent theater. It met with little success. Perhaps because of their limited popularity as stage vehicles, Shaw published seven of his early plays in two series, *Plays Pleasant and Unpleasant* (1898). In lengthy prefaces he commented on the technical and social qualities of the plays and expanded the stage directions into full descriptions, character sketches, and analyses, thus adapting the play to a public accustomed to the reading of novels.

Shaw's period of activity in the theater and in literature extended for almost sixty years. During this time he expressed himself on all subjects with great frankness, sometimes with wisdom, and always with wit; the prefaces to his published plays contain the best expressions of his philosophy. He was for most of his life an ardent vegetarian and a teetotaler.

School

What makes school life irksome until you get used to it and easy when you get used to it, is that it is a routine. You have to get up at a fixed hour, wash and dress, take your meals, and do your work all at fixed hours. Now the worst of a routine is that, though it is supposed to suit everybody, it really suits nobody.

◆━◆━◆

A BBC radio talk to sixth-form students, delivered on June 23, 1937. Reprinted by permission of The Society of Authors on behalf of the Bernard Shaw Estate.

Hallo, Sixth Forms! I have been asked to speak to you because I have become celebrated through my eminence in the profession of Eschylus, Sophocles, Euripides, and Shakespear. Eschylus wrote in school Greek, and Shakespear is "English Literature," which is a school subject. In French schools I am English Literature. Consequently, all the sixth forms in France shudder when they hear my name. However, do not be alarmed: I am not going to talk to you about English literature. To me there is nothing in writing a play; anyone can write one if he has the necessary natural turn for it; and if he hasn't he can't: that is all there is to it.

However, I have another trick for imposing on the young. I am old: over eighty, in fact. Also I have a white beard; and these two facts are somehow associated in people's minds with wisdom. That is a mistake. If a person is a born fool, the folly will get worse, not better, by a long life's practice. Having lived four times as long as you gives me only one advantage over you. I have carried small boys and girls in my arms, and seen them grow into sixth-form scholars, then into young men and women in the flower of youth and beauty, then into brides and bridegrooms who think one another much better and lovelier than they really are, then into middle-aged paterfamiliases and anxious mothers with elderly spreads, and finally I have attended their cremations.

Now you may not think much of this; but just consider. Some of your schoolfellows may surprise you by getting hanged. Others, of whom you may have the lowest opinion, will turn out to be geniuses, and become the great men of your time. Therefore, always be nice to young people. Some little beast who is no good at games and whose head you may possibly have clouted for indulging a sarcastic wit and a sharp tongue at your expense may grow into a tremendous swell, like Rudyard Kipling. You never can tell.

It is no use reading about such things or being told about them by your father. You must have known the people personally, as I have. That is what makes a difference between your outlook on the world and mine. When I was as young as you the world seemed to me to be unchangeable, and a year seemed a long time. Now the years fly past before I have time to look around. I am an old man before I have quite got out of the habit of thinking of myself as a boy. You have fifty years before you, and therefore must think carefully about your future and about your conduct. I have no future and need not care what I say or do.

You all think, don't you, that you are nearly grown up. I thought so when I was your age; and now, after eighty-one years of that expectation, I have not grown up yet. The same thing will happen to you. You will escape from school only to discover that the world is a bigger school, and that you are back again in the first form. Before you can work your way up into the sixth form again you will be as old as I am.

The hardest part of schooling is, fortunately, the early part when you are a very small kid and have to be turned into a walking ready reckoner. You have to know up to twelve times twelve, and how many shillings there are in any number of pence up to 144 without looking at a book. And you must understand a printed page just as you understand people talking to you. That is a stupendous feat of sheer learning: much the most difficult I have ever achieved; yet I have not the faintest recollection of being put through it, though I remember the governess who did it. I cannot remember any time at which a printed page was unintelligible to me, nor at which I did not know without counting that fifty-six pence make four and eightpence. This seems so magical to me now that I sometimes regret that she did not teach me the whole table of logarithms and the binomial theorem and all the other mathematical short cuts and ready reckonings as well. Perhaps she would have if she had known them herself. It is strange that if you learn anything when you are young you remember it forever. Now that I am old I forget everything in a few seconds, and everybody five minutes after they have been introduced to me. That is a great happiness, as I don't want to be bothered with new things and new people; but I still cannot get on without remembering what my governess taught me. So cram in all you can while you are young.

But I am rambling. Let us get back to your escape from your school or your university into the great school of the world; and remember that you will not be chased and brought back. You will just be chucked out neck and crop and the door slammed behind you.

What makes school life irksome until you get used to it, and easy when you do get used to it, is that it is a routine. You have to get up at a fixed hour, wash and dress, take your meals, and do your work all at fixed hours. Now the worst of a routine is that, though it is supposed to suit everybody, it really suits nobody. Sixth-form scholars are like other people: they are all different. Each of you is what is called an individual case, needing individual attention. But you cannot have it at school. Nobody has time enough nor money enough to provide each of you with a separate teacher and a special routine carefully fitted to your individual personality, like your clothes and your boots.

I can remember a time when English people going to live in Germany were astonished to find that German boots were not divided into rights and lefts: a boot was a boot and it did not matter which foot you put it on, your foot had to make the best of it. You may think that funny; but let me ask you how many of you have your socks knitted as rights and lefts? I have had mine knitted that way for the last fifty years. Some knitters of socks actually refuse my order and say that it can't be done. Just think of that? We are able to make machines that can fly round the world and instruments that can talk round the world, yet we think we cannot knit socks as rights and lefts, and I am considered a queer sort of fellow because I want it done and insist that it can be done. Well, school routines are like the socks and the old German boots: they are neither rights or lefts, and consequently they don't fit any human being properly. But we have to manage with them somehow.

And when we escape from school into the big adult world, we have to choose between a lot of routines: the college routine, the military routine, the naval routine, the court routine, the civil service routine, the legal routine, the clerical routine, the theatrical routine, or the parliamentary routine, which is the worst of the lot. To get properly stuck into one of these grooves you have to pass examinations; and this you must set about very clearheadedly or you will fail. You must not let yourself get interested in the subjects or be overwhelmed by the impossibility of anyone mastering them all even at the age of five hundred, much less twenty. The scholar who knows everything is like the little child who is perfectly obedient and perfectly truthful: it doesn't exist and never will. Therefore you must go to a crammer. Now, what is a crammer? A crammer is a person whose whole life is devoted to doing something you have not time to do for yourself: that is, to study all the old examination papers and find out what are the questions that are actually asked, and what are the answers expected by the examiners and officially recognized as correct. You must be very careful not to suppose that these answers are always the true answers. Your examiners will be elderly gentlemen, and their knowledge is sure to be more or less out-of-date. Therefore begin by telling yourself this story.

Imagine yourself a young student early in the fifteenth century being examined as to your knowledge of the movements of the sun and moon, the planets and stars. Imagine also that your father happens to know Copernicus, and that you have learnt from his conversation that the planets go round not in circles but in ellipses. Imagine that you have met the painter Leonardo da Vinci, and been allowed to peep at his funny notebook, and, by holding it up to a mirror, read the words "the earth is a moon of the sun." Imagine that on being examined you gave the answers of Copernicus and Leonardo, believing them to be the true answers. Instead of passing at the head of the successful list you would have been burnt alive for heresy. Therefore you would have taken good care to say that the stars and the sun move in perfect circles, because the circle is a perfect figure and therefore answers to the perfection of the Creator. You would have said that the motion of the sun round the earth was proved by the fact that Joshua saw it move in Gibeon and stopped it. All your answers would be wrong, but you would pass and be patted on the head as a young marvel of Aristotelian science.

Now, passing examinations today is just what it was in the days of Copernicus. If you at twenty years of age go up to be examined by an elderly gentleman of fifty, you must find out what people were taught thirty years ago and stuff him with that, and not with what you are taught today.

But, you will say, how are you possibly to find out what questions are to be asked and what answers are expected? Well, you cannot; but a good crammer can. He cannot get a peep at the papers beforehand, but he can study the old examination papers until he knows all the questions the examiners have to keep asking over and over again; for, after all, their number is not infinite. If only you will swot hard enough to learn them all you will pass with flying colors. Of course, you will not be able to learn them all, but your chances will be good in proportion to the number you can learn.

The danger of being plucked for giving up-to-date answers to elderly examiners is greatest in the technical professions. If you want to get into the navy, or practise medicine, you must get specially trained for some months in practices that are quite out of date. If you don't you will be turned down by admirals dreaming of the Nelson touch, and surgical baronets brought up on the infallibility of Jenner and Lister and Pasteur. But this does not apply to all examinations. Take the classics, for instance. Homer's Greek and Virgil's Latin, being dead languages, do not change as naval and medical practice changes. Suppose you want to be a clergyman. The Greek of the New Testament does not change. The creeds do not change. The Thirty-nine Articles do not change, though they ought to, for some of them are terribly out of date. You can cram yourself with these subjects and save your money for lessons in elocution.

In any case you may take it as a safe rule that if you happen to have any original ideas about examination subjects you must not air them in your examination papers. You may very possibly know better than your examiners, but do not let them find out that you think so.

Once you are safely through your examinations you will begin life in earnest. You will then discover that your education has been very defective. You will find yourself uninstructed as to eating and drinking and sleeping and breathing. Your notions of keeping yourself fit will consist mostly of physical exercises which will shorten your life by twenty years or so. You may accept me as an educated man because I have earned my living for sixty years by work which only an educated man, and even a highly educated one, could do. Yet the subjects that educated me were never taught in my schools. As far as I know, my schoolmasters were utterly and barbarously ignorant of them. School was to me a sentence of penal servitude. You see, I was born with what people call an artistic temperament. I could read all the masterpieces of English poets, playwrights, historians, and scientific pioneers, but I could not read schoolbooks, because they are written by people who do not know how to write. To me a person who knew nothing of all the great musicians from Palestrina to Edward Elgar, or of the great painters from Giotto to Burne-Jones, was a savage and an ignoramus even if he were hung all over with gold medals for school classics. As to mathematics, to be imprisoned in an ugly room and set to do sums in algebra without ever having had the meaning of mathematics explained to me, or its relation to science, was enough to make me hate mathematics all the rest of my life, as so many literary men do. So do not expect too much from your school achievements. You may win the Ireland scholarship and then find that none of the great business houses will employ a university don on any terms.

As to your general conduct and prospects, all I have time to say is that if you do as everyone does and think as everyone thinks you will get on very well with your neighbors, but you will suffer from all their illnesses and stupidities. If you think and act otherwise you must suffer their dislike and persecution. I was taught when I was young that if people would only love one another, all would be well with the world. This seemed simple and very nice; but I found when I tried to put it in practice not only that other people were seldom lovable, but that I was not very lovable myself. I also found that to love anyone is to take a liberty with them which is quite unbearable unless they happen to return your affection, which you have no right to expect. What you have to learn if you are to be a good citizen of the world is that, though you will certainly dislike many of your neighbors, and differ from some of them so strongly that you could not possibly live in the same house with them, that does not give you the smallest right to injure them or even to be personally uncivil to them. You must not attempt to do good to those who hate you: for they do not need your officious services, and would refuse to be under any obligation to you. Your difficulty will be how to behave to those whom you dislike, and cannot help disliking for no reason whatever, simply because you were born with an antipathy to that sort of person. You must just keep out of their way as much as you can; and when you cannot, deal as honestly and civilly with them as with your best friend. Just think what the world would be like if everyone who disliked you were to punch your head.

The oddest thing about it is that you will find yourself making friends with people whose opinions are the very opposite to your own, whilst you cannot bear the sight of others who share all your beliefs. You may love your dog and find your nearest relatives detestable. So don't waste your time arguing whether you *ought* to love all your neighbors. You can't help yourself, and neither can they.

You may find yourself completely dissatisfied with all your fellow creatures as they exist at present and with all their laws and institutions. Then there is nothing to be done but to set to work to find out exactly what is wrong with them, and how to set them right. That is perhaps the best fun of all; but perhaps I think so only because I am a little in that line myself. I could tell you a lot more about this, but time is up, and I am warned that I must stop. I hope you are sorry.

JAMES THURBER

James Thurber (1894–1961), American humorist, cartoonist, short-story writer, and editor, was born and grew up in Columbus, Ohio. World War I interrupted his college studies. During the war, he worked in Washington and Paris as a code clerk in the State Department. After the war, Thurber returned to Ohio State University and completed his degree. After a stint on several newspapers, Thurber, through his friend E. B. White, joined the newly organized *New Yorker* magazine and became its managing editor. After he relinquished this position, he continued on as one of the mainstays of The *New Yorker*'s distinguished list of contributors.

Until his eyesight failed, Thurber drew the inimitable cartoons and illustrations for his own writings. Among his best-known works are *The Owl in the Attic and Other Perplexities* (1931), *The Seal in the Bedroom and Other Predicaments* (1932), and *My Life and Hard Times* (1933).

Here Lies Miss Groby

The fierce light that Miss Groby brought to English literature was the light of Identification. Perhaps, at the end, she could no longer retain the dates of birth and death of one of the Lake poets. That would have sent her to the principal of the school with her resignation.

———◆◆———

Miss Groby taught me English composition thirty years ago. It wasn't what prose said that interested Miss Groby; it was the way prose said it. The shape of a sentence crucified on a blackboard (parsed, she called it) brought a light to her eye. She hunted for Topic Sentences and Transitional Sentences the way little girls hunt for white violets in springtime. What she loved most of all were Figures of Speech. You remember her. You must have had her, too. Her influence will never die out of the land. A small schoolgirl asked me the other day if I could give her an example of metonymy. (There are several kinds of metonymies, you may recall, but the one that will come to mind most easily, I think, is Container for the Thing Contained). The vision of Miss Groby came clearly before me when the little girl mentioned the old, familiar word. I saw her sitting at her desk, taking the rubber band off the roll-call cards, running it back upon the fingers of her right hand, and surveying us all separately with quick little henlike turns of her head.

Here lies Miss Groby, not dead, I think, but put away on a shelf with the other T squares and rulers whose edges had lost their certainty. The fierce light that Miss Groby brought to English literature was the light of Identification. Perhaps, at the end, she could no longer retain the dates of the birth and death of one of the Lake poets. That would have sent her to the principal of the school with her resignation. Or perhaps she could not remember, finally, exactly how many Cornish-men there were who had sworn that Trelawny should not die, or precisely how many springs were left to Housman's lad in which to go about the woodlands to see the cherry hung with snow.

Verse was one of Miss Groby's delights because there was so much in both its form and content that could be counted. I believe she would have got an enormous thrill out of Words-worth's famous lines about Lucy if they had been written this way:

> *A violet by a mossy stone*
> *Half hidden from the eye,*
> *Fair as a star when ninety-eight*
> *Are shining in the sky.*

It is hard for me to believe that Miss Groby ever saw any famous work of literature from far enough away to know what it meant. She was forever climbing up the margins of books and crawling between their lines, hunting for the little gold of phrase, making marks with a pencil. As Palamides hunted the Questing Beast, she hunted the Figure of Speech. She hunted it through the clangorous halls of Shakespeare and through the green forests of Scott.

Night after night, for homework, Miss Groby set us to searching in *Ivanhoe* and *Julius Caesar* for metaphors, similes, metonymies, apostrophes, personifications, and all the rest. It got so that figures of speech jumped out of the pages at you, obscuring the sense and pattern of the novel or play you were trying to read. "Friends, Romans, countrymen, lend me your ears." Take that, for instance. There is an unusual but perfect example of Container for the Thing Contained. If you read the funeral oration unwarily—that is to say, for its meaning—you might easily miss the C.F.T.T.C. Antony is, of course, not asking for their ears in the sense that he wants them cut off and handed over; he is asking for the function of those ears, for their power to hear, for, in a word, the thing they contain.

At first I began to fear that all the characters in Shakespeare and Scott were crazy. They confused cause with effect, the sign for the thing signified, the thing held for the thing holding it. But after a while I began to suspect that it was I myself who was crazy. I would find myself lying awake at night saying over and over, "The thinger for the thing contained." In a great but probably misguided attempt to keep my mind on its hinges, I would stare at the ceiling and try to think of an example of the Thing Contained for the Container. It struck me as odd that Miss Groby had never thought of that inversion. I finally hit on one, which I still remember. If a woman were to grab up a bottle of Grade A and say to her husband, "Get away from me or I'll hit you with the milk," that would be a Thing Contained for the Container. The next day in class I raised my hand and brought my curious discovery straight out before Miss Groby and my astonished schoolmates. I was eager and serious about it and it never occurred to me that the other children would laugh. They laughed loudly and long. When Miss Groby had quieted them she said to me rather coldly, "That was not really amusing, James." That's the mixed-up kind of thing that happened to me in my teens.

In later years I came across another excellent example of this figure of speech in a joke long since familiar to people who know vaudeville or burlesque (or radio, for that matter). It goes something like this:

A: What's your head all bandaged up for?
B: I got hit with some tomatoes.
A: How could that bruise you up so bad?
B: These tomatoes were in a can.

I wonder what Miss Groby would have thought of that one.

I dream of my old English teacher occasionally. It seems that we are always in Sherwood Forest and that from far away I can hear Robin Hood winding his silver horn. "Drat that man for making such a racket on his cornet!" cries Miss Groby. "He scared away a perfectly darling Container for the Thing Contained, a great, big, beautiful one. It leaped right back into its context when that man blew that cornet. It was the most wonderful Container for the Thing Contained I ever saw here in the Forest of Arden."

"This is Sherwood Forest," I say to her.

"That doesn't make any difference at all that I can see," she says to me.

Then I wake up, tossing and moaning.

BETTY SMITH

Betty Smith (1904–   ) was born in Brooklyn, New York. She left school after the eighth grade. When her children were old enough, she continued her studies at the University of Michigan, where she won the Avery Hopwood award in drama. She has written more than seventy one-act plays and has acted in stock and on the radio. In 1943, her partly autobiographical novel of a Brooklyn slum childhood, *A Tree Grows in Brooklyn*, was published and became a best seller. More than two million copies of the book were sold in the United States. Later, with George Abbott, she turned the novel into a successful musical play (1951). Two other novels by Betty Smith are *Tomorrow Will Be Better* (1948) and *Maggie-Now* (1958).

Francie's Great Expectations
FROM *A Tree Grows in Brooklyn*

Brutalizing is the only adjective for the public schools of that district around 1908 and '09. . . . Teaching requirements were easy: graduation from high school and two years at Teachers Training school. Few teachers had the true vocation of their work. They taught because it was one of the few jobs open to them; because it was better paying than factory work; because they had a long summer vacation . . . they got a pension when they retired. They taught because no one wanted to marry them. Married women were not allowed to teach in those days, hence most of the teachers were women made neurotic by starved love instincts. These barren women spent their fury on other women's children in a twisted authoritative manner.

———◆◆———

School days were eagerly anticipated by Francie. She wanted all of the things that she thought came with school. She was a lonely child and she longed for the companionship of other children. She wanted to drink from the school water fountains in the yard. The faucets were inverted and she thought that soda water came out instead of plain water. She had heard mama and papa speak of the school room. She wanted to see the map that pulled down like a shade. Most of all, she wanted "school supplies"; a notebook and tablet and a pencil box with a sliding top filled with new pencils, an eraser, a little tin pencil sharpener made in the shape of a cannon, a pen wiper, and a six-inch, soft wood, yellow ruler. . . .

Francie expected great things from school. Since vaccination taught her instantly the difference between left and right, she thought that school would bring forth even greater miracles. She thought she'd come home from school that first day knowing how to read and write. But all she came home with was a bloody nose gained by an older child slamming her head down on the stone rim of the water trough when she had tried to drink from the faucets that did not gush forth soda water after all.

Francie was disappointed because she had to share a seat and desk (meant only for one) with another girl. She had wanted a desk to herself. She accepted with pride the pencil the monitor passed out to her in the morning and reluctantly surrendered it to another monitor at three o'clock.

She had been in school but half a day when she knew that she would never be a teacher's pet. That privilege was reserved for a small group of girls . . . girls with freshly-curled hair, crisp clean pinafores and new silk hairbows. They were the children of the prosperous storekeepers of the neighborhood. Francie noticed how Miss Briggs, the teacher, beamed on them and seated them in the choicest places in the front row. These darlings were not made to share seats. Miss Briggs' voice was gentle when she spoke to these fortune-favored few, and snarling when she spoke to the great crowd of unwashed.

Francie, huddled with other children of her kind, learned more that first day than she realized. She learned of the class system of a great Democracy. She was puzzled and hurt by teacher's attitude. Obviously the teacher hated her and others like her for no other reason than that they were what they were. Teacher acted as though they had no right to be in the school but that she was forced to accept them and was doing so with as little grace as possible. She begrudged them the few crumbs of learning she threw at them. Like the doctor at the health center, she too acted as though they had no right to live.

It would seem as if all the unwanted children would stick together and be one against the things that were against them. But not so. They hated each other as much as the teacher hated them. They aped teacher's snarling manner when they spoke to each other.

There was always one unfortunate whom the teacher singled out and used for a scapegoat. This poor child was the nagged one, the tormented one, the one on whom she vented her spinsterly spleen. As soon as a child received this dubious recognition, the other children turned on him and duplicated the teacher's torments. Characteristically, they fawned on those close to teacher's heart. Maybe they figured they were nearer to the throne that way.

Three thousand children crowded into this ugly brutalizing school that had facilities for only one thousand. Dirty stories went the rounds of the children. One of them was that Miss Pfieffer, a bleached blond teacher with a high giggle, went down to the basement to sleep with the assistant janitor those times when she put a monitor in charge and explained that she had to "step out to the office." Another, passed around by little boys who had been victims, was that the lady principal, a hard-bitten, heavy cruel woman of middle years who wore sequin-decorated dresses and smelled always of raw gin, got recalcitrant boys into her office and made them take down their pants so that she could flay their naked buttocks with a rattan cane. (She whipped the little girls through their dresses.)

Of course, corporal punishment was forbidden in the schools. But who, outside, knew? Who would tell? Not the whipped children, certainly. It was a tradition in the neighborhood that if a child reported that he had been whipped in school, he would receive a second home-whipping because he had not behaved in school. So the child took his punishment and kept quiet, leaving well enough alone.

The ugliest thing about these stories was that they were all sordidly true.

Brutalizing is the only adjective for the public schools of that district around 1908 and '09. Child psychology had not been heard of in Williamsburg in those days. Teaching requirements were easy: graduation from high school and two years at Teachers Training School. Few teachers had the true vocation for their work. They taught because it was one of the few jobs open to them; because it was better paying than factory work; because they had a long summer vacation; because they got a pension when they retired. They taught because no one wanted to marry them. Married women were not allowed to teach in those days, hence most of the teachers were women made neurotic by starved love instincts. These barren women spent their fury on other women's children in a twisted authoritative manner.

The cruelest teachers were those who had come from homes similar to those of the poor children. It seemed that in their bitterness towards those unfortunate little ones, they were somehow exorcizing their own fearful background.

Of course, not all of the teachers were bad. Sometimes one who was sweet came along, one who suffered with the children and tried to help them. But these women did not last long as teachers. Either they married quickly and left the profession, or they were hounded out of their jobs by fellow teachers.

The problem of what was delicately called "leaving the room" was a grim one. The children were instructed to "go" before they left home in the morning and then to wait until lunch hour. There was supposed to be a time at recess but few children were able to take advantage of that. Usually the press of the crowd prevented a child's getting near the washrooms. If he was lucky enough to get there (where there were but ten lavoratories for five hundred children), he'd find the places pre-empted by the ten most brutalized children in the school. They'd stand in the doorways and prevent entrance to all comers. They were deaf to the piteous pleas of the hordes of tormented children who swarmed before them. A few exacted a fee of a penny which few children were able to pay. The overlords never relaxed their hold on the swinging doors until the bell clanged the end of recess. No one ever ascertained what pleasure they derived from this macabre game. They were never punished since no teacher ever entered the children's washrooms. No child ever snitched. No matter how young he was, he knew that he mustn't squeal. If he tattled, he knew he would be tortured almost to death by the one he reported. So this evil game went on and on.

Technically, a child was permitted to leave the room if he

asked permission. There was a system of coy evasion. One finger held aloft meant that a child wished to go out but a short time. Two fingers meant desire for a longer stay. But the harassed and unfeeling teachers assured each other that this was just a subterfuge for a child to get out of the classroom for a little while. They *knew* the child had ample opportunity at recess and at lunch time. Thus they settled things among themselves.

Of course, Francie noted, the favored children, the clean, the dainty, the cared-for in the front seats, were allowed to leave at any time. But that was different somehow.

As for the rest of the children, half of them learned to adjust their functions to the teachers' ideas of such things and the other half became chronic pants-wetters. . . .

Katie's campaign against vermin and disease started the day her children entered school. The battle was fierce, brief, and successful.

Packed closely together, the children innocently bred vermin and became lousy from each other. Through no fault of their own, they were subjected to the most humiliating procedure that a child could go through.

Once a week, the school nurse came and stationed herself with her back to the window. The little girls lined up and when they came to her, turned round, lifted their heavy braids and bent over. Nurse probed about the hair with a long thin stick. If lice or nits were in evidence, the little one was told to stand aside. At the end of the examination, the pariahs were made to stand before the class while Nurse gave a lecture about how filthy those little girls were and how they had to be shunned. The untouchables were then dismissed for the day with instructions to get "blue ointment" from Knipe's Drug Store and have their mothers treat their head. When they returned to school, they were tormented by their peers. Each offender would have an escort of children following her home, chanting:

"Lousy, ye'r lousy! Teacher said ye'r lousy. Hadda go home, hadda go home, hadda go home because ye'r lousy."

It might be that the infected child would be given a clean bill next examination. In that case, she, in turn, would torment those found guilty, forgetting her own hurt at being tormented. They learned no compassion from their own anguish. Thus their suffering was wasted.

There was no room in Katie's crowded life for additional

trouble and worry. She wouldn't accept it. The first day that Francie came home from school and reported that she sat next to a girl who had bugs walking up and down the lanes of her hair, Katie went into action. She scrubbed Francie's head with a cake of her coarse strong yellow scrubwoman's soap until her scalp tingled with rawness. The next morning, she dipped the hair brush into a bowl of kerosene oil, brushed Francie's hair vigorously, braided it into braids so tight that the veins on Francie's temples stuck out, instructed her to keep away from lighted gas jets and sent her off to school.

Francie smelled up the whole classroom. Her seat sharer edged as far away from her as possible. Teacher sent a note home forbidding Katie to use kerosene on Francie's head. Katie remarked that it was a free country and ignored the note. Once a week she scrubbed Francie's head with the yellow soap. Every day she anointed it with the kerosene.

When an epidemic of mumps broke out in the school, Katie went into action against communicable diseases. She made two flannel bags, sewed a bud of garlic in each one, attached a clean corset string and made the children wear them around their necks under their shirts.

Francie attended school stinking of garlic and kerosene oil. Everyone avoided her. In the crowded yard, there was always a cleared space around her. In crowded trolley cars, people huddled away from those Nolan children.

And it worked! Now whether there was a witch's charm in the garlic, whether the strong fumes killed the germs or whether Francie escaped contracting anything because infected children gave her a wide berth, or whether she and Neeley had naturally strong constitutions, is not known. However, it was a fact that not once in all the years of school were Katie's children ever sick. They never so much as came down with a cold. And they never had lice.

Francie, of course, became an outsider shunned by all because of her stench. But she had become accustomed to being lonely. She was used to walking alone and to being considered "different." She did not suffer too much.

Francie liked school in spite of all the meanness, cruelty, and unhappiness. The regimented routine of many children, all doing the same thing at once, gave her a feeling of safety. She felt that she was a definite part of something, part of a community gathered under a leader for the one purpose. The Nolans were individualists. They conformed to nothing except what was essential to their being able to live in their world. They followed their own standards of living. They were part of no set social group. This was fine for the making of individualists but sometimes bewildering to a small child. So Francie felt a certain safety and security in school. Although it was a cruel and ugly routine, it had a purpose and a progression.

School was not all unrelieved grimness. There was a great golden glory lasting a half hour each week when Mr. Morton came to Francie's room to teach music. He was a specialized teacher who went around to all the schools in that area. It was holiday time when he appeared. He was so vibrant, gay and jolly—so intoxicated with living—that he was like a god come from the clouds. He was homely in a gallant vital way. He understood and loved children and they worshipped him. The teachers adored him. There was a carnival spirit in the room on the day of his visit. Teacher wore her best dress and wasn't quite so mean. Sometimes she curled her hair and wore perfume. That's what Mr. Morton did to those ladies.

He arrived like a tornado. The door burst open and he flew in with his coattails streaming behind him. He leaped to the platform and looked around smiling and saying, "well-well," in a happy voice. The children sat there and laughed and laughed out of happiness and Teacher smiled and smiled.

He drew notes on the blackboard; he drew little legs on them to make them look as though they were running out of the scale. He'd make a flat note look like humpty-dumpty. A sharp note would rate a thin beet-like nose zooming off it. All the while he'd burst into singing just as spontaneously as a bird. Sometimes his happiness was so overflowing that he couldn't hold it and he'd cut a dance caper to spill some of it out.

He taught them good music without letting them know it was good. He set his own words to the great classics and gave them simple names like "Lullaby" and "Serenade" and "Street Song" and "Song for a Sunshine Day." Their baby voices shrilled out in Handel's "Largo" and they knew it merely by the title of "Hymn." Little boys whistled part of Dvorak's *New World Symphony* as they played marbles. When asked the name of the song, they'd reply "Oh, 'Going Home.'" They played potsy, humming "The Soldiers' Chorus" from *Faust* which they called "Glory."

Not as well loved as Mr. Morton, but as much admired, was Miss Bernstone, the special drawing teacher who also came once a week. Ah, she was from another world, a world of beautiful dresses of muted greens and garnets. Her face was sweet and tender, and, like Mr. Morton, she loved the vast hordes of unwashed and unwanted children more than she loved the cared-for ones. The teachers did not like *her*. Yes, they fawned on her when she spoke to them and glowered at her when her back was turned. They were jealous of her charm, her sweetness and her lovely appeal to men. She was warm and glowing and richly feminine. They knew that she didn't sleep alone nights as they were forced to do.

She spoke softly in a clear singing voice. Her hands were beautiful and quick with a bit of chalk or a stick of charcoal. There was magic in the way her wrist turned when she held a crayon. One wrist twist and there was an apple. Two more twists and there was a child's sweet hand holding the apple. On a rainy day, she wouldn't give a lesson. She'd take a block of paper and a stick of charcoal and sketch the poorest, meanest kid in the room. And when the picture was finished, you didn't see the dirt or the meanness; you saw the glory of innocence and the poignancy of a baby growing up too soon. Oh, Miss Bernstone was grand.

These two visiting teachers were the gold and silver sun-splash in the great muddy river of school days, days made up of dreary hours in which Teacher made her pupils sit rigid with their hands folded behind their back while she read a novel hidden in her lap. If all the teachers had been like Miss Bernstone and Mr. Morton, Francie would have known plain what heaven was. But it was just as well. There had to be the dark and muddy waters so that the sun could have something to background its flashing glory.

FRANCES GRAY PATTON

Frances Gray Patton (1906–   ) was born in North Carolina and has always lived there. She was graduated from Duke University, where her husband teaches English. She has been interested in writing since she was a young girl, and has had many of her short stories published in *The New Yorker*. *The Ladies' Home Journal* ran some short incidents and one long story about Miss Dove. *Good Morning, Miss Dove* was published as a full-length book in 1954. Other works by Frances Gray Patton include *The Finer Things of Life* (1951), *A Piece of Luck and Other Stories* (1955), and *28 Stories* (1969). In 1955 Mrs. Patton won the Christopher Award.

The Unknown Miss Dove
FROM *Good Morning, Miss Dove*

All in all, in bearing and clothing and bony structure, Miss Dove suggested that classic portrait of the eternal teacher that small fry, generation after generation, draw upon fences and sidewalks with nubbins of purloined chalk. . . . But there was more to Miss Dove. There was something that defies analysis.

———◆◆———

By eight-thirty, some two hundred and fifty children, ranging in age from six to twelve, were safely inside the school building. In various home-rooms they gauged, with the uncanny shrewdness of innocence, the various moods of various teachers. How far dared they go today?

But as morning progressed and the classes went, in turn, to spend forty-five minutes in the geography room with Miss Dove, they dropped their restless speculation.

For Miss Dove had no moods. Miss Dove was a certainty. She would be today what she had been yesterday and would be tomorrow. And so, within limits, would they. Single file they would enter her room. Each child would pause on the threshold as its mother and father had paused, more than likely, and would say—just as the policeman had said—in distinct, formal accents: "Good morning, Miss Dove." And Miss Dove would look directly at each of them, fixing her eyes directly upon theirs, and reply: "Good morning, Jessamine," or "Margaret," or "Samuel." (Never "Sam," never "Peggy," never "Jess." She eschewed familiarity as she wished others to eschew it.) They would go to their appointed desks. Miss Dove would ascend to hers. The lesson would begin.

There was no need to waste time in preliminary admonitions. Miss Dove's rules were as fixed as the signs of the zodiac. And they were known. Miss Dove rehearsed them at the beginning of each school year, stating them as calmly and dispassionately as if she were describing the atmospheric effects of the Gulf Stream. The penalties for infractions of the rules were also known. If a child introduced a foreign object—a pencil, let us say, or a wad of paper, or a lock of hair—into his mouth, he was required to wash out his mouth with the yellow laundry soap that lay on the drainboard of the sink in the corner by the sand table. If his posture was incorrect he had to go and sit for a while upon a stool without a back-rest. If a page in his notebook was untidy, he had to copy it over. If he emitted an uncovered cough, he was expected to rise immediately and fling open a window, no matter how cold the weather, so that a blast of fresh air could protect his fellows from the contamination of his germs. And if he felt obliged to disturb the class routine by leaving the room for a drink of water (Miss Dove loftily ignored any other necessity) he did so to an accompaniment of dead silence. Miss Dove would look at him—that was all—following his departure and greeting his return with her perfectly expressionless gaze and the whole class would sit idle and motionless, until he was back in the fold again. It was easier—even if one had eaten salt fish for breakfast—to remain and suffer.

Of course, there were flagrant offenses that were dealt with in private. Sometimes profanity sullied the air of the geography room. Sometimes, though rarely, open rebellion was displayed. In those instances, the delinquent was detained, minus the comfort of his comrades, in awful seclusion with Miss Dove. What happened between them was never fully known. (Did she threaten him with legal prosecution? Did she beat him with her long map-pointer?) The culprit, himself, was unlikely to be communicative on the subject or, if he were, to overdo the business with a tale that revolved to an incredible degree around his own heroism. Afterward, as was duly noted, his classroom attitude was subdued and chastened.

Miss Dove had no rule relating to prevarication. A child's word was taken at face value. If it happened to be false—well, that was the child's problem. A lie, unattacked and undistorted by defense, remained a lie and was apt to be recognized as such by its author.

Occasionally a group of progressive mothers would contemplate organized revolt. "She's been teaching too long," they would cry. "Her pedagogy hasn't changed since we were in Cedar Grove. She rules the children through fear!" They would turn to the boldest one among themselves. "*You* go," they would say. "You go talk to her!"

The bold one would go, but somehow she never did much talking. For there in the geography room, she would begin to feel—though she wore her handsomest tweeds and perhaps a gardenia for courage—that she was about ten years old and her petticoat was showing. Her throat would tickle. She would wonder desperately if she had a clean handkerchief in her bag. She would also feel thirsty. Without firing a shot in the cause of freedom she would retreat ingloriously from the field of battle.

And on that unassaulted field—in that room where no leeway was given to the personality, where a thing was black or white, right or wrong, polite or rude, simply because Miss Dove said it was, there was a curiously soothing quality. The children left it refreshed and restored, ready for fray or frolic. For within its walls they enjoyed what was allowed them nowhere else—a complete suspension of will.

On this particular Wednesday the first-graders, to whom Miss Dove gave a survey course in the flora and fauna of the Earth, drew pictures of robins. They drew them in crayon on eight-by-eleven sheets of manila paper. They did not draw them from memory. They copied the bird Miss Dove had drawn for them on the blackboard. (She knew exactly how a robin looked and saw no sense in permitting her pupils to rely upon their own random observations.) They left an inch-wide margin, measuring it with a ruler, around each picture. (Miss Dove believed in margins—except for error!) All the first grade's robins would look alike. Which was as it should be. Which was true of robins everywhere. Miss Dove was concerned with facts, not with artistic impressions.

She divided the second grade into activity groups. One group cut scenic photographs from old magazines and pasted them in a scrapbook. Another modeled clay caribou for the sand table. Still another drew a colored mural on the rear blackboard. The groups did not talk among themselves, asking questions and pooling advice. They had no need to. Miss Dove had told them what to do.

The third grade recited the states of the Union. It was Miss Dove's experience that the eight-year-old mind learned best by rote.

At a quarter past eleven the fourth grade filed in. This grade was studying economic geography—the natural resources of different regions and their manifold uses in civilized life—and on Monday was to take a proficiency test prepared by the state Board of Education. Each year in April all grammar-grade students—students in the fourth, fifth and sixth grades—were so examined. Regarding these tests, Miss Dove's sentiments were mixed. She resented them as an intrusion upon her privacy and as an implication that her efficiency was open to question. But she recognized in them, grudgingly, a certain practice-value to the children.

For in every life—once, if not oftener—there was a proficiency test. A time came when one was put to the proof. One stood alone. He was what he was. He knew what he knew. He did what he could. And he had no source of strength outside himself. Certainly, such a time had come to Miss Dove.

And on a plane more human than sublime, Miss Dove's vanity had always been flattered by the results of the test. Cedar Grove led the state in geography.

"You may utilize this period for review, children," she said. "Open your books to page ninety-three. Memorize the agricultural products of the Argentine pampas."

At that moment Miss Dove was first aware of a pain in her back. The pain was small in area but it was acute. It thrust like a knife into her spine. It was so intense, so unfamiliar, and so unexpected that she hardly believed in it. It descended along her right thigh. Miss Dove counted ten. The pain was easier. It was gone. It had been only a threat.

Tension, she thought. Anxiety about the proficiency tests. She was displeased with herself. She despised women who had backaches. *I must tranquilize my mind*, she told herself. *I will think of the Alps. White. Clean. Lofty. Rising above Lake Lucerne. The lake is blue; it reflects the evening star.* So she concentrated her thoughts upon mountains and water that she had never seen. And after a while she was sure she had imagined that stab of agony in her spine.

She slipped a rubber band from a sheaf of fifth-grade essay papers. She took a red pencil and began to correct them. But part of her mind stayed with the class that was present. She knew, for instance, when Vicky Evans, who was disposed to day-dreams, tired of her book and started gazing out the window. "Come back, Victoria," she said.

She heard when David Burnham sighed and muttered something exceedingly improper under his breath. "Hell and damn," David said.

"You will remain after class, David," Miss Dove said without glancing up from the fifth-grade papers.

"Yes, Miss Dove," said David.

At noon an electric buzzer, operated from a switch in the principal's office, shrilled through Cedar Grove School. It was the signal for lunch and "big recess." In almost every room children slammed their books shut, shuffled their feet, sloshed their paint-water, and made a mass lunge toward food and freedom. Different teachers reacted according to their different temperaments. The art teacher, for instance, was a full-blown, husky girl who had been a college hockey star as well as an esthetics major. She made a flying leap and reached the door ahead of her class. "Clean your paint brushes!" she yelled. "Police up your desks!" Her thick, wiry hair stood out around her face and—so the enchanted children claimed—was heard to crackle. "It's nothing to me if you starve!" The music teacher began to play the piano. "Softly, softly!" she begged in her sweet, tinkly voice. "Trippingly on our toes! Let's all be elves and fairies!" The literature teacher was not sorry to be interrupted; she had been

ading aloud from *Hiawatha*, a work she considered unworthy of her critical talents. She shrugged, not caring what
the children did so long as they went away, and began a letter
to her fiancé, who was pursuing his doctorate at Purdue.
"Lover," she wrote, "I am sinking in an intellectual quagmire."

But in the geography room there was no disorder. Forty-
three children sat quietly in their places. They did not look
up. Their posture was superb. Their brows were puckered
in thought as they read on of wheat and beef and leather.
From this room they were not to be becked or called by
mechanical noises. Here they acknowledged one sole authority which, in due time, would speak.

"Attention, please," said Miss Dove in the serene voice of
one who expects to be obeyed.

Forty-three children folded their hands on their desks and
raised limpid eyes to her face.

"Close your books, please," said Miss Dove.

Forty-three books were closed, not slammed, in the re-
spectful manner due to books.

"The class will rise," said Miss Dove.

The class rose. So did its teacher. The pain returned. It
nibbled at a vertebra like some small rodent with sharp,
burrowing teeth. But it was bearable, as most things are in
moments sustained by duty.

Miss Dove continued standing there on her raised platform
as she did at the end of every class period. (To sit down
would be to show weakness. And no teacher, Miss Dove was
convinced, could afford to show weakness if she wished her
pupils to show strength.) On the desk before her, like an orb
and scepter, were her map-pointer and her globe. On the
wall behind her, like a tapestry depicting far-flung dominions,
hung the map of the world.

"The class is dismissed," said Miss Dove.

Forty-two children, one by one—without scrambling or
pushing—filed out into the hall. David Burnham remained
standing in the aisle.

For an instant Miss Dove was tempted to let David go with
the others—to excuse him with a reprimand or, at least, to
defer his punishment until the next day. If she could rest
during the whole lunch hour, sitting perfectly still and even
(though the notion was unorthodox) putting her head down
upon her desk— But no. David's character was in her
keeping.

Miss Dove understood, quite as well as David's parent did, the child's motivation. (She had taught other ministers sons.) But unlike them she did not care whether David loved or hated her. She cared only that he conform to the rules.

She had pondered the new psychology which held that in the depths of human nature lay wild-animal instincts of greed, anger, idleness, and discourtesy. She could credit that theory. She had no rosy concept of human nature. But what did the theory prove? The thing that distinguished a man from a brute—a gentleman from a savage—was not instinct but performance.

David knew she had heard his naughty oath. He had meant her to hear it. In vulgar parlance, he had "asked for it" and he had a right to "get it."

Miss Dove looked at David. Her gaze was not contemptuous. Not impressed. She saw no hero in the aisle and no monster, either. She saw a nine-year-old boy who had gone a little further than he now wished he had.

And what did David see as he looked at Miss Dove? How did any of Miss Dove's pupils, past or present, see her? Off hand, that would seem an easy question. There was nothing elusive about Miss Dove's appearance and it had, moreover, remained much the same for more than thirty-five years. When she had begun to teach geography her figure had been spare and angular and it was still so. Her hair was more shadowy than it had once been but, twisted into a meager little old-maid's-knot, it had never had a chance to show much color. Her thin, unpainted mouth bore no sign of those universal emotions—humor, for instance, and love, and uncertainty—that mark most mouths in the course of time. Her pale, bleached-out complexion never flushed with emotion—a slight pinkness at the tip of her pointed nose was the only visible indication that ordinary human blood ran through her veins. She wore round-toed black shoes with low, rubber-tapped heels that did not clatter when she walked. Her dress, of some dull-surfaced dark material, was close cousin to the one in which she had made her pedagogical debut: It had the same long sleeves, the same high neck, and the same white linen handkerchief (or one very like) fluted into a fan and pinned to its left bosom. (The handkerchief was not for use—Miss Dove did not cough or sneeze in public—, nor was it for ornament. It was a caution to its owner's pupils that it behooved each of them to possess a clean handkerchief, too.) All in all, in bearing and clothing and bony structure, Miss Dove suggested that classic portrait of the eternal teacher that small fry, generation after generation, draw upon fences and sidewalks with nubbins of purloined chalk; a grown-up stranger, catching his first glimpse of her, might be inclined to laugh with a kind of relief, as if he'd seen some old, haunting ogress of his childhood turned into a harmless joke. And then Miss Dove would look at him and all the comedy would ebb from his mind. Her large eyes were quite naked (for she had retained perfect vision) and gray like a flat, calm sea on a cloudy day. They were shrewd and unillusioned; and when one stood exposed to their scrutiny feeling uncomfortably that they penetrated veil upon veil of one's private life and perceived, without astonishment, many hidden—and often unlovely—truths in the deep recesses of one's nature, it was impossible to see anything about Miss Dove as ridiculous. Even the elevated position of her desk— a position deplored by modern educators who seek to introduce equality into the teacher-student relation—was right and proper. The dais of aloof authority suited her as a little hill near Ratisbon suited Napoleon Bonaparte.

But there was more to Miss Dove. There was something that defies analysis. She had an extra quality as compelling as personal charm (which she did *not* have and would have scorned to cultivate) that captured the imagination. She gave off a sort of effulgence of awe and terror. But the terror did not paralyze. It was terror that caused children to flex their moral muscles and to dream of enduring, without a whimper, prolonged ordeals of privation and fatigue. Sometimes, if their ideal of courage was high, it caused them even to dare Miss Dove's disapproval.

The little ones, the six-year olds, whose geographical primer was entitled "At Home with Birds and Beasts," often pictured Miss Dove in the guise of some magnificent creature, furred or feathered. She was a huge black grizzly reared on its hind legs to block a mountain pass; she was a camel—bigger than other camels—leading a caravan across the desert; she was a Golden Eagle on a crag in Scotland. Later, when they had progressed to the intellectual sophistication of the fourth, the fifth, or the sixth and final grade of Cedar Grove School they were likely to cast her in the image of symbol. (One fanciful child had likened her to the Pharos watching little skiffs in the harbor of Alexandria.) But David Burnham was not fanciful; he was scared. Had he been pressed, at the moment, to describe Miss Dove, he would have said: "She looks like a teacher."

Miss Dove would have been gratified. A teacher was what she was and what she wished to be.

HORTENSE CALISHER

Hortense Calisher (1911–   ), Manhattan-born and educated at Hunter College and Barnard College, tried her hand
at various jobs upon her graduation from college in 1932:
salesclerk, model, social worker. She married in 1935 and
settled down with her husband and two children in the Hud-
son River Valley.

The publication of Calisher's first collection of short stories,
In the Absence of Angels (1951), immediately identified her
as one of America's important short-story writers. Her style
is caustic and disciplined, and one of her preoccupations is
the strain of marriage.

A Wreath for Miss Totten

Perhaps with the teachers, as with us, she was neither
admired nor loathed but simply ignored. . . . And
though all of us had a raffish hunger for metaphor, we
never dubbed Miss Totten with a nickname.

———◆◆◆———

Children growing up in the country take their images of in-
tegrity from the land. The land with its changes is always
about them, a pervasive truth, and their midget foregrounds
are criss-crossed with minute dramas which are the animal-
cules of a larger vision. But children who grow in a city
where there is nothing greater than the people brimming up
out of subways, rivuleting in the streets—these children must
take their archetypes where and if they find them.

In P.S. 146, between periods, when the upper grades were
shunted through the halls in that important procedure known

as "departmental," most of the teachers stood about chatting relievedly in couples; Miss Totten, however, always stood at the door of her "home room," watching us straightforwardly, alone. As, straggling and muffled, we lined past the other teachers, we often caught snatches of upstairs gossip which we later perverted and enlarged; passing before Miss Totten we deflected only that austere look, bent solely on us.

Perhaps with the teachers, as with us, she was neither admired nor loathed but simply ignored. Certainly none of us ever fawned on her as we did on the harshly blond and blue-eyed Miss Steele, who never wooed us with a smile but slanged us delightfully in the gym, giving out the exercises in a voice like scuffed gravel. Neither did she obsess us in the way of the Misses Comstock, two liverish, stunted women who could have had nothing so vivid about them as our hatred for them. And though all of us had a raffish hunger for metaphor, we never dubbed Miss Totten with a nickname.

Miss Totten's figure, as she sat tall at her desk or strode angularly in front of us rolling down the long maps over the blackboard, had that instantaneous clarity, one metallic step removed from the real, of the daguerreotype. Her clothes partook of this period too—long, saturnine waists and skirts of a stuff identical with that in a good family umbrella. There was one like it in the umbrella stand at home—a high black one with a seamed ivory head. The waists enclosed a vestee of dim but steadfast lace; the skirts grazed narrow boots of that etiolated black leather, venerable with creases, which I knew to be a sign of both respectability and foot trouble. But except for the vestee, all of Miss Totten, too, folded neatly to the dark point of her shoes, and separated from these by her truly extraordinary length, her face presided above, a lined, ocher ellipse. Sometimes, on drowsy afternoons, her face floated away altogether and came to rest on the stand at home. Perhaps it was because of this guilty image that I was the only one who noticed Miss Totten's strange preoccupation with Mooley Davis.

Most of us in Miss Totten's room had been together as a group since first grade, but we had not seen Mooley since down in second grade, under the elder and more frightening of the two Comstocks. I had forgotten Mooley completely but when she reappeared I remembered clearly the incident which had given her her name.

That morning, very early in the new term, back in Miss Comstock's, we had lined up on two sides of the classroom for a spelling bee. These were usually a relief to good and bad spellers alike, since they were the only part of our work which resembled a game, and even when one had to miss and sit down there was a kind of dreamy catharsis in watching the tenseness of those still standing. Miss Comstock always rose for these occasions and came forward between the two lines, standing there in an oppressive close-up in which we could watch the terrifying action of the cords in her spindling gray neck and her slight smile as someone was spelled down. As the number of those standing was reduced, the smile grew, exposing the oversize slabs of her teeth, through which the words issued in a voice increasingly unctuous and soft.

On this day the forty of us still shone with the first fall neatness of new clothes, still basked in that delightful anonymity in which neither our names nor our capacities were already part of the dreary foreknowledge of the teacher. The smart and quick had yet to assert themselves with their flying, staccato hands; the uneasy dull, not yet forced into recitations which would make their status clear, still preserved in the small, sinking corners of their hearts a lorn, factitious hope. Both teams were still intact when the word "mule" fell to the lot of a thin colored girl across the room from me, in clothes perky only with starch, her rusty fuzz of hair drawn back in braids so tightly sectioned that her eyes seemed permanently widened.

"Mule," said Miss Comstock, giving out the word. The ranks were still full. She had not yet begun to smile.

The girl looked back at Miss Comstock, soundlessly. All her face seemed drawn backward from the silent, working mouth, as if a strong, pulling hand had taken hold of the braids.

My turn, I calculated, was next. The procedure was to say the word, spell it out and say it again. I repeated it in my mind: Mule. M-u-l-e. Mule.

Miss Comstock waited quite a long time. Then she looked around the class, as if asking them to mark well and early her handling of this first malfeasance.

"What's your name?" she said.

"Ul—ee." The word came out in a glottal, molasses voice, hardly articulate, the *l*'s scarcely pronounced.

"Lilly?"

The girl nodded.

"Lilly what?"

"Duh—avis."

"Oh. Lilly Davis. Mmmm. Well, spell 'mule,' Lilly." Miss Comstock trilled out the name beautifully.

The tense brown bladder of the girl's face swelled desperately, then broke at the mouth. "Mool," she said, and stopped. "Mmm—ooo—"

The room tittered. Miss Comstock stepped closer.

"Mule!"

The girl struggled again. "Mool."

This time we were too near Miss Comstock to dare laughter. Miss Comstock turned to our side. "Who's next?"

I half raised my hand.

"Go on." She wheeled around on Lilly, who was sinking into her seat. "No. Don't sit down."

I lowered my eyelids, hiding Lilly from my sight. "Mule," I said. "M-u-l-e. Mule."

The game continued, words crossing the room uneventfully. Some children survived. Others settled, abashed, into their seats, craning around to watch us. Again the turn came around to Lilly.

Miss Comstock cleared her throat. She had begun to smile. "Spell it now, Lilly," she said. "Mule."

The long-chinned brown face swung from side to side in an odd writhing movement. Lilly's eyeballs rolled. Then the thick sound from her mouth was lost in the hooting, uncontrollable laughter of the whole class. For there was no doubt about it: the long, coffee-colored face, the whitish glint of the eyeballs, the bucking motion of the head suggested it to us all—a small brown quadruped, horse or mule, crazily stubborn or at bay.

"Quiet!" said Miss Comstock. And we hushed, although she had not spoken loudly. For the word had smirked out from a wide, flat smile and on the stringy neck beneath there was a creeping, pleasurable flush which made it pink as a young girl's.

That was how Mooley Davis got her name, although we had a chance to use it for only a few weeks, in a taunting singsong when she hung up her coat in the morning or as she flicked past the little dustbin of a store where we shed our pennies for tasteless, mottoed hearts. For after a few weeks, when it became clear that her cringing, mucoused talk was getting worse, she was transferred to the "ungraded" class. This group, made up of the mute, the shambling and the oddly tall, some of whom were delivered by bus, was housed

a basement, with a separate entrance which was forbidden
not only by rule but by a lurking distaste of our own.

The year Mooley reappeared in Miss Totten's room, a
dispute in the school system had disbanded all the ungraded
classes in the city. Here and there in the back seat of a class
now there would be some grown-size boy who read haltingly
from a primer, fingering the stubble on his slack jaw. Down
in 4-A there was a shiny, petted doll of a girl, all crackling
hair bow and nimble wheel chair, over whom the teachers
shook their heads feelingly, saying, "Bright as a dollar!
Imagine!" as if there were something sinister in the fact that
useless legs had not impaired the musculature of a mind. And
in our class, in harshly clean, faded dresses which were always a little too infantile for her, her spraying ginger hair
cut short now and held by a round comb which circled the
back of her head like a snaggle-toothed tiara which had
slipped, there was this boney, bug-eyed wraith of a girl who
raised her hand instead of saying "Present!" when Miss Totten
said "Lilly Davis?" at roll call, and never spoke at all.

It was Juliet Hoffman who spoke Mooley's nickname first.
A jeweler's daughter, Juliet had achieved an eminence even
beyond that due her curly profile, embroidered dresses and
prancing, leading-lady ways when, the Christmas before, she
had brought as her present to teacher a real diamond ring.
It had been a modest diamond, to be sure, but undoubtedly
real, and set in real gold. Juliet had heralded it for weeks before and we had all seen it—it and the peculiar look on the
face of the teacher, a young substitute whom we hardly
knew, when she had lifted it from the pile of hankies and
fancy note paper on her desk. The teacher, over the syrupy
protests of Mrs. Hoffman, had returned the ring, but its
sparkle lingered on, iridescent around Juliet's head.

On our way out at three o'clock that first day with Miss
Totten, Juliet nudged at me to wait. Obediently, I waited
behind her. Twiddling her bunny muff, she minced over to
the clothes closet and confronted the new girl.

"I know you," she said. "Mooley Davis, that's who you
are!" A couple of the other children hung back to watch.
"Aren't you? Aren't you Mooley Davis?"

I remember just how Mooley stood there because of the
coat she wore. She just stood there holding her coat against
her stomach with both hands. It was a coat of some pale,
vague tweed, cut the same length as mine. But it wrapped
the wrong way over for a girl and the revers, wide ones,

came all the way down and ended way below the pressin
hands.

"Where you been?" Juliet flipped us all a knowing grin
"You been in ungraded?"

One of Mooley's shoulders inched up so that it almos
touched her ear, but beyond that she did not seem able to
move. Her eyes looked at us, wide and fixed. I had the feelin
that all of her had retreated far, far back behind the eyes
which, large and light and purposefully empty, had bee
forced to stay.

My back was to the room but on the suddenly woode
faces of the others I saw Miss Totten's shadow. Then sh
loomed thinly over Juliet, her arms, which were crossed a
her chest, hiding the one V of white in her garments so tha
she looked like an umbrella tightly furled.

"What's *your* name?" she asked, addressing not so muc
Juliet as the white muff, which, I noticed now, was slightly
soiled.

"Jooly-ette."

"Hmm. Oh, yes. Juliet Hoffman."

"Jooly-ette, it is." She pouted creamily up at Miss Totten
her glance narrow with the assurance of finger rings to come

Something flickered in the nexus of yellow wrinkles aroun
Miss Totten's lips. Poking out a bony forefinger, she held i
against the muff. "You tell your mother," she said slowly
"that the way she spells it, it's *Juliet*."

Then she dismissed the rest of us but put a delaying hand
on Mooley. Turning back to look, I saw that she had knel
down painfully, her skirt hem graying in the floor dust, and,
staring absently over Mooley's head, she was buttoning up
the wrongly shaped coat.

After a short, avid flurry of speculation we soon lost interes
in Mooley and in the routine Miss Totten devised for her.
At first, during any kind of oral work, Mooley took her place
at the blackboard and wrote down her answers, but later Miss
Totten sat her in the front row and gave her a small slate.
She grew very quick at answering, particularly in "mental
arithmetic" and in the card drills when Miss Totten held up
large manila cards with significant locations and dates inscribed in her Palmer script, and we went down the rows,
snapping back the answers.

Also, Mooley had acquired a protector in Ruby Green, the
other Negro girl in the class—a huge, black girl with an arm-
flailing, hee-haw way of talking and a rich contralto singing

oice which we had often heard in solo at Assembly. Ruby, boasting of her singing in night clubs on Saturday nights, of a father who had done time, cowed us all with these pungent nklings of the world on the other side of the dividing line of Amsterdam Avenue, that deep, velvet murk of Harlem which she lit for us with the flash of razors, the honky-tonk beat of the "numbahs" and the plangent wails of the mugged. Once, hearing David Hecker, a doctor's son, declare, "Mooley has a cleft palate, that's what," Ruby wheeled and put a large hand on his shoulder in menacing caress.

"She ain' got no cleff palate, see? She talk sometime, roun' home." She glared at us each in turn with such a pug scowl that we flinched, thinking she was going to spit. Ruby giggled. "She got no cause to talk, roun' here. She just don' need to bother." She lifted her hand from David, spinning him backward, and joined arms with the silent Mooley. "Me neither!" she added, and walked Mooley away, flinging back at us her gaudy, syncopated laugh.

Then one day, lolloping home after three, I suddenly remembered my books and tam and above all my homework assignment, left in the pocket of my desk at school. I raced back there. The janitor, grumbling, unlocked the side door at which he had been sweeping and let me in. In the mauve, settling light the long maw of the gym held a rank, uneasy stillness. I walked up the spiral metal stairs feeling that I thieved on some part of the school's existence not intended for me. Outside the ambushed quiet of Miss Totten's room I stopped, gathering breath. I heard voices, one surely Miss Totten's dark, firm tones, the other no more than an arrested gurgle and pause.

I opened the door slowly. Miss Totten and Mooley raised their heads. It was odd, but although Miss Totten sat as usual at her desk, her hands clasped to one side of her hat, lunch box and the crinkly boa she wore all spring, and although Mooley was at her own desk in front of a spread copy of our thick reader, I felt the distinct, startled guilt of someone who interrupts an embrace.

"Yes?" said Miss Totten. Her eyes had the drugged look of eyes raised suddenly from close work. I fancied that she reddened slightly, like someone accused.

"I left my books."

Miss Totten nodded and sat waiting. I walked down the row to my desk and bent over, fumbling for my things, my haunches awkward under the watchfulness behind me. At the door, with my arms full, I stopped, parroting the formula of dismissal. "Good afternoon, Miss Totten."

"Good afternoon."

I walked home slowly. Miss Totten, when I spoke, had seemed to be watching my mouth, almost with enmity. And in front of Mooley there had been no slate.

In the class the next morning, as I collected the homework in my capacity as monitor, I lingered a minute at Mooley's desk, expecting some change perhaps in her notice of me, but there was none. Her paper was the same as usual, written in a neat script quite legible in itself but in a spidery back-hand that just faintly silvered the page, like a communiqué issued out of necessity but begrudged.

Once more I had a glimpse of Miss Totten and Mooley together, on a day when I had joined the slangy, athletic Miss Steele, who was striding capably along in her Ground Grippers on the route I usually took home. Almost at once I had known I was unwelcome, but I trotted desperately in her wake, not knowing how to relieve her of my company. At last a stitch in my side forced me to stop, in front of a corner fishmonger's.

"Folks who want to walk home with me have to step on it!" said Miss Steele. She allotted me one measuring, stone-blue glance and moved on.

Disposed on the bald white window stall of the fish store there was a rigidly mounted eel that looked as if only its stuffing prevented it from growing onward, sinuously, from either impersonal end. Beside it were several tawny shells. A finger would have to avoid the spines on them before being able to touch their rosy, pursed throats. As the pain in my side lessened, I raised my head and saw my own face in the window, egg-shaped and sad. I turned away. Miss Totten and Mooley stood on the corner, their backs to me, waiting to cross. A trolley clanged by, then the street was clear, and Miss Totten, looking down, nodded gently into the black boa and took Mooley by the hand. As they passed down the hill to St. Nicholas Avenue and disappeared, Mooley's face, smoothed out and grave, seemed to me, enviably, like the serene, guided faces of children seen walking securely under the restful duennaship of nuns.

Then came the first day of Visiting Week, during which, according to convention, the normal school day would be on display but for which we had actually been fortified with rapid-fire recitations which were supposed to erupt from us in sequence—like the somersaults which climax acrobatic acts. On this morning, just before we were called to order, Dr. Piatt, the principal, walked in. He was a gentle man, keeping to his office like a snail, and we had never succeeded in making a bogey of him, although we tried. Today he shepherded a group of mothers and two men, officiously dignified, all of whom he seated on some chairs up front at Miss Totten's left. Then he sat down too, looking upon us benignly, his head cocked a little to one side in a way he had, as if he hearkened to some unseen arbiter who whispered constantly to him of how bad children could be but he benevolently, insistently continued to disagree.

Miss Totten, alone among the teachers, was usually immune to visitors, but today she strode restlessly in front of us, and as she pulled down the maps one of them slipped from her hand and snapped back up with a loud, flapping roar. Fumbling for the roll book, she sat down and began to call the roll, something she usually did without looking at the book, favoring each of us with a warming nod instead.

"Arnold Ames?"

"Pres-unt!"

"Mary Bates?"

"Pres-unt!"

"Wanda Becovic?"

"Pres-unt!"

"Sidney Cohen?"

"Pres-unt!"

"L—Lilly Davis?"

It took us a minute to realize that Mooley had not raised her hand. A light impatient groan rippled over the class. But Mooley, her face uplifted in its blank, cataleptic stare, was looking at Miss Totten. Miss Totten's own lips moved. There seemed to be a cord between her lips and Mooley's. Mooley's lips moved, opened.

"Pres-unt!" said Mooley.

The class caught its breath, then righted itself under the sweet, absent smile of the visitors. With flushed, lowered lids but in a rich, full voice, Miss Totten finished calling the roll. Then she rose and came forward with the manila cards. Each time, she held up the name of a State and we answered with its capital city.

Pennsylvania.

"Harrisburg!" said Arnold Ames.

Illinois.

"Springfield!" said Mary Bates.

Arkansas.

"Little Rock!" said Wanda Becovic.

North Dakota.

"Bismarck!" said Sidney Cohen.

Idaho.

We were afraid to turn our heads.

"Buh . . . Boise!" said Mooley Davis.

After this we could hardly wait for the turn to come around to Mooley again. When Miss Totten, using a pointer against the map, indicated that Mooley was to "bound" the State of North Carolina, we focused with such attention that the visitors, grinning at each other, shook their heads at such zest. But Dr. Piatt was looking straight at Miss Totten, his lips parted, his head no longer to one side.

"N-North Cal . . . Callina." Just as the deaf gaze at the speaking, Mooley's eyes never left Miss Totten's. Her voice issued, burred here, choked there, but unmistakably a voice. "Bounded by Virginia on the north . . . Tennessee on the west . . . South Callina on the south . . . and on the east . . . and on the east . . ." She bent her head and gripped her desk with her hands. I gripped my own desk, until I saw that she suffered only from the common failing—she had forgotten. She raised her head.

"And on the east," she said joyously, "and on the east by the Atlantic Ocean."

Later that term Miss Totten died. She had been forty years in the school system, we heard in the eulogy at Assembly. There was no immediate family, and any of us who cared to might pay our respects at the chapel. After this, Mr. Moloney, who usually chose "Whispering" for the dismissal march, played something slow and thrumming which forced us to drag our feet until we reached the door.

Of course none of us went to the chapel, nor did we bother to wonder whether Mooley went. Probably she did not. For now that the girl withdrawn for so long behind those rigidly empty eyes had stepped forward into them, they flicked about quite normally, as captious as anyone's.

Once or twice in the days that followed we mentioned Miss Totten, but it was really death that we honored, clicking our tongues like our elders. Passing the umbrella stand at home I sometimes thought of Miss Totten, furled forever in her coffin. Then I forgot her too, along with the rest of the class. After all, this was only reasonable in a class which had achieved Miss Steele.

But memory, after a time, dispenses its own emphasis, making a feuilleton of what we once thought most ponderable, laying its wreath on what we never thought to recall. In the country, the children stumble upon the griffin mask of the mangled pheasant and they learn; they come upon the murderous love knot of the mantis and they surmise. But in the city, although no man looms very large against the sky, he is silhouetted all the more sharply against his fellows. And sometimes the children there, who know so little about the natural world, stumble upon that unsolicited good which is perhaps only a dislocation in the insensitive rhythm of the natural world. And if they are lucky, memory holds it in waiting. For what they have stumbled upon is their own humanity—their aberration and their glory. That is why I find myself wanting to say aloud to someone: "I remember . . . a Miss Elizabeth Totten."

TERENCE RATIGAN

Terence Rattigan (1911–   ) was born in London and educated at Harrow and at Trinity College, Oxford. He was a
flight lieutenant in World War II. He achieved an interna-
tional reputation as a playwright in 1946 with *The Winslow
Boy*. His other plays include *The Deep Blue Sea* (1952) and
Separate Tables (1955). *The Browning Version* (1949) ex-
plores, among other themes, what constitutes good teaching
and who is a good teacher. The play is constructed with con-
summate craftsmanship and involves the reader in an en-
grossing experience.

Mr. Gilbert's Revelation
FROM *The Browning Version*

It didn't take much discernment on my part to realize I
had become an utter failure as a schoolmaster. Still,
stupidly enough, I hadn't realized that I was also feared.

◆•◆

GILBERT: . . . I thought perhaps you could tell me something about the lower fifth.

ANDREW: What would you like to know?

GILBERT: Well, sir, quite frankly, I'm petrified.

ANDREW: I don't think you need to be. May I give you
some sherry?

(He comes down left to the cupboard.)

GILBERT: Thank you.

ANDREW: They are mostly boys of about fifteen or sixteen. They are not very difficult to handle.

(He takes out a bottle and a glass.)

GILBERT: The headmaster said you ruled them with a rod of iron. He called you "the Himmler of the lower fifth."

ANDREW: *(turning, bottle and glass in hand)*: Did he? "The Himmler of the lower fifth." I think he exaggerated. I hope he exaggerated. "The Himmler of the lower fifth."

(He puts the bottle on the desk, then fills the glass.)

GILBERT: *(puzzled)*: He only meant that you kept the most wonderful discipline. I must say I do admire you for that. I couldn't even manage that with eleven-year-olds, so what I'll be like with fifteens and sixteens I shudder to think.

(He moves below the chair right of the desk.)

ANDREW: It is not so difficult. *(He hands* GILBERT *the glass.)* They aren't bad boys. Sometimes a little wild and unfeeling, perhaps—but not bad. "The Himmler of the lower fifth." Dear me!

(He turns to the cabinet with the bottle.)

GILBERT: Perhaps I shouldn't have said that. I've been tactless, I'm afraid.

ANDREW: Oh no. *(He puts the bottle in the cupboard.)* Please sit down.

(He stands by the downstage end of the desk.)

GILBERT: Thank you, sir.

(He sits right of the desk.)

ANDREW: From the very beginning I realized that I didn't possess the knack of making myself liked—a knack that you will find you do possess.

GILBERT: Do you think so?

ANDREW: Oh yes. I am quite sure of it. *(He moves up left of the desk.)* It is not a quality of great importance to a schoolmaster though, for too much of it, as you may also find, is as great a danger as the total lack of it. Forgive me lecturing, won't you?

GILBERT: I want to learn.

ANDREW: I can only teach you from my own experience. For two or three years I tried very hard to communicate to the boys some of my own joy in the great literature of the past. Of course I failed, as you will fail, nine hundred and ninety-nine times out of a thousand. But a single success can atone, and more than atone, for all the failure in the world.

And sometimes—very rarely, it is true—but sometimes I had that success. That was in the early years.

GILBERT (*eagerly listening*): Please go on, sir.

ANDREW: In early years too, I discovered an easy substitute for popularity. (*He picks up his speech.*) I had of course acquired—we all do—many little mannerisms and tricks of speech, and I found that the boys were beginning to laugh at me. I was very happy at that, and encouraged the boys' laughter by playing up to it. It made our relationship so very much easier. They didn't like me as a man, but they found me funny as a character, and you can teach more things by laughter than by earnestness—for I never did have much sense of humor. So, for a time, you see, I was quite a success as a schoolmaster . . . (*He stops.*) I fear this is all very personal and embarrassing to you. Forgive me. You need have no fears about the lower fifth.

(*He puts the speech into his pocket and turns to the window.* GILBERT *rises and moves above the desk.*)

GILBERT (*after a pause*): I'm afraid I said something that hurt you very much. It's myself you must forgive, sir. Believe me, I'm desperately sorry.

ANDREW (*turning down stage and leaning slightly on the back of the swivel chair*): There's no need. You were merely telling me what I should have known for myself. Perhaps I did in my heart, and hadn't the courage to acknowledge it. I knew, of course, that I was not only not liked, but now positively disliked. I had realized too that the boys—for many long years now—had ceased to laugh at me. I don't know why they no longer found me a joke. Perhaps it was my illness. No, I don't think it was that. Something deeper than that. Not a sickness of the body, but a sickness of the soul. At all events it didn't take much discernment on my part to realize I had become an utter failure as a schoolmaster. Still, stupidly enough, I hadn't realized that I was also feared. "The Himmler of the lower fifth." I suppose that will become my epitaph. (GILBERT *is now deeply embarrassed and rather upset, but he remains silent. He sits on the upstage end of the window seat. With a mild laugh.*) I cannot for the life of me imagine why I should choose to unburden myself to you—a total stranger—when I have been silent to others for so long. Perhaps it is because my very unworthy mantle is about to fall on your shoulders. If that is so I shall take a prophet's privilege and foretell that you will have a very great success with the lower fifth.

HEYWOOD BROUN

Heywood Broun (1888–1939) was born in Brooklyn and educated at the Horace Mann High School and Harvard University. During World War I, he served as an overseas war correspondent. When he returned to New York, he worked as a sports reporter, then as a widely syndicated columnist for various newspapers. He was founder and president of the New York Newspaper Guild.

Broun was one of the most widely read writers of his time. A skillful humorist, satirist, and commentator, Broun grew increasingly concerned over the scarred lives of so many of his fellow Americans. He was active in many causes, always championing the underdog.

Broun had a sharp yet kindly eye for human weakness and pretension. He wrote about people in an easy, disarming style gently touched with his puckish humor.

Kittredge's Farewell

. . . and without another word he left fifty years of teaching behind him. . . . it may be that like Christian he felt relieved of his burden. It is even possible that he went straight to his library and, taking down a copy of *Hamlet*, said, "Now for the first time in fifty years I can read this for fun and find out if it really is any good."

———◆•◆———

Once I wrote that no man ever knows just when to stop. Human beings time themselves badly in the matter of making exits. We all stay on too long. So it must be admitted that Professor Kittredge did rather well. For my taste his farewell to Harvard University was a shade too theatrical, but it was effective, and, after all, he had taught Shakespeare for forty or fifty years.

He did not dramatize himself in the manner of Lear or Mercutio or Macbeth. I wish I knew more about Shakespeare, but that can't be blamed on Kittredge. He did his best or, if not that, at least he put no obstacles in my way. However, I have a vague recollection that somewhere in *Julius Caesar* Brutus and Cassius sit down in a tent and talk together very quietly. Perhaps that's the thing called "the quarrel scene." In any case I refer to the part before they get to fighting.

That would be the mood of Professor Kittredge's farewell. The high and florid tradition of Shakespeare was revised into the swaggering underemphasis of New England.

Professor Kittredge has a long white beard but insufficient showmanship to swing it, and so when he came to the river's brink he made no oration but set up his tent and placed upon it the sign "Business as Usual." In addition to the pupils in his course some three hundred other students had gathered to hear "Kitty" take off.

If any expected him to weep or sing *The Last Round-Up* they were disappointed. He did fetch Shakespeare out and saddle the old word painter for a final foray, but it was done without benefit of bugle calls. The absent-minded professor gave no indication of noticing the studio audience. He addressed his remarks solely to those enrolled in English 2.

The class was at work on Gene Tunney's old favorite, *A Winter's Tale*. Where they had left off on the previous occasion they took up again. No hint was given by the preceptor that this was an occasion having anything of unusual significance. It was just a segment of that same old course—a course, I might add, in which the bones of many luckless Harvard seekers after knowledge lie moldering. But it's too late now. There is no spot this side of Judgment Day where I can argue to have my D minus raised to a simple D.

A little before his hour was up he informed the class that he would not be able to finish the play at that morning session. He suggested that they might use the printed notes in the book, although he added that they were hardly as good as he could furnish. And then quite casually, too casually I fear, he said, "We'll stop here."

From now on Harvard will have to find Shakespeare without the aid of George Lyman Kittredge, the last of the Old Guard of distinguished scholars at Cambridge. And since he had taught his subject in the same place and the same room for very nearly fifty years, perhaps he may be pardoned for departing at the end a little from the honored tradition of Harvard. He did not, as he might have done, step directly toward the door and so out into the yard and through the gate and home from Harvard. He blew himself for a full minute to the privilege of behaving like a leading man or a Yale professor in the department of English. He stood poised at the edge of the platform and took his full sixty seconds of applause from the three hundred.

George Lyman Kittredge did not bow or blow kisses to the crowd or in any way acknowledge the plaudits of the undergraduates. No flashlight photographers had been bidden to be present. He kept clearly in his mind that this was not New Haven.

Nor is there any reason to be captious about the way things are done among the Elis. "Each man to his taste," as the Yale senior said when he signed up to take the course on Robert Browning with William ("Billy") Lyon Phelps. To be sure, Kittredge might have stood his ground indefinitely and run no risk that any one of Harvard's sons would dare to call him "Kitty." But precisely at the end of a minute the Professor indicated with his hand that he wanted the aisle cleared.

It used to be a cloak he wore, if I remember. But in any case he threw something over his shoulders and without another word he left fifty years of teaching behind him. And as he walked under the elms in the direction of his house it may be that like Christian he felt relieved of his burden. It is even possible that he went straight to his library and, taking down a copy of *Hamlet*, said, "Now for the first time in fifty years I can read this for fun and find out if it really is any good."

GEORGE ORWELL

George Orwell or Eric Blair (1903–1950), was an English novelist, essayist, and critic. A fiercely independent socialist, his early works dealt with the life and culture of the working class. His *Down and Out in Paris and London* (1933) deals with his vagabonding years doing odd jobs for a living. His *Homage to Catalonia* (1938) expresses his disillusionment with Communism. Orwell's best-known works are *Animal Farm* (1946) and *1984* (1949). *Animal Farm* is a devastating satire of Soviet Russian history. In *1984* Orwell projects the world in the making and the world to be. Essentially Orwell was concerned with the politics and culture of his time, with the values destroyed by the "catastrophe of Communism in Russia" and the failures of Socialism in Western Europe. V.S. Pritchett has called Orwell the "conscience of his generation." "Such, Such Were the Joys" was found among Orwell's papers after his death.

Such, Such Were the Joys . . .

"Here is a little boy," said Bingo, indicating me to the strange lady, "who wets his bed every night. Do you know what I am going to do if you wet your bed again?" she added, turning to me. "I am going to get the Sixth Form to beat you."

❖❖❖

Soon after I arrived at Crossgates (not immediately, but after a week or two, just when I seemed to be settling into the routine of school life) I began wetting my bed. I was now aged eight, so this was a reversion to a habit which I must have grown out of at least four years earlier.

Excerpted from "Such, Such Were the Joys" in *Such, Such Were the Joys* by George Orwell, copyright 1945, 1952, 1953 by Sonia Brownell Orwell. Reprinted by permission of Harcourt Brace Jovanovich, Inc. and Mrs. Sonia Brownwell Orwell and Martin Secker and Warburg.

Nowadays, I believe, bed-wetting in such circumstances is taken for granted. It is a normal reaction in children who have been removed from their homes to a strange place. In those days, however, it was looked on as a disgusting crime which the child committed on purpose and for which the proper cure was a beating. For my part I did not need to be told it was a crime. Night after night I prayed, with a fervour never previously attained in my prayers, "Please God, do not let me wet my bed! Oh, please God, do not let me wet my bed!" but it made remarkably little difference. Some nights the thing happened, others not. There was no volition about it, no consciousness. You did not properly speaking *do* the deed: you merely woke up in the morning and found that the sheets were wringing wet.

After the second or third offence I was warned that I should be beaten next time, but I received the warning in a curiously roundabout way. One afternoon, as we were filing out from tea, Mrs. Simpson, the headmaster's wife, was sitting at the head of one of the tables, chatting with a lady of whom I know nothing, except that she was on an afternoon's visit to the school. She was an intimidating, masculine-looking person wearing a riding habit, or something that I took to be a riding habit. I was just leaving the room when Mrs. Simpson called me back, as though to introduce me to the visitor.

Mrs. Simpson was nicknamed Bingo, and I shall call her by that name for I seldom think of her by any other. (Officially, however, she was addressed as Mum, probably a corruption of the "Ma'am" used by public school boys to their housemasters' wives.) She was a stocky square-built woman with hard red cheeks, a flat top to her head, prominent brows and deepset, suspicious eyes. Although a great deal of the time she was full of false heartiness, jollying one along with mannish slang (*"Buck* up, old chap!" and so forth), and even using one's Christian name, her eyes never lost their anxious, accusing look. It was very difficult to look her in the face without feeling guilty, even at moments when one was not guilty of anything in particular.

"Here is a little boy," said Bingo, indicating me to the strange lady, "who wets his bed every night. Do you know what I am going to do if you wet your bed again?" she added, turning to me. "I am going to get the Sixth Form to beat you."

The strange lady put on an air of being inexpressibly shocked, and exclaimed "I-should-think-so!" And here occurred one of those wild, almost lunatic misunderstandings which are part of the daily experience of childhood. The Sixth Form was a group of older boys who were selected as having "character" and were empowered to beat smaller boys. I had not yet learned of their existence, and I mis-heard the phrase "the Sixth Form" as "Mrs. Form." I took it as referring to the strange lady—I thought, that is, that her name was Mrs. Form. It was an improbable name, but a child has no judgement in such matters. I imagined, therefore, that it was *she* who was to be deputed to beat me. It did not strike me as strange that this job should be turned over to a casual visitor in no way connected with the school. I merely assumed that "Mrs. Form" was a stern disciplinarian who enjoyed beating people (somehow her appearance seemed to bear this out) and I had an immediate terrifying vision of her arriving for the occasion in full riding kit and armed with a hunting whip. To this day I can feel myself almost swooning with shame as I stood, a very small, round-faced boy in short corduroy knickers, before the two women. I could not speak. I felt that I should die if "Mrs. Form" were to beat me. But my dominant feeling was not fear or even resentment: it was simply shame because one more person, and that a woman, had been told of my disgusting offence.

A little later, I forget how, I learned that it was not after all "Mrs. Form" who would do the beating. I cannot remember whether it was that very night that I wetted my bed again, but at any rate I did wet it again quite soon. Oh, the despair, the feeling of cruel injustice, after all my prayers and resolutions, at once again waking between the clammy sheets! There was no chance of hiding what I had done. The grim statuesque matron, Daphne by name, arrived in the dormitory specially to inspect my bed. She pulled back the clothes, then drew herself up, and the dreaded words seemed to come rolling out of her like a peal of thunder:

"REPORT YOURSELF to the headmaster after breakfast!"

I do not know how many times I heard that phrase during my early years at Crossgates. It was only very rarely that it did not mean a beating. The words always had a portentous sound in my ears, like muffled drums or the words of the death sentence.

When I arrived to report myself, Bingo was doing something or other at the long shiny table in the ante-room to the study. Her uneasy eyes searched me as I went past. In the study Mr. Simpson, nicknamed Sim, was waiting. Sim was a round-shouldered curiously oafish-looking man, not large but ambling in gait, with a chubby face which was like that of an overgrown baby, and which was capable of good humour. He knew, of course, why I had been sent to him, and had already taken a bone-handled riding crop out of the cupboard, but it was part of the punishment of reporting yourself that you had to proclaim your offence with your own lips. When I had said my say, he read me a short but pompous lecture, then seized me by the scruff of the neck, twisted me over and began beating me with the riding crop. He had a habit of continuing his lecture while he flogged you, and I remember the words "you dir-ty little boy" keeping time with the blows. The beating did not hurt (perhaps as it was the first time, he was not hitting me very hard), and I walked out feeling very much better. The fact that the beating had not hurt was a sort of victory and partially wiped out the shame of the bed-wetting. I was even incautious enough to wear a grin on my face. Some small boys were hanging about in the passage outside the door of the ante-room.

"D'you get the cane?"

"It didn't hurt," I said proudly.

Bingo had heard everything. Instantly her voice came screaming after me:

"Come here! Come here this instant! What was that you said?"

"I said it didn't hurt," I faltered out.

"How dare you say a thing like that? Do you think that is a proper thing to say? Go in and REPORT YOURSELF AGAIN!"

This time Sim laid on in real earnest. He continued for a length of time that frightened and astonished me—about five minutes, it seemed—ending up by breaking the riding crop. The bone handle went flying across the room.

"Look what you've made me do!" he said furiously, holding up the broken crop.

I had fallen into a chair, weakly snivelling. I remember that this was the only time throughout my boyhood when a beating actually reduced me to tears, and curiously enough I was not even now crying because of the pain. The second beating had not hurt very much either. Fright and shame seemed to have anesthetised me. I was crying partly because I felt that this was expected of me, partly from genuine repentance, but partly also because of a deeper grief which is peculiar to childhood and not easy to convey: a sense of desolate loneliness and helplessness, of being locked up not

only in a hostile world but in a world of good and evil when
the rules were such that it was actually not possible for m
to keep them.

I knew that bed-wetting was (a) wicked and (b) outsid
my control. The second fact I was personally aware of, an
the first I did not question. It was possible, therefore, t
commit a sin without knowing that you committed it, with
out wanting to commit it, and without being able to avoi
it. Sin was not necessarily something that you did: it migh
be something that happened to you. I do not want to clain
that this idea flashed into my mind as a complete novelty a
this very moment, under the blows of Sim's cane: I must hav
had glimpses of it even before I left home, for my early
childhood had not been altogether happy. But at any rate thi
was the great, abiding lesson of my boyhood: that I was in a
world where it was *not possible* for me to be good. And the
double beating was a turning-point, for it brought home to
me for the first time the harshness of the environment into
which I had been flung. Life was more terrible, and I was
more wicked, than I had imagined. At any rate, as I sat on
the edge of a chair in Sim's study, with not even the self-
possession to stand up while he stormed at me, I had a conviction of sin and folly and weakness, such as I do not remember to have felt before.

In general, one's memories of any period must necessarily
weaken as one moves away from it. One is constantly learning new facts, and old ones have to drop out to make way
for them. At twenty I could have written the history of my
schooldays with an accuracy which would be quite impossible
now. But it can also happen that one's memories grow sharper
after a long lapse of time, because one is looking at the past
with fresh eyes and can isolate and, as it were, notice facts
which previously existed undifferentiated among a mass of
others. Here are two things which in a sense I remembered,
but which did not strike me a strange or interesting until quite
recently. One is that the second beating seemed to me a just
and reasonable punishment. To get one beating, and then to
get another and far fiercer one on top of it, for being so
unwise as to show that the first had not hurt—that was quite
natural. The gods are jealous, and when you have good
fortune you should conceal it. The other is that I accepted the
broken riding crop as my own crime. I can still recall my
feeling as I saw the handle lying on the carpet—the feeling
of having done an ill-bred clumsy thing, and ruined an ex-

ensive object. *I* had broken it: so Sim told me, and so I believed. This acceptance of guilt lay unnoticed in my memory or twenty or thirty years.

So much for the episode of the bed-wetting. But there is one more thing to be remarked. This is that I did not wet my bed again—at least, I did wet it once again, and received another beating, after which the trouble stopped. So perhaps his barbarous remedy does work, though at a heavy price, I have no doubt.

Crossgates was an expensive and snobbish school which was in process of becoming more snobbish, and, I imagine, more expensive. The public school with which it had special connections was Harrow, but during my time an increasing proportion of the boys went on to Eton. Most of them were the children of rich parents, but on the whole they were the unaristocratic rich, the sort of people who live in huge shrubberied houses in Bournemouth or Richmond, and who have cars and butlers but not country estates. There were a few exotics among them—some South American boys, sons of Argentine beef barons, one or two Russians, and even a Siamese prince, or someone who was described as a prince.

Sim had two great ambitions. One was to attract titled boys to the school, and the other was to train up pupils to win scholarships at public schools, above all Eton. He did, towards the end of my time, succeed in getting hold of two boys with real English titles. One of them, I remember, was a wretched little creature, almost an albino, peering upwards out of weak eyes, with a long nose at the end of which a dewdrop always seemed to be trembling. Sim always gave these boys their titles when mentioning them to a third person, and for their first few days he actually addressed them to their faces as "Lord So-and-so." Needless to say he found ways of drawing attention to them when any visitor was being shown round the school. Once, I remember, the little fair-haired boy had a choking fit at dinner, and a stream of snot ran out of his nose onto his plate in a way horrible to see. Any lesser person would have been called a dirty little beast and ordered out of the room instantly: but Sim and Bingo laughed it off in a "boys will be boys" spirit.

All the very rich boys were more or less undisguisedly favoured. The school still had a faint suggestion of the Victorian "private academy" with its "parlour boarders," and when I later read about that kind of school in Thackeray I immediately saw the resemblance. The rich boys had milk and biscuits in the middle of the morning, they were given riding lessons once or twice a week, Bingo mothered them and called them by their Christian names, and above all they were never caned. Apart from the South Americans, whose parents were safely distant, I doubt whether Sim ever caned any boy whose father's income was much above £2,000 a year. But he was sometimes willing to sacrifice financial profit to scholastic prestige. Occasionally, by special arrangement, he would take at greatly reduced fees some boy who seemed likely to win scholarships and thus bring credit on the school. It was on these terms that I was at Crossgates myself: otherwise my parents could not have afforded to send me to so expensive a school.

I did not at first understand that I was being taken at reduced fees; it was only when I was about eleven that Bingo and Sim began throwing the fact in my teeth. For my first two or three years I went through the ordinary educational mill: then, soon after I had started Greek (one started Latin at eight, Greek at ten), I moved into the scholarship class, which was taught, so far as classics went, largely by Sim himself. Over a period of two or three years the scholarship boys were crammed with learning as cynically as a goose is crammed for Christmas. And with what learning! This business of making a gifted boy's career depend on a competitive examination, taken when he is only twelve or thirteen, is an evil thing at best, but there do appear to be preparatory schools which send scholars to Eton, Winchester, etc., without teaching them to see everything in terms of marks. At Crossgates the whole process was frankly a preparation for a sort of confidence trick. Your job was to learn exactly those things that would give an examiner the impression that you knew more than you did know, and as far as possible to avoid burdening your brain with anything else. Subjects which lacked examination-value, such as geography, were almost completely neglected, mathematics was also neglected if you were a "classical," science was not taught in any form—indeed it was so despised that even an interest in natural history was discouraged—and the books you were encouraged to read in your spare time were chosen with one eye on the "English Paper." Latin and Greek, the main scholarship subjects, were what counted, but even these were deliberately taught in a flashy, unsound way. We never, for example, read right through even a single book of a Greek or Latin author: we merely read short passages which were picked out because they were the kind of thing likely to be set as an "unseen translation." During the last year or so before we went up for our scholarships, most of our time was spent in simply working our way through the scholarship papers of previous years. Sim had sheaves of these in his possession, from every one of the major public schools. But the greatest outrage of all was the teaching of history.

There was in those days a piece of nonsense called the Harrow History Prize, an annual competition for which many preparatory schools entered. At Crossgates we mugged up every paper that had been set since the competition started. They were the kind of stupid question that is answered by rapping out a name or a quotation. Who plundered the Begams? Who was beheaded in an open boat? Who caught the Whigs bathing and ran away with their clothes? Almost all our historical teaching was on this level. History was a series of unrelated unintelligible but—in some way that was never explained to us—important facts with resounding phrases tied to them. Disraeli brought peace with honour. Clive was astonished at his moderation. Pitt called in the New World to redress the balance of the Old. And the dates, and the mnemonic devices! (Did you know, for example, that the initial letters of "A black Negress was my aunt: there's her house behind the barn" are also the initial letters of the battles in the Wars of the Roses?) Bingo, who "took" the higher forms in history, revelled in this kind of thing. I recall positive orgies of dates, with the keener boys leaping up and down in their places in their eagerness to shout out the right answers, and at the same time not feeling the faintest interest in the meaning of the mysterious events they were naming.

"1587?"

"Massacre of St. Bartholomew!"

"1707?"

"Death of Aurangzeeb!"

"1713?"

"Treaty of Utrecht!"

"1773?"

"The Boston Tea Party!"

"1520?"

"Oh, Mum, please, Mum—"

"Please, Mum, please, Mum! Let me tell him, Mum!"

"Well; 1520?"

"Field of the Cloth of Gold!"

And so on.

But history and such secondary subjects were not bad fun. It was in "classics" that the real strain came. Looking back, I realise that I then worked harder than I have ever done since, and yet at the time it never seemed possible to make quite the effort that was demanded of one. We would sit round the long shiny table, made of some very pale-coloured, hard wood, with Sim goading, threatening, exhorting, sometimes joking, very occasionally praising, but always prodding, prodding away at one's mind to keep it up to the right pitch of concentration, as one might keep a sleepy person awake by sticking pins into him.

"Go on, you little slacker! Go on, you idle, worthless little boy! The whole trouble with you is that you're bone and horn idle. You eat too much, that's why. You wolf down enormous meals, and then when you come here you're half asleep. Go on, now, put your back into it. You're not *thinking*. Your brain doesn't sweat."

He would tap away at one's skull with his silver pencil, which, in my memory, seems to have been about the size of a banana, and which certainly was heavy enough to raise a bump: or he would pull the short hairs round one's ears, or, occasionally, reach out under the table and kick one's shin. On some days nothing seemed to go right, and then it would be: "All right, then, I know what you want. You've been asking for it the whole morning. Come along, you useless little slacker. Come into the study." And then whack, whack, whack, whack, and back one would come, red-wealed and smarting—in later years Sim had abandoned his riding crop in favour of a thin rattan cane which hurt very much more— to settle down to work again. This did not happen very often, but I do remember, more than once being led out of the room in the middle of a Latin sentence, receiving a beating and then going straight ahead with the same sentence, just like that. It is a mistake to think such methods do not work. They work very well for their special purpose. Indeed, I doubt whether classical education ever has been or can be successfully carried on without corporal punishment. The boys themselves believed in its efficacy. There was a boy named Beacham, with no brains to speak of, but evidently in acute need of a scholarship. Sim was flogging him towards the goal as one might do with a foundered horse. He went up

for a scholarship at Uppingham, came back with a consciousness of having done badly, and a day or two later received
a severe beating for idleness. "I wish I'd had that caning before I went up for the exam," he said sadly—a remark which
I felt to be contemptible, but which I perfectly well understood. . . .

I had learned early in my career that one can do wrong
against one's will, and before long I also learned that one can
do wrong without ever discovering what one has done or
why it was wrong. There were sins that were too subtle to
be explained, and there were others that were too terrible to
be clearly mentioned. For example, there was sex, which
was always smouldering just under the surface and which
suddenly blew up into a tremendous row when I was about
twelve.

At some preparatory schools homosexuality is not a problem, but I think that Crossgates may have acquired a "bad
tone" thanks to the presence of the South American boys,
who would perhaps mature a year or two earlier than an
English boy. At that age I was not interested, so I do not
actually know what went on, but I imagine it was group mas-
turbation. At any rate, one day the storm suddenly burst over
our heads. There were summonses, interrogations, confessions,
floggings, repentances, solemn lectures of which one understood nothing except that some irredeemable sin known as
"swinishness" or "beastliness" had been committed. One of
the ringleaders, a boy named Horne, was flogged, according
to eyewitnesses, for a quarter of an hour continuously before
being expelled. His yells rang through the house. But we
were all implicated, more or less, or felt ourselves to be
implicated. Guilt seemed to hang in the air like a pall of
smoke. A solemn, black-haired imbecile of an assistant master,
who was later to be a Member of Parliament, took the older
boys to a secluded room and delivered a talk on the Temple
of the Body.

"Don't you realise what a wonderful thing your body
is?" he said gravely. "You talk of your motor-car engines,
your Rolls-Royces and Daimlers and so on. Don't you understand that no engine ever made is fit to be compared with
your body? And then you go and wreck it, ruin it—for life!"

He turned his cavernous black eyes on me and added
sadly:

"And you, whom I'd always believed to be quite a decent

person after your fashion—you, I hear, are one of the very worst."

A feeling of doom descended upon me. So I was guilty too. I too had done the dreadful thing, whatever it was, that wrecked you for life, body and soul, and ended in suicide or the lunatic asylum. Till then I had hoped that I was innocent, and the conviction of sin which now took possession of me was perhaps all the stronger because I did not know what I had done. I was not among those who were interrogated and flogged, and it was not until the row was well over that I even learned about the trivial incident that had connected my name with it. Even then I understood nothing. It was not till about two years later that I fully grasped what that lecture on the Temple of the Body had referred to.

At this time I was in an almost sexless state, which is normal, or at any rate common, in boys of that age; I was therefore in the position of simultaneously knowing and not knowing what used to be called the Facts of Life. At five or six, like many children, I had passed through a phase of sexuality. My friends were the plumber's children up the road, and we used sometimes to play games of a vaguely erotic kind. One was called "playing at doctors," and I remember getting a faint but definitely pleasant thrill from holding a toy trumpet, which was supposed to be a stethoscope, against a little girl's belly. About the same time I fell deeply in love, a far more worshipping kind of love than I have ever felt for anyone since, with a girl named Elsie at the convent school which I attended. She seemed to me grown up, so I suppose she must have been fifteen. After that, as so often happens, all sexual feelings seemed to go out of me for many years. At twelve I knew more than I had known as a young child, but I understood less, because I no longer knew the essential fact that there is something pleasant in sexual activity. Between roughly seven and fourteen, the whole subject seemed to me uninteresting and, when for some reason I was forced to think of it, disgusting. My knowledge of the so-called Facts of Life was derived from animals, and was therefore distorted, and in any case was only intermittent. I knew that animals copulated and that human beings had bodies resembling those of animals: but that human beings also copulated I only knew, as it were reluctantly, when something, a phrase in the Bible perhaps, compelled me to remember it. Not having desire, I had no curiosity and was willing o leave many questions unanswered. Thus, I knew in principle how the baby gets into the woman, but I did not know how it gets out again, because I had never followed the subject up. I knew all the dirty words, and in my bad moments I would repeat them to myself, but I did not know what the worst of them meant, nor want to know. They were abstractly wicked, a sort of verbal charm. While I remained in that state, it was easy for me to remain ignorant of any sexual misdeeds that went on about me, and to be hardly wiser even when the row broke. At most, through the veiled and terrible warnings of Bingo, Sim and all the rest of them, I grasped that the crime of which we were all guilty was somehow connected with the sexual organs. I had noticed, without feeling much interest, that one's penis sometimes stands up of its own accord (this starts happening to a boy long before he has any conscious sexual desires), and I was inclined to believe, or half-believe, that *that* must be the crime. At any rate, it was something to do with the penis— so much I understood. Many other boys, I have no doubt, were equally in the dark.

After the talk on the Temple of the Body (days later, it seems in retrospect: the row seemed to continue for days), a dozen of us were seated at the long shiny table which Sim used for the scholarship, under Bingo's lowering eye. A long, desolate wail rang out from a room somewhere above. A very small boy named Ronald, aged no more than about ten, who was implicated in some way, was being flogged, or was recovering from a flogging. At the sound, Bingo's eyes searched our faces, and settled on me.

"You see," she said.

I will not swear that she said, "You see what you have done," but that was the sense of it. We were all bowed down with shame. It was *our fault*. Somehow or other we had led poor Ronald astray: *we* were responsible for his agony and his ruin. Then Bingo turned upon another boy named Heath. It is thirty years ago, and I cannot remember for certain whether she merely quoted a verse from the Bible, or whether she actually brought out a Bible and made Heath read it; but at any rate the text indicated was:

"Who shall offend one of these little ones that believe in me, it were better for him that a millstone were hanged about his neck, and that he were drowned in the depth of the sea."

That, too, was terrible. Ronald was one of these little ones
we had offended him; it were better that a millstone were
hanged about our necks and that we were drowned in the
depth of the sea.

"Have you thought about that, Heath—have you thought
what it means?" Bingo said. And Heath broke down into
tears.

Another boy, Beacham, whom I have mentioned already
was similarly overwhelmed with shame by the accusation that
he "had black rings round his eyes."

"Have you looked in the glass lately, Beacham?" said
Bingo. "Aren't you ashamed to go about with a face like
that? Do you think everyone doesn't know what it mean
when a boy has black rings round his eyes?"

Once again the load of guilt and fear seemed to settle down
upon me. Had *I* got black rings round my eyes? A couple of
years later I realised that these were supposed to be a symp-
tom by which masturbators could be detected. But already
without knowing this, I accepted the black rings as a sure
sign of depravity, *some* kind of depravity. And many times
even before I grasped the supposed meaning, I have gazed
anxiously into the glass, looking for the first hint of that
dreaded stigma, the confession which the secret sinner writes
upon his own face.

These terrors wore off, or became merely intermittent,
without affecting what one might call my official beliefs. . . .
Some months later it happened that I once again saw Horne,
the ringleader who had been flogged and expelled. Horne was
one of the outcasts, the son of poor middle-class parents,
which was no doubt part of the reason why Sim had handled
him so roughly. The term after his expulsion he went on to
South Coast College, the small local public school, which
was hideously despised at Crossgates and looked upon as "not
really" a public school at all. Only a very few boys from
Crossgates went there, and Sim always spoke of them with
a sort of contemptuous pity. You had no chance if you went
to a school like that: at the best your destiny would be a
clerkship. I thought of Horne as a person who at thirteen
had already forfeited all hope of any decent future. Phys-
ically, morally and socially he was finished. Moreover I assumed that his parents had only sent him to South Coast
College because after his disgrace no "good" school would
have him.

During the following term, when we were out for a walk, we passed Horne in the street. He looked completely normal. He was a strongly built, rather good-looking boy with black hair. I immediately noticed that he looked better than when I had last seen him—his complexion, previously rather pale, was pinker—and that he did not seem embarrassed at meeting us. Apparently he was not ashamed either of having been expelled, or of being at South Coast College. If one could gather anything from the way he looked at us as we filed past, it was that he was glad to have escaped from Crossgates. But the encounter made very little impression on me. I drew no inference from the fact that Horne, ruined in body and soul, appeared to be happy and in good health. I still believed in the sexual mythology that had been taught me by Bingo and Sim. The mysterious, terrible dangers were still there. Any morning the black rings might appear round your eyes and you would know that you too were among the lost ones. Only it no longer seemed to matter very much. These contradictions can exist easily in the mind of a child, because of its own vitality. It accepts—how can it do otherwise?—the nonsense that its elders tell it, but its youthful body, and the sweetness of the physical world, tell it another story.

ALFRED KAZIN

Alfred Kazin (1915–   ), American literary critic, editor, anthologist, and educator, was born in New York and educated at the City College of New York and at Columbia University. Kazin has served as lecturer and professor at various colleges and universities. He was editor of the *New Republic* from 1942 to 1943. He has also edited anthologies and special editions of poems and essays.

Kazin has written moving and poignant books about growing up in America. He is highly regarded for his forthright, perceptive attempts to catch the essence of the American spirit and especially of New York intellectual life. His books include *On Native Grounds* (1942), *A Walker in the City* (1951), *Starting out in the Thirties* (1965), and *New York Jew* (1979).

The Blessed Dismissal Gong
FROM *A Walker in the City*

The school—from every last stone in the courtyard to the battlements frowning down at me from the walls—was only the stage for a trial. I felt that the very atmosphere of learning that surrounded us was fake—that every lesson, every book, every approving smile was only a pretext for the constant probing and watching of me, that there was not a secret in me that would not be decimally measured into that white record book. All week long I lived for the blessed sound of the dismissal gong at three o'clock on Friday afternoon.

◆◆◆

All my early life lies open to my eye within five city blocks. When I passed the school, I went sick with all my old fear of it. With its standard New York public-school brown brick courtyard shut in on three sides of the square and the pretentious battlements overlooking that cockpit in which I can still smell the fiery sheen of the rubber ball, it looks like a factory over which has been imposed the façade of a castle. It gave me the shivers to stand up in the courtyard again; I felt as if I had been mustered back into the service of those Friday morning "tests" that were the terror of my childhood.

It was never learning I associated with that school: only the necessity to succeed, to get ahead of the others in the daily struggle to "make a good impression" on our teachers, who grimly, wearily, and often with ill-concealed distaste watched against our relapsing into the natural savagery they expected of Brownsville boys. The white, cool, thinly ruled record book sat over us from their desks all day long, and had remorselessly entered into it each day—in blue ink if we had passed, in red ink if we had not—our attendance, our conduct, our "effort," our merits and demerits; and to the last possible decimal point in calculation, our standing in an unending series of "tests"—surprise tests, daily tests, weekly tests, formal midterm tests, final tests. They never stopped trying to dig out of us whatever small morsel of fact we had managed to get down the night before. We had to prove that we were really alert, ready for anything, always in the race. That white thinly ruled record book figured in my mind as the judgment seat; the very thinness and remote blue lightness of its lines instantly showed its cold authority over me; so much space had been left on each page, columns and columns in which to note down everything about us, implacably and forever. As it lay there on a teacher's desk, I stared at it all day long with such fear and anxious propriety that I had no trouble believing that God, too, did nothing but keep such record books, and that on the final day He would face me with an account in Hebrew letters whose phonetic dots and dashes looked strangely like decimal points counting up my every sinful thought on earth.

All teachers were to be respected like gods, and God Himself was the greatest of all school superintendents. Long after I had ceased to believe that our teachers could see with the back of their heads, it was still understood, by me, that they knew everything. They were the delegates of all visible and invisible power on earth—of the mothers who waited on the stoops every day after three for us to bring home tales of our daily triumphs; of the glacially remote Anglo-Saxon principal, whose very name was King; of the incalculably important Superintendent of Schools who would someday rubberstamp his name to the bottom of our diplomas in grim acknowledgment that we had, at last, given satisfaction to him, to the Board of Superintendents, and to our benefactor the Ctiy of New York—and so up and up, to the government of the United States and to the great Lord Jehovah Himself. My belief in teachers' unlimited wisdom and power rested not so much on what I saw in them—how impatient most of them looked, how wary—but on our abysmal humility, at least in those of us who were "good" boys, who proved by our ready compliance and "manners" that we wanted to get on. The road to a professional future would be shown us only as we pleased *them*. *Make a good impression the first day of the term, and they'll help you out. Make a bad impression, and you might as well cut your throat.* This was the first article of school folklore, whispered around the classroom the opening day of each term. You made the "good impression" by sitting firmly at your wooden desk, hands clasped; by silence for the greatest part of the live-long day; by standing up obsequiously when it was so expected of you; by sitting down noiselessly when you had answered a question; by "speaking nicely," which meant reproducing their painfully exact enunciation; by "showing manners," or an ecstatic submissiveness in all things; by outrageous flattery; by bringing little gifts at Christmas, on their birthdays, and at the end of the term—the well-known significance of these gifts being that they came not from us, but from our parents, whose eagerness in this matter showed a high level of social consideration, and thus raised our standing in turn.

It was not just our quickness and memory that were always being tested. Above all, in that word I could never hear without automatically seeing it raised before me in gold-plated letters, it was our *character*. I always felt anxious when I heard the word pronounced. Satisfactory as my "character" was, on the whole, except when I stayed too long in the playground reading; outrageously satisfactory, as I can see now, the very sound of the word as our teachers coldly gave it out from the end of their teeth, with a solemn weight on each dark syllable, immediately struck my heart cold with fear—they could not believe I really had it. Character was never something you had; it had to be trained in you, like a technique. I was never very clear about it. On our side *character* meant demonstrative obedience; but teachers already had it—how else could they have become teachers? They had it; the aloof Anglo-Saxon principal whom we remotely saw only on ceremonial occasions in the assembly was positively encased in it; it glittered off his bald head in spokes of triumphant light; the President of the United States had the greatest conceivable amount of it. Character belonged to great adults. Yet we were constantly being driven onto it; it was the great threshold we had to cross. *Alfred Kazin, having shown proficiency in his course of studies and having displayed satisfactory marks of character* . . . Thus someday the hallowed diploma, passport to my further advancement in high school. But there—I could already feel it in my bones —they would put me through even more doubting tests of character; and after that, if I should be good enough and bright enough, there would be still more. *Character* was a bitter thing, racked with my endless striving to please. The school—from every last stone in the courtyard to the battlements frowning down at me from the walls—was only the stage for a trial. I felt that the very atmosphere of learning that surrounded us was fake—that every lesson, every book, every approving smile was only a pretext for the constant probing and watching of me, that there was not a secret in me that would not be decimally measured into that white record book. All week long I lived for the blessed sound of the dismissal gong at three o'clock on Friday afternoon.

EVAN HUNTER

Evan Hunter (1926–   ), American novelist and play-
wright, was born and educated in New York City and received his B.A. from Hunter College in 1950. He has written
many novels, plays, and screenplays under the names Evan
Hunter, Hunt Collins, Richard Marsten, and Ed McBain.

Hunter's best-known work is his novel *The Blackboard
Jungle*. In writing this novel, he drew on his brief teaching
experiences in New York City. When it was published, *The
Blackboard Jungle* was recognized as a forceful, realistic account of life in a New York City vocational high school.

Mr. Dadier's First Days at North
Manual Trades High School
FROM *The Blackboard Jungle*

"As you know," he said, "this is English 55-206, and
we're here to learn English. I know a lot of you will be
wondering why on earth you have to learn English. Will
English help you get a job as a mechanic, or an electrician? The answer is yes, English will. Besides, no
matter what you've thought of English up to now, I
think you'll enjoy this class, and you might be surprised
to find English one of your favorite subjects before the
term is finished."

"I'll be s'prised, all right," Miller said.

———— ✦✦✦ ————

The first thing he noticed when he entered the room was that the class was a small one, not more than twenty or so boys. He was happy about that because it's easier to teach a small group. He didn't know, of course, that there were thirty-five boys in 55-206, and that most of them had already begun cutting on this first day of the term.

The second thing he noticed was the well-built Negro boy with the white tee shirt and dungarees. The boy noticed him at the same moment, and the charming grin broke out on his handsome face.

"Well," he said, "hello, Chief."

"Gregory Miller," Rick said.

"You did remember the name, dintchoo, Chief?"

"Sit down, Miller," Rick said. "And *my* name is Mr. Dadier. I think you'd better start remembering that."

Miller took his seat, and Rick looked over to the other boys who were standing in clusters around the room, talking or laughing.

"All right," he said, "let's sit down. And let's make it fast."

The boys looked up at him, but they made no move toward their seats.

"You deaf back there? Let's break it up."

"Why?" one of the boys asked.

"What?" Rick said, surprised.

"I said 'Why?'"

"I heard you, smart boy. Get to your seat before you find a seat in the principal's office."

"I'm petrified," the tall boy said. He had stringy blond hair, and the hair was matted against his forehead. His face was a field of ripe acne, and when he grinned his lips contorted crookedly in a smile that was boyishly innocent and mannishly sinister at the same time. He continued smiling as he walked to the middle of the room and took the seat alongside Miller. The other boys, taking his move as a cue, slowly drifted back to the seats and turned their attention to Rick.

"You may keep the seats you now have," Rick said, reaching into his briefcase for the Delaney cards. He distributed the cards as he'd done with his official class, and said, "I'm sure you know how to fill these out."

"We sure do," the blond boy said.

"I didn't get your name," Rick said pointedly.

"Maybe 'cause I didn't give it," the boy answered, the crooked smile on his mouth again.

"His name is Emmanuel, too," Miller said. He smiled at the private joke which only he and Rick shared.

"Is it?" Rick asked innocently.

"No," the blond boy said.

"Then what is it?"

"Guess," the blond boy said. "It begins with a W."

"I'd say 'Wiseguy' offhand, but I'm not good at guessing. What's your name, and make it snappy."

"West," the boy said. "Artie West."

Rick smiled, suddenly reversing his tactics, hoping to throw the boys off balance. They were expecting a hard man, so he'd wisecrack a little, show them that he could exchange a gag when there was time for gagging. "Any relation to Mae West?" he asked.

West answered so quickly that Rick was certain he'd heard the same question many times before. "Only between my eyes and her tits," he said, the crooked grin on his mouth.

His answer provided Rick with a choice. He could drop the banter immediately and clamp down with the mailed fist again, or he could show that he wasn't the kind of person who could be bested in a match of wits. For some obscure reason that probably had a smattering of pride attached to it, he chose to continue the match.

"Watch your language," he said, smiling. "My mother's picture is in my wallet."

"I didn't know you had one," West said.

Again there was the choice, only this time West had penetrated deeper. A warning buzzer sounded at the back of Rick's mind. He saw the grinning faces of the boys in 55-206, and he knew they wanted him to continue the battle of half-wits. He would have liked to continue it himself, despite the incessant warning that screamed inside his head now. The truth was, however, he could not think of a comeback, and rather than spout something inadequate, he fled behind the fortress of his desk and said, "All right, let's knock it off now, and fill out the Delaney cards."

West smiled knowingly, and winked at Miller. He was a sharp cookie, West, and Miller was just as sharp—and if the two were friends, there'd probably be trouble in 55-206, Rick figured.

Rick looked out over the boys as they filled out the Delaney

cards. There was a handful of Negroes in the class, and the
rest of the boys were white, including a few Puerto Ricans.
They all appeared to be between sixteen and seventeen, and
most of them wore the tee shirt and dungarees which Rick
assumed to be the unofficial uniform of the school.

"As you know," he said, "this is English 55-206, and we're
here to learn English. I know a lot of you will be wondering why on earth you have to learn English. Will English
help you get a job as a mechanic, or an electrician? The answer is yes, English will. Besides, no matter what you've
thought of English up to now, I think you'll enjoy this class,
and you might be surprised to find English one of your favorite subjects before the term is finished."

"I'll be s'prised, all right," Miller said.

"I don't want any calling out in the classroom," Rick said
sternly. "If you have anything to say, you raise your hand.
Is that understood? My name, incidentally, is Mr. Dadier."

"We heard of you, Daddy-oh," a boy at the back of the
room said.

"Pronunciation is an important part of English," Rick said
coldly. "I'd hate to fail any boy because he couldn't learn to
pronounce my name. It's Mr. Dadier. Learn it, and learn it
now. Believe me, it won't break my heart to fail all of you."

A small Negro boy wearing a porkpie hat suddenly got to
his feet. He put his hands on his hips, and a sneer curled
his mouth. "You ever try to fight thirty-five guys at once,
teach?" he asked.

Rick heard the question, and it set off a trigger response
in his mind which told him, *This is it, Dadier. This is it, my
friend.* He narrowed his eyes and walked slowly and purposefully around his desk. The boy was seated in the middle
of the room, and Rick walked up the aisle nearest his desk,
realizing as he did so that he was placing himself in a
surrounded-by-boys position. He walked directly to the boy,
pushed his face close to his, and said, "Sit down, son, and
take off that hat before I knock it off."

He said it tightly, said it the way he'd spoken the lines for
Duke Mantee when he'd played *The Petrified Forest* at Hunter. He did not know what the reaction would be, and he
was vaguely aware of a persistent fear that crawled up his
spine and into his cranium. He knew he could be jumped by
all of them in this single instant, and the knowledge made
him taut and tense, and in that short instant before the boy

reacted, he found himself moving his toes inside his shoes to relieve the tension, to keep it from breaking out in the form of a trembling hand or a ticcing face.

The room was dead silent, and it seemed suddenly cold, despite the September sunshine streaming through the windows.

And even though the boy reacted almost instantly, it seemed forever to Rick.

The boy snatched the hat from his head, all his bravado gone, his eyes wide in what appeared to be fright. "I'm sorry, teach," he said, and then he instantly corrected it to "Mr. Dadier."

He sat immediately, and he avoided Rick's eyes, and Rick stood near his desk and continued to look down at the boy menacingly for a long while. Then he turned his back on the boy and walked back to the front of his room and his own desk. His face was set tightly, and he made his nostrils flare, the way he'd learned to do a long time ago in his first dramatics class.

He flipped open his Delaney book, stared down at it, and then raised his head slowly, the mock cold anger still in his eyes and in the hard line of his mouth. "Pass the Delaney cards to the front of the room. Pass down your program cards, too, and I'll sign them. You there, in the first row, collect them all and bring them to my desk."

The boy in the first seat of the first row smiled at Rick vacuously, and he made no move to start collecting the cards which were already being passed down to the front of each row.

"Did you hear me?" Rick asked.

"Yes," the boy said, still smiling vacuously.

"Then let's move," Rick said tightly.

The boy rose, still smiling that stupid, empty smile. *Another wise guy*, Rick thought. *The room is full of wise guys*.

The stupidly smiling boy collected all the cards, and brought them to Rick. Rick inserted the Delaney cards into his book, and then began mechanically signing the program cards in the spaces provided, a system which made it impossible for a boy to miss being enrolled in the class to which he had been assigned. When the program cards were returned to the official teachers the next day, any delinquent would automatically be exposed. It was an effective system.

"We won't accomplish much today, other than getting

acquainted. Tomorrow we'll get our books from the book room, and begin work."

He shifted his glance to the boy in the first seat of the first row. The boy was still smiling. The smile was plastered onto his thin face. He looked as if he were enjoying something immensely. Rick turned away from him, irritated, but not wanting another showdown so soon after his brush with the other boy.

"Our trip to the book room shouldn't take more than . . ."

"Is this trip necessary?" one of the boys called out.

Third seat, second row. Rick automatically tabulated the boy, and then fingered his card in the Delaney book. "What'd you say, Belazi?" he asked, reading the boy's name from the card.

"I said, is this trip necessary?"

"Yes, it is. Does that answer your question?"

"Yes, it does," the boy said.

"I'm glad it does, Belazi. Do you have any other important questions to ask?" He recalled something about sarcasm being a bad weapon to use against a class, but he shrugged the memory aside.

"Nope," Belazi answered.

"Well, good. May I go on with what I was saying then, with your kind permission?"

"Sure," Belazi said, smiling.

"Thank you. I appreciate your thoughtfulness."

"He the most thoughtful cat in this class," Miller said emphatically.

"Nobody asked you, Miller," Rick snapped.

"I ony just volunteerin' the information."

"I appreciate it," Rick said, unsmiling. "But I'll try to manage without your help."

"Think you'll make it, teach?" West asked.

"I'll tell you what, West," Rick said. "I'll be here until four this afternoon, planning tomorrow's lesson for this class. Since you're so worried, why don't you join me, and we'll plan it together."

"You can handle that case alone," West said.

"Aw, go on, help him," another boy called.

Rick located the card in the Delaney book. "Antoro? Is that your name?"

"Yeah," the boy said, proud to be in the act.

"Do you know what Toro means in Spanish?" Rick asked.

"My name ain't Toro," Antoro replied.

"Nonetheless, do you know what it means?"

"No. What?"

"Bull. Plain, old ordinary, common BULL."

Antoro, plainly insulted, retreated behind a sullen visage. Rick turned away from him and looked directly at the boy in the first seat of the first row. The boy was still smiling that blank, stupid smile.

"What's so funny?" Rick asked.

The boy continued to smile.

"You," Rick snapped. He looked at the card in the Delaney book. "Santini. What's so funny?"

"Me?" Santini asked, smiling vacuously.

"Yes, you. What's so funny?"

"Nothin'," Santini said, smiling broadly.

"Then why are you . . ."

"He the smilinest cat in the whole school," Miller informed Rick. "He smile all the time. Thass cause he an idiot."

"What?" Rick asked, turning.

Miller tapped his temple with one brown forefinger. "Lotsa muscles," he said, "but no brains."

Rick looked at Santini. The boy was still smiling, and the smile *was* an idiotic one. There was no mirth behind it. It perched on his mouth like a plaster monkey. He felt suddenly embarrassed for having brought the smile to the attention of the class. Surely, the boy was not an idiot, but his intelligence was probably so low that . . .

"Well, try to pay attention here," Rick said awkwardly.

"I'm payin' attention," Santini said innocently, still smiling.

Rick cleared his throat and passed out the signed program cards. He hated these damned orientation classes. The beginning was bound to be difficult, and it was made doubly difficult by the fact that there was really nothing to do without books and without . . . without a plan, he reluctantly admitted, realizing he should have planned out these first, difficult, getting-acquainted periods.

"We'll cover a lot of interesting topics this term," he said. "We'll learn all about newspapers, and we'll read a lot of interesting short stories, and several good novels, and we'll cover some good plays, too, perhaps acting them out right here in class."

"Tha's for me," Miller said suddenly. Rick smiled, pleased because he thought he'd struck a responsive chord.

"The acting, you mean?" he asked.

"Man, man," Miller said. "I'm a real Ty-rone Power type. You watch me, Chief. I'll lay 'em in the aisles."

The boys all laughed suddenly, and for the a moment Rick didn't now what the joke was. He understood suddenly and completely. Miller had used the word "lay" and that was always good for a yak. He wondered whether or not Miller had chosen the word purposely, or had simply blundered into the approving laughter of the boys. Whatever the case, Miller basked in his glory, soaking up the laughs like sunshine.

"Well, you'll get plenty of opportunity to act," Rick said, pretending he didn't understand what the laughter was about. "And we'll have all sorts of contests, too, for letter-writing, and for progress made. I'm thinking of awarding prizes to the boys who show me they're really working. Like tickets to football games and hockey games, things like that. Provided I get some co-operation from you."

"You ever hear of Juan Garza, teach?" one of the boys piped.

"No, I don't believe so," Rick said. "Who was Juan Garza?"

"He used to be in my class," the boy said. Rick had located his card now in the Delaney book. The boy's name was Maglin.

"What about Juan Garza, Maglin?" Rick asked.

Maglin smiled. "Nothing. He just used to be in my class, that's all."

"Why'd you ask if I knew him?"

"I just thought you might have heard about him. He used to be in my class."

"I gather he was a celebrity of some sort," Rick said dryly.

"He sure was," Maglin said, and all the boys laughed their approval.

"Well, it's a shame he's not in the class now," Rick said, and for some reason all the boys found this exceptionally funny. He was ready to pursue the subject further when the bell rang. He rose quickly and said, "I'll see you all tomorrow. Miller, I'd like to talk to you for a moment."

Miller's brow creased into a frown, and the frown vanished before a confident smile. He came to the front of the room, and while the rest of the boys sauntered out, he stood uneasily by the desk, shifting his weight from one foot to the other.

Rick waited until the other boys were all gone. He knew exactly what he was going to do, but he wanted to do it alone, with just him and Miller present. Its effectiveness would depend upon Miller's response, and he was sure the response would be a good one, once he separated Miller from the pack. When the other boys had all drifted out, he said, "Man to man talk, Miller. Okay?"

"Sure," Miller said uneasily, staring down at his shoelaces.

"I've checked your records," he lied. "You've got the makings of a leader, Miller. You're bright and quick, and the other boys like you."

"Me?" Miller asked, lifting his eyes, surprised. "Me?"

The flattery was beginning to work, and Rick pressed his advantage, smiling paternally now. "Yes, Miller, you. Come now, let's have no modesty here. You know you're head and shoulders above all of these boys."

Miller smiled shyly. "Well, I don't know. I mean . . ."

"Here's the point, Miller. We're going to have a damned fine class here." He used the word "damned" purposely, to show Miller he was not above swearing occasionally. "I can sense that. But I want it to be an outstanding class, and I can't make it that without your help."

"Me?" Miller asked again, really surprised now, and Rick wondered if he hadn't carried the flattery angle too far.

"Yes, you," he pushed on. "Come on, boy, let's lay our cards on the table."

"I don't know what you want, Ch . . . Mr. Dadier," Miller said.

"I want you to be the leader in this class, the way you're entitled to be. I want you to set the example for the rest of the boys. I want you to give me all your co-operation, and the other boys will automatically follow suit. That's what I want, Miller. If you help me, we can make this class the best one in the school."

"Well, I don't know," Miller said dubiously.

"I do know," Rick insisted. "What do you say, boy?"

"Well . . . sure, I'll help all I can. Sure, if you think so."

"That's my boy," Rick said, rising and clapping Miller on the shoulder. "I'll see you tomorrow, Miller." He walked Miller to the doorway, his arm around the boy. "Now take it easy."

"Sure," Miller said, puzzled. His brow furrowed once, and then he smiled again. "Sure," he said. And then, almost arrogantly, "Sure!"

Rick watched him go down the corridor, and then he went back into the room and packed his briefcase. He had been smooth there, all right. Brother, he had pulled the wool clear down over Miller's eyes, clear down over his shoelaces, too. Once he put Miller in his pocket, he'd get West, too. And once he got the two troublemakers, the clowns, the class was his. He'd used flattery, the oldest of weapons, and Miller had taken the hook without once suspecting any trickery. A leader, indeed! *Rickie*, he told himself, *you are a bloody goddamned genius!* The class had been troublesome, true, but he'd put his finger on the trouble spot and immediately weeded it out. That was the way to do it, despite what Solly Klein preached. These kids *were* humans, and not animals to be penned up and ignored. All you had to do was hit the proper chord. . . .

[The following Thursday] the boys were talking when he entered Room 206, but they took their seats immediately and stared at Rick as he went to his desk. Miller watched him with raised eyebrows. The room was dead silent.

Good, Rick thought. *That's the way it should be.*

He put his Delaney book on the desk, opened it, and quickly took the attendance. West, he noted with satisfaction, was absent. That was good, too. He'd be able to concentrate on Miller exclusively.

He reached into his briefcase and pulled out a blue-jacketed book titled *Graded Units in Vital English*. He opened the book on his desk, reading the stamped lettering on the title page:

NORTH MANUAL TRADES HIGH SCHOOL

This book is loaned to the pupil with the distinct understanding that he will not deface it in any way and that his responsibility for it will not cease until he has returned it to his teacher and received a receipt therefor.

Keep the Book Covered

He wondered if they understood any of the high-falutin' language therein, turned his attention therefrom, and said, "I'd like to pinpoint some of your most common grammatical faults today, so that I'll be able to plan the remedial work we'll need throughout the term."

He said it coldly, and the boys eyed him coldly, showing neither distaste nor enthusiasm for his project.

"Antoro," he said, "will you get these books from the closet back there and distribute them to the class?"

Antoro rose without a sound. He was a good-looking boy, with sandy-brown hair and brown eyes. He walked to the

front of the room, extended his hand for the key Rick offered
and then walked back to the book closet and opened it.

"You'd better give him a hand, Belazi," Rick said. Belazi
rose as soundlessly as Antoro had, walked quickly to the back
of the room, and then began carrying the blue books through
the aisles, dropping one on each desktop. Antoro started on
the other end of the room, and the book distribution was
accomplished neatly in a very few moments. Both boys returned to their seats after Antoro gave the key back to Rick.

"If you'll all turn to page one," Rick said, and he watched
the boys move like automatons, heard the whispering pages
as the boys flipped past the *Preface*, and the *To the Teacher*
section, and the *Suggested Aids for Study* section, and the
Correction Chart, and the *Bibliography*, and the *Table of
Contents*.

"Page one," Rick repeated. "Have you all got that? It's an
Achievement Test. If you'll all look at part A, now. It says,
'*Select the correct word or words in each parenthesis.*' Have
you all found that?"

No one in the class answered Rick. He frowned slightly,
and then went on.

"There's an example there of what's to be done." He
paused, and then read aloud: "EXAMPLE: He (done, did)
what he was told. *Answer:* did." He paused again. "Do you
all get the idea? There are thirty-five sentences in this first
section, more than enough for all of us. I'll call on you, and
you'll take the sentences in order. Don't be afraid of making
mistakes. That's what I want to find out. When I discover
your weak spots, I'll be able to fix them. Is that clear?"

The class remained silent. The boys looked up from their
books expectantly, but no one said a word.

"All right," Rick said, "will you take the first one, Miller?"

He had chosen Miller purposely, hoping the boy would
start things off right, especially after his chat with him the
other day. A lot of things had happened since that chat,
though, and Rick didn't know exactly where he stood with
the colored boy. Miller made a motion to rise, and Rick
quickly said, "We can do this seated, boys."

Miller made himself comfortable in his seat again, and
then studied the first sentence. Rick wasn't really anticipat-
ing too much difficulty with the test. This was a fifth-term
class, and they'd had most of this material pounded into their
heads since they were freshmen. The first sentence read:
Henry hasn't written (no, any) answer to my letter.

Rick read the sentence, and then looked at Miller. "Well, Miller, what do you say?"

Miller hesitated for a just a moment. "Henry hasn't written no answer to my letter," he said.

Rick stared at Miller, and then he looked out at the class. Something had come alive in their eyes, but there was still no sound. The silence was intense, pressurized almost. "No," Rick said. "It should be 'Henry hasn't written *any* answer.' Well, that's all right. I want to learn your mistakes. Will you take the next one, Carter?"

Carter, a big red-headed boy, looked at the second sentence in the test.

If I were (he, him), I wouldn't say that.

"If I were him," he said rapidly, "I wouldn't say that."

Rick smiled. "Well," he said, "if I were you, I wouldn't say that, either. 'He' is correct."

Something was happening out there in the class, but Rick didn't know what it was yet. There was excitement showing in the eyes of the boys, an excitement they could hardly contain. Miller's face was impassive, expressionless.

"Antoro, will you take the next one, please?" Rick said. He had been making notes in his own book as he went along, truly intending to use this test as a guide for future grammar lessons. He looked at the third sentence now.

It was none other than (her, she).

"It was none other than her," Antoro said quickly.

"No," Rick said. "The answer is 'she.' Take the next one, Levy."

Levy spoke almost as soon as his name was called. "George throwed the ball fast," he said.

"Throwed the ball?" Rick said, lifting his eyebrows. "*Throwed?* Come now, Levy. Surely you know 'threw' is correct."

Levy said nothing. He studied Rick with cold eyes.

"Belazi," Rick said tightly, "take the next one."

"It is them who spoke," Belazi said.

He knew the game now. He knew the game, and he was powerless to combat it. Miller had started it, of course, and the other kids had picked it up with an uncanny instinct for following his improvisation. Now Rick would never know if they were really making errors or were just purposely giving wrong answers even when they knew the right ones. The "he-him," "she-her" business may have thrown them, but nobody used "throwed" for "threw." No, he couldn't buy that.

He listened to scattered sentences throughout the test as he called on every boy in the class.

Won't anyone borrow *you a pen?*

The player stealed *a base.*

Last term the class choose *Mary Wilson as president.*

She speaks worst *than her brother.*

Where was *you when the policeman came?*

Where was I indeed, Rick thought, when the brains (was, were) passed out?

"We didn't do too well on that, did we?" he asked.

The class was silent.

Okay, Rick thought, we can play this game from both sides of the goddamn fence. If we're going to be little smart guys, let's all be little smart guys.

"Since we've gone over all the sentences in class now, and since I gave you the correct answer for each sentence, the homework for tonight should be fairly simple," he said.

"Home . . ." one of the boys started, and Miller turned in instant reproval. The word "Shut . . ." burst from his mouth before he could stop it, but he never finished the sentence, never added the "up," apparently realizing the completed sentence would be too incriminating.

But Rick knew the whole story now, and the class sensed it, and they kept their silence only with the greatest effort. A battle of wills raged before Rick's desk, and he watched it with amazement, because it was obviously Miller who was holding the minds of his classmates captive in a clenched fist. He had given Miller a leadership pitch on Monday, but he hadn't for a moment believed that Miller was really a leader. A troublemaker, yes, someone to laugh at, but not a person to follow seriously. He revised his thinking rapidly now, and he even wondered if he hadn't, like Frankenstein, helped create this monster. Damnit, had he established Miller as a leader in Miller's own mind?

He watched the battle out there, watched the students' protest, like sand held in the tightest fist, slowly seeping through Miller's closed fingers. It was one thing to play games with the new snot-nose teacher, but when that teacher began dropping homework on their skulls, the game wasn't so hilarious anymore. Rick smiled, sensing the conflict, wanting to bring the battle to a head.

"Yes, homework," he said, still smiling. "And since I don't want you to take these books home, you can begin copying all thirty-five questions into your notebooks right now."

"Hey, what the hell!" Carter shouted. Carter's outburst started it. His words were livid with outrage, and his carrot-topped head seemed to lend fiery pictorial support to his indignation.

De la Cruz, a pale, thin boy with a reedy voice, shouted, "Homework? How come we have thees . . ."

"It ain't even the first week of school!"

"Goddamnit, talk about slave drivers . . ."

"I go to work after school, teach!"

"That's enough of that!" Rick shouted. He tightened his jaws and calmly said, "Start copying the sentences now. The homework will count as one of the tests the class receives during the term. It may very well decide whether you pass or fail this course."

The rebellion ended as suddenly as it had started. Miller smiled at his classmates coldly, his face telling them they were all jackasses for having protested in the first place. It all led to the same thing anyway, didn't it, and now the teacher had the satisfaction of having heard them whine. He flipped open his notebook with weary superiority, and the other boys followed suit while Rick watched them copying the sentences.

"Better get them all," he said, almost enjoying his power now. "The test will be marked on the basis of thirty-five questions."

This time, the class was silent. They had apparently grasped the meaning of the Miller-Gandhi method of attack. They wouldn't give Rick any more satisfaction. They would be separate stones now, held together by a mute mortar that bound them into a wall as solid as any fortress. Rick sat at his desk and watched them laboriously transcribing the sentences. His victory, if considered such at all, had been a hollow one. And aside from the momentary elation he'd felt when they'd finally broken to his will, he felt no real joy.

The silence out there was an almost tangible thing. He wanted to reach out and probe it with his finger, push at it like some gelatinous mass. He could hear the scratching of pen on looseleaf paper, could see the tops of the boys' heads as they worked.

What the hell goes on inside those heads? he wondered.

Probably nothing. Zero. Perfect vacuum.

This is a job for a man with a vacuum cleaner, he mused.

How do you go about cleaning a vacuum? Do vacuums get dirty? How do you get inside a vacuum to begin with? Someday we'll discuss vacuums in class. And for the best ten thousand word thesis following our discussion, I'll award a hollow loving cup, the hollow symbolizing the vacuum, and the loving cup symbolizing the mutual love and affection the boys and I share.

That was fun, he thought wryly, *what'll we play next?*

Probably charades for the rest of the term if this goddamned silent treatment persisted. The silence, of course, could be broken easily enough. Just shock them out of it, that's all. Like using insulin on a schizophrenic. Steady now, sir, easy now. WHAM! I beg your pardon, doctor, but did you see the top of my skull? I'm sure I had one when I came in.

Shock always worked, one way or another. Cure them or kill them.

It had its definite setbacks, though, the way this sudden homework assignment did. The shock may have goosed them out of their silence, but once the shock wore off the silence returned, and with it the memory of the shock to increase the formidability of the silence. Vicious circle. Elementary, my dear Watson.

Well, my dear Watson, just what do you propose? Shall we allow the silence to smother activity, like a dense London fog? Or shall we pierce the fog occasionally, knowing it will return anyway? Well, my dear Watson, what the hell's wrong with you, old boy? No answers? No suggestions? Nothing? Hell of a help, all right, you are.

Or should we treat the disease rather than the symptoms? If so, just what was the disease? Resentment, of course. They didn't like his interference in the rape. Well, he didn't like it much either, so they were even. Nobody likes polio much, for that matter, but everyone recognizes it as a disease. You can't discount something simply because it doesn't appeal to you.

Well, there was nothing to be done about the rape intervention. That was history, dead and gone, and rightfully in the province of the Social Studies department, with George Katz perhaps teaching a sparkling course on The Rise and Fall of Richard Dadier.

But, as with any disease, you can isolate the germ—or at least the germ-carrier. He knew who the germ-carrier was in this ward, by God. His finger unconsciously tapped the Delaney card in its slot in the book.

Miller, Gregory.

He sounds like a movie star, Rick thought.

Only you and I, Watson, know that he is in reality a germ-carrier.

Shall we operate?

We shall operate. Scalpel, please. Sponge. Suture. Scotch tape . . .

The bell sounded.

"Thats all," Rick said. "Pass the books down to the front of your row. Belazi and Antoro, collect them please and take them to the closet. Your homework is due tomorrow when we meet again." He paused. "Miller, I'd like to talk to you. Would you mind waiting?"

The class began filing out silently as Belazi and Antoro picked up the grammar books. Rick gave Antoro the key, and Miller waited alongside Rick's desk until the books were back in the closet. When Antoro and Belazi left, Rick faced Miller squarely.

"What do you say, Miller?" he said.

Miller did not smile. His face was in complete repose. He eyed Rick levelly and asked, "About what, Chief?"

"I thought we had a little talk."

"So?"

"You led them today," Rick said earnestly, being completely honest with the boy, using the same hook he'd used on Monday, but really meaning it this time. "But you led them the wrong way. Why?"

"Maybe you should of ought to minded your own business, Chief," Miller said. "Ain't many guys who like whut happened to Douglas Murray."

"That wasn't my fault, Miller," Rick said seriously. "You should know that. You'd have done the same thing in my position."

"Would I of? You don't know me so good, Chief."

"You're angry because I intervened, is that it?"

"Murray's goan to jail, you know that?"

"I had nothing to do with pressing charges, Miller."

"No?"

"No."

"You jus' pure-white innocent, that's all," Miller said.

"But what about our talk the other day, Miller? I thought we . . ."

"Mr. Dad-yay," Miller said, "s'pose we jus' forget that li'l snowjob, okay?"

"I wasn't snowing you," Rick lied. All right, he had snowed Miller. That was before he knew. This was different now.

"Man," Miller said, "the snow was knee-deep."

Rick stared at the boy, feeling curiously like the fellow who'd cried wolf. He'd tried to capture Miller's loyalty on a false peg Monday. The peg had turned out to be a true enough one, and now Miller had turned the tables. He hadn't believed Rick then, and he wasn't buying anything Rick sold from now on.

"I mean it, Miller," Rick said fervently.

"Man, you know that li'l poem, don't choo?" Miller asked.

"What poem?"

Miller smiled. "The wind blew, and the crap flew, and for days the vision was bad." He paused and studied Rick's face, still smiling.

"I don't see the point," Rick said slowly.

"You don't, huh? Well, what I mean, Chief, the vision is jus' now beginnin' to clear up a little. I can see fine now."

"You *are* a leader," Rick said, almost desperately this time, the realization overwhelming.

"I got a class now," Miller said. "Mind if I go, Chief?"

He walked across the room and hesitated at the door, seemingly about to say something further. Then he smiled, shrugged, and left Rick sitting at his desk with an Unassigned period.

JOHN UPDIKE

John Hoyer Updike (1932–   ), American novelist and
poet, is considered one of the best of our contemporary
writers—a fresh original, vigorous, highly talented man. Born
in Pennsylvania, he attended Harvard University and spent a
year at Oxford. From 1955 to 1957, Updike worked for *The
New Yorker* contributing verse, essays, parodies, and short
stories. His novels, beginning with *The Poorhouse Fair* (in
1959), have been widely acclaimed. His short stories are particularly popular.

Tomorrow and Tomorrow
and So Forth

Mark winced, pierced by the awful clarity with which his
students saw him. Through their eyes, how queer he
looked, with his chalky hands, and his horn-rimmed
glasses, and his hair never slicked down, all wrapped up
in "literature" . . .

———◆◆———

Whirling, talking, 11D began to enter Room 109. From the
quality of the class's excitement Mark Prosser guessed it
would rain. He had been teaching high school for three years,
yet his students still impressed him; they were such sensitive
animals. They reacted so infallibly to merely barometric
pressure.

In the doorway, Brute Young paused while little Barry
Snyder giggled at his elbow. Barry's stagy laugh rose and
fell, dipping down toward some vile secret that had to be
tasted and retasted, then soaring like a rocket to proclaim
that he, little Barry, shared such a secret with the school's

fullback. Being Brute's stooge was precious to Barry. The
fullback paid no attention to him; he twisted his neck to
stare at something not yet coming through the door. He
yielded heavily to the procession pressing him forward.

Right under Prosser's eyes, like a murder suddenly appearing in an annalistic frieze of kings and queens, someone stabbed a girl in the back with a pencil. She ignored
the assault saucily. Another hand yanked out Geoffrey
Langer's shirt-tail. Geoffrey, a bright student, was uncertain whether to laugh it off or defend himself with anger,
and made a weak, half-turning gesture of compromise, wearing an expression of distant arrogance that Prosser instantly
coördinated with baffled feelings he used to have. All along
the line, in the glitter of key chains and the acute angles of
turned-back shirt cuffs, an electricity was expressed which
simple weather couldn't generate.

Mark wondered if today Gloria Angstrom wore that
sweater, an ember-pink angora, with very brief sleeves. The
virtual sleevelessness was the disturbing factor: the exposure
of those two serene arms to the air, white as thighs against
the delicate wool.

His guess was correct. A vivid pink patch flashed through
the jiggle of arms and shoulders as the final knot of youngsters
entered the room.

"Take your seats," Mr. Prosser said. "Come on. Let's go."

Most obeyed, but Peter Forrester, who had been at the
center of the group around Gloria, still lingered in the doorway with her, finishing some story, apparently determined to
make her laugh or gasp. When she did gasp, he tossed his
head with satisfaction. His orange hair, preened into a kind
of floating bang, bobbed. Mark had always disliked redheaded
males, with their white eyelashes and puffy faces and thyroid
eyes, and absurdly self-confident mouths. A race of bluffers.
His own hair was brown.

When Gloria, moving in a considered, stately way, had
taken her seat, and Peter had swerved into his, Mr. Prosser
said, "Peter Forrester."

"Yes?" Peter rose, scrabbling through his book for the
right place.

"Kindly tell the class the exact meaning of the words
'Tomorrow, and tomorrow, and tomorrow/Creeps in this
petty pace from day to day.' "

Peter glanced down at the high-school edition of *Macbeth*
lying open on the desk. One of the duller girls tittered ex-

pectantly from the back of the room. Peter was popular with the girls; girls that age had minds like moths.

"Peter. With your book shut. We have all memorized this passage for today. Remember?" The girl in the back of the room squealed in delight. Gloria laid her own book face-open on her desk, where Peter could see it.

Peter shut his book with a bang and stared into Gloria's. "Why," he said at last, "I think it means pretty much what it says."

"Which is?"

"Why, that tomorrow is something we often think about. It creeps into our conversation all the time. We couldn't make any plans without thinking about tomorrow."

"I see. Then you would say that Macbeth is here referring to the, the date-book aspect of life?"

Geoffrey Langer laughed, no doubt to please Mr. Prosser. For a moment, he *was* pleased. Then he realized he had been playing for laughs at a student's expense.

His paraphrase had made Peter's reading of the lines seem more ridiculous than it was. He began to react. "I admit—"

But Peter was going on; redheads never know when to quit. "Macbeth means that if we quit worrying about tomorrow, and just live for today, we could appreciate all the wonderful things that are going on under our noses."

Mark considered this a moment before he spoke. He would not be sarcastic. "Uh, without denying that there is truth in what you say, Peter, do you think it likely that Macbeth, in his situation, would be expressing such"—he couldn't help himself—"such sunny sentiments?"

Geoffrey laughed again. Peter's neck reddened; he studied the floor. Gloria glared at Mr. Prosser, the indignation in her face clearly meant for him to see.

Mark hurried to undo his mistake. "Don't misunderstand me, please," he told Peter. "I don't have all the answers myself. But it seems to me the whole speech, down to "Signifying nothing,' is saying that life is—well, a *fraud*. Nothing wonderful about it."

"Did Shakespeare really think that?" Geoffrey Langer asked, a nervous quickness pitching his voice high.

Mark read into Geoffrey's question his own adolescent premonitions of the terrible truth. The attempt he must make was plain. He told Peter he could sit down and looked through the window toward the steadying sky. The clouds were gaining intensity. "There is," Mr. Prosser slowly began,

"much darkness in Shakespeare's work, and no play is darker
than *Macbeth*. The atmosphere is poisonous, oppressive. One
critic has said that in this play, humanity suffocates." He felt
himself in danger of suffocating, and cleared his throat.

"In the middle of his career, Shakespeare wrote plays about
men like Hamlet and Othello and Macbeth—men who aren't
allowed by their society, or bad luck, or some minor flaw in
themselves, to become the great men they might have been.
Even Shakespeare's comedies of this period deal with a world
gone sour. It is as if he had seen through the bright, bold
surface of his earlier comedies and histories and had looked
upon something terrible. It frightened him, just as some day
it may frighten some of you." In his determination to find
the right words, he had been staring at Gloria, without meaning to. Embarrassed, she nodded, and, realizing what had happened, he smiled at her.

He tried to make his remarks gentler, even diffident. "But
then I think Shakespeare sensed a redeeming truth. His last
plays are serene and symbolical, as if he had pierced through
the ugly facts and reached a realm where the facts are again
beautiful. In this way, Shakespeare's total work is a more
complete image of life than that of any other writer, except
perhaps for Dante, an Italian poet who wrote several centuries earlier." He had been taken far from the Macbeth
soliloquy. Other teachers had been happy to tell him how the
kids made a game of getting him talking. He looked toward
Geoffrey. The boy was doodling on his tablet, indifferent.
Mr. Prosser concluded, "The last play Shakespeare wrote is
an extraordinary poem called *The Tempest*. Some of you
may want to read it for your next book reports—the ones due
May 10th. It's a short play."

The class had been taking a holiday. Barry Snyder was
snicking BBs off the blackboard and glancing over at Brute
Young to see if he noticed. "Once more, Barry," Mr. Prosser
said, "and out you go." Barry blushed, and grinned to cover
the blush, his eyeballs sliding toward Brute. The dull girl in
the rear of the room was putting on lipstick. "Put that away,
Alice," Prosser said. "This isn't a beauty parlor." Sejak, the
Polish boy who worked nights, was asleep at his desk, his
cheek white with pressure against the varnished wood, his
mouth sagging sidewise. Mr. Prosser had an impulse to let
him sleep. But the impulse might not be true kindness, but
just the self-congratulatory, kindly pose in which he sometimes discovered himself. Besides, one breach of discipline

encouraged others. He strode down the aisle and squeezed Sejak's shoulder; the boy awoke. A mumble was growing at the front of the room.

Peter Forrester was whispering to Gloria, trying to make her laugh. The girl's face, though, was cool and solemn, as if a thought had been provoked in her head—as if there lingered there something of what Mr. Prosser had been saying. With a bracing sense of chivalrous intercession, Mark said, "Peter. I gather from this noise that you have something to add to your theories."

Peter responded courteously. "No, sir, I honestly don't understand the speech. Please, sir, what *does* it mean?"

This candid admission and odd request stunned the class. Every white, round face, eager, for once, to learn, turned toward Mark. He said, "I don't know. I was hoping *you* would tell *me*."

In college, when a professor made such a remark, it was with grand effect. The professor's humility, the necessity for creative interplay between teacher and student were dramatically impressed upon the group. But to 11D, ignorance in an instructor was as wrong as a hole in a roof. It was as if Mark had held forty strings pulling forty faces taut toward him and then had slashed the strings. Heads waggled, eyes dropped, voices buzzed. Some of the discipline problems, like Peter Forrester, smirked signals to one another.

"Quiet!" Mr. Prosser shouted. "All of you. Poetry isn't arithmetic. There's no single right answer. I don't want to force my own impression on you; that's not why I'm here." The silent question, *Why are you here?* seemed to steady the air with suspense. "I'm here," he said, "to let you teach yourselves."

Whether or not they believed him, they subsided, somewhat. Mark judged he could safely reassume his human-among-humans pose. He perched on the edge of the desk, informal, friendly, and frankly beseeching. "Now, honestly. Don't any of you have some personal feeling about the lines that you would like to share with the class and me?"

One hand, with a flowered handkerchief balled in it, unsteadily rose. "Go ahead, Teresa," Mr. Prosser said. She was a timid, sniffly girl whose mother was a Jehovah's Witness.

"It makes me think of cloud shadows," Teresa said.

Geoffrey Langer laughed. "Don't be rude, Geoff," Mr. Prosser said sideways, softly, before throwing his voice forward: "Thank you, Teresa. I think that's an interesting and valid impression. Cloud movement has something in it of the slow, monotonous rhythm one feels in the line 'Tomorrow, and tomorrow, and tomorrow.' It's a very gray line, isn't it, class?" No one agreed or disagreed.

Beyond the windows actual clouds were bunching rapidly, and erratic sections of sunlight slid around the room. Gloria's arm, crooked gracefully above her head, turned gold. "Gloria?" Mr. Prosser asked.

She looked up from something on her desk with a face of sullen radiance. "I think what Teresa said was very good," she said, glaring in the direction of Geoffrey Langer. Geoffrey snickered defiantly. "And I have a question. What does 'petty pace' mean?"

"It means the trivial day-to-day sort of life that say, a bookkeeper or a bank clerk leads. Or a schoolteacher," he added, smiling.

She did not smile back. Thought wrinkles irritated her perfect brow. "But Macbeth has been fighting wars, and killing kings, and being a king himself, and all," she pointed out.

"Yes, but it's just these acts Macbeth is condemning as 'nothing.' Can you see that?"

Gloria shook her head. "Another thing I worry about— isn't it silly for Macbeth to be talking to himself right in the middle of this war, with his wife just dead, and all?"

"I don't think so, Gloria. No matter how fast events happen, thought is faster."

His answer was weak; everyone knew it, even if Gloria hadn't mused, supposedly to herself, but in a voice the entire class could hear, "It seems so *stupid*."

Mark winced, pierced by the awful clarity with which his students saw him. Through their eyes, how queer he looked, with his chalky hands, and his horn-rimmed glasses, and his hair never slicked down, all wrapped up in "literature," where, when things get rough, the king mumbles a poem nobody understands. He was suddenly conscious of a terrible tenderness in the young, a frightening patience and faith. It was so good of them not to laugh him out of the room. He looked down and rubbed his fingertips together, trying to erase the chalk dust. The class noise sifted into unnatural quiet. "It's getting late," he said finally. "Let's start the recitations of the memorized passage. Bernard Amilson, you begin."

Bernard had trouble enunciating, and his rendition began " 'T'mau 'n' t'mau 'n' t'mau.' " It was reassuring, the extent to which the class tried to repress its laughter. Mr. Prosser wrote "A" in his marking book opposite Bernard's name. He always gave Bernard A on recitations, despite the school nurse, who claimed there was nothing organically wrong with the boy's mouth.

It was the custom, cruel but traditional, to deliver recitations from the front of the room. Alice, when her turn came, was reduced to a helpless state by the first funny face Peter Forrester made at her. Mark let her hang up there a good minute while her face ripened to cherry redness, and at last relented. "Alice, you may try it later." Many of the class knew the passage gratifyingly well, though there was a tendency to leave out the line "To the last syllable of recorded time" and to turn "struts and frets" into "frets and struts" or simply "struts and struts." Even Sejak, who couldn't have looked at the passage before he came to class, got through it as far as "And then is heard no more."

Geoffrey Langer showed off, as he always did, by interrupting his own recitation with bright questions. " 'Tomorrow, and tomorrow, and tomorrow,' " he said, " 'creeps in'— shouldn't that be *'creep* in,' Mr. Prosser?"

"It is 'creeps.' The trio is in effect singular. Go on. Without the footnotes." Mr. Prosser was tired of coddling Langer. The boy's black hair, short and stiff, seemed deliberately ratlike.

" 'Creep*sss* in this petty pace from day to day, to the last syllable of recorded time, and all our yesterdays have lighted fools the way to dusty death. Out, out—' "

"No, no!" Mr. Prosser jumped out of his chair. "This is poetry. Don't mushmouth it! Pause a little after 'fools.' "

Geoffrey looked genuinely startled this time, and Mark himself did not quite understand his annoyance and, mentally turning to see what was behind him, seemed to glimpse in the humid undergrowth the two stern eyes of the indignant look Gloria had thrown Geoffrey. He glimpsed himself in the absurd position of acting as Gloria's champion in her private war with this intelligent boy. He sighed apologetically. "Poetry is made up of lines," he began, turning to the class. Gloria was passing a note to Peter Forrester.

The rudeness of it! To pass notes during a scolding that she herself had caused! Mark caged in his hand the girl's frail

wrist and ripped the note from her fingers. He read it to himself, letting the class see he was reading it, though he despised such methods of discipline. The note went:

Pete—I think you're *wrong* about Mr. Prosser. I think he's
wonderful and I get a lot out of his class. He's heavenly
with poetry. I think I love him. I really do *love* him. So
there.

Mr. Prosser folded the note once and slipped it into his
side coat pocket. "See me after class, Gloria," he said. Then,
to Geoffrey, "Let's try it again. Begin at the beginning."

While the boy was reciting the passage, the buzzer
sounded the end of the period. It was the last class of the
day. The room quickly emptied, except for Gloria. The noise
of lockers slamming open and books being thrown against
metal and shouts drifted in.

"Who has a car?"

"Lend me a cig, pig."

"We can't have practice in this slop."

Mark hadn't noticed exactly when the rain started, but it
was coming down hard now. He moved around the room
with the window pole, closing windows and pulling down
shades. Spray bounced in on his hands. He began to talk
to Gloria in a crisp voice that, like his device of shutting the
windows, was intended to protect them both from embarrass-
ment.

"About note passing." She sat motionless at her desk in the
front of the room, her short, brushed-up hair like a cool
torch. From the way she sat, her naked arms folded at her
breasts and her shoulders hunched, he felt she was chilly.
"It is not only rude to scribble when a teacher is talking, it
is stupid to put one's words down on paper, where they look
much more foolish than they might have sounded if spoken."
He leaned the window pole in its corner and walked toward
his desk.

"And about love. 'Love' is one of those words that illustrate what happens to an old, overworked language. These
days, with movie stars and crooners and preachers and
psychiatrists all pronouncing the word, it's come to mean
nothing but a vague fondness for something. In this sense, I
love the rain, this blackboard, these desks, you. It means nothing, you see, whereas once the word signified a quite explicit
thing—a desire to share all you own and are with someone

else. It is time we coined a new word to mean that, and when you think up the word *you* want to use, I suggest that you be economical with it. Treat it as something you can spend only once—if not for your own sake, for the good of the language." He walked over to his own desk and dropped two pencils on it, as if to say, "That's all."

"I'm sorry," Gloria said.

Rather surprised, Mr. Prosser said, "Don't be."

"But you don't understand."

"Of course I don't. I probably never did! At your age, I was like Geoffrey Langer."

"I bet you weren't." The girl was almost crying; he was sure of that.

"Come on, Gloria. Run along. Forget it." She slowly cradled her books between her bare arm and her sweater, and left the room with that melancholy shuffling teen-age gait, so that her body above her thighs seemed to float over the desktops.

What was it, Mark asked himself, these kids were after? What did they want? Glide, he decided, the quality of glide. To slip along, always in rhythm, always cool, the little wheels humming under you, going nowhere special. If Heaven existed, that's the way it would be there. *He's heavenly with poetry.* They loved the word. Heaven was in half their songs.

"Christ, he's humming." Strunk, the physical ed teacher, had come into the room without Mark's noticing. Gloria had left the door ajar.

"Ah," Mark said, "a fallen angel, full of grit."

"What the hell makes you so happy?"

"I'm not happy, I'm just heavenly. I don't know why you don't appreciate me."

"Say." Strunk came up an aisle with a disagreeably effeminate waddle, pregnant with gossip. "Did you hear about Murchison?"

"No." Mark mimicked Strunk's whisper.

"He got the pants kidded off him today."

"Oh dear."

Strunk started to laugh, as he always did before beginning a story. "You know what a goddam lady's man he thinks he is?"

"You bet," Mark said, although Strunk said that about every male member of the faculty.

"You have Gloria Angstrom, don't you?"

"You bet."

"Well, this morning Murky intercepts a note she w[as] writing, and the note says what a damn neat guy she think[s] Murchison is and how she *loves* him!" Strunk waited f[or] Mark to say something, and then, when he didn't, continue[d]. "You could see he was tickled pink. But—get this—it tur[ns] out at lunch that the same damn thing happened to Fryebur[g] in history yesterday!" Strunk laughed and crackled h[is] knuckles viciously. "The girl's too dumb to have thought it u[p] herself. We all think it was Peter Forrester's idea."

"Probably was." Mark agreed. Strunk followed him out t[o] his locker, describing Murchison's expression when Fryebur[g] (in all innocence, mind you) told what had happened to him[.]

Mark turned the combination of his locker, 18–24–3[.] "Would you excuse me, Dave?" he said. "My wife's in tow[n] waiting."

Strunk was too thick to catch Mark's anger. "I got to g[et] over to the gym. Can't take the little darlings outside in th[e] rain; their mommies'll write notes to teacher." He waddle[d] down the hall and wheeled at the far end, shouting. "No[w] don't tell You-know-who!"

Mr. Prosser took his coat from the locker and shrugge[d] it on. He placed his hat upon his head. He fitted his rubber[s] over his shoes, pinching his fingers painfully, and lifted hi[s] umbrella off the hook. He thought of opening it right there i[n] the vacant hall, as a kind of joke, and decided not to. Th[e] girl had been almost crying; he was sure of that.

ROBERT GRAVES

Robert Graves (1895–   ) was born in Wimbledon, England. He went from school to World War I, where he became a captain of the Welch Fusiliers. Apart from a year spent as professor of English literature at Cairo University in 1926, Graves has lived by his writing. His historical novels include *I, Claudius, Claudius the God, Sergeant Lamb of the Ninth, Count Belisarius, Wife to Mr. Milton, Proceed, Sergeant Lamb, The Golden Fleece, They Hanged My Saintly Billy,* and *The Isles of Unwisdom.* He wrote his autobiography, *Goodbye to All That,* in 1929. His two most controversial books are *The White Goddess* and *The Nazarene Doctrine Restored.* He has translated Apuleius, Lucan, and Suetonius, and compiled the first modern dictionary of Greek mythology, *The Greek Myths.* In 1961 he became Professor of Poetry at Oxford. He has made his home in Majorca since 1929.

Treacle Tart

"Eat your tart," snapped Mr. Lees
"But I never eat treacle tart—sir!"
"It's my duty to see that you do so, every Monday."
Julius smiled. "What a queer duty!" he said incredulously.

------◆◆------

The news travelled from group to group along the platform of Victoria Station, impressing our parents and kid-sisters almost as much as ourselves. A lord was coming to our prep school. A real lord. A new boy, only eight years old. Youngest son of the Duke of Downshire. A new boy, yet a lord. Lord Julius Bloodstock. Same name! Crikey!

Reprinted by permission of Curtis Brown, Ltd. From *Catacrok* by Robert Graves, copyright © 1956 by Robert Graves.

Excitement strong enough to check the rebellious tears of home-lovers, and make our last good-byes all but casual. None of us having had any contact with the peerage, it was argued by some, as we settled in our reserved Pullman carriage, that on the analogy of policemen there couldn't be boy-lords. However, Mr. Lees, the Latin Master (declined: *Lees, Lees, Lem, Lei, Lei, Lee*) confirmed the report. The lord was being driven to school that morning in the ducal Rolls-Royce. Crikey again! *Cricko, Crickere, Crikey, Crictum!*

Should we be expected to call him "your Grace," or "Sire," or something? Would he keep a coronet in his tuck-box? Would the masters dare cane him if he broke school rules or didn't know his prep?

Billington Secundus told us that his father (the famous Q.C.) had called Thos a "tuft-hunting toad-eater," as meaning that he was awfully proud of knowing important people such as bishops and Q.C.s and lords, To this Mr. Lees turned a deaf ear, though making ready to crack down on any further disrespectful remarks about the Rev. Thomas Pearce, our Headmaster. None came. Most of us were scared stiff of Thos; besides, everyone but Billington Secundus considered pride in knowing important people an innocent enough emotion.

Presently Mr. Lees folded his newspaper and said: "Bloodstock, as you will learn to call him, is a perfectly normal little chap, though he happens to have been born into the purple—if anyone present catches the allusion. Accord him neither kisses nor cuffs (*nec oscula, nec verbera*, both neuter) and all will be well. By the way, this is to be his first experience of school life. The Duke has hitherto kept him at the Castle under private tutors."

At the Castle, under private tutors! Crikey; *Crikey, Crikius, Crikissime!*

We arrived at the Cedars just in time for school dinner. Thos, rather self-consciously, led a small, pale, fair-haired boy into the dining-hall, and showed him his seat at the end of the table among the other nine new-comers. "This is Lord Julius Bloodstock, boys," he boomed. "You will just call him Bloodstock. No titles or other honorifics here."

"Then I prefer to be called Julius." His first memorable words.

"We happen to use only surnames at Brown Friars," chuckled Thos; then he said Grace.

None of Julius's table-mates called him anything at all, to begin with, being either too miserable or too shy even to say "Pass the salt, please." But after the soup, and half-way through the shepherd's pie (for once not made of left-overs) Billington Tertius, to win a bet, leant boldly across the table and asked: "Lord, why didn't you come by train, same as the rest of us?"

Julius did not answer at first, but when his neighbours nudged him, he said: "The name is Julius, and my father was afraid of finding newspaper photographers on the platform. They can be such a nuisance. Two of them were waiting for us at the school gates, and my father sent the chauffeur to smash both their cameras."

This information had hardly sunk in before the third course appeared: treacle tart. Today was Monday: onion soup, shepherd's pie and carrots, treacle tart. Always had been. Even when Mr. Lees-Lees-Lem had been a boy here and won top scholarship to Winchester. "Treacle. From the Greek *theriace*, though the Greeks did not, of course . . ." With this, Mr. Lees, who sat at the very end of the table, religiously eating treacle tart, looked up to see whether anyone were listening; and noticed that Julius had pushed away his plate, leaving the oblong of tough burned pastry untouched.

"Eat it, boy!" said Mr. Lees. "Not allowed to leave anything here for Mr. Good Manners. School rule."

"I never eat treacle tart," explained Julius with a little sigh.

"You are expected to address me as 'sir,' " said Mr. Lees.

Julius seemed surprised. "I thought we didn't use titles here, or other honorifics," he said, "but only surnames?"

"Call me 'sir,' " insisted Mr. Lees, not quite certain whether this were innocence or impertinence.

"Sir," said Julius, shrugging faintly.

"Eat your tart," snapped Mr. Lees.

"But I never eat treacle tart—sir!"

"It's my duty to see that you do so, every Monday."

Julius smiled. "What a queer duty!" he said incredulously.

Titters, cranings of necks. Then Thos called jovially down the table: "Well, Lees, what's the news from your end? Are the summer holidays reported to have been wearisomely long?"

"No, Headmaster. But I cannot persuade an impertinent boy to sample our traditional treacle tart."

"Send him up here, plate and all! Oliver Twist asking for less, eh?"

When Thos recognized Julius, his face changed and he swallowed a couple of times, but having apparently lectured the staff on making not the least difference between duke's son and shopkeeper's son, he had to put his foot down. "My dear boy," he said, "let me see you eat that excellent piece of food without further demur; and no nonsense."

"I never eat treacle tart, Headmaster."

Thos started as though he had been struck in the face. He said slowly: "You mean perhaps: 'I have lost my appetite, sir.' Very well, but your appetite will return at supper time, you mark my words—and so will the treacle tart."

The sycophantic laughter which greeted this prime Thossism surprised Julius but did not shake his poise. Walking to the buttery-table, he laid down the plate, turned on his heel, and walked calmly back to his seat.

Thos at once rose and said Grace in a challenging voice.

"Cocky ass, I'd like to punch his lordly head for him," growled Billington Secundus later that afternoon.

"You'd have to punch mine first," I said. "He's a . . . the thing we did in Gray's *Elegy*—a village Hampden. Standing up to Lees and Thos in mute inglorious protest against that foul treacle tart."

"You're a tuft-hunting toad-eater."

"I may be. But I'd rather eat toads than Thos's treacle tart."

A bell rang for supper, or high tea. The rule was that tuck-box cakes were put under Matron's charge and distributed among all fifty of us while they lasted. "Democracy," Thos called it (I can't think why); and the Matron, to cheer up the always dismal first evening, had set the largest cake she could find on the table: Julius's. Straight from the ducal kitchens, plastered with crystallized fruit, sugar icing and marzipan, stuffed with raisins, cherries and nuts.

"You will get your slice, my dear, when you have eaten your treacle tart," Matron gently reminded Julius. *"Noblesse oblige."*

"I never eat treacle tart, Matron."

It must have been hard for him to see his cake devoured by strangers before his eyes, but he made no protest; just sipped a little tea and went supperless to bed. In the dormitory he told a ghost story, which is still, I hear, current in the school after all these years: about a Mr. Gracie (why "Gracie"?) who heard hollow groans in the night, rose to investigate and was grasped from behind by an invisible hand. He found that his races had caught on the door knob; and, after other har-owing adventures, traced the groans to the bathroom, where Mrs. Gracie . . .

Lights out! Sleep. Bells for getting up; for prayers; for breakfast.

"I never eat treacle tart." So Julius had no breakfast, but we pocketed slices of bread and potted meat (Tuesday) to slip him in the playground afterwards. The school porter intervened. His orders were to see that the young gentleman had no food given him.

Bell: Latin. Bell: Maths. Bell: long break. Bell: Scripture. Bell: wash hands for dinner.

"I never eat treacle tart," said Julius, as a sort of response to Thos's Grace; and this time fainted.

Thos sent a long urgent telegram to the Duke, explaining his predicament: school rule, discipline, couldn't make excep-tions, and so forth.

The Duke wired back non-committally: "Quite so. Stop. The lad never eats treacle tart. Stop. Regards. Downshire."

Matron took Julius to the sickroom, where he was allowed milk and soup, but no solid food unless he chose to call for treacle tart. He remained firm and polite until the end, which came two days later, after a further exchange of telegrams.

We were playing kick-about near the Masters' Wing, when the Rolls-Royce pulled up. Presently Julius, in overcoat and bowler hat, descended the front steps, followed by the school porter carrying his tuck-box, football boots and hand-bag. Billington Secundus, now converted to the popular view, led our three cheers, which Julius acknowledged with a gracious tilt of his bowler. The car purred off; and thereupon, in token of our admiration for Julius, we all swore to strike against treacle tart the very next Monday, and none of us eat a single morsel, even if we liked it, which some of us did!

When it came to the point, of course, the boys sitting close to Thos took fright and ratted, one after the other. Even Billington Secundus and I, not being peers' sons or even village Hampdens, regretfully conformed.

S. J. WILSON

S. J. Wilson (1932–   ) is an American novelist, educated
from grade school through college in the city of New York.
Mr. Wilson is the author of *To Find a Man*, a novel which
was made into a movie by Columbia motion picture company.
Mr. Wilson is also engaged in the creative aspects of adver-
tising.

Miss Diamond's Difficult Day
FROM *Hurray for Me*

The dirt flew in the first barrage. It was followed by
bombardments of erasers, cheese boxes, tin cans, chalk,
paper clips, paint boxes, raffia, rolls of colored paper,
piano music sheets, story books, crayons, beanbags, the
bird's nest, blocks, Libby's imitation-leather schoolbag
whatever else in the room proved throwable.

◆◆◆

We had come to where the class line was forming when Libby
stopped and said, "Ooh, what we forgot."

"What?" I asked. She pointed to the line. Most of the
children were carrying empty cream-cheese boxes and paper
bags. Gerard Shuminsky could hardly stand under the weight
of a large potato sack and an enormous enamel bowl into
which holes had been bored.

Libby then explained that this was the day we were to do
indoor planting, that we were supposed to bring a planter and
dirt with us, and that she couldn't imagine the kind of punishment we would get for having forgotten. All I could remember was Miss Diamond's shaking the packet of seeds at

us, and nothing more. However, assuming that Gerard Shuminsky had more than enough dirt in his sack, I broke out
of line and ran back to help him in the hope he would share
some with me.

I took the bowl from him as he trailed behind, tugging at
the sack and swearing eternal friendship between gasps.

The class was in the room when we arrived. Seeing us,
Miss Diamond asked to know whose sack it was.

"It's mine," said Gerard Shuminsky proudly.

"What's in it?" she asked.

"Planting dirt," said Gerard Shuminsky, hurt that she did
not recognize at once the greater effort he had made.

"It looks to me as if you're planning to bury somebody,"
Miss Diamond said, and throwing back her head, she cackled
at the ceiling.

But instead of joining in as usual, the class became a hive.
Everyone buzzed hatred for Miss Diamond into everyone
else's ears. Gerard Shuminsky developed tears. Even the class
knew he had tried so hard.

Miss Diamond's laughter snapped in mid-sound. She went
to her desk, rapped with her ruler. "Quiet . . . quiet! What
is the meaning of this whispering?"

The class gaped at her through sullen, pouting, even rebellious faces. We all knew to what lengths Gerard Shuminsky
had gone to please her; that the only reason he wet his pants
every day just before lunchtime was because he wouldn't
raise his hand and interrupt her to ask to leave the room; that
he thought she was the most wonderful person in the world;
and that ever since she had been appointed first monitor,
Leatrice Aronowitz had become as welcome as a pebble in a
shoe.

I put the bowl down on the floor, went to my seat.

"I think we ought to bury her with it," Libby whispered
as I sat.

Miss Diamond shushed her, warned her that she was supposed to be on her very best behavior or she would insist
that her mother come to school.

Libby stood and said, "I 'pologize Miss Diamond for opening up my mouth." She curtsied, sat and quickly whispered,
"That old shtinkfoose."

Miss Diamond, who had seemingly turned her attention
to the rest of the class, barked, "What was that?"

Libby looked around and behind, her face as innocent as milk, her eyes assuring Miss Diamond that she must have heard someone else.

"Libby! Stand up!"

Libby obeyed.

"Now, what did you say?"

Twisting the ends of her neckerchief, Libby complained, "I don't know why you always pick on me like I did everything wrong in the whole class when I try to be as good as gold and maybe better. I didn't say nothing after I 'pologized so nice before. And now you say I said something and I'm always wrong and you're always right, even if someone else said it I have to be wrong. I wish the ground would open up before me so I could disappear into it. I suffer too much. I wish God doesn't leave me here to the end of my days. I am a good woman, a good mother, so if He takes the good first, why not me?"

"What are you talking about?" Miss Diamond looked lost. "What was that business about the ground opening up before you?"

"Oh, that was what my mother said before she found out my father wasn't dead."

"That, Libby Jackson," Miss Diamond spoke thunderbolts, "is all I am going to take from you now and forever." She strode across the room, grabbed Libby's arm; and as Libby tried to pull away, told Leatrice Aronowitz to keep the class in order and led a weeping, wrestling Libby from the room.

The door closed.

A blackboard eraser hit Leatrice Aronowitz. Leatrice Aronowitz demanded whoever threw it to stand up or else she would report the whole class. Another eraser sailed, missed Leatrice Aronowitz and hit Honora Wasserman. Honora Wasserman stood, looked around slowly, suspiciously, and having made up her mind who the culprit was, went to the blackboard, picked up the pointer and, charging at Gerard Shuminsky, hit him over the head. Gerard Shuminsky began to cry.

I ran over, pulled the pointer out of Honora Wasserman's fist and whipped it across her behind. Honora Wasserman screamed virtuous rage. I lashed the pointer again for Johnny's sake—and again, for luck.

A girl, I suspected Felicia Bluestone but wasn't sure, dumped a bag of dirt on my head.

Solly Mink with a great battle-rousing "Yaaaaah!" ran into Leatrice Aronowitz, knocked her down and with the help of one or two other boys, dumped dirt into her bloomers.

Not that she felt sorry for Leatrice Aronowitz, but rather in the defense of all womanhood, Marcia Weissbaum slapped her hands and stamped her foot, ordered them to release Leatrice Aronowitz at once. For her efforts, Solly Mink stuffed a handful of dirt into her mouth. Marcia Weissbaum sputtered dirt and rage, flung whatever came to hand—and the full-scale war was on.

The boys were in one camp, the girls the other. The dirt flew in the first barrage. It was followed by bombardments of erasers, cheese boxes, tin cans, chalk, paper clips, paint boxes, raffia, rolls of colored paper, piano music sheets, story-books, crayons, beanbags, the bird's nest, blocks, Libby's imitation-leather schoolbag and whatever else in the room proved throwable.

Just as the boys were beginning to show signs of conquering and as Herman Zuckerman and Generoso Puppi were stuffing Gazella Caccialanza into Gerard Shuminsky's sack, we heard Miss Diamond screech. "CHILDREN!" like a trolley making a sudden downhill stop.

We became stone.

When we had put our seats back in their places and stood penitent in front of them, Miss Diamond composed herself like a cat's fur. "You will all be punished very severely for this. And as for you, Leatrice Aronowitz—stop jigging when I'm talking to you—I cannot tell you how disappointed I am in you for not keeping this class in order. It seems to me that only Gerard knows how to keep such a bunch of ruffians in good behavior."

Gerard Shuminsky stiffened to attention. I was sorry. As long as it had lasted, I liked him better when he slumped.

"I want you all to sit on your hands," Miss Diamond continued. "And I want Gerard to stand up front right next to my desk. If anyone moves his hands from under him or says one word, I want Gerard to report him to me at once. And that person's mother will have to come to school tomorrow."

Gerard Shuminsky raised his hand to attract Miss Diamond's attention.

"What is it?" she asked.

"I can't be monitor now," he said sadly.

"Why not?"

"Because I got lots of dirt in my shoes and it hurts my feet when I stand."

"Then take your shoes off and empty them on the floor. I have to get the custodian up here anyway to clean up this horrid mess you children made."

"I can't take my shoes off," Gerard Shuminsky complained. He was very unhappy.

"Gerard," Miss Diamond asked loftily, "is this your idea of a joke?"

"No, Miss Diamond."

I thought he was going to cry.

"Then why can't you take your shoes off?"

"Because . . ." The words wouldn't come from between his lips. A tear swam up into each eye.

"Well, Gerard, speak up!"

"Because . . ." and then he quickly sputtered, "I can't tie my laces again."

"Neither can I," I volunteered.

"I can't neither," said Marcia Weissbaum.

At once the entire class admitted and confessed that they didn't know how to tie their shoelaces.

Miss Diamond rapped the desk to bring us to attention. "In that case," she said, "after the custodian cleans up—and you are going to help him—we will spend the rest of the day, if necessary, learning how to tie our shoelaces."

We applauded, and Miss Diamond smiled and bowed, smiled and bowed like old Mother Niddity Nod.

All this time I imagined Libby standing, crying in the corner of Mr. Pierce's office. During lunch, I thought of her standing, crying, starving in Mr. Pierce's office. While we were having rest period, I could see her as a crumpled heap in the corner.

We were back to sitting with shoes in our laps, practicing tying, when there was a knock on the door. Miss Diamond crossed the room with the determination of a diver striding a springboard in preparation for a difficult jump, and opened it. "Yes?" With a gracious, flowing arm she waved in Libby and her mother.

That Mrs. Jackson should finally consent to appear raised Miss Diamond's stature a mile for me. Mrs. Jackson was, as she herself would have said, "dolled up," her lips were painted, her cheeks rouged. The tips of her ears shone with the frost of diamond earrings. And she wore high heels.

Miss Diamond led the way back to her desk, pulled a chair up on the platform for Mrs. Jackson, invited her to sit; and they bit and chewed words as if they had the opposite ends of a frankfurter in their mouths and were gobbling toward its middle. At times, Mrs. Jackson would glare at Libby, who stood in front of the desk as unconcerned as sunshine.

After the face-to-face conference was over, both women rose sighing with satisfaction. Mrs. Jackson stepped from the platform and, loud enough for us to all hear, told Libby that she now had the "whole picktchoor."

Libby replied, "You do?"

"Yairse, I do," her mother countered. "And I orlso know how to straighten it owt!" She bowed once more to Miss Diamond and left tipper-tricking on her high heels.

JAMES JOYCE

James Joyce (1842–1941) was born into a lower-middle-class family in Dublin. There was no hint in his background that he would become one of the most significant writers of his time. His father was an undistinguished civil servant more interested in drinking and arguing about politics than in reading literature. His mother, although more artistically inclined, had, unlike her son, a conventional mind.

Young Joyce got through a thorough Jesuit education at Clongowes Wood School and later at Belvedere College and University College in Dublin. While in school, he thought he might become a priest, but upon graduation in 1902, he turned his back, like his creation Stephen Dedalus, on home, religion, and country.

The originality of Joyce's style and his realistic, antiromantic view of Irish life made it difficult for him to get his work published. *Ulysses*, Joyce's crowning achievement in the novel, was published in 1922 only with the help of friends. Joyce's most startlingly original work, *Finnegans Wake*, appeared in book form in 1939. Because the increasing complexity of his style attracted only sophisticated readers, Joyce was never able to support himself and his family by his writing.

Joyce was forced to endure a series of extremely painful and only partially successful eye operations. Although his last years brought him some measure of fame among his more literate contemporaries, this period was marred by his increasing blindness, concern for his mentally ill daughter, and the approach of World War II. Joyce died in Zurich.

The Caning

FROM *A Portrait of the Artist as a Young Man*

Stephen closed his eyes and held out in the air his trembling hand with the palm upwards. He felt the prefect of studies touch it for a moment at the fingers to straighten it and then the swish of the sleeve . . . as the pandybat was lifted to strike.

———◆◆◆———

The door opened quietly and closed. A quick whisper ran through the class: the prefect of studies. There was an instant of dead silence and then the loud crack of a pandybat on the last desk. Stephen's heart leapt up in fear.

—Any boys want flogging here, Father Arnall? cried the prefect of studies. Any lazy idle loafers that want flogging in this class?

He came to the middle of the class and saw Fleming on his knees.

—Hoho! he cried. Who is this boy? Why is he on his knees? What is your name, boy?

—Fleming, sir.

—Hoho, Fleming! An idler of course. I can see it in your eye. Why is he on his knees, Father Arnall?

—He wrote a bad Latin theme, Father Arnall said, and he missed all the questions in grammar.

—Of course he did! cried the prefect of studies, of course he did! A born idler! I can see it in the corner of his eye.

He banged his pandybat down on the desk and cried:

—Up, Fleming! Up, my boy!

Fleming stood up slowly.

—Hold out! cried the prefect of studies.

Fleming held out his hand. The pandybat came down on it with a loud smacking sound: one, two, three, four, five, six.

—Other hand!

The pandybat came down again in six loud quick smacks.

—Kneel down! cried the prefect of studies.

Fleming knelt down squeezing his hands under his armpits, his face contorted with pain, but Stephen knew how hard his hands were because Fleming was always rubbing rosin into them. But perhaps he was in great pain for the noise of the pandybat was terrible. Stephen's heart was beating and fluttering.

—At your work, all of you! shouted the prefect of studies. We want no lazy idle loafers here, lazy idle little schemers. At your work, I tell you. Father Dolan will be in to see you every day. Father Dolan will be in tomorrow.

He poked one of the boys in the side with the pandybat, saying:

—You, boy! When will Father Dolan be in again?

—Tomorrow, sir, said Tom Furlong's voice.

—Tomorrow and tomorrow and tomorrow, said the prefect of studies. Make up your minds for that. Every day Father Dolan. Write away. You, boy, who are you?

Stephen's heart jumped suddenly.

—Dedalus, sir.

—Why are you not writing like the others?

—I . . . my . . .

He could not speak with fright.

—Why is he not writing, Father Arnall?

—He broke his glasses, said Father Arnall, and I exempted him from work.

—Broke? What is this I hear? What is this? Your name is? said the prefect of studies.

—Dedalus, sir.

—Out here, Dedalus. Lazy little schemer. I see schemer in your face. Where did you break your glasses?

Stephen stumbled into the middle of the class, blinded by fear and haste.

—Where did you break your glasses? repeated the prefect of studies.

—The cinderpath, sir.

—Hoho! The cinderpath! cried the prefect of studies. I know that trick.

Stephen lifted his eyes in wonder and saw for a moment Father Dolan's whitegrey not young face, his baldy whitegrey head with fluff at the sides of it, the steel rims of his spectacles and his nocoloured eyes looking through the glasses. Why did he say he knew that trick?

—Lazy idle little loafer! cried the prefect of studies. Broke my glasses! An old schoolboy trick! Out with your hand this moment!

Stephen closed his eyes and held out in the air his trembling hand with the palm upwards. He felt the prefect of studies touch it for a moment at the fingers to straighten it and then the swish of the sleeve of the soutane as the pandybat was lifted to strike. A hot burning stinging tingling blow like the loud crack of a broken stick made his trembling hand crumple together like a leaf in the fire: and at the sound and the pain scalding tears were driven into his eyes. His whole body was shaking with fright, his arm was shaking and his crumpled burning livid hand shook like a loose leaf in the air. A cry sprang to his lips, a prayer to be let off. But though the tears scalded his eyes and his limbs quivered with pain and fright he held back the hot tears and the cry that scalded his throat.

—Other hand! shouted the prefect of studies.

Stephen drew back his maimed and quivering right arm and held out his left hand. The soutane sleeve swished again as the pandybat was lifted and a loud crashing sound and a fierce maddening tingling burning pain made his hand shrink together with the palms and fingers in a livid quivering mass. The scalding water burst forth from his eyes and, burning with shame and agony and fear, he drew back his shaking arm in terror and burst out into a whine of pain. His body shook with a palsy of fright and in shame and rage he felt the scalding cry come from his throat and the scalding tears falling out of his eyes and down his flaming cheeks.

—Kneel down! cried the prefect of studies.

Stephen knelt down quickly pressing his beaten hands to his sides. To think of them beaten and swollen with pain all in a moment made him feel so sorry for them as if they were not his own but someone else's that he felt sorry for. And as he knelt, calming the last sobs in his throat and feeling the burning tingling pain pressed into his hands, he thought of the hands which he had held out in the air with the palms up and of the firm touch of the prefect of studies when he had steadied the shaking fingers and of the beaten swollen reddened mass of palm and fingers that shook helplessly in the air.

NIKOS KAZANTZAKIS

Nikos Kazantzakis (1883–1957), Greek poet and novelis
was born in Crete. After getting his law degree in Athen
he traveled widely. Between 1919 and 1947 he held a variet
of governmental posts. In the middle and late 1920's he con
verted to Communism and made three pilgrimages to Russi
but he soon became disenchanted with the restraints and th
unresolvable conflicts he saw in the Russian system.

Kazantzakis' thinking and writing were much influence
by Bergson and Nietzsche. He saw himself as a kind of mod
ern Odysseus: "I am a mariner of Odysseus with heart o
fire but with mind ruthless and clear."

Kazantzakis' reputation rests on the creative output of th
last eleven years of his life. His important works includ
Zorba the Greek (1946), which introduced him to America
audiences; *The Greek Passion* (1948); *The Temptation o
Christ* (1951); and *Report to Greco* (1956).

The First Schoolday
FROM *Report to Greco*

"This is my son," my father said.
Untangling my hand from his own, he turned me over to
the teacher.
"His bones are mine, his flesh is yours. Don't feel sorry
for him. Thrash him and make a man of him."

❖

With my ever-magic eye, my buzzing bee- and honey-filled
mind, a red woolen cap on my head and sandals with red
pompons on my feet, I set out one morning, half delighted,

lf dismayed. My father held me by the hand; my mother
ad given me a sprig of basil (I was supposed to gain courage
y smelling it) and hung my golden baptismal cross around
y neck.

"God's blessings upon you, and my blessings too," she
urmured, looking at me proudly.

I was like a small sacrificial victim weighted down with
rnaments. Within me I felt both pride and fear, but my
and was wedged deeply in my father's grasp, and I bore
yself with manly courage. We marched and marched
rrough the narrow lanes, reached Saint Minas's, turned, and
ntered an old building with a wide courtyard. Four great
ooms occupied the corners and a dust-covered plane tree the
niddle. I hesitated, turning coward; my hand had begun to
remble in the large warm palm.

Bending over, my father touched my hair and patted me.
gave a start, for as far as I could remember, this was the
rst time he had ever caressed me. Lifting my eyes, I glanced
t him fearfully. He saw that I was afraid and withdrew his
and.

"You're going to learn to read and write here so you can
ecome a man," he said. "Cross yourself."

The teacher appeared in the doorway. He was holding a
ong switch and seemed like a savage to me, a savage with
uge fangs. I pinned my eyes on the top of his head to see
f he had horns. But I was unable to see, because he was
wearing a hat.

"This is my son," my father said.

Untangling my hand from his own, he turned me over to
he teacher.

"His bones are mine, his flesh is yours. Don't feel sorry for
im. Thrash him and make a man of him."

"Don't worry, Captain Michael," said the teacher, pointing
o his switch. "Right here is the tool which makes men."

A pile of heads remains fixed in my memory from those
elementary school days, a pile of children's heads glued one to
he next like skulls. Most of them must actually have become
skulls by now. But remaining in me above and beyond those
heads, undying, are my four teachers.

Paterópoulos in the first grade: a little old man, very short,
ierce-eyed, with drooping mustache, and the switch constantly in hand. He hunted us down, collected us, then set us
out in a row as though we were ducks and he were taking us

to market to sell. "The bones are mine, the flesh is your
Teacher," every father instructed him as he turned over h
wild goat of a son. "Thrash him, thrash him until he become
a man." And he thrashed us pitilessly. All of us, teacher an
students alike, awaited the day when these many beating
would turn us into men. When I grew older and philanthrop
theories began to mislead my mind, I termed this metho
barbarous. But when I came to know human nature sti
better, I blessed, and still bless, Paterópoulos's holy switch
It was this that taught us that suffering is the greatest guid
along the ascent which leads from animal to man.

Tityros—"What-cheese"—reigned over the second grad
reigned, poor fellow, but did not govern. He was pale, wit
spectacles, starched collar and shirt, pointed down-at-hee
patent leather shoes, a huge hairy nose, and slender finger
yellowed from tobacco. His real name wasn't What-cheese
it was Papadákis. But one day his father, who was the prie
in an outlying village, came to town bringing him a larg
head of cheese as a present. "What cheese is this, Father?
said the son [pompously using academic rather than popula
Greek for this homely question]. A neighbor happened to b
at the house. She overheard, spread the word, and the poo
teacher was roasted over the coals and given this nickname
What-cheese did not thrash, he entreated. He used to rea
us *Robinson Crusoe*, explaining each and every word. The
he gazed at us with tenderness and anguish, as though beg
ging us to understand. But we were thumbing through th
book and gazing ecstatically at the poorly printed pictures o
tropical forests, trees with great fat leaves, Robinson in hi
broad-brimmed straw hat with an expanse of deserted ocea
on all sides. Bringing out his tobacco pouch, poor What
cheese would roll a cigarette to smoke during recess, lool
at us imploringly, and wait.

One day when we were doing Sacred History, we came t
Esau, who sold his birthright to Jacob for a pottage of lentils
When I went home for dinner, I asked my father what birth
right meant. "Go ask Uncle Nikoláki," he said, scratchin,
his head and coughing.

This uncle had finished elementary school, which mad
him the family's most educated member. He was my mother'
brother: a stubby little Tom Thumb, bald, with large timor
ous eyes and monstrous hands all covered with hair. He ha
married above him, and his jaundiced, venom-nosed wife fel

nothing but scorn for him. She was also jealous. Every night
he tied his foot to the bedpost with rope to keep him from
getting up during the night and going to visit their plump
big-breasted servant, who slept downstairs. In the morning
he released him. My poor uncle endured this martyrdom for
five years, but then the Lord willed that the venom-nosed
should die (this is why we call Him the All-good) and this
time my uncle married a solid, kindhearted, foul-mouthed
peasant girl, who did not tie him. He used to come to our
house, all elated, and find my mother.

"How are you getting along now with your new wife,
Nikoláki?" she inquired.

"Marghí, no need to ask how happy I am! She doesn't tie
me."

Afraid of my father, he never lifted his eyes to look him
in the face but gazed constantly at the street door, rubbing
his hairy hands together. On this day, as soon as he heard
that Captain Michael was calling him, he rose from table
with his mouth still full of food and sped to our house.

What could the ogre want with me now? he asked himself
with irritation, swallowing his last mouthful. How does my
poor sister stand him? Recalling his first wife, he smiled con-
tentedly and murmured, "I, at least, was saved. Praise the
Lord!"

"Come here," my father said as soon as he saw him. "You
went to school. Explain this."

The two of them held council, bending over the book.

"Birthright means hunting costume," said my father after
much reflection.

My uncle shook his head.

"I think it means musket," he objected. But his voice was
trembling.

"Hunting costume," roared my father. He knitted his
brows, and my uncle cowered.

The next day the teacher asked, "What does birthright
mean?"

I jumped up. "Hunting costume."

"What nonsense! What ignorant fool told you that?"

"My father."

The teacher quailed. Afraid like everyone else of my father,
how could he dream of contradicting him?

"Yes," he said, swallowing hard, "yes, certainly, sometimes, but very rarely, it can mean hunting costume. Here,
however . . ."

Sacred History was my favorite subject. It was a stran[ge] intricate and somber fairy tale with serpents who talke[d] floods and rainbows, thefts and murders. Brother kill[ed] brother, a father wanted to slaughter his only son, God inte[r]vened every two minutes and did His share of killing, peop[le] crossed the sea without wetting their feet.

We did not understand. We asked the teacher, and [he] coughed, raised his switch angrily, and shouted, "Stop th[is] impertinence! How many times do I have to tell you—[no] talking!"

"But we don't understand, sir," we whined.

"These are God's doings," the teacher answered. "We'[re] not supposed to understand. It's a sin!"

A sin! We heard that terrible word and shrank back [in] fright. It wasn't a word, it was a serpent, the same serpe[nt] that had beguiled Eve, and it was coming down from th[e] teacher's platform and opening its mouth in order to eat u[s]. We shrank into our desks and did not utter a sound.

Another word which horrified me when I first heard it w[as] *Abraham*. Those two *ah*'s reverberated inside me; they seeme[d] to come from far away, out of some deep, dark, and dange[r]ous well. I whispered "Abraham, Abraham" secretly to myse[lf] and heard footsteps and panting behind me—someone wit[h] huge bare feet was pursuing me. When I learned that he ha[d] taken his son one day in order to slaughter him, I becam[e] terror-stricken. Without a doubt he was the one who slaugh[-] tered little children, and I hid behind the back of my des[k] to keep him from discovering me and carrying me off. Whe[n] the teacher told us that whoever follows God's commmand[-] ments goes to Abraham's bosom, I swore inwardly to trans[-] gress all the commandments in order to save myself fro[m] that bosom.

I felt the identical agitation when, in the same subjec[t] Sacred History, I first heard the word *Habakkuk*. This wor[d] also seemed extremely dark to me. Habakkuk was a bogeyma[n] who came to lurk in our courtyard every time the darknes[s] fell (I knew just where he crouched: behind the well). Onc[e] when I dared to venture all alone into the yard at night, h[e] sprang from behind the well, reached out his hand, an[d] shouted at me: "Habakkuk!" In other words, "Stop! I'[m] going to eat you!"

The sound of certain words excited me terribly—it wa[s] fear I felt most often, not joy. Especially Hebrew words, fo[r]

I knew from my grandmother that on Good Friday the Jews took Christian children, tossed them into a trough lined with spikes, and drank their blood. Oftentimes it seemed to me that a Hebrew word from the Old Testament—and above all the word *Jehovah*—was a spikelined trough and that someone wanted to throw me in.

In the third grade we had Periander Krasákis. What merciless godfather gave the name of Corinth's savage tyrant to this sickly runt of a man with his high starched collar to conceal the scrofula on his neck, his skinny grasshopper legs, the little handkerchief always at his mouth so that he could spit, spit, and spit as though breathing his last? This one had a mania for cleanliness. Every day he inspected our hands, ears, nose, teeth, and nails. He did not thrash, did not entreat; he shook his oversized head which was covered with pimples, and shouted at us:

"Beasts! Pigs! If you don't wash every day with soap, you'll never, never become men. You know what being a man means? It means washing with soap. Brains aren't enough, you poor devils, soap is needed too. How are you going to appear before God with hands like that? Go out to the yard and get washed."

He drove us to distraction for hours on end—which vowels were long, which short, whether to use an acute or circumflex accent—while we listened to the voices in the street—vegetable mongers, kouloúri boys, donkeys braying, women laughing—and waited for the bell to ring so that we could escape. We watched the teacher sweating away at his desk as he repeated the points of grammar over and over again in an effort to make them stick in our minds. But our thoughts were outside in the sun, on pebble warfare. We adored this game and often came to school with broken heads.

One divine spring day the windows were open. A tangerine tree was in bloom across the street, and its perfume entered the classroom. Each of our minds had turned into a blossoming tangerine tree; we could not bear to hear anything more about acute and circumflex accents. A bird came just then, perched on the plane tree in the schoolyard and began to sing. At that point a pale redheaded student who had arrived that year from his village, Nikoliós by name, was unable to control himself. He raised his finger.

"Be quiet, sir," he cried. "Be quiet and let us hear the bird."

Poor Periander Krasákis! One day we buried him. He h
rested his head calmly on his desk, palpitated a moment li
a fish, and given up the ghost. Terror-stricken at the sight
death right in front of our eyes, we rushed screaming in
the yard. The next day we donned our Sunday clothes, wash
our hands carefully (in order not to deny him anything
that point) and took him to the old cemetery by the sea.
was springtime; the heavens were laughing, the soil smell
of camomile. The coffin lay uncovered. The dead man's fa
was full of oozing pimples; it had begun to turn green a
yellow. And when his students leaned over one by one to gi
him the parting kiss, the spring no longer smelled of camomil
but of rotting flesh.

In grade four we had the principal of the school, who bo
reigned and governed. He was short, as tubby as a stora,
jar, and had a small pointed beard, gray eyes that were alwa
angry, and bowlegs. "Good God, just look at his legs," w
used to say to each other in hushed voices so that he wou
not hear. "Just look how they wrap around each other. Ar
listen to him cough. He isn't a Cretan!" He had come to
from Athens, freshly educated, apparently bringing Ne
Pedagogy with him. We thought it must be some woma
named Pedagogy [the word *new* in Greek can also mea
young woman], but when we confronted him for the fir
time, he was alone. Pedagogy wasn't there; she must hav
stayed at home. He was holding a small braided cowhide. H
lined us up and began to lecture us. We must see and touc
whatever we learned, he said, or else draw it on some pap
covered with dots. And we were to look sharp. He wasn
going to stand for any nonsense, not even laughing and shou
ing during recess. We were to keep our arms crossed, ar
whenever we saw a priest in the street, kiss his hand. "Loc
sharp, poor devils, because otherwise—see this?" He pointe
to the cowhide. "I'm not just talking; you'll see that I mea
business!" And indeed we did see. When we were disorderl
or when he felt in a bad mood, he unbuttoned us, lower
our shorts, and thrashed our bare skin with the cowhid
And when he was too lazy to undo the buttons, he lashed
across the ears until blood flowed.

One day I fortified my heart, raised my finger, and aske
"Teacher, where is New Pedagogy? Why doesn't she come
school?"

He bounded out of his chair and removed the cowhide from its hook on the wall.

"Come here, you impudent brat," he cried. "Unbutton your pants!"

He was too lazy to do it himself.

"Here! Here! Here!" he bellowed as he struck. When he had worked up a sweat, he stopped.

"That's where New Pedagogy is," he said. "Next time shut up!"

But he was also a sly little devil, this husband of New Pedagogy. One day he said to us, "Tomorrow I'm going to tell you about Christopher Columbus, how he discovered America. But so you'll understand better I want each of you to be holding an egg in his hands, and whoever doesn't have an egg at home, let him bring some butter."

He had a daughter of marriageable age named Terpsichore: short, but very delectable. Though she had many suitors, he did not want her to marry. "I won't have any such abominations in my house," he used to say. And when the toms came out in January and began miaowing on the pantiles, he got a ladder, climbed onto the roof, and chased them away. "Nature be damned," he murmured, "it has no morals."

On Good Friday he took us to church to do obeisance to the Crucified. Afterwards he brought us back to school to explain what we had seen, whom we had worshiped, and what crucifixion meant. We fell into formation in our seats, tired and disgusted because we had eaten nothing that day except sour lemons and had drunk nothing except vinegar so that we too might taste Christ's suffering. Whereupon, New Pedagogy's spouse began in a deeply solemn voice to explain how God descended to earth, how he became Christ, suffered, and was crucified in order to deliver us from sin. Exactly what this sin was we did not understand very clearly, but we did understand clearly that he had twelve disciples, one of whom—Judas—had betrayed him.

"And Judas was like . . . like whom?"

The teacher left his platform and began to proceed slowly, threateningly, from desk to desk, eying us one by one.

"Judas was like . . . like . . ."

His index finger was extended; he shifted it from pupil to pupil, trying to find which of us Judas was like. We all quailed and trembled lest the terrible finger come to rest upon us. Suddenly the teacher emitted a cry, and his finger halted at a pallid, poorly dressed boy with beautiful reddish-blond hair. It was Nikoliós, the same who the year before in third grade had called out. "'Be quiet, Teacher, and let us hear the bird."

"There, like Nikoliós!" cried the teacher. "Identical! The same pallor, the same clothes. And Judas had red hair. Deep red, like the flames of hell!"

When poor Nikoliós heard this, he burst into tears. The rest of us, no longer in danger, eyed him with ferociously hateful glances and passed the word secretly from desk to desk that as soon as school was out we would beat him to a pulp because he had betrayed Christ.

Satisfied at having followed New Pedagogy and shown us tangibly what Judas was like, the teacher dismissed the class. We hemmed Nikoliós in as soon as we reached the street and began to spit on him and beat him up. He ran off in tears, but we pursued him with stones, jeering "Judas! Judas!" at him until he reached his home and slipped inside.

Nikoliós never appeared again in class, never set foot again in school. Thirty years later, when I had returned to Crete after my stay in Europe, there was a knock on our door. It was Holy Saturday. My father had ordered us all new shoes for Easter, and a pale, feeble man with red hair and beard stood on the threshold. He was delivering the shoes, which were neatly wrapped in a colored cloth. He stood shyly on the threshold, looked at me, and shook his head.

"Don't you know me?" he said. "Don't you remember me?" And as he said this, I recognized him.

"It's Nikoliós!" I cried, clasping him in my arms.

"Judas," he said, and he smiled bitterly.

ELIE WIESEL

Elie Wiesel (1928–   ) was born in Sighet, Romania, and educated at the Sorbonne and the University of Paris. He served as foreign correspondent in Israel, Paris, and New York since 1949 for *Yedioth Ahronoth* (Tel Aviv), *L'Arche* (Paris), and the *Jewish Daily Forward* (New York).

All of Wiesel's writings are translated from the French: *Night* (1960), *The Accident* (1960), *The Gates of the Forest* (1966), *Legends of Our Time* (1968), *Zalmen of the Madness of God* (1968), and *The Jews of Silence: A Personal Report on Soviet Jewry* (1966).

Wiesel was a prisoner in a Nazi concentration camp, where he saw his family die. The personal and cosmic significance of the Holocaust are central themes in all his writings. In a sense, Wiesel is the hero of all his books. The constant leitmotif that runs through his writings is that "man's greatest sin is his apathy toward evil."

My Teachers
FROM *Legends of Our Time*

. . . the act of writing is for me often nothing more than the secret or conscious desire to carve words on a tombstone: to the memory of a town forever vanished, to the memory of a childhood in exile, to the memory of all those I loved and who, before I could tell them I loved them, went away.

My teachers were among them.

❖❖❖

For some, literature is a bridge linking childhood to death. While the one gives rise to anguish, the other invites nostalgia. The deeper the nostalgia and the more complete the fear, the purer, the richer the word and the secret.

But for me writing is a *matzeva*, an invisible tombstone, erected to the memory of the dead unburied. Each word corresponds to a face, a prayer, the one needing the other so as not to sink into oblivion.

This is because the Angel of Death too early crossed my childhood, marking it with his seal. Sometimes I think I see him, his look victorious, not at the end of the journey but at its starting point. He fuses into the very beginning, the first élan, rather than into the abyss which cradles the future.

Thus, I evoke the solitary victor with nostalgia, almost without fear. Perhaps this is because I belong to an uprooted generation, deprived of cemeteries to visit the day after the New Year, when, according to custom, we fall across the graves and commune with our dead. My generation has been robbed of everything, even of our cemeteries.

I left my native town in the spring of 1944. It was a beautiful day. The surrounding mountains, in their verdure, seemed taller than usual. Our neighbors were out strolling in their shirt-sleeves. Some turned their heads away, others sneered.

After the war I had several opportunities to return. Temptation was not lacking, each reasonable: to see which friends had survived, to dig up the belongings and valuable objects we had hidden the night before our departure, to take possession once again, even fleetingly, of our property, of our past.

I did not return. I began to wander across the world, knowing all the while that to run away was useless: all roads lead home. It remains the only fixed point in this seething world. At times I tell myself that I have never really left the place where I was born, where I learned to walk and to love: the whole universe is but an extension of that little town, somewhere in Transylvania, called Màrmarosszighet.

Later, as student or journalist, I was to encounter in the course of my wanderings strange and sometimes inspiring men who were playing their parts or creating them: writers, thinkers, poets, troubadours of the apocalypse. Each gave me something for my journey: a phrase, a wink, an enigma. And I was able to continue.

But at the moment of *Heshbon-Hanefesh*, of making an

accounting, I recognized that my real teachers are waiting, to guide and urge me forward, not in awesome, distant places, but in the tiny classrooms filled with shadows and with song, where a boy I used to resemble still studies the first page of the first tractate of the Talmud, certain of finding there answers to all questions. Better: all answers *and* all questions.

Thus, the act of writing is for me often nothing more than the secret or conscious desire to carve words on a tombstone: to the memory of a town forever vanished, to the memory of a childhood in exile, to the memory of all those I loved and who, before I could tell them I loved them, went away.

My teachers were among them.

The first was an old man, heavy-set, with a white beard, a roguish eye and anemic lips. His name escapes me. In fact, I never knew it. In town, people referred to him as "the teacher from Betize," doubtless because he came from the village of that name. He was the first to speak to me lovingly about language. He put his heart and soul into each syllable, each punctuation mark. The Hebrew alphabet made up the frame and content of his life, contained his joys and disappointments, his ambitions and memories. Outside the twenty-two letters of the sacred tongue, nothing existed for him. He would say to us with tenderness: "The Torah, my children, what is it? A treasure chest filled with gold and precious stones. To open it you need a key. I will give it to you, make good use of it. The key, my children, what is it? The alphabet. So repeat after me, with me, aloud, louder: *Aleph, bet, gimmel!* Once more, and again, my children, repeat with force, with pride: *Aleph, bet, gimmel.* In that way the key will forever be part of your memory, of your future: *Aleph, bet, gimmel.*"

It was "Zeide the Melamed" who later taught me Bible and, the following year, Rashi's commentaries. Eternally in mourning, this taciturn teacher, with his bushy black beard, filled us with uneasiness mixed with fear. We thought him severe if not cruel. He never hesitated to rap the knuckles of anyone who came late or distorted the meaning of a sentence. "It's for your own good," he used to explain. He was quick to fly into a rage and whenever he did we lowered our heads and, trembling, waiting for the lull. But he was, in truth, a tormented and sentimental man. While punishing a recalcitrant

pupil he suffered; he did not allow it to show because he did
not want us to think him weak. He revealed himself only to
God. Why was so much slander spread about him? Why was
he credited with a meanness he did not have? Perhaps because he was hunchbacked, because he lowered his eyes when
he spoke. The children, who unwittingly frightened him, like
to believe that ugliness is the ally of meanness if not its
expression.

His school was in a ramshackle house, at the end of the
court, and consisted of only two rooms. He held forth in the
first. In the other, his assistant, a young scholar named
Itzhak, opened for us the heavy doors of the Oral Tradition.
We began with the tractate of *Baba-Metzia:* it dealt with a
dispute between two persons who found a garment, to whom
did it belong? Itzhak read a message and we repeated it in
the customary *niggun.* By the end of the semester we were
able to absorb an entire page a week. Next year came the
study of the *Tossafot,* which comment on the commentaries.
And our brains, slowly sharpening, pierced the meaning of
each word, released the illumination it has contained for as
long as the world has been world. Who came closest to that
light: the school of Shammai, the intransigent? or that of
Hillel, his interlocutor and rival? Both. All trees are nour-
ished by the same sap. Yet I felt closer to the House of
Hillel; it strove to make life more tolerable, the quest more
worthwhile.

At the age of ten I left Itzhak and became a student of
the "Selishter Rebbe," a morose character with wild eyes, a
raucous, brutal voice. In his presence no one dared open his
mouth or fall into daydream. He terrorized us. Whenever he
distributed slaps—which happened often, and often for no
reason—he did so with all his strength; and he had strength
to spare. That was his method of enforcing discipline and
preparing us for the Jewish condition.

At twilight, between *Minhah* and *Maariv* prayers, he used
to force us to listen as he read a chapter from the literature
of *Mussar.* As he described the tortures suffered by the sinner
in his grave, even before appearing before the heavenly tri-
bunal, sobs would shake his entire body. He would stop and
bury his head in his hands. It was as if he experienced the
pangs of the last judgment in advance. I shall never forget
his detailed descriptions of hell which, in his naïveté, he situated in a precise spot, in the heavens.

On the Sabbath he became a different person, almost unrecognizable. He made his appearance at the synagogue opposite the Little Market. Standing next to the stove to the right of the entrance, looking hunted, he lost himself in prayer, seeing no one. I would greet him but he did not respond. He would not hear me. It was as if he no longer knew who I was, or that I was there at all. The seventh day of the week he consecrated to the creator and he saw nothing of what surrounded him, not even himself. He prayed in silence, apart; he did not follow the cantor, his lips scarcely moved. A distant sadness hovered over his distracted gaze. Weekdays, I was less afraid of him.

I had decided to change schools and I became the student of three successive teachers; they too were natives of nearby villages.

Their attitude was more humane. We already considered ourselves "grownups" who could take on a *sugya*, even a difficult passage, without assistance. Every now and then, when at an impasse, we would ask them to show us how to continue; the moment the problems posed in the commentaries of the *Marsha* or the *Maharam* were unraveled, their swift clarity dazzled us. To emerge suddenly from the entanglement of a Talmudic thought always brought me intense joy; each time I would find myself on the threshold of a luminous, indestructible universe, and I used to think that over and beyond the centuries and the funeral-pyres, there is always a bridge that leads somewhere.

Then the Germans invaded our little town and the nostalgic singing of the pupils and their teachers was interrupted. To hear it once more, I would give all I possess, all that has been promised me.

From time to time I sit down again with a tractate of the Talmud. And a paralyzing fear comes over me: it is not that I have forgotten the words, I would still know how to translate them, even to comment on them. But to speak them does not suffice: they must be sung and I no longer know how. Suddenly my body stiffens, my glance falters, I am afraid to turn around: behind me my masters are gathered, their breath burning, they are waiting, as they did long ago at examination time, for me to read aloud and demonstrate to the past generations that their song never dies. My masters are waiting and I am ashamed to make them wait. I am ashamed, for they have not forgotten the song. In them the song has remained alive, more powerful than the forces that annihilated them, more obstinate than the wind that scattered their ashes. I want to plead with them to return to their graves, no longer to interfere with the living. But they have nowhere to go; heaven and earth have rejected them. And so, not to humiliate them, I force myself to read a first sentence, then I reread it in order to open it, close it again, before joining it to the next. My voice does not rise above a murmur. I have betrayed them: I no longer know how to sing.

With but a single exception, all my masters perished in the death factories invented and perfected for the glory of the national German genius.

I saw them, unshaved, emaciated, bent; I saw them make their way, one sunny Sunday, toward the railroad station, destination unknown. I saw "Zeide the Melamed," his too-heavy bundle bruising his shoulders. I was astonished: to think that this poor wanderer had once terrorized us. And the "Selishter Rebbe," I saw him too in the middle of the herd, absorbed in his own private world as if in a hurry to arrive more quickly. I thought: his face has taken on the expression of Shabbat, and yet it is Sunday. He was not weeping, his eyes no longer shot forth fire; perhaps at last he was going to discover the truth—yes, hell does exist, just as this fire exists in the night.

And so for the tenth time I read the same passage in the same book, and my masters, by their silence, indicate their disapproval: I have lost the key they entrusted me.

Today other books hold me in their grip and I try to learn from other storytellers how to pierce the meaning of an experience and transform it into legend. But most of them talk too much. Their song is lost in words, like rivers in the sand.

It was the "Selishter Rebbe" who told me one day: "Be careful with words, they're dangerous. Be wary of them. They beget either demons or angels. It's up to you to give life to one or the other. Be careful, I tell you, nothing is as dangerous as giving free rein to words."

At times I feel him standing behind me, rigid and severe. He reads over my shoulder what I am trying to say; he looks and judges whether his disciple enriches man's world or impoverishes it, whether he calls forth angels, or on the contrary kneels before demons of innumerable names.

Were the "Selishter Rebbe" with his wild eyes not standing behind me, I should perhaps have written these lines differently; it is also possible that I have written nothing.

Perhaps I, his disciple, am nothing more than his tombstone.

JOHN O'HARA

John O'Hara (1905–1970), American novelist and short
story writer, was born in Pottsville, Pennsylvania, and brought
up as a Catholic. The untimely death of his father prevented
O'Hara's going to Yale. His early employment included such
varied jobs as ship steward, railroad freight clerk, gas-meter
reader, and guard in an amusement park.

O'Hara's newspaper career took him from reporter on
two Pennsylvania papers to the *Mirror, Morning Telegraph,*
and *Herald Tribune* in New York. He worked as movie
critic and as football editor of *The New Yorker*. He also
wrote for *Time* and served as screenwriter for four moving-
picture companies. His first novel, *Appointment in Samarra*
(1934), brought him success and critical acclaim, and his
most ambitious work, *A Rage to Live* (1949), was very popular. His style is vigorous and immensely readable.

Do You Like It Here?

". . . I say to you, I do not know who stole this watch,
or who returned it to my rooms. But by God, Roberts,
I'm going to find out. I'm going to find out, if it's the
last thing I do. If it's the last thing I do. That's all,
Roberts. You may go."

———◆◆◆———

The door was open. The door had to be kept open during
study period, so there was no knock, and Roberts was startled
when a voice he knew and hated said, "Hey, Roberts. Wanted
in Van Ness's office." The voice was Hughes's.

"What for?" said Roberts.

"Why don't you go and find out what for, Dopey?" said
Hughes.

"Phooey on you," said Roberts.

From *The O'Hara Generation*, published by Random House in 1969.
Reprinted by permission of Random House, Inc. Originally published
in *The New Yorker*.

"Phooey on *you*," said Hughes, and left.

Roberts got up from the desk. He took off his eyeshade and put on a tie and coat. He left the light burning.

Van Ness's office, which was *en suite* with his bedroom, was on the ground floor of the dormitory, and on the way down Roberts wondered what he had done. It got so after a while, after going to so many schools, that you recognized the difference between being "wanted in Somebody's office" and "Somebody wants to see you." If a master wanted to see you on some minor matter, it didn't always mean that you had to go to his office; but if it was serious, they always said, "You're wanted in Somebody's office." That meant Somebody would be in his office, waiting for you, waiting specially for you. Roberts didn't know why this difference existed, but it did, all right. Well, all he could think of was that he had been smoking in the shower room, but Van Ness never paid much attention to that. Everybody smoked in the shower room, and Van Ness never did anything about it unless he just happened to catch you.

For minor offences Van Ness would speak to you when he made his rounds of the rooms during study period. He would walk slowly down the corridor, looking in at each room to see that the proper occupant, and no one else, was there; and when he had something to bawl you out about, something unimportant, he would consult a list he carried, and he would stop in and bawl you out about it and tell you what punishment went with it. That was another detail that made the summons to the office a little scary.

Roberts knocked on Van Ness's half-open door and a voice said, "Come in."

Van Ness was sitting at his typewriter, which was on a small desk beside the large desk. He was in a swivel chair and when he saw Roberts he swung around, putting himself behind the large desk, like a damn judge.

He had his pipe in his mouth and he seemed to look over the steel rims of his spectacles. The light caught his Phi Beta Kappa key, which momentarily gleamed as though it had diamonds in it.

"Hughes said you wanted me to report here," said Roberts.

"I did," said Van Ness. He took his pipe out of his mouth and began slowly to knock the bowl empty as he repeated, "I did." He finished emptying his pipe before he again spoke. He took a long time about it, and Roberts, from his years of experience, recognized that as torture tactics. They always

made you wait to scare you. It was sort of like the third degree. The horrible damn thing was that it always did scare
you a little, even when you were used to it.

Van Ness leaned back in his chair and stared through his
glasses at Roberts. He cleared his throat. "You can sit down,"
he said.

"Yes, sir," said Roberts. He sat down and again Van Ness
made him wait.

"Roberts, you've been here now how long—five weeks?"

"A little over. About six."

"About six weeks," said Van Ness. "Since the seventh of
January. Six weeks. Strange. Strange. Six weeks, and I really
don't know a thing about you. Not much, at any rate. Roberts, tell me a little about yourself."

"How do you mean, Mister?"

"How do I mean? Well—about your life, before you decided to honor us with your presence. Where you came from,
what you did, why you went to so many schools, so on."

"Well, I don't know."

"Oh, now. Now, Roberts. Don't let your natural modesty
overcome the autobiographical urge. Shut the door."

Roberts got up and closed the door.

"Good," said Van Ness. "Now, proceed with this—uh—
dossier. Give me the—huh—huh—*lowdown* on Roberts,
Humphrey, Second Form, McAllister Memorial Hall, et
cetera."

Roberts, Humphrey, sat down and felt the knot of his tie.
"Well, I don't know. I was born at West Point, New York.
My father was a first lieutenant then and he's a major now.
My father and mother and I lived in a lot of places because
he was in the Army and they transferred him. Is that the kind
of stuff you want, Mister?"

"Proceed, proceed. I'll tell you when I want you to—uh—
halt." Van Ness seemed to think that was funny, that "halt."

"Well, I didn't go to a regular school till I was ten. My
mother got a divorce from my father and I went to school
in San Francisco. I only stayed there a year because my
mother got married again and we moved to Chicago, Illinois."

"Chicago, Illinois! Well, a little geography thrown in, eh,
Roberts? Gratuitously. Thank you. Proceed."

"Well, so then we stayed there about two years and then
we moved back East, and my stepfather is a certified public
accountant and we moved around a lot."

"Peripatetic, eh, Roberts?"

"I guess so. I don't exactly know what that means." Roberts paused.

"Go on, go on."

"Well, so I just went to a lot of schools, some day and some boarding. All that's written down on my application blank here. I had to put it all down on account of my credits."

"Correct. A very imposing list it is, too, Roberts, a very imposing list. Ah, to travel as you have. Switzerland. How I've regretted not having gone to school in Switzerland. Did you like it there?"

"I was only there about three months. I liked it all right, I guess."

"And do you like it here, Roberts?"

"Sure."

"You do? You're sure of that? You wouldn't want to change anything?"

"Oh, I wouldn't say that, not about any school."

"Indeed," said Van Ness. 'With your vast experience, naturally you would be quite an authority on matters educational. I suppose you have many theories as to the strength and weaknesses inherent in the modern educational systems."

"I don't know. I just—I don't know. Some schools are better than others. At least I like some better than others."

"Of course. Of course." Van Ness seemed to be thinking about something. He leaned back in his swivel chair and gazed at the ceiling. He put his hands in his pants pockets and then suddenly he leaned forward. The chair came down and Van Ness's belly was hard against the desk and his arm was stretched out on the desk, full length, fist closed.

"Roberts! Did you ever see this before? Answer me!" Van Ness's voice was hard. He opened his fist, and in it was a wristwatch.

Roberts looked down at the watch. "No, I don't think so," he said. He was glad to be able to say it truthfully.

Van Ness continued to hold out his hand, with the wristwatch lying in the palm. He held out his hand a long time, fifteen seconds at least, without saying anything. Then he turned his hand over and allowed the watch to slip onto the desk. He resumed his normal position in the chair. He picked up his pipe, slowly filled it, and lit it. He shook the match back and forth long after the flame had gone. He swung around a little in his chair and looked at the wall, away from Roberts. "As a boy I spent six years at this school. My brothers, my two brothers, went to this school. My *father* went to this

school. I have a deep and abiding and lasting affection fo
this school. I have been a member of the faculty of this schoo
for more than a decade. I like to think that I am part of thi
school, that in some small measure I have assisted in it
progress. I like to think of it as more than a mere stepping
stone to higher education. At this very moment there are in
this school the sons of men who were my classmates. I hav
not been without my opportunities to take a post at this and
that college or university, but I choose to remain here. Why
Why? Because I love this place. I love this place, Roberts.
cherish its good name." He paused, and turned to Roberts
"Roberts, there is no room here for a thief!"

Roberts did not speak.

"There is no room here for a thief, I said!"

"Yes, sir."

Van Ness picked up the watch without looking at it. He
held it a few inches above the desk. "This miserable watch wa
stolen last Friday afternoon, more than likely during the
basketball game. As soon as the theft was reported to me I immediately instituted a search for it. My search was unsuccess-
ful. Sometime Monday afternoon the watch was put here,
here in my rooms. When I returned here after classes Monday afternoon, this watch was lying on my desk. Why? Because the contemptible rat who stole it knew that I had
instituted the search, and like the rat he is, he turned yellow
and returned the watch to me. Whoever it is, he kept an entire dormitory under a loathsome suspicion. I say to you, I do
not know who stole this watch, or who returned it to my
rooms. But by God, Roberts, I'm going to find out, if it's
the last thing I do. If it's the last thing I do. That's all,
Roberts. You may go." Van Ness sat back, almost breathless.

Roberts stood up. "I give you my word of honor, I—"

"I said you may go!" said Van Ness.

Roberts was not sure whether to leave the door open or to
close it, but he did not ask. He left it open.

He went up the stairs to his room. He went in and took
off his coat and tie, and sat on the bed. Over and over again,
first violently, then weakly, he said it, "The bastard, the
dirty bastard."

LEO ROSTEN

Leo Calvin Rosten (1908–   ) was born in Lodz, Poland, and educated at the University of Chicago and the London School of Economics. Rosten has had an extraordinarily varied career, serving in various governmental capacities as consultant and researcher. He also worked as editorial adviser to *Look* magazine, and adviser to various charitable foundations.

Probably Rosten's most famous book is *T*H*E E*D*U*C*A*T*I*O*N O*F H*Y*M*A*N K*A*P*L*A*N*, inspired by Rosten's experiences teaching English to adults in night school during the Depression. *The Joys of Yiddish* (1968) is another of Rosten's vastly popular books, beloved by Jews and Christians alike. Rosten has also written for the movies under the pseudonym Leonard Ross. His *Captain Newman, M.D.*, enjoyed widespread critical acclaim.

Dear Miss O'Neill

FROM *People I Have Loved, Known or Admired*

Nothing disturbed Miss O'Neill's tight, shipshape classroom. She was unruffable. She simply ignored, or outflanked, the ruses and traps and malingerings of our minor Machiavellis. Nothing impeded the steady pace and purpose of her tutelage. . . . I was exhilarated by what I can only call the incorruptibility of her instruction.

◆·◆

On the hellish hot days (and the only city more hellish than Chicago, where this happened, is Bombay), Miss O'Neill would lift her wig and scratch her pate. She did it absently, without interrupting whatever she was saying or doing.

I always watched this with fascination. Miss O'Neill wa our seventh-grade teacher, and it was the consensus of my cynical classmates that Miss O'Neill had, until very recently been—a *nun*. That was the only way they could explain the phenomenal fact of her wig. Miss O'Neill, they whispered had been nudged out of her holy order for dire, mysterious heart-rending reasons, and the punishment her stern su periors had decreed was that she teach the emphatically non-Catholic heathens in the George Howland Elementary School on Sixteenth Street.

None of us ever knew Miss O'Neill's first name (actually teachers never *had* a first name), and when my mother once asked me how old she was, I answered, "Oh, she's *old*." "Old" meant at least thirty, even forty—which, to an eleven-year old, is as decrepit and remote and meaningless as, say, sixty or seventy, though not one hundred.

Miss O'Neill was dumpy, moonfaced, sallow, colorless and we hated her. We hated her as only a pack of West Side barbarians could hate a teacher of arithmetic. She did not teach arithmetic—but that is how much we hated her. She taught English. She was a thirty-third-degree perfectionist who drilled us—constantly, endlessly, mercilessly—in spelling and grammar and diction and syntax. She had a hawk's eye for error, for a dangling participle or an upright *non sequitur*, a "not *quite* right" word or a fruity solecism. (Did you know that "solecism" comes from the contempt of Greek patricians for the dialect that thrived in Soloi?)

Whenever one of our runny-nosed congregation made a mistake, in composition *or* recitation, Miss O'Neill would send the malefactor to the blackboard to "diagram" the sentence. Going to the blackboard for the public self-exposure of a grammatical tort, which in Miss O'Neill's eyes partook of at least venial sin, was the classroom torture we most resented.

Miss O'Neill's diagramming made us lay bare the solid, irreducible anatomy of a sentence. We had to separate subject from predicate, the accusative from the dative. We had to explain how each part of a sentence works, and how the parts fit together, and how they mesh and move to wheel out meaning. We had to uncover our mistakes ourselves, "naked to our enemies," then offer a correction and explain the reason for *that*—all as Miss O'Neill impassively waited. She waited as if she could sit there until Gabriel blew his kazoo, as our devastating humor had it.

And if an offered correction was itself wrong, Miss O'Neill compounded the heartlessness of her discipline by making the culprit parse *that* on the board, and see where and why *that* was in error, and how *that* must now be remedied. It was inhuman.

Some kids broke into the sweats as they floundered around at the blackboard, guessing at (and failing to pinpoint) their mistake, praying that Miss O'Neill would end the fearful ordeal either by identifying the awful error herself or, at least, by hinting, eyebrowing, murmuring a sound (positive or negative) that might guide them to the one true redeeming answer. But that Miss O'Neill would never do; instead, she shifted her inquisition from the criminal at the blackboard to the helots in the chairs. "Well, class? Who sees the mistake? . . . Jacob? No? . . . Sylvia . . . My, my . . . Harold? . . . Annie . . . Joseph? . . . Come, come, class; you must concentrate. There is an error—an error in grammar—on that blackboard. . . ." So pitiless and unyielding was her method.

Each afternoon, as we poured out of George Howland, like Cheyennes en route to a massacre, we would pause for a time in the schoolyard to pool our misery and voice our indignation over the fate that had condemned us to such an abecedarian. Had we known Shakespeare, we would have added one word to Hamlet's command to Ophelia, making it, with feeling, "Get thee *back* to a nunnery."

What added frustration to our grievance was the fact that Miss O'Neill never lost her patience, never grew angry, never even raised her voice. Worse, she was impervious to the sly infractions, the simulated incomprehensions, with which our most talented saboteurs baited and riled other teachers. Nothing disturbed Miss O'Neill's tight, shipshape classroom. She was unrufflable. She simply ignored, or outflanked, the ruses and traps and malingerings of our minor Machiavellis. Nothing impeded the steady pace and purpose of her tutelage.

I say that my comrades and I hated Miss O'Neill—but that is not entirely true. I only pretended to hate her. In our sidewalk conclaves, on weekends, when we chortled over the latest *tour de force* of Douglas Fairbanks, who could hold off fifty of Richelieu's swordsmen with his single blade, or outwit a platoon of Pancho Villa's ruffians with no more than his acrobatics and celestial smile; or when we mourned the unaccountable defeat of our noble Cubs by the disgusting White Sox; or when we matched extravagances about

what we would do if we happened to find *ten million dolla*
at that very moment; or when we licked our Eskimo Pi
and, for the umpteenth time, shared fantasies about the ho
breathed surrender of one or another seventh-grade nymp
to our lascivious fumblings—sooner or later Miss O'Nei
would be damned by some indignant freeman, and I woul
at once join in the howlings about her cold-blooded despo
tism, cursing her as fervently as any of my companions: S
strong is the desire of a boy to "belong," to be no differer
from the grubbiest of his fellows.

But secretly, my respect for Miss O'Neill—nay, even m
affection—mounted, week by week. I was exhilarated b
what I can only call the incorruptibility of her instruction
I found stirring within myself a sense of excitement, of dis
covery, a curious quickening of the spirit that attends initia
tion into a new world.

Though I could not have explained it in these words,
sensed that frumpy Miss O'Neill was leading me, not throug
the musty labyrinth of English Composition, but into a sunli
realm of order and meaning. Her iron rules, her inflexibl
demands, her meticulous corrections, were not, to me, th
torment or irritation they were to my companions. They
were sudden flashes of light, giddying glimpses of the magic
that hides within the arrangement of words, intoxicating
visions of that universe that awaits understanding. It was
as if a cloak of wonder had been wrapped around the barren
bones of grammar.

For it was not just grammar or diction or syntax to which
Miss O'Neill, whether she knew it or not, was introducing
me. She was revealing language as the vehicle for thinking,
grammar as the servant of logic, diction as a chariot for the
imagination, the prosaic sentences as the beautiful, beating
life of the mind at work. She was teaching what an earlier
generation called "right reason."

The most astonishing thing about Miss O'Neill was that
she proceeded on the assumption that she *could* teach a pack
of potential poolroom jockeys how to write clear, clean, correct sentences, organized into clear, clean, correct paragraphs
—in their native tongue.

I do not think Miss O'Neill had the slightest awareness of
her influence on me, or anyone else. She was not especially
interested in me. She never betrayed an iota of preference
for any of her captive and embittered flock.

Nor was Miss O'Neill much interested in the high, grand aches of the language whose terrain she so briskly charted. e was a technician, pure and simple—efficient, conscien-us, immune to excuses or flattery or subterfuge. Nothing railed her from her professionalism.

And that is the point. Miss O'Neill did not try to please . She did not try to like us. She certainly made no effort make us like her. She valued results more than affection, d, I suspect, respect more than popularity.

She was not endowed with either loving or lovable at-ibutes, and she did not bother regretting it or denying it trying to compensate for it. She went about her task with forthright "I want" or "You go" instead of the sanctimo-ous "Shall we?" She concentrated solely on the transmission her knowledge and the transferring of her skill.

I think Miss O'Neill understood what foolish evangelists f education are bound to rediscover: that drill and discipline e not detestable; that whether they know it or not, chil-ren prefer competence to "personality" in a teacher; that ommunication is more significant than camaraderie; that hat is hard to master gives students special rewards (pride, lf-respect, the unique gratification of having succeeded) recisely because difficulties have been conquered, ramparts aled, battles won; that there may be no easy road at all to arning some things, and no "fascinating" or "fun" way of arning some things really well.

Popular teachers often leave residues of uncertainty in heir pupils, I think, suspicions of things untested, therefore nresolved. Children's unease with ambiguity, especially hen it is the product and the price of lenience, surely leads discontent. But "hard" teachers earn gratitude—perhaps ot immediately, perhaps not articulated, no doubt grudging —for respecting the *subject* no less than the student, for eaching that refuses to diminish the subject's size or debase ts importance.

I do not know whether Miss O'Neill infected any other armint in the seventh grade with a passion for, or even n abiding interest in, English. To me, she was a force of nlightenment.

Miss O'Neill must long ago have retired from her mission o elementary-school aborigines. Perhaps she has been called rom this unkind world to don wings—and, I hope, golden ocks, to replace the wig under whose gauzy base she scratched er relief from itching on those broiling days in Chicago. If

she is still alive, she must be in her dotage: I hope she som
how gets word of these thanks, so long belated, for a ta
so well performed.

I have never forgotten what she taught me.

To this day, whether I am wrestling a slipshod senten
or stand glazed before a recalcitrant phrase; when I mu
drive myself to tame a rebellious paragraph, or burn out tl
fog of careless prose; whether I begin to puff over an i
voluted passage in Proust or get knocked cold by an u
saintly clause in Talcott Parsons, I promptly find myse
thinking of dear Miss ((What-oh-what?) O'Neill—and, sig
ing, reach for a sheet of paper and proceed to diagram tl
English until I know—and know *why*—it is right or wron
and how it can be swept clean of that muddleheadedne
that doth plague us all.

FRANCINE du PLESSIX GRAY

Francine du Plessix Gray (1930–   ) was born in France
and came to the United States in 1941. She was educated at
Bryn Mawr, Black Mountain College, and Barnard College.

Gray worked as a UPI reporter, editorial assistant at
Réalités, and staff writer for *The New Yorker*. In the spring
of 1975, she was Distinguished Visiting Professor at the City
University of New York.

Gray has won many awards for her writing, among them
the Putnam Creative Writing Award, the National Catholic
Book Award, the Front Page Award, and the award of the
Newswomen's Club of New York. She is the author of *Divine
Disobedience: Profiles in Catholic Radicalism* (1970) and
has contributed articles and stories to various popular
periodicals.

For Lycidas Is Dead

Mrs. B. was the most feared and revered teacher at the
Spence School in the 1940's, a vengeful, autocratic,
beady-eyed tyrant who carried much of published poetry
in her head. No one made us lose more hours of our
precious leisure, no one made us weep more bitterly. Yet,
upon those rare occasions when we had social contact
with our teachers . . . I believe that we polished our
shoes, brushed our hair, rehearsed our conversation for
the sole purpose of trying to carve out some space in
Mrs. B.'s steel-hard heart.

◆◆◆

Whenever we whispered or passed notes in class she mercilessly kept us at school after hours to memorize still more
stanzas from *The Viking Book of Poetry of the English-
Speaking World*. ("Du Plessix," she'd thunder, " 'The Grecian

Urn'! THE WHOLE THING!") And so we ended up com
mitting a good deal of that book to memory, seeing that
typical year of Mrs. B.'s assignments included the 40 openin
lines of Chaucer's "Canterbury Tales" (in Middle English
and over 500 lines of Shakespeare, Keats, Shelley, Milton
Wordsworth, Coleridge, Whitman.

Mrs. B. was the most feared and revered teacher at th
Spence School in the 1940's, a vengeful, autocratic, beady
eyed tyrant who carried much of published poetry in th
head. No one made us lose more hours of our preciou
leisure, no one made us weep more bitterly as we walked away
from her office down the halls replete with odors of gym
floor wax and cooking meat loaf, ornate with busts of Keats
and papier-mâché models of the Globe Theater. And yet
upon those rare occasions when we had social contact with
our teachers—a student-faculty tea or dinner—I believe that
we polished our shoes, brushed our hair, rehearsed our con
versation for the sole purpose of trying to carve out some
space in Mrs. B.'s steel-hard heart. Once in her company, she
was the sole magnet of our attention, we sat at her feet in a
mesmerized circle as she meted out her wry comments on
Shelley's atheism or Pope's *Dunciad*. And I now know that
if she commanded so much more of our terror and reverence
than the equally autocratic heads of the Latin or math depart
ments, it was because she doled out the single most shamanis-
tic, magical element of any education: that mnemonic skill,
perhaps lost in our time, of committing great poetry to
memory.

"Weep no more, woeful shepherds, weep no more,/For
Lycidas, your sorrow, is not dead,/Sunk though he be beneath
the watery floor. . . ." Those lines of Milton's floated through
me as I visited my old school recently and walked by the
immense grandfather clock past which I'd rushed every morning at 8:18, rehearsing that day's assigned verses in the hope
of an impeccable recitation. I had come to observe a few
English classes. And some minutes later I was seated among
a remarkable group of girls—15 years old, most of them—
engaged with an equally remarkable teacher in an elective
course entitled "The Mysteries of Identity: A Theme in Modern Literature."

When I told them about Mrs. B.'s enforced recitations
they gasped as if I were talking about compulsory Hebrew.
With that excited glance characteristic of the contemporary
student confronting the totally arcane, one of them exclaimed,

"Actually, that might be kind of exotic!" Then a bell rang and they ran off to their next class, perhaps to "The Disappearance of the Wilderness in American Fiction."

"Upper-school girls are awfully independent these days," one of their English teachers commented as we chatted about that exceptional class. "It would not be *fun* or *profitable* for them to be forced to memorize, so there *is* no memorization beyond simple poems such as "The Tyger," in seventh or eighth grade . . ." ". . . Sometime in the middle to late 1960's, both private and public schools totally did away with the tradition of committing poetry to memory. . . ." "At a time when the young spend more hours a week watching television than they do in the classroom, one has to design attractive electives which will lure students toward works they would not otherwise read. . . ."

My old school, I reflected upon leaving, still offered a more splendid literary education than any I had visited this decade. And yet, with some bitterness, I resented the loss of the litanic recitations enforced by the wizardly Mrs. B. What, precisely, had been lost? Nothing less than myth, magic and ritual.

To have been led to memorize poems such as Milton's "Lycidas" by my mother and the formidable Mrs. B. is one of the most profoundly relevant gifts I have ever received. To know "Lycidas" by heart is not only to be endowed for life with some of the most sumptuous cadences in the English language, it is also to comprehend the sum and substance of Frazer's "The Golden Bough." And it is to carry in one's head forever an infernally beautiful system of mantras, an entire mode of meditation. For "Lycidas" is at once a symbol of the diurnal rhythms of nature, an archetype of the man-God who dies and is resurrected, a sign of reconciliation with our fear of mortality and our hunger for eternity. And I am at a loss to know what preoccupations are more relevant, at any time, to our psychic survival.

THEODORE H. WHITE

Theodore H. White (1915–   ) is an American editor,
journalist, and historian. White attended the Boston Latin
School and Harvard University, where he majored in history.
During World War II, he served as a war correspondent in
China. He remained in Europe following the war, reporting
on the recovery of Western Europe.

Since the middle '50s, White has devoted his time largely to
writing about American politics. He has written for such
publications as *Life, Look, The Reporter, The New York
Times Magazine, New York Magazine, The Saturday Review.*

White's major work is *The Making of the President* series.
For the first volume in this series, he won a Pulitzer Prize.

Among White's other writings is *Fire In the Ashes*, a highly
perceptive analysis of the regeneration of Western Europe
after the second World War. Here White focuses a sharp,
courageous intelligence on America's policies and respon-
sibilities. *Breach of Faith: The Fall of Richard Nixon* deals
with one of the most sordid, most frightening episodes in
American history.

Despite what he has seen of the American political process
up close, White believes that "America brings forth more
good men and more good government than any other system
in the world."

Fond Memories of Schooldays
FROM *In Search of History*

How can I say what a ten-year-old boy remembers of a
schoolteacher lost in time? She was stout, gray-haired,
dimpled, schoolmarmish, almost never angry. She was
probably the first Protestant I ever met; she taught history vigorously; and she was special, the first person who

made me think I might make something of myself. She
was the kind of teacher who could set fire to the imaginations of the ordinary children who sat in lumps
before her, and to do so was probably the chief reward
she sought.

———◆◆———

In the descent of ideas, therefore, family came first, street
next—and then public school.

Whatever the general theory of the Boston School Com-
mittee was, in the state in which Horace Mann had first
broached the idea of free public education, its practice, when
I was going to school, was excellent.

As the Boston public-school system absorbed me, it was
simple. Each neighborhood had an elementary school within
a child's walking distance—kindergarten through third grade.
At the level of the William E. Endicott School, where I began, the Irish had replaced the Yankee schoolmarms and my
teachers were Miss Phelan, Miss Brennan, Miss Murray,
Miss Kelly. They were supposed to teach us to read, write
(by the Palmer method) and add. They also made us memorize poetry, and the poetry was all New England—Henry
Wadsworth Longfellow, James Russell Lowell, John Greenleaf Whittier. But memory was essential, as it was in Hebrew
school, where one memorized the Bible.

Each neighborhood also had an intermediate school—in
my case, the Christopher Gibson School. There segregation
began, boys separated from girls for special periods. In the
fourth grade, boys had special periods to learn carpentry,
girls to learn sewing. In the fifth grade, it was electricity
and wiring for boys, cooking for girls. Vocational and book
learning were taught in the same building. I can still tell a
ripsaw from a crosscut saw by what was taught me (by a
lady carpentry teacher, Miss Sprague) in the fourth grade. I
can still wire lamps in series or in parallel, insulate or install
cutoff switches by what was taught me in the fifth grade. But
—most importantly—I first became aware of the word "history" in the sixth grade at the Christopher Gibson School—
and my teacher was Miss Fuller.

How can I say what a ten-year-old boy remembers of a
schoolteacher lost in time? She was stout, gray-haired, dimpled, schoolmarmish, almost never angry. She was probably
the first Protestant I ever met; she taught history vigorously;
and she was special, the first person who made me think I

might make something of myself. She was the kind of teacher who could set fire to the imaginations of the ordinary children who sat in lumps before her, and to do so was probably the chief reward she sought.

Her course in American history began, of course, at a much later date than the history we were taught at Hebrew school. In Boston, history began in 1630—when the Puritans came. It then worked back and forth, but every date had to be impeccably remembered; Columbus was 1492, Cabot was 1497. Cortés was 1519, as was Magellan; and so on, moving through Jamestown, 1607; New York, 1614; Plymouth Colony, 1620; then other dates that led up to the settlement of Boston— 1630! 1630! 1630! We also had to know the names in the tests: William Penn, Sir George Carteret, King James (which had to be written King James I, or else you were marked wrong).

Miss Fuller did not stop with names and dates. First you had to get them right, but then they became the pegs on which connections between events were to be hung. In this she was far ahead of most of the teachers of her day. For example: Thanksgiving. How did it come about? What would you have thought that first winter in Plymouth, if you had come from England, and survived? How would you invite the Indians to your feast? She decided we would have a play the day before Thanksgiving, a free-form play in the classroom, in which we would all together explore the meeting of Puritans and Indians, and the meaning of Thanksgiving. She divided the class, entirely Jewish, into those children who were American-born and spoke true English, and those who were recent arrivals and spoke only broken English or Yiddish. I was Elder William Bradford, because I spoke English well. "Itchie" Rachlin, whose father was an unemployed trumpet player recently arrived from Russia, and who spoke vivid Yiddish, was Squanto, our Indian friend. Miss Fuller hoped that those who could not speak English would squawk strange Indian sounds while I, translating their sounds to the rest of the Puritans, all of us in black cardboard cone hats, would offer good will and brotherhood. "Itchie" and the other recently arrived immigrant children played the game of being "Indian" for a few minutes, then fell into Yiddish, pretending it was Indian talk. Miss Fuller could not, of course, understand them, but I tried nevertheless to clean up their Yiddish vulgarities in my translation to the other little Puritans, who could not help but giggle. (*"Vos is dos vor traef?*" said Itchie, meaning: "You want us to eat pig food?" and I would translate in English: "What kind of strange food is this before us?") Miss Fuller became furious as we laughed our way through the play; and when I tried to explain, she was hurt and upset. Thanksgiving was sacred to her.

But she was a marvelous teacher. Once we had learned the names and dates from 1630 to the Civil War, she let us talk and speculate, driving home the point that history connected to "now," to "us." America for her was all about freedom, and all the famous phrases from "Give me liberty or give me death" to the Gettysburg Address had to be memorized by her classes—and understood.

She was also a very earnest, upward-striving teacher. I realize now that she must have been working for an advanced degree, for she went to night school at Boston University to take education courses. This, too, reached from outside to me. One day she told my mother about a project her night-school seminar was conducting in how much independent research a youngster of ten or eleven could do on his own— one of those projects now so commonplace in progressive schools. Would my mother mind, she asked, if I was given such an assignment, and then reported on it to her seminar? My mother said yes after Miss Fuller promised to bring me home herself afterwards.

My assignment was to study immigration, and then to speak to the seminar about whether immigrants were good or bad for America. Her seminar mates would question me to find out how well I had mastered the subject. The Immigration Act of 1924—the "Closing of the Gates"—had just been passed; there was much to read in both papers and magazines about the controversy, but my guide was my father. He put it both ways: the country had been built by immigrants, so immigrants were not bad. He had been an immigrant himself. On the other hand, as a strong labor man, he followed the A.F. of L. line of those days. The National Association of Manufacturers (the capitalists) wanted to continue unrestricted immigration so they could sweat cheap labor. But the American Federation of Labor wanted immigration restricted to keep the wages of American workingmen from being undercut by foreigners. This was a conundrum for my father: he was against the capitalists and for the A.F. of L.; but he was an immigrant himself, as were all our friends and neighbors. He helped me get all the facts, and I made a speech on the platform of a classroom at Boston University Teachers

College at nine one night, explaining both sides of the story and taking no position. I enjoyed it all, especially when the teachers began asking me questions; I had all the dates and facts, and an attentive audience, but no answers then just as I have none now. I must have done well, for Miss Fuller kissed me and bought me candy to eat on the streetcar. It became clear to me, as we talked on the way home, that immigrants were history, too. History was happening now, all about us, and the gossip of Erie Street and the problem of whether someone's cousin could get a visa back in the old country and come here were really connected to the past, and to Abraham Lincoln, Henry Clay, Sam Adams, Patrick Henry and the elder William Bradford.

If I went on to the Boston Public Latin School, I think it was because of Miss Fuller and my mother; it was Miss Fuller who persuaded my mother that there was something more than a lump in the boy, and pointed me in the direction of the Latin School.

The Boston school system offered then what seems to me still a reasonable set of choices after intermediate school. You could go to a local high school—Charlestown High School, Roxbury Memorial High School, South Boston High School. Or, if your parents chose, you could go to a "downtown" high school. Today these central schools would be called "magnet schools," "enrichment schools," "elite schools." They served the entire Boston community—a Commerce High School to learn bookkeeping and trade, a Mechanic Arts High School to learn blueprints, welding, machining, and, at the summit, the Boston Public Latin School, the oldest public school in America, founded in 1635. It was free choice: you could walk to your local community high school, or you could go downtown to the central, quality schools. There were no school buses then, so if you did want to take the half-hour trolley ride to a downtown school, you bought student tickets, beige-brown tabs at five cents each, half the price of the dime fare for a regular rider on the Boston transit system. Ten cents a day, five days a week, for carfare was a considerable sum. You had to *want* to go.

My mother, my father, myself all agreeing, I chose the Latin School.

The Boston Public Latin School reeked of history. Harvard had been founded only in 1636, a year after the Latin School, because, so the school boasted, there had to be a college to take its first graduates. The school had sat originally on Beacon Hill, before being moved ultimately to the Fenway, where it was when I attended. The original school on the hill had given its name to the street which is still there: School Street in Boston. We learned that the legendary boys who had outfaced the British on the hill, and thrown snowballs at the Redcoats who put cinders on the icy streets where they sleighed, were Latin School boys. They were the first recorded student demonstrators in American history. In our Latin School assembly hall, the frieze bore proudly the names of boys who had graduated to mark American history. From Franklin, Adams and Hancock, on through Emerson, Motley, Eliot, Payne, Quincy, Sumner, Warren, Winthrop—the trailblazers pointed the way. The frieze might later have listed a Kennedy, a Bernstein, a Wharton. But all this history translated quite precisely to the immigrant parents of Boston. The Latin School was the gateway to Harvard—as much so in 1928, when I entered, as it had been for hundreds of years before. No longer is it so.

In my day, the Latin School was a cruel school—but it may have been the best public school in the country. The old Boston version of "Open Admissions" held that absolutely anyone was free to enter. And the school was free to fail and expel absolutely anyone who did not meet its standards. It accepted students without discrimination, and it flunked them—Irish, Italians, Jewish, Protestant, black—with equal lack of discrimination. Passing grade was fifty, and to average eighty or better was phenomenal. Our monthly tests were excerpts from the College Board examinations of previous years—and we learned "testmanship" early, beginning at age fourteen. The entire Latin School was an obstacle course in "testmanship," a skill which, we learned, meant that one must grasp the question quickly; answer hard, with minimum verbiage; and do it all against a speeding clock. If you scored well in Latin School classroom tests in arithmetic, the College Boards held no peril—you would do better in those exams; and at Harvard, almost certainly, you would qualify for the advanced section of Mathematics A.

The Latin School taught the mechanics of learning with little pretense of culture, enrichment or enlargement of horizons. Mr. Russo, who taught English in the first year, had the face of a prizefighter—a bald head which gleamed, a pug nose, a jut jaw, hard and sinister eyes which smiled only when a pupil scored an absolute triumph in grammar. He was less interested in the rhymes of *The Idylls of the King* or "Evangeline," or the story in *Quentin Durward*, than in drubbing into us the structure of paragraph and sentence. The paragraph began with the "topic sentence"—that was the cornerstone of all teaching in composition. And sentences came with "subjects," "predicates," "metaphors," "similes," "analogies." Verbs were transitive, intransitive and sometimes subjunctive. He taught the English language as if he were teaching us to dismantle an automobile engine or a watch and then assemble it again correctly. We learned clean English from him. Mr. Graetsch taught German in the same way, mechanically, so that one remembered all the rest of one's life that six German prepositions take the dative case—*aus-bei-mit, nach-von-zu*, in alphabetical order. French was taught by Mr. Scully. Not only did we memorize passages (*D'un pas encore vaillant et ferme, un vieux prêtre marche sur la route poudreuse*), but we memorized them so well that long after one had forgotten the title of the work, one remembered its phrases; all irregular French verbs were mastered by the end of the second year.

What culture was pumped in came in ancient history, taught by Mr. Hayes; American history taught by Mr. Nemzoff, who enlarged on what Miss Fuller had taught in the sixth grade; and Latin itself, taught by "Farmer" Wilbur. "Farmer" Wilbur was a rustic who raised apples on his farm outside Boston, and would bring them in by the bushel to hand out to the boys who did well. Latin was drudgery; one learned Caesar, one groaned through Cicero, one went on to Virgil. I did badly in Latin, although ancient history fascinated me; and not until I came many years later to American politics did I realize how much of "Farmer" Wilbur's teaching of Caesar and Cicero had flaked off into the sediment of my thinking.

Yet, though the choice had been my own, my first three years at the Latin School were an unrelieved torment. I barely managed a sixty average, which put me somewhere in the lower third of my class. But then in June 1931 my father died, and I was plunged into an education that remains for all men and women of my generation their great shaping experience—the lessons taught by the Great Depression.

LIANE ELLISON NORMAN

Liane Ellison Norman (1937–   ) is an American teacher and essayist. Mrs. Norman is a graduate of Grinnell College and holds advanced degrees from Brandeis University. She has taught on various academic levels at Chatham College, Kalamazoo College, Brandeis University, and the University of Pittsburgh. Like so many of her contemporaries, Mrs. Ellison's life encompasses several careers: she is wife, mother, and teacher.

Thornley's Legacy
FROM Writers for Life

There were dozens of teachers before Thornley, some good, some indifferent, some incompetent, some probably insane. . . . Thornley alone, among the events and personalities of my adolescent years, refuses to petrify. . . . He is not a fossil artifact of memory, but—though he is now dead—an active influence on me. . . . What a gift that small man, Thornley of the attentive smile, gave me.

———◆◆◆———

We called him Thornley. We called other teachers by their last names, too, but not with the same affection. "Who d'you have for History?" one would ask. "Peterson," or "Smith," would be the answer. Sometimes it came with a grimace or a groan. Sometimes it made no difference and the answer was noncommittal. But we never said "Thornley" with that scorn, loathing, or neutrality. About Thornley there was no adolescent edge of secret superiority.

Wilson R. Thornley was the one man I have thought to be a real wizard, a man of irreversible and lasting sorcery. I

Reprinted with permission from *The Center Magazine*, a publication of the Robert Maynard Hutchins Center for the Study of Democratic Institutions, Santa Barbara, California.

don't remember, any longer, how we qualified to be in his enchanted circle—Creative Writing class. It may have been we had to have good grades, but I rather think his reputation served to warn off all but the gifted and disciplined. In my case, Thornley's influence penetrated our lives, bound us together, and outlasted our association. . . .

Thornley lived a few blocks from my home, in a neat brick house separated from the street by a row of tall evergreens. All week long he gave himself without stint to students, but evenings and weekends he retreated to fir-fenced privacy and to "the Missus," who, when she sent me her husband's obituary, wrote, "My perfect marriage life is over. . . ." Other teachers sometimes talked about their private lives, usually to kill time or to boast. Thornley spoke of his family to illustrate points he wanted to make, and perhaps to suggest how close interesting people were—under our very noses and down the block. I remember feeling that it was a rare privilege to have Thornley let us in a little on his life. . . .

But I knew Thornley best in class, leaning against the window wall of the clean, undecorated schoolroom, wearing a tweed sports coat, his shirt with its tiny checkered pattern buttoned to the top without a necktie. He was a small man, tidy and compact. He wore rimless glasses. A flame of hair sprang up around the edges of a bald head. His voice was a little wry, quick and precise. He had a way of cocking his head like a bird when he smiled. He would tip his head, raise an eyebrow, and smile so deeply and so attentively that he conferred a kingdom on each of us. It wasn't a kingdom where you lived happily ever after in a haze of golden stupidity: it was a kingdom to govern. . . .

Now that I am a writing teacher, I know how hard he worked for the apparent simplicity of his teaching. Then it never seemed that he *did* much. No striding or ranting or joking or audiovisual aids or checking up, no exams or pop quizzes, no stratagems or penalties. That used to puzzle me, for school was a tense contest of wit and power between most students and most teachers. But no one would have considered misbehaving in Thornley's class, nor even thought the absence of misbehavior odd. His authority was unchallenged, though as far as I could tell, he never pulled rank nor used any of the fragile defenses teachers have. In fact, Creative Writing seemed to conduct itself, once the initial assignments had been completed and considered.

Those assignments were what Thornley called reporting, and they were hard. He meant by reporting using our senses to gather concrete and exact information. The maxim was not, write about what you know, but know about what you write. Report on running water, he said. And then, report on the moon. After that, report on the produce counter at the market in two ways: so that the produce is attractive, and so that it isn't. And after that, report five minutes at the lunch counter at Kress's. And then report people under stress.

What we learned was to use all five senses, completely and precisely, to find the exact words to tell what it was our senses had perceived. In most of our classes, we were learning higher falutin' abstractions than in our earlier years, but in Thornley's class, we learned to look and listen, to smell and feel and taste, and we discovered that we normally overlooked a good deal that went on around us. We discovered that the moon was always new as long as you looked at it with your own eyes, but that clichés made it any old moon. We discovered that a detail could lead one to the conclusion that a tomato was fresh or rotten without ever naming the conclusion; indeed, I believe we learned that our conclusions came from evidence, and that as writers we could supply the same evidence for our readers, and then get out of the reader's way. We discovered, watching people on the surgical floor of the hospital or in traffic court, that it was mere conclusion to say that this woman was nervous or that man was sad. We couldn't know these things. But we could observe all sorts of telling details and give them to our readers. The woman clasped and unclasped her chapped hands. She kneaded her fingers. She slid her rings back and forth, working them over her knuckles. She chafed at her nose, played with a strand of hair, fidgeted her blouse buttons. She chewed on her lips, licked them, lined them with lipstick, pressed them together, chewed them and licked them. The man paced, arched his shoulders back, sat and slid in the smooth chair, stretching his legs in front of him, and sighed. He took off his glasses and pressed the heels of his hands into his eye sockets. He straightened up and stared at the floor. And so on. Green could mean a thousand colors, but the green of oxidized copper meant something limited and specific, and you could be pretty sure a reader would know what you had in mind. "Beautiful" described your own conclusion, but a sunset that flamed and billowed like a forest fire, blue near the horizon, ignited a reader's knowledge and memory.

We went from assigned reports to essays, stories, and
poems, using the same principles of reporting—exactitude,
concreteness, carefully defined points of view. I don't remember that Thornley made assignments, but we wrote constantly, then gave him our manuscripts to be discussed in
class, then rewrote and learned the habits of revision. Thornley read each manuscript without comment. He would clip
off the author's name and give the manuscript to another
student ahead of time to prepare to read aloud; it was important to do justice to every manuscript by reading it well.
When it was read, discussion and criticism followed. It wasn't
gentle criticism. We tore into one another's work. Sometimes
the author tore in, too (hearing, in someone else's reading,
flaws hitherto unnoticed), sometimes defended, sometimes
sat quiet. The important thing was that there were readers
for everything we wrote—not only the teacher who dealt the
grades—and we had to take those readers into account when
we wrote. They weren't indolent readers, but careful and
exacting. I think, too, we helped to raise our readers' expec-
tations by expecting a good deal of them. Standards were
high because writers and readers took one another with great
seriousness.

That seriousness was something new. All the schools expected us, the students, to take the school, the principal, the
teachers, our studies seriously, but never ourselves. If we
were taken seriously it was as a problem. Sometimes, of
course, our seriousness in Creative Writing led us into sen-
tentious solemnity. We were full of adolescent revelation and
epiphany and, tippling this heady new wine of intentional
creation, wrote gravely of our transcendent experiences, finding God in a field of timothy grass or some such. One boy
got tired of what we were doing and wrote a poem about the
town drunk's funeral, and another wrote a mystery story in
which a sausage maker turned his nagging wife into link
sausages. By and large, however, we lacked humor but made
it up in intensity.

When I went to college, I took it for granted that writers
valued tough criticism, for I didn't know then how extraordinary Thornley's class had been. But I found that the habits
I had developed in his class—the rigorous scrutiny and criticism that I had come to expect with regard to my work—
wounded the tender sensibilities of my new classmates, many
of whom were neither as gifted nor as determined as those
who wrote under Thornley's demanding aegis. Nearly all of

my college writing classmates wrote with their own expressive needs uppermost; few had in their minds the need for readers, and consequently did not so much consider the effects of their words on readers as they guarded their own egos.

Those of us who were Thornley's students in high school felt ourselves an anointed group. This feeling was some protection against the hurly-burly pain of late adolescence, against our self-contempt. Through all of my school years, I was sore with division. I was intellectually eager, in most things "the brain," and thus suspect in the eyes of my classmates. I wanted dimples, naturally curly hair, and an easy way with boys more than anything else, and yet I guarded the secret life of my mind fiercely. Outside of Creative Writing class, we were assaulted by teenage life—students necking in shadowy places in the halls, barbaric pep rallies before football games, incessant doom of pimples, crises of dances and dates. The pressures were continual and acute, but Thornley's class provided a thin envelope of protective self-esteem. It wasn't only that we competed in the National Scholastic writing competitions—and won, year after year, in record numbers—but that we were in charge of the process of communication, that we made decisions and governed ourselves without losing sight of those we would speak to. I think of those high-school years in terms of ferocity—nature red in tooth and claw, a time of life short, nasty, and brutish—with the exception of Creative Writing, where the civilizing arts of communication, respect, conservation, and community flowered.

Thornley stood out—stands out still—because he changed us in ways that made us both more self-sufficient and more generous. There were dozens of teachers before Thornley, some good, some indifferent, some incompetent, some probably insane. What impresses me now is my inability to discern what, if anything, I learned from them. Probably there is considerable bedrock in what I know that came from them, yet I have little sense of what it was or who they were. Those I remember best were the eccentrics, memories of whom stand out sharply in my mind like still lifes or like spare skeleton trilobites pressed into and preserved by the earth's capacity to remember outlines. I don't often think of them, but I can dig their outlines out of the decomposition of other memories. Thornley alone, among the events and personalities of my adolescent years, refuses to petrify. He is

not a fossil artifact of memory, but—though now he is dead—
an active influence on me as I observe, write, daily use lan
guage, and teach writing. He healed that awful division in me
between kids and teachers, between what I thought, knew
perceived, felt, and had thought fit to keep secret, and the
life I lived in public. It was under his teaching that I realized
that my mind was not an antisocial aberration. . . .

My writing class last term did not go well. My students
sat in their seats as if anesthetized. They seemed to me in
curious, sullen, uninterested in language. They used words—
both writing and speaking—merely to approximate what they
meant, rather than to find out just what it is and to share it.
The pursuit of exactitude did not excite them. Writing did
not seem to be, for them, a way to discover. I asked what
newspaper columnists they regularly read; it turned out that
none of them, though they all expect to make their living by
writing, read any columnist at all. In fact, none read a newspaper regularly. Only one read books and he alone wrote well.
It was a dull class. It went nowhere. It bored and depressed
me and probably bored and depressed them. One student
hinted that I had hurt his feelings by criticizing his paper.
What would Thornley do? Aha! I had forgotten. The student
with the hurt feelings ought not to be writing for me, but for
his classmates. I find myself going back to inquire regularly,
to test what I do against the principles I have distilled from
what Thornley did. . . .

We did not rely, in those days, on dittos, mimeos, or photo-
copies. Since manuscripts were read aloud, we had to listen
carefully, to remember what we heard. The sound of language mattered, as did timing. But there were other lessons
about reading. One day we discussed the several poems on the
blackboard, written out in Thornley's Palmer-method long-
hand. One, full of classical allusions, did not fare as well as
the others. Why? Thornley asked. What did the allusions do?
What did they refer to? No one knew, although the poems had
been on the board—with a note to the janitor, "Do Not Erase"
—for nearly a week. "You're not ready to talk about this
poem yet," said Thornley, and explained that readers had to
work, too, particularly when a writer's frame of reference
was not familiar. There were ways of finding out what unfamiliar words meant, and as readers, we had to avail ourselves of them. Ignorance, as of the law, was no excuse. It
turned out that the poem was Milton's and that the efforts

to read him opened wide avenues of resonance. As I recall, most of us went through heavily allusive phases after that, making our poems treasure hunts full of clues to our new-found erudition.

The reciprocal disciplines of writing and reading were what kept the language healthy and elastic. From Thornley I got the idea that we hold language in trust, generation after generation. It isn't a private property. It can't be possessed or alienated. To be usable at all, it must be shared on terms mutually accepted, generally understood, and relatively stable. We come to the great estate of language, entitled by birth to use it freely, to utilize its fertility and draw on its wealth. But that entitlement settles upon us an entail as well. We can do with language what we will on one condition, that we transmit it with care, an unalienable inheritance, to those who come after. . . .

I have lost track of my Thornley classmates. My sisters, though, took Creative Writing in their turn, and remember Thornley much as I do, though I was the only one to grow up calling herself a writer. So I may be wrong to say that Thornley affected others as he did me, though we shared several years, five hours a week, of priceless, transforming time with him. I should really speak only for myself. His effect on me was to make me radically conservative, that is, to make me conscious of a language capable of radical originality, particularity, skepticism, dissent, even heresy—a language, using which, one's intellectual and artistic freedom is unconditional: yet a language that, in order to work, must be conserved, its roots acknowledged, its conventions observed, its rules kept.

In that creative care there was, I believe, the most important recognition of all. It was that as a writer, I was part of a community of people who needed language. Without that need, there was no possibility that I could write. It was a way of combining my sense of myself as a particular individual, unlike any other in the world—ever—with my sense of belonging and contributing to a common social purpose. I could be myself, develop my own direction, grow in my own way, say what I liked. But at the same time, I was not alone, not stranded in difference or isolated. Through language, I belonged. What I made, I could share—in fact, I had to, if the making had any value.

What a gift that small man, Thornley of the attentive smile, gave me. I'm sad that he is dead, that the Missus' perfect marriage is over. But a man like Thornley never really dies, for those he touched, as teacher or spouse, carry him in the marrow of their bones and the tingle of their nerve ends.

WILLIAM HOLMES McGUFFEY

William Holmes McGuffey (1800–1873) was an American preacher, educator, and textbook writer. After graduating from Washington College in 1826, McGuffey taught Latin, Greek, and Hebrew at Miami University in Oxford, Ohio. In 1829, he became a preacher in the Presbyterian church. McGuffey served at various times as president of Cincinnati College, president of Ohio University, and professor of moral philosophy at the University of Virginia.

McGuffey is best remembered for his famous series of readers. In their time, they served as virtual libraries to millions of people in rural and small-town America. Heavily didactic and moralistic in tone and content, they were, nonetheless, vastly better than anything else that had appeared before them. They provided young America with a taste for real literature. These readers shaped students' attitudes as no other single American book or individual has ever done. Over 122,000,000 copies of McGuffey's readers were sold. As late as 1920, they were still in use in some parts of our country. "From 1836 until near the close of the century," says Hugh Fullerton, "Professor McGuffey exerted the greatest influence culturally of any person in American history."

The Last Lesson

FROM

McGUFFEY'S
FIRST
ECLECTIC READER

làst   slātes   wrīte   wāste
nēat   tāk′en   clēan   lēarn
rēad′er   pâr′ents   sĕc′ond

We have come to the last lesson in this book. We have finished the First Reader.

You can now read all the lessons in it, and can write them on your slates.

Have you taken good care of your book? Children should always keep their books neat and clean.

Are you not glad to be ready for a new book?

Your parents are very kind to send you to school. If you are good, and if you try to learn, your teacher will love you, and you will please your parents.

Be kind to all, and do not waste your time in school.

When you go home, you may ask your parents to get you a Second Reader.